ALSO BY DARCY COATES

HOW BAD THINGS CAN GET

DARCY COATES

Poisoned Pen
PRESS

Published by Poisoned Pen Press, an imprint of Sourcebooks
1935 Brookdale RD, Naperville, IL 60563-2773
(630) 961-3900
sourcebooks.com

Cataloging-in-Publication Data is on file with the Library of Congress.

Printed and bound in the United States of America.
VP 10 9 8 7 6 5 4 3 2 1

1.

"You have to die, Josanna. It doesn't work if you don't die."

The voice echoed along the concrete hallways. It was beseeching and sweet, but beneath the sing-song tones was the poorly hidden bite of irritation.

Josanna crawled. The hallways were dark. The lights had been shut off, and even though she knew the compound as well as she knew the planes of her own face, Josanna didn't dare stand. The halls were full of new obstacles. She'd already tripped over one, heavy and padded, and she didn't want to risk it again. She couldn't make any noise.

Not if she hoped to live.

And she did—she wanted to live so, so badly. As wrong as it was. As bad as it made her. She wanted to *live*.

"Come back to me." There was a scrape, metal against concrete. The voice stayed sweet, but it simmered like a pot of sugar about to burn. "I'll help you, dear one. But you can't fail us now. You know how important this is."

She crept forward. There were ways out of the compound. Narrow windows she could worm through, hidden doors, little hatches, loose boards. She wasn't yet eight. She was still small enough to fit through the tiny gaps when she tried. She just had to find one they'd forgotten to seal.

Her hands were numb as she felt her way along the gritty floor. The heat had gone out at the same time as the lights, and the rooms were like ice chests. Josanna wore one of the adults' coats. She didn't know who it belonged to. She hadn't been able to see them in the dark; she could only feel the fabric as she dragged the jacket off their stiff arms.

There was a door along this hall. The elders liked to use it to get into the private rooms in the east quadrant, and those rooms had a little square window to outside. Maybe they'd forgotten to seal it. She just needed to—

"Josanna, don't you want to fix this? Don't you want to save them?"

The voice bounced from wall to wall. The compound had never echoed before. It had never been so *empty*.

She reached out. Her knees ached as they shuffled across the hard floor.

And then her fingers touched something.

Not concrete. Not metal. Something that was both firm and soft, all at once.

Skin.

She'd touched skin—a person, someone who had fallen in the hall and had been left where they dropped. They were as cold as the frigid air.

She felt a nose. The corners of lips. The skin was tacky, and as her hands moved across it, she understood why.

Their face would be covered in red. Rivers of blood poured out of the cavities where they'd gouged out their own eyes.

Ruth snapped up, a gasp seizing in her throat, the air not making it to her lungs.

Aching from the cold, echoing, empty halls. The tack of drying blood sticking to her fingertips.

The sensations lasted for just a second and then crumbled. She inhaled again, more deliberately, and instead of the acrid tang of early rot, her lungs filled with briny air.

People crowded across the deck, dressed in bright colors and flowing fabrics, laughing. Music played from concealed speakers, drowning out the sounds of the ocean.

Her dreams were always vivid. Sometimes so vivid they bled into reality, but never for more than a few seconds. Just long enough to make sure she wouldn't forget them.

She subtly rubbed her hands together, reassuring herself that they weren't coated with tacky blood. As she did, she glanced across the row of lounge chairs that ran along the cruise liner's deck.

Ruth froze. Carson was staring at her.

And his expression…

A woman shrieked with laughter. Ruth's chair rattled as a group bumped her, phones held high on selfie sticks as they ran past. One of them shouted an apology as they wove through the crowd.

She looked back at Carson. He no longer faced her, but stared along the deck. His familiar grin stretched his sun-reddened face.

Ruth wiped at clammy cheeks with the back of her hand. She'd only known Carson for six months, but in that time, he'd been nothing but friendly and jovial toward her.

The way he'd been staring at her, though…

He'd seemed cold. Closed off.

The nightmare looped through her mind: the halls, the bodies, the distant, cooing voice.

He couldn't have known what she'd seen. Those images lived in Ruth's head alone.

He couldn't know. He *couldn't*.

A hand pressed into Ruth's shoulder. Her pulse spiked, and she fought the impulse to flinch from the touch.

"Hey," Zach said. He leaned down and held out a tall glass. Ice and pale liquid glittered in the sun, beads of condensation already trailing down the surface. "I know you said you weren't thirsty, but I felt bad about you being the only one without a drink. You can leave it if you don't want it."

Drinks. That's right. Zach and Hayleigh were going to get drinks.

She glanced back at Carson. His face lit up as he waved to Hayleigh through the crowd.

"Thanks," Ruth managed, and took the glass, even though she felt breathless and queasy. Zach ducked in and quickly kissed her cheek, his stubble both scratchy and comforting, before dropping into the chair beside her.

She wanted to say something. But she didn't know if she could. Zach and Carson had been friends since they were six. Ruth was the new addition to the group.

She was trying so hard not to ruin the trip. But she was afraid she was, anyway. Seasickness had dogged her for the two days they'd been on the water. That and the nightmares made it hard to sleep. She felt ragged and uneasy, and she couldn't match the group's energy.

Maybe that's all it is. I'm tired and stressed, and I misread Carson. Maybe… it was a joke?

It hadn't felt like one.

I only saw it for a second. He might not have even been looking at me. Don't overthink it.

Hayleigh sauntered along the deck, swinging her Saran Wrapped hips in an exaggerated fashion as she navigated between the other festivalgoers, holding the drinks high above her head like trophies. Carson laughed and clapped as she curtsied, placing the drinks on the small ledge between their chairs.

"I return victorious," she said, wriggling as she settled back into her lounge, her blond hair fluffing up against the towel. "The battle was vicious, but the prizes made it worth it."

"My queen, the undefeated champion of busy bars." Carson picked up his drink and clinked it against Hayleigh's. His broad face was pink, his smile huge and infectious.

No trace of revulsion. No apparent hostility toward Ruth.

But, even when he turned to talk to Zach, he didn't look at her. Not once.

She sipped the drink so she'd at least seem like she was doing something. It was the lychee mocktail, the one she'd had at dinner the night before. She'd liked it, and Zach had remembered. That brought a little spark of joy. Zach's hand rested over the side of his lounge chair and she took it, wrapping their fingers together.

The music cut out. There was a *click*, and a woman's voice flooded the deck, loud but pleasant.

"Good afternoon, valued guests," she said, and the chattering voices fell silent as heads turned toward the concealed speakers. "I'm pleased to say we are nearly at our destination and will be anchoring in approximately an hour. A tender will bring you to shore. As you disembark, a crew member will pass out gift bags. Inside, you will find treats from our sponsors as well as something very special: an invitation to the first game of the festival."

A flood of murmurs rose through the crowd.

"Do you think they'll have prizes?" Hayleigh asked, grasping Carson's forearm, her eyes bright.

"It wouldn't be an Eton game if they didn't," Carson said.

Ruth turned to look behind her. Only a thin railing separated her from endless, violently blue ocean.

A hazy landform had appeared at the horizon. Sweat bloomed on her palms and mixed with the condensation trailing down the icy glass.

She'd seen that silhouette before. Many times. The jagged outline had haunted her nightmares, growing larger and clearer with each new rendition.

The announcer's final words settled on Ruth heavily, like a cold hand had blocked out the sun.

"Welcome, guests, to Prosperity Island."

Petra released her hold on the announcement button. The script for their welcome message was highlighted on her digital pad, and she tagged and archived it with several quick taps.

One more task done. A thousand still to go. All of them urgent, most of them behind schedule, and at least a dozen of them on the verge of blooming into fully formed disasters.

She could juggle them, though. She knew how. She'd been juggling for her whole life.

The view from the bridge was phenomenal. Below, nearly all their six hundred guests mingled on the deck. Beyond that, white crests paved the way to the mass in the distance.

The island wasn't leased. Eton owned it. She'd helped him navigate the purchase eight months prior, at the same time he'd started talking about hosting a festival that would never be forgotten.

She'd seen how much Eton paid for the island. A staggering amount, the kind of number that stopped feeling real. She could visualize ten thousand dollars. She could visualize a hundred thousand. But twenty-two million? Those were just words strung together. Game currency. No longer tethered to reality.

Being allowed to play with game currency was the privilege of very few people.

Eton stood behind her, looking younger than his thirty years, his posture easy and his smile lopsided as he stared at the distant island. He dressed the same way he always did in his videos—a cheap T-shirt and a red beanie that was fraying at the edges.

The rich could afford to wear whatever they liked, but Petra knew his clothing choices weren't driven by comfort. It was Eton's brand. The brand she liked to think of as *Best Friend to All*. It was what had helped him amass his millions of followers and billions of video views. And he almost never let that mask slip.

"We still need to assign a safety officer before the game," she said, scrolling through her notes. "Do you want me to set that up?"

"Don't worry about it, Pet; I'll sort it out later."

She felt a twinge of frustration, even as he smiled at her. Eton hated red tape, but he usually didn't put up too much of a fuss as long as he didn't have to be involved. But she'd been nudging him about this for weeks.

"It's just that *later* has become *now*. If you want the first game to start before nightfall, we need to prep a safety briefing. The course is too dangerous to ignore—"

"Pet, it's okay!" He laughed, easy and happy, and leaned over the dash to get a better view of the horizon. "Scratch it off your list and leave it to me. Right now, I just want to make sure all our guests make it to the beach."

Petra looked back at her screen, each task tagged for category and color-coded by urgency. The shades blurred together.

She knew Eton well enough to see what he was doing.

Eton hadn't been neglecting to name a safety officer because he didn't care about it. Indifference wasn't the problem.

He actively didn't want one.

And she didn't know why.

2.

Ruth didn't start breathing properly until her feet plunged through the surf and touched wet sand.

They'd spent two full days on the cruise ship that had brought them from New York to the Caribbean. Two days of an open bar and live entertainment and their choice of restaurants. And Ruth had suffered the entire trip.

Seasickness was supposed to be less of a problem on cruise ships, she'd been told. Their size dampened the ocean's incessant rocking. But Ruth had never been on anything deeper than a lake. And, while the ocean liner had been bad, the small chugging boat that ferried them through the shallow water was so much worse.

Zach leaped off the tender behind her, crisp water splashing up his thighs. He placed a bracing hand on her back as they followed their group out of the surf and toward the welcome booth. "There you go," he said. "Just breathe."

Ruth swallowed. Her body still felt like it swayed. She looked up, fighting to fix her eyes on the landscape ahead. On something, anything, solid.

A crescent-shaped beach spread out around them. The sand was a clean, creamy white, contrasting against the jewel tones of the water behind them: emerald green in the shallows, sapphire blue closer to the cruise ship.

Above, the island's ridgeline sawed across the late afternoon sky, blanketed in thick green.

The nausea rose up again, bile in the back of her throat.

She'd seen those jagged ridgelines in her dreams. They'd alternated with visions of the compound: the dark, the rot, the cold, followed by glimpses of azure blue and deep forest green and vivid red.

It shouldn't have been possible for her to recognize the island's silhouette. It had never been shown in any of the promotional videos—only glimpses of the jungle and the beach.

Stop. Don't overthink. You're tired, you're sick, and you're making connections where they don't exist. You pictured an island in your dreams, and it was blurry and vague and approximately the right shape, but that's as far as the similarities go.

Though…

Her eyes moved to the highest point of the island. A lopsided ridge, green on one side, bare rock on the other, like a flag.

That had been in her dreams too.

"Okay?" Zach asked, rubbing her back.

Ruth made herself smile. She was *not* going to ruin this. "Yes! Just excited to finally be here."

"Me too," Hayleigh gasped. She was a few paces ahead of them, one hand holding her wide-brimmed hat in place as she spun giddily, drinking in the sights. "This is amazing."

Prosperity Island truly did seem like paradise.

Carson jogged after his girlfriend. By the time he caught up with Hayleigh, he was laughing.

The final guests had left the tender, and its motor rattled as it turned to make another trip back to the cruise ship. They were one of the last groups brought to land.

A queue led toward a small welcome tent. Beyond that, clusters of festivalgoers spread out across the beach. Rustic wooden shacks had been constructed just ahead of where the sand rose to meet the jungle, and banners hung on their eaves, advertising a bar, snack food, and an information desk that offered towels, sunscreen, and umbrella loans.

A stage had been built to the right, the sand packed around its edges, precariously close to the amplifiers. Ruth didn't know any of the advertised acts, but Zach had seemed excited when he'd read the list to her.

"Name?"

Ruth snapped back to herself. The queue to the welcome booth had emptied, leaving her on the threshold. Two women stood at the bench, cartons of tote bags behind them, digital pads propped in front.

"Zachary Waldon," Zach said, while the second assistant, smile flawless, repeated, "Name, please?"

"Oh. Ruth. Phillips."

The woman tapped buttons on her screen, and her smile widened as she nodded. She dug into one of the crates and passed a tote across the counter. "Welcome, Ruth. You'll find a map of the island and an itinerary inside your bag. Feel free to look around or get a drink, but don't travel far. An announcement will be happening soon. Enjoy!"

The bag was heavier than she'd expected. Ruth thanked the woman before joining Zach as they crossed to meet up with their group.

Carson and Hayleigh had already dropped onto the beach and were emptying their totes' contents onto the sand. They talked simultaneously, their excitement making them flushed and a little too loud.

Ruth took a spot between Zach and Hayleigh, forming a sort of circle. Heat from the sand soaked through her skirt.

She pulled open her own tote, seeking a distraction. A good part of its weight came from a water bottle made of silver metal. A logo—a flame surrounded by a swirl—had been engraved on the front.

That was Eton's symbol.

She'd tried to watch his videos, but something about his smile had left her unnerved. It wasn't fake, not like some of the smiles she'd seen on TV, but it was…too much.

Zach had promised her she wouldn't need to know anything about Eton to enjoy the festival. Unlike Ruth, the other three friends had been subscribed to the creator for years. *We're not, like, mega fans,* Hayleigh had explained one time. *I mean, I bought a T-shirt to support him. But I mostly just watch his videos to help me fall asleep at night. They're relaxing, you know?*

And Ruth had thought of the riotous music, of how Eton's excitement had him on the verge of yelling, of how no shot lasted more than three seconds, and she wished she could trade brains with Hayleigh.

I don't click on him much these days, Zach had added. *He was better a couple of years ago, when he did more gaming.*

They'd all agreed with Zach. And yet, when the festival was announced, it became the only topic they wanted to talk about.

Ruth found herself a little bit envious. The others had been watching Eton's videos since they were teenagers; they'd bonded over him. They had years of fond memories and nostalgia to boost their excitement when Zach won the sweepstakes for admission to the festival.

All of Ruth's childhood idols were dead.

She put the bottle aside. Beneath that was an assortment of trinkets. A beanie, in the style of Eton's, also marked with his logo. Sunblock, which Hayleigh gushed over—"La-Mure Vivace! This stuff's so expensive!"—as well as snack-sized bags of pretzels and nuts, glowing wristbands, a tightly-wrapped microfiber towel, and so much more.

"What's this?" Hayleigh pulled a smooth pebble from her bag. A black circle had been painted in its center.

"I've got one too," Zach said, fishing his own out. "Do you think this is the invitation to the game?"

"It's got to be." Carson held his up, examining it as though it might reveal more clues. The rock was small enough to fit into his palm, and the black circle was shiny and glossy. "Maybe it's like…an entry ticket? Maybe this is going to be our currency?"

The conversation faded into the background. Ruth had found the one item she'd been looking for: the island's map. Like the other gifts, it could have been made cheaply, but the organizers had opted for a touch of luxury instead. She abandoned the tote's contents and unfurled the thick paper.

Prosperity Island was printed across the top. The illustration beneath was clearly intended to be a keepsake from the festival, maybe even framed. A shipwreck had been drawn in one corner of the ocean, mermaids in another. Little tags marked notable locations.

The island itself had a central mass—the raised peak that marked where a volcano had broken through millions of years before—and then multiple ridges and spits that reached into the ocean. Beaches formed between each of the arms, giving the island three large coves and two smaller ones. The largest ridge stretched far into the water, nearly doubling the island's length before curving into ocean-swept rocks at the end.

Ruth found the beach they were on. The stage and stalls had been drawn on the stretch of gently arching yellow. She let her eyes trail outward; not far away, in the jungle, was a clearing marked *The Village*. And the next nearest beach, another large one, was tagged *Endurance Cove*. A skull had been drawn beneath the name.

The air hummed. Ruth snapped her head up. The crowd quieted and eyes turned toward the stage, where the amplifiers had come to life, filling the beach with dead noise.

A woman stood onstage, one hand caressing the microphone stand. Her short dark hair was styled elegantly, curling behind her ears. The linen shirt and loose gray pants draped off her effortlessly. She looked immaculately casual, and yet Ruth felt a tightly wound intensity radiating out of her.

"That's Petra," Zach whispered, leaning close to Ruth. "Eton's project manager. She's been in a couple of videos."

"She's so pretty," Hayleigh cooed.

This had to be the announcement they'd been warned about. Which meant the final guests had been brought to shore.

The dead noise faded. Music, loud and poppy, played. Then Petra flashed a smile, showing blinding white teeth, and raised a hand. "Welcome, guests, to your private paradise!"

Whooping cheers and applause burst from the groups spread about the beach. Many of them had already made use of the bar.

"My name's Petra, and you'll be seeing plenty of me over the next five days." She unhooked the microphone from the stand and began to walk along the edge of the stage. "You can also look forward to spending time with someone you're already very familiar with. Our host and our games master. *Eton.*"

A second figure leaped onto stage. He held up both hands, waving, his smile lopsided and delighted.

The hollering applause was much louder and lasted much longer. It drowned out even the music.

Eton's walk transformed into a comical dance as he crossed the platform. Laughter burst from the audience, including the three friends next to Ruth. She smiled, trying to play along, but something about the scene was making her uneasy, and she didn't know why.

Eton came to a halt next to Petra. He made shushing motions, and it still took the crowd a painful stretch of time to fall quiet. Once they did, Petra spoke.

"Momentarily, we'll show you to where you'll be living for the next five days," she said. "I'm sure you're excited to see your cabins. But it wouldn't be an Eton experience without a game, now would it? I hope you're ready to play!"

More cheers. Hands thrust into the air, trying to get noticed.

Eton took the microphone. He gave one more little wave, then said, "Hey, welcome to my island!"

His voice had an odd lilt to it. His red beanie looked too hot for the tropical island; his stubble was shaggy. He wasn't classically handsome, and he wasn't trying to seem cool.

But the audience *loved* him.

And, as Ruth gazed up at him onstage, she understood why.

He was charismatic. Incredibly, powerfully, and magnetically.

It had taken her a second to recognize the magnetism because he wore it humbly. Almost sheepishly. When he smiled, it was like he was asking the audience, *Hey, can we be friends?*

And that recognition let Ruth finally understand why the scene had made her so uncomfortable. She'd seen it all before.

A warmly smiling figure onstage. Hungry adoration from the audience. Music, yelling, clapping.

She'd lived this at Petition.

Ruth pulled her arms around herself as their host beamed down at them.

"Okay, okay, okay," Eton called, laughing as he tried to make himself heard over the clamor. "It's time for a game. We have a good one today. And there are only going to be *ten* contestants. That's right, just ten. You were picked at random when you stepped onto the island, and you didn't even know it. Each of you has a little rock in your bag, about this big."

He made the shape with his spare hand. Rustling sounds rose across the beach as guests dug into their totes.

"Most of you will have a rock with a *black* dot on it," Eton continued. "If that's you, relax, take it easy, enjoy the island! You're the spectators this time around! But for ten lucky individuals, your dot is red. And you'll be competing to win a prize."

Ruth's stomach turned to ice. Her group had their stones out, checking the color. Theirs were all painted black.

She hadn't seen hers yet. But she already knew.

The woman at the welcome booth, the one who'd checked her name against the list, had reached deep into the crate to get her tote bag. Not picked from on top, like the others. But pulled from beneath.

He said it was random.

He lied. He wanted them to think they all had an equal chance. But he'd handpicked these first players. He'd wanted to craft a group that would be entertaining.

Which means he knows. He knows, somehow, he knows—

She bit the inside of her cheek until it hurt. He didn't know. He couldn't. Petition was a closely guarded secret. The most precious and the most dangerous secret she'd ever kept.

"Did you check yours?" Hayleigh asked, nudging Ruth. She barely heard the question over the clamoring and the music and the heat and the rushing in her ears.

She felt numb as she reached into the tote. Her fingers searched its depths and closed around a cool, smooth rock. She drew it out.

The painted circle shone in the late afternoon light.

Red as blood.

3.

Sophia Holmsten had killed a man.

At least, the public believed she had.

News sites reported a hit-and-run at two in the morning after a night of drinking at a bar in Manaus. Her rental car was caught on cameras near the scene, swerving as it tried to stay in its lane.

The local courts dismissed the case. The public, not so much.

Logan tapped the camera on his phone, taking a discreet photo. It captured her lounging on her beach towel, strawberry blond hair cascading down her back, her strappy bathing suit wrapping across her curves.

Her reputation had been shredded in most online spaces. While she still had a very loyal following of fans who believed in her innocence—or, perhaps, didn't care about her lack of it—the public no longer saw her as a glamorous but sweet model. Search bars now autofilled *murderer* after her name.

She'd come to the festival as part of her image rehabilitation, Logan guessed. Someone on her team might have suggested it. Sophia Holmsten, with her 6.8 million social followers and a persona of curated elegance, would normally never want to be associated with Eton and his tween-friendly content.

But it was a good chance to be seen in public in a controlled, safe way. She'd post beachside photos of her skin bathed in glowing sunsets, and she'd let the other attendees take candid pictures with her as she sat with an entourage six-strong, in case any guests wanted to make a scene.

Maybe she'd connect with Eton, even. Being associated with more wholesome creators wasn't a terrible plan, and she might already be considering cross-promotion possibilities. She certainly wouldn't be the only one.

Logan had also spotted Ryan Sherman, more commonly known as Trigger. His kid-focused channel mostly featured upsized versions of popular toys: Lego forts built from blocks the size of pillows, inflatable pools filled with slime. He'd recently finished probation after drug possession charges, though his audience was young enough to remain largely oblivious.

Elsewhere among the crowd were models and video essayists, influencers and travelogue hosts. Internet celebrities from a dozen unrelated paths had been lured to the festival by the promise of pristine beaches, publicity, and the chance to cross paths with their peers.

Logan's motives were shades of the same cloth. He ran a channel that unearthed and documented the secrets that online personalities tried to keep hidden. The scandals, the criminal charges, the legal backstabbings.

People sometimes called him a drama channel. But he'd always fought to be more than that. Drama channels took existing gossip and whipped it up into a storm; Logan sought original stories, and he often spent months on each project before laying out the narrative, documentary-style.

And, as petty as it was to insist on the distinction, it was the difference between being a tabloid and a newspaper. His pride insisted on the latter. It made it possible to pretend that his very expensive journalism degree had a purpose.

Onstage, Eton was hyping up the audience. Logan was surprised they were having a game so soon after arrival. There were only a few hours of daylight left; he'd expected the guests would be shown to their accommodations and given the remainder of the day to unwind.

But then, the trip only lasted five days. Eton must have wanted to use every available minute.

Commotion broke out as painted rocks were unveiled. Logan had already checked his: black. A tangible relief. He was here to observe, not perform.

His two most popular series had recently wrapped up. A promising line of inquiry into a new story had turned out to be hollow. His audience was willing to wait for quality, but Logan was also very aware of how fickle the algorithms could be. He'd requested a ticket to the festival as a last-second long shot and had been surprised to be accepted. Now he just needed the island to produce something. Even just a fluffy one-video stopgap to tide him over to his next major project.

Logan let his gaze skip over the pockets of excitement, the hot spots where winning rocks had been uncovered. He sat up straighter.

One of those groups held a familiar face. Zachary Waldon.

Logan hadn't noticed him on the cruise liner. And he certainly hadn't expected to see him at the festival. Zachary Waldon wasn't a celebrity. In fact, Logan was likely the only person on the beach who would recognize the man.

There were two kinds of tickets to the festival. Forty tickets—plus entourage accommodations—went to bona fide celebrities and online personalities. That was how Logan had gotten in. He knew every other name on the list, and Zachary hadn't appeared on it. Which meant he'd gotten in through the lucky draw.

All remaining tickets—five hundred and sixteen, at last count—had been given out randomly. As Eton had explained in his promotional video, it was the only way to keep it fair. He didn't want spots to go to the highest bidders; he wanted the festival to be for actual fans.

The entry form included questions like the entrant's age, how long they had been watching Eton's videos, and how many tickets they wanted. Because, in Eton's words, *A party is only fun if you get to bring your friends.*

Apparently, Zachary Waldon had entered. And won.

Or, at least, someone in his group had.

Logan angled his phone and took a photo. It was a distant shot and badly framed, but that was fine. Logan never published the images. They functioned as a visual journal and helped him remember threads he wanted to follow later. The photos not only captured the subject but also gave environmental context, a time stamp, and room for notes.

Obvious ones, like Sophia Holmsten, didn't require any commentary. But jotting down his thoughts in the moment could be useful mental triggers later. He tapped to add a caption to the picture. Text appeared under Zachary's distant, grainy photo.

THAT NIGHTMARE WITH THE PODCAST RESURFACES AGAIN.

4.

Hayleigh shrieked. She clutched at Ruth. "You got it! You actually got one of them!"

Nearby guests heard. They craned to get a glimpse of the coveted ticket into the game, some of them applauding her, and any hope Ruth had of quietly passing off the rock vanished.

"Ruth, that's amazing!" Zach's face lit up. He looked so happy for her, and she hated that she couldn't match his energy. "You've got some luck on your side today."

Except I don't. I was picked. Because of who I am. Because of Petition.

Stop it. That's paranoia. If you keep linking every event in your life back to Petition, you'll never be free.

But the sightings—

Dreams. They're just dreams. There's no such thing as sightings.

She should have left the nausea behind on the ship, but her stomach felt cold and heavy. She looked past Zach, toward the stage, half convinced that Eton would be standing at its edge, staring at her, cold and calculating.

He was doing his dance again, fists pumping and hips swinging as he celebrated for the winners. He didn't seem to notice Ruth.

See? Paranoia.

"Ruth?" Zach's hand was on her shoulder, gentle but concerned. "What's wrong?"

"I'm not feeling well." That was the truth, at least. "Do any of you want my rock?"

She held it out toward the group.

Hayleigh inhaled with desire, but she made no move to take it. Zach's eyebrows rose as he glanced at the offered gift.

For them, the rock was more than being allowed to play a game or win a prize. It was a chance to stand in front of Eton. To be *seen* by him. To impress him.

Only Carson didn't seem to want the stone. He was staring at Ruth. The joy was gone from his face. Even his body language had shifted, growing colder. The others, too mesmerized by the offering, didn't notice.

Hayleigh spoke first. "Ruthie, don't be ridiculous. You won it; you get to play."

"Is it the seasickness?" Zach asked. "Do you want to try some more ginger tablets?"

"Do we have our winners?" Eton yelled, his voice distorting as he leaned too close to the microphone. He held a hand up. "Let me see you!"

"Here!" Hayleigh called, waving and pointing at Ruth before Ruth could stop her. More attendees stood up through the scattered clusters, holding their red-painted stones above their heads, shouting triumphantly.

"There you are!" Eton yelled. At his side, Petra applauded them. Eton pointed at his audience. "Let me show you what you're competing for."

He thrust a hand into his shorts pocket. And he brought out a thick stack of notes, fastened together in the center with a band.

"Ten *thousand*," he said, fanning the package. "Cash, all yours to take home."

"Whoa," Zach whispered.

"And we're going to find out who wins it *right now*." Eton gestured over their heads.

They turned. Behind the audience, near the space where the sand sloped up to meet the jungle, stood five figures in bright yellow shirts. The word CREW was printed across their chests in thick black ink. The center figure held a staff, an orange-and-black pennant flag hanging from its tip.

As eyes turned toward them, the center figure began to move toward a path leading into the jungle, the flag undulating behind him. The other four crew members beckoned to the festival attendees.

"Let's go," Eton yelled. Then he thrust the microphone back toward his assistant and scrambled over the edge of the stage, landing heavily in the sand.

All around, the guests snapped into a frenzy, shouting and laughing as they stuffed trinkets back into their gift bags and collected their drinks. People ran past Ruth, kicking up sand as they raced to catch up with the flag leading them into the jungle.

Ruth's breathing whistled between her teeth. It was too much, happening too fast. She didn't want to play games. She didn't want an audience.

"Ruth?" Zach was still watching her, concern creasing the gap between his thick eyebrows. When she didn't answer, he held out a hand. "Let's talk. Somewhere quieter."

They left Hayleigh and Carson to gather their gift bags as they pressed against the flow of festival guests. The sun was hot, and Zach's hand was hotter.

"Is something wrong?" he asked, stopping in a clear area where they couldn't be overheard.

Ruth shook her head. It was hard to explain the crawling, itching discomfort that had burrowed under her skin since Eton had taken the stage. Or how she hated the way she felt cornered into participating. Like someone had shone a spotlight on her and told her to dance. "I don't even know what the game is. Can you take my rock? Please? You'll have more fun."

He gave a very soft smile. "I'll talk to one of the organizers and see what they can do."

The beach was emptying, and it made it easier to see the additional yellow-shirted staff members spaced around the perimeter. They stood with their hands behind their backs, attentively watching the crowd.

Zach jogged toward the nearest, a woman who couldn't have been older than twenty. Ruth couldn't hear them, so instead, she watched Zach's hands form gestures as he talked. The woman smiled, all helpful cheer, and shook her head.

Ruth turned away, not wanting to see any more.

The cruise liner they'd arrived on was growing smaller as it departed. They would be isolated on the island until it returned in five days' time.

On her other side, Eton had vanished into the jungle, along with most of the procession. Their beach was nearly empty save for stragglers who were ordering drinks or renting hats and buying sunscreen.

"Okay." Zach, slightly breathless, stopped at Ruth's side. "So, she says we're not allowed to trade or give away the rocks. They don't want game tickets being swapped for money or favors, so they have a blanket rule that they're only valid for the original owner. But you *can* withdraw from the game."

Some of the aching pressure left Ruth's back. "I can."

"Absolutely. You don't have to play if you don't want to."

Ruth knew what he was thinking. Because those same words were living in her own head. If Zach wasn't going to say them, she would.

"Ten thousand dollars is a lot of money."

Zach hesitated. "Sure, but the whole point of this festival is to have a break. You've been working hard. The last thing you need is to work *harder*. If you're not excited to play, then let's turn it down and join the audience."

She gazed up at him. His smile was always very slightly crooked, his eyebrows so thick that they were the first thing anyone noticed about him.

Zach said they were there to relax, but for Ruth, it was something more.

She had to get up before dawn for her job; Zach's shifts saw him arriving home late at night. The festival was a chance to really and truly spend time together. As a couple, and also with his friends. She'd hoped that, maybe, by the end of the week, they might feel like her friends too.

But she'd spent the cruise queasy and sleep-deprived. And now, given the chance to take part in a competition, all she wanted to do was hide.

That wasn't the person she wanted them to see.

It wasn't even the person she wanted to *be*.

"To hell with it," she said, and turned the rock over in her hand. "It's just a game. Let's play."

"Are you sure?"

"Yes. I want to do this." She gave him a smile she didn't fully feel.

Zach offered her his hand. As they crossed the beach, Ruth let her gaze turn to the vanishing procession.

Hayleigh and Carson waited for them at the jungle's edge. They were imitating Eton's quirky dance. Hayleigh, who had been taking classes since she was a child, managed to make the swinging hips and pumping fists seem choreographed. Carson scooped her up, over his shoulder. Hayleigh shrieked with laughter, sandals falling off her kicking feet as Carson spun them in a circle.

The question spilled out of Ruth: "Is Carson upset about something?"

"Hmm?" Zach raised his eyebrows. "I don't think so. Why do you ask?"

He doesn't like me, all of a sudden. The friendliest person I've ever met doesn't like me, and I don't know why.

"It's nothing," she said.

The trail into the jungle was a narrow dirt ribbon. Trees pressed in on them, leaves brushing across Ruth's bare skin. The temperature dropped and the sounds changed; the crashing surf was dampened and replaced by insect chatter and birdcalls.

Signs had been nailed to trees at regular intervals, marking the trail. One arrow pointed back the way they'd come: SUNSET BEACH. Another arrow ushered them forward: ENDURANCE COVE. The one the map had marked with a skull.

They mingled into the procession, Hayleigh skipping over roots as she chattered about influencers she'd spotted on the beach, Carson laughing at her jokes.

And then, before Ruth felt ready for it, they were at Endurance Cove.

Guests spilled onto sand textured with ocean debris. Jagged rock ridges walled the cove in on either side, spilling out of the jungle and pushing deep into the crashing waves. With the thick greenery to their backs, it made the beach feel like a capsule. As though, once you stepped onto it, there would be no way out.

A platform had been built not far from the path. It was smaller than the stage but also taller, reminiscent of a lifeguard tower. Behind that was a large screen, the size of a movie theater's. It was blank.

Eton and his assistant stood near the tower, waiting for the guests to filter out of the trees.

"Find yourself a good vantage point!" Eton had to yell to be heard. "Unless you're a player! If you're a player, hustle over here!"

"I'll be cheering for you," Zach said. He had to bend close to be heard, and he pressed a kiss to her cheek.

"Good luck!" Hayleigh squeezed Ruth into an intense hug. "You're going to be amazing!"

Carson didn't say anything.

Ruth wasn't sure she could speak, so she gave them a shaky nod as her group split away to join the audience.

It left her feeling very alone.

She turned her eyes toward what she knew had to be the stage for their game. A massive structure stretched out toward the ocean.

Gnawing fear built in her stomach.

Too late for second thoughts. No matter what the game was, she would have to find a way to hold her own against the ten strangers she'd be facing in the arena.

It was time to play.

5.

Logan hung back at the jungle's edge, using the trees for shade. Umbrellas had been set up around the cove, but there weren't enough for the swarming guests, and he didn't want to fight for one of the coveted spaces when they were already packed with overheated bodies.

It was easier to get a feel for the crowd from a distance too. They were growing rowdy. The drinks stand offered water, but it wasn't a popular option, not when the alcohol was free.

In the distance, closer to the game, Eton was ushering guests into the cove. He craned to look toward the forest, likely trying to gauge how many attendees were still coming, and his gaze locked onto Logan.

They hadn't crossed paths yet. Logan raised a hand, a voiceless acknowledgment.

For a split second, Eton remained frozen. Then he gave Logan a thumbs-up—an awkward gesture, which fit his slightly dorky brand—and turned back to the crowd.

"Huh," Logan whispered to himself. He slid his phone out and snapped a photo of Eton beaming at a guest, then added a caption.

AM I A SURPRISE?

It was hard to be sure from the distance, but he thought he'd caught a flash of shock on Eton's face. Which shouldn't have been possible. Logan was one of the VIP guests, a list Eton would have personally curated.

He'd need to leave the shade after all. Eton's reaction might be nothing, but it was just strange enough to be worth pursuing.

"Afternoon, sir."

A staff member had appeared behind him, stepping out of the forest. The yellow shirt hung loose off his slight frame, but he was clean-cut, and his body language was deferential and cheerful as he dipped his head. "I just wanted to check that you're doing okay. If you're looking for shade, I can fetch a spare umbrella for you."

Even for a VIP guest, it was more attentiveness than he'd been expecting. "I'm good. Thank you, though."

The man smiled, revealing large, slightly crooked teeth and half an inch of red gums. "Glad to hear it. We're always about, so just give myself or a colleague a wave if we can do anything for you."

A line of perspiration trailed down between Logan's shoulders as the staff member moved toward the crowd.

He'd had a unique smile.

And Logan had seen it before.

He had a strong memory for faces. Usually, he could also bring up a name. Not this time. The smile was familiar but only distantly.

Which meant Logan had most likely crossed paths with him just briefly.

He could have been part of the crowd at one of Logan's live events. Or maybe he'd appeared in a few seconds of video posted by one of the creators Logan followed.

It wasn't even that statistically unlikely. Eton was likely hiring staff workers who were familiar with his content and with online spaces in general, so the smiling staff member probably came from within the giant bubble online personalities crafted around themselves.

But...

Even though Logan couldn't remember where he'd seen that smile, he'd felt a pang of discomfort from it. As though the previous encounter had been tinged with unpleasantness.

Logan aimed his phone. The smiling staff member was speaking with guests at the edge of the audience. Logan took his picture, then added a caption.

SOMETHING'S WRONG HERE.

Ruth's throat tightened as she gazed up at the structure filling the better part of the cove.

Her first impression was of jagged lines and sharp angles.

It was made of wood. She thought of shipwrecks. Not the fresh ones with solid hulls, but the wrecks that had been decayed and weathered until all the wood had rotted away except for the frame.

This structure wasn't old, though. Its timber was raw enough to feel brutally out of place on the uninhabited beach.

It's a maze.

Or something like it.

Posts had been planted into the sand. They supported beams of wood that zigzagged across the cove, interlocking with one another. There didn't seem to be any pattern to the design; if anything, the beams seemed to have been arranged with deliberate erraticism.

Ruth suspected that, if viewed from above, it would have seemed uncannily like one of the house floor plans she and Zach had been looking at on real estate sites, except this house would have upward of eighty rooms. The suspended beams not only filled a large part of the cove, but they extended over the foaming ocean as well.

"Hustle time, contestants!" Eton called. He pulled his beanie off to run his fingers through damp hair, then replaced the hat, grinning at them. "If you have a red rock, you're wanted over here!"

It's a game. Ruth couldn't tear her eyes off the structure as she moved toward their host. *Games are designed to be fun. Games are designed so that anyone can play. Right?*

There were ladders leading up to the beams. She had a suspicion they would need to climb them.

"First up, I'm going to need your names," Eton said.

The group had clustered around him in a loose semicircle. Petra stood beside Eton, a sleek silver digital pad held in one hand, a stylus in the other. Eton pointed at the nearest contestant, a tall, broad-shouldered man.

"Trigger," he said, and snapped his fingers for emphasis. He was a performer, Ruth thought. She wouldn't be surprised if he had his own social media following.

Eton then pointed at Ruth, his smile wide, the full force of his unassuming charisma directed at her.

She was tempted to lie. Give him a fake name, maybe say she was Hayleigh. She wanted to see if his smile changed, or catch a flash of confusion. Any hint that he already knew her name.

But lies were like half-wild dogs. They could just as easily turn around and bite you as defend you.

Ruth was already carrying several powerful, dangerous lies. And she'd learned that it was risky to stack too many more on top. Too much weight and the whole tower would topple.

"Ruth," she said, reluctant to give him her surname.

Eton moved on without skipping a beat. The other contestants gave their names while the assistant jotted them down, but they blended into a muddy slurry in Ruth's ears. The crowd of festival attendees were making noise behind them as they fought for position around the game's stage. No one seemed to know what it was.

"That's great," Eton said, rocking on the balls of his feet. "We're ready to start! I'll explain the rules over the speakers in a moment, but right now, you just need to take your starting positions. There are ten ladders around the border of our game board. Each of you needs to find one and climb it. No sharing! There's a platform at the top, and you'll wait there. Everyone good with that?"

There were murmurs of agreement, broken by Trigger's question: "Are some starting places better than others?"

Eton's smile widened. "Maybe."

That single word was like lightning zapping through the group. Three of them broke away, racing toward the structure. A second of hesitation, then the others started after them. Eton laughed, clapping, then turned toward his announcer's podium.

Ruth joined the race but kept her pace easy. She was fairly sure she'd need to conserve her stamina for the actual game.

The other contestants' strategies varied. Some ran for the closest ladders—the ones nearest the audience—and latched onto them. Others ran farther down the beach or into the crashing surf, assessing each potential starting point before moving on.

Ruth reached the closest edge. The three ladders there had all been claimed, so she kept moving.

Eton had called it a game board. As she passed underneath the suspended planks, she squinted upward and tried to get a read on how the gameplay might unfold. Colorful flags flapped in the wind at various points. Some beams were painted different colors. If the design was based on any tabletop game, she didn't recognize it.

If she didn't know the rules, there was no way to guess which starting places might have an advantage. Which meant any would do. Ruth aimed for a ladder on the board's left-hand side, but another contestant, a woman with curly dark hair, beat her to it. She slammed into the wood frame, eyes wild, as though prepared to fight Ruth for it.

Ruth showed her palms, signaling that she wasn't competition, and turned away.

Available ladders were vanishing quickly. A few contestants on the other side of the board were still running between options, but as she watched, they each picked their positions and started climbing.

One ladder was left. Near the board's back, half submerged in the ocean.

Water splashed across Ruth's legs and filled her shoes as she waded out.

The adrenaline was hitting her, and she couldn't even tell if the water was warm or icy. She reached her ladder, gripped the smooth wood rungs, and began to climb.

It's just a game. Games are designed to be fun.

But Ruth didn't feel it. The ladder seemed to go on forever. As she crawled onto the four-foot circular platform at the ladder's top, all she felt was fear and twisting vertigo.

The platform was at least twelve feet above the swelling water.

She glanced to her side. Two other platforms were along that section of the board, and each already held their contestants: a small, shy-looking woman and a man who was kneeling, fingers digging into the wood, as though afraid he would fall if he let go.

Below them, a dark line rippled beneath the waves. Rocks, Ruth realized. Jagged rocks, hidden just under the water.

This isn't safe.

The taste of metal flooded her mouth. It was suddenly hard to breathe.

Shouldn't there be harnesses? A safety instructor, helmets, knee guards?

Weren't there laws about this kind of thing?

Laws only matter if there's someone to enforce them.

This was Eton's island. Eton's game. Eton's rules.

The audience moved like a haze. They were cheering. Not a single one of them seemed to question the contest.

No one was going to stop it.

Creaking rose from the supports as the ocean swelled. Ruth braced her hands on the platform and felt rough wood burrs against her palms.

She faced toward the announcer's podium, her mouth dry, her heart beating fast, waiting for her instructions.

Tell me how bad it's going to be.

6.

Logan leaned his back against the announcer's platform.

He'd planted himself there while Eton was speaking with the contestants. Eton's online persona was goofy, friendly, happy. A bit like a golden retriever in human form. But Logan suspected he was a lot smarter, and significantly more perceptive, than he acted in his videos.

You didn't get to be a self-made millionaire otherwise.

But, no matter how observant Eton actually was, the event created enough chaos that Logan could get close unseen. He'd guessed that Eton would take his place on top of the platform, and that guess had been right.

He held his phone in one languid hand and maintained a disinterested face. If anyone on the beach looked at him, it would seem like he was using the platform for shade.

But the location put him just ten feet below Eton. And the angle meant Eton would need to lean over the railing to see him.

In the distance, the contestants ran for the game's structure, jostling to pick ladders.

It looked unsafe. It might even give Logan the video he'd come to the island for: a poorly planned game exposing Eton to legal liability. Not exactly deep journalism, but enough.

He could have gone for that instead. Tried to get some footage, maybe jotted down time stamps as the game unfolded.

But there were dozens of phone cameras already aimed at the stage. He was the only person close enough to Eton and his assistant to hear them.

And his hunch paid dividends.

"Is Logan Lloyd here?"

Eton's voice still held its usual joviality, but there was a clipped under-current of tension.

His assistant must have heard it too. Her answer seemed hedged. "He was a last-minute VIP invite. Kamille Faux had to pull out, and Lloyd didn't need any additional tickets, so we slotted him in."

"You didn't warn me, Pet."

Warn. An unusual word choice.

"It was in one of the memos. That was the weekend we lost our IT lead, so you might have skimmed past it." She sounded uneasy. "What's wrong with Logan Lloyd?"

Silence. Logan held on to his bored facade, one thumb moving above his phone as though he was playing on it, but every muscle was keyed rigid. Wood creaked above his head as someone shifted their weight. The announcer's podium, like the game's structure, was a recent construction, and it sounded like it was in pain.

"What's wrong with Logan Lloyd?" Petra's voice dropped, and she became hard to hear. "He has a decent reputation. A large audience. He's a video essayist, and you said you wanted more of those. I thought he was a safe bet."

"He shreds reputations, Pet." Eton laughed, and it was a sudden, jarring noise, as though he wished he could erase his previous words. "Never mind that. Looks like the contestants are nearly in place."

"Eton, I doubt he's after you. He doesn't target people without cause. And some of the other VIP guests should be plenty of fodder for him."

"You're very right, of course—I'm being a goose. Let's get on with this game, yeah? Let's have some fun."

The words were light, happy, energetic.

Logan tipped his head back. Pressed against the platform's side, he could only see one part of Eton. A hand, wrapped around the wooden railing.

The knuckles were white.

———————————

Ruth crouched on the platform. Wind, full of brine, buffeted at her back. She thought she could feel the wooden structure sway.

The platform was only four feet wide. It felt like nothing.

Two beams connected to her platform: one to her left, and one that led straight ahead. They connected to more planks, and those to still more, creating dozens of splitting pathways.

It didn't seem safe to stand. But she had to. She needed to see the game's layout. To see what was coming.

Flags fluttered at regular intervals. Beneath each was a white box with a red number painted on it, one to five.

Ten contestants. Five boxes. We need to collect something from them, don't we?

The beams seemed very narrow. The ground very far away. She tried to get a read on the other contestants' reactions. Some were scanning the pathways, trying to memorize the map.

"Welcome," Eton's voice boomed across the cove, "to your first game."

The screen behind the raised platform was massive. Even from the distance, Ruth could see it clearly. Text flashed up: Survive the Maze. Beneath was an illustrated skull, matching the one on the map.

"Spread around the maze are five boxes," Eton said. "Inside each box is a numbered piece. Your aim is to collect all five and then hang them on the pole in the maze's center."

Ruth glanced toward the central pole. It rose higher than any other. Shining metal hooks had been fastened around it, though they looked uncomfortably out of reach.

"Easy, right?" The words on the screen were replaced with Eton's grinning face as an unseen camera magnified him a hundredfold. "Of course, it wouldn't be an Eton game without a few twists."

The crowd spread across the beach, filling the gap between Eton's platform and the game. Ruth looked for Zach, but the electric panic had gotten into her head, and she couldn't see him.

"Some planks are painted *red*," Eton said, enunciating clearly. Ruth fought to focus on his words. "Red planks are shortcuts. But, beware: they're narrower than the regular paths. You'll have to weigh that risk against the time saved."

He wasn't joking, Ruth saw. The unpainted beams looked about six inches wide. The red ones were half that.

"If you touch the ground—or the water, for that matter—you're out of the game. I repeat: you *cannot* leave the platforms or else you'll be disqualified. Otherwise, the board is yours to use how you like. If you think you can make a jump, you're welcome to try. It might save you some valuable time."

No. No chance. The gaps between the beams were at minimum five feet wide. The platform swayed again, and Ruth fought against the vertigo crashing through her.

"Inside two of the boxes, alongside the numbers you'll need to retrieve, you'll also find a big red button. Press it, and a siren will play."

Eton held up a finger. On cue, a wailing, whooping sound blared out of the speakers. Ruth flinched. It sounded very much like police sirens.

"When you hear that noise, everyone has to freeze," Eton said. His grin was getting wider and wider. He seemed delighted. "If you so much as wobble, you'll be disqualified. That applies to everyone... except the contestant that presses the button. If you activate the siren, you'll get a full ten seconds advantage. You can keep moving while everyone else holds still. And ten seconds can count for a *lot* in a game like this."

The panic was still running hot through Ruth, but it was starting to condense, to sharpen into focus.

She saw Zach. He'd pushed toward the front of the crowd and raised his hands above his head to applaud. His eyes were fixed on her, his smile full of pride.

"Wait for my mark," Eton called, and the speakers were so powerful that sound waves reverberated through Ruth's bones. "Count down from ten."

She took a breath. She was starting to see more clearly. *Think* more clearly.

"Ten," Eton called. His face vanished from the screen, replaced with a countdown. The audience joined in. "Nine! Eight!"

Some contestants dropped into a crouch, preparing. Eton had described the game as a race, and that was how they were treating it.

But that was a mistake. The goal shouldn't be speed.

The goal was to *stay on the boards.*

Falling was an instant disqualification. It was the only way to truly lose.

And none of them had any practice on the suspended beams.

"Seven! Six!"

Ruth wasn't athletic enough to compete on speed. So she'd play to her strengths. She'd move cautiously and deliberately.

She stood straight, gaining as much height as she could, to try to map the puzzle's layout. She ignored the red beams—she wasn't confident she could cross them without falling. Instead, she let her gaze zigzag across the unpainted paths, figuring out her route to the first two numbers.

"Five! Four!"

Some of the other contestants had the same idea. She could see them mouthing as they tried to memorize the path. One woman slipped her phone out of her pocket, held it high above her head, and took a photo. A smart idea, except Ruth knew it would be hard to use as soon as she left her starting space.

"Three! Two!"

She filled her lungs with briny air. The platform swayed. Her palms were hot and prickling.

"One!" Eton raised his fist into the air. "*Go!*"

A boom shook them. Colored smoke billowed out of concealed cannons around the cove's edge.

The race began.

7.

Ruth stepped off her platform.

The boards were six inches wide. That should have been plenty, but Ruth's balance wavered. She lowered herself, sinking her center of weight, and poised one hand over the wood.

The beam shuddered—reverberations caused by the contestant to her right as he ran. She spared him a glance. Curling flaxen hair was cut into a mullet and held back from his face with a bandanna, and it bounced with each leaping step.

Too eager. Too ready to treat it like a race.

But his agility was better than Ruth's. The pathways shook as he charged along them.

To her left, the meek-looking girl shuffled forward, bent over to hold onto the planks with both hands. She might have been afraid of heights. Or maybe she'd seen the ridge of rocks beneath her.

Ruth focused on keeping her movements smooth. She could be fast without actually running. And she'd memorized the route she'd need to take to the nearest box. That let her keep her eyes on the beam beneath her feet.

"Blake, Trigger, and Makayla are going full tilt." Eton's voice boomed over the shouts and cheers from the audience. "Blake's nearly at his first box. He's—oh!"

There was movement in her peripheral vision. Blake, the mulleted contestant, had tried to cut a corner. His sneakers slipped on the wood.

One hand lashed out, reaching for the nearest beam, but only managed to scrape it.

Ruth's heart filled her throat as she watched him drop. His lithe body twisted in the air, then he hit the sand hard.

Hard enough that Ruth swore she could feel the reverberations.

We're so fragile inside. We're not designed to fall. Organs can burst. Cartilage pops, muscles snap. Not a single part of our body is supposed to withstand that kind of impact.

She stared, fixated with horror, at Blake's pained grimace. Then he rolled onto his side and got to his knees, and an embarrassed smile softened his face.

"Blake's out!" Eton yelled. "He's out, and Makayla is first to a box! She's got her number, and she's moving again!"

Two staff members jogged to Blake, and he laughed as they helped him limp into the roaring, deafening crowd.

They were all letting the game continue. As though nothing had even happened.

"Jessica and Ruth are both still hanging by the starting line," Eton called, and Ruth flinched to hear her own name amplified by the speakers. "Meanwhile, Ricky's gotten turned around. Vincent and Yu made it to Box Four at the same time, and there's a fight on for who gets to claim their number first. Looks like it's Yu!"

She had to keep moving.

A humming sound filled the air. She glanced up. Something hovered over the game, all sharp angles, and Ruth's first thought was of an enormous, wasplike insect. Then she realized it was both higher and larger than she'd first thought. A drone.

The screen behind Eton displayed a list of the contestant names running down one side. One turned red: Blake, disqualified.

The rest of the screen was filled with an aerial view of the game. Ruth saw herself, hunched and hesitant, uncannily still as the others moved like colored dots across the map.

Are they recording this? Is it going on Eton's channel? Don't they need permission to do that?

Panic left a bitter tang on her tongue. She dropped her head, letting her hair fall forward to disguise her face.

That's paranoia. Stop it.

But what if—

No one could possibly recognize you.

The ringing in her ears was rising again. It was drowning out the clarity, dulling her senses. She lurched forward, faster than was wise, just to snap through the paralysis.

"Cia has her first number!" Eton's narration washed over the riotous audience. "And Mateo is in a standoff with Ricky. Makayla has just snatched her *second* number, pulling into a strong lead!"

Ruth's first box was close. She jogged the final few steps, feeling the board shudder under her feet, and clutched at the post.

A flip lid hid the box's contents. She shoved it up.

A vivid red button caught her eye. It had been set into the back of the box, invisible from outside. The first of two alarms.

No one had been to this box yet. She could press it, gain ten seconds of uninterrupted advantage. Maybe disqualify some other contestants if they couldn't hold still enough.

It meant every eye would be fixed on her for those ten seconds. She might even become a target if the other contestants thought she'd gained too much ground.

She was playing a cautious game. She ignored the button.

Beneath were ten palm-sized circles of wood, the number *3* painted on them. Ribbons had been woven through a hole, making them look like medals.

They were meant to be worn, Ruth realized. She pulled one out and looped it over her neck, then dropped the lid back in place.

"Ruth has her first number!" Eton yelled. "So does Trigger! And—wait—we've just lost another contestant! Cia's down!"

The drone was racing toward the other side of the game. Ruth's eyeline followed its trajectory and saw a woman in the sand, getting to her feet. The game was shallower on that side. A five-foot drop instead of ten, and Cia was already walking away.

The screen behind Eton had been updated. Two names were now red. The rest had numbers next to them, tracking their scores. Most were on one. Makayla and Yu both had two. Only Jessica, shuffling on hands and knees, hadn't reached a box.

Ruth had already planned her next path. She pushed away from the post, then held her arms out for balance as she paced along the board and took a left turn. Eton was narrating, but she let the words fade out of her focus.

And then the siren blared.

Ruth flinched and nearly lost her balance. She remembered, just in time, that she was supposed to freeze. Her toes dug into the wood beam, fighting to hold herself steady, her arms held out awkwardly like a posed doll.

"The first advantage!" Eton's voice was turning ragged. He thumped a fist onto the observation tower's railing. "Trigger has it! Only Trigger can move!"

Trigger howled in triumph, both fists held above him, one clutching his most recently claimed token, as he jogged along the maze. Ruth half expected him to fall, but he vaulted along his route, wavering.

Am I playing it too safe? Was this a mistake?

"Vincent: disqualified!" Eton yelled, as a figure in Ruth's peripherals rocked, arms swiveling as he fought to hold his balance. "Find a ladder back to the beach, Vincent!"

The sirens cut out.

Ruth sucked in a breath, then leaned forward and took a right turn. Her next box was close. Someone was already at it. The dark-haired girl who'd claimed the ladder Ruth had wanted. She snatched out her token and slung it around her neck.

"Makayla's at three!" Eton called. "She's been flawless so far; can she keep that up for the last two tokens?"

The girl turned toward Ruth and began advancing along the beam.

"Wait—" Ruth held up a hand. There was no way they could pass one another. But Makayla didn't seem to care.

The ocean swelled beneath them. White-tipped waves caressed the hidden line of rocks.

She's going to push me off. Ruth couldn't even tell if she was being irrational. Makayla's face was fixed, her jaw rigid. And she was moving so much faster than Ruth could.

Ruth backtracked, breathless and unsteady. They were just a few paces apart.

"I'm going straight," Makayla yelled, and Ruth realized she was at a turnoff, where a converging route intersected. She sidestepped onto it, nearly toppling, and a second later, Makayla barreled past.

"Looks like Makayla won that confrontation," Eton said. "Ruth lost time, but she stayed in the game. Meanwhile, Mateo is at his second box, and Trigger's trying his luck on a red beam."

Ruth stepped back onto her route. Her legs trembled, but she pushed herself forward.

The audience gasped, then roared. "Still in!" Eton yelled, and Ruth knew, even without looking, that Trigger had come close to falling off the red beam.

She hit the box, shoved the lid up, and pulled out a token. The pile was smaller than in the first box.

She slung the token around her neck. Then she took several precious seconds to assess the board.

Figures moved across it. Some, like Makayla and Trigger, actually ran, their pounding sneakers shaking dust off the unsteady wood.

There was a struggle on the island side of the board. Two men had tried to cross the same beam, much like Ruth and Makayla, but neither of them was giving space. They grappled, trying to skirt around one another without falling. Ruth watched, horrified, as the taller man's shoe slipped. He threw out his arm, catching it around the beam on the way past.

"Ricky's down!" Eton yelled. "Wait—can he—is he—"

Ricky hung suspended, one arm hooked around the beam, feet kicking at air. The other man leaped across him. Ricky tried to pull himself up, his face straining, searching for purchase with his spare hand. Then his face slumped in defeat, and he let himself drop.

"Ricky's out!"

Another name changed color on the board.

Four red. Six black.

And Ruth had found her path to the next box.

She moved forward, faster than before. Eagerness was growing, and it was crowding out the anxiety. Four contestants were out. And Ruth was close to getting another token.

Was this what people meant when they said games were *fun*?

The drone raced overhead, and its insectlike whir mixed with Eton's voice. "Disaster! Trigger went to a box he's already visited! That's going to cost him dearly. This might be Makayla's game to lose. She's nearly at her fourth box, and—yes—she's got it!"

The siren surged to life. Makayla had gotten to the first box Ruth had visited. It was in the far corner of the map, over the ocean, and it seemed like most of the contestants were saving it for last.

Ruth froze, half crouched. Numbers flashed up on the screen, counting down from ten.

"Mateo can't hold still!" Eton crowed. "Disqualified, my friend!"

From her angle, Ruth didn't have to turn her head to see Makayla.

The woman slung the token around her neck and then broke into a sprint. She just needed one more to win. She seemed to have a good sense of the maze, and looped around it in a path that would carry her over the deepest part of the map.

And Ruth was in the perfect place to see it all unfold.

Makayla flew across one of the longest beams in the maze. It was at least twenty feet, bolted into posts at either end.

The beam reverberated with each well-placed step. Makayla was moving fast, and it seemed like she was no longer racing the other contestants but was racing herself.

One of the precious bolts holding the path in place snapped free.

The beam twisted. Splinters bristled along the fracturing wood.

Makayla's ankle turned along with the surface. She tried to correct, bringing her other foot across, but there was no recovering when the beam was no longer stable.

She threw out her arms as she slipped off the side. She was trying to catch the beam on the way past, stop her fall like Vincent had, possibly even pull herself back up.

And, maybe, she could have managed it. If the surface hadn't been wrenched into a ridge of ugly shards as the board splintered.

Makayla's hand grasped the ridges. Skin tore.

Ruth's mouth opened, a silent gasp, as blood gushed across the wood. More sprayed as Makayla's hand broke free, splinters embedded in it. Droplets scattered in an arc and were snatched away by the ocean-borne wind.

And Makayla kept falling.

Into the swells of gem blue and frosting white—and the twisting, distorted line of rocks.

8.

"Help!" Ruth screamed.

"And Makayla's down!" Eton's narration, booming from the speakers, sounded strange. It held all of his joviality and eagerness, but a tinge of uncertainty caught at the edges, making the cadence off-kilter.

He hadn't seen it as clearly as Ruth had. He was too far away. But it must have looked bad, even from his distance.

"Help!" Ruth hunched, gripping the path she stood on, vertigo thick and her blood hot as it pumped through her head. "Help her! She needs help!"

A drop of blood oozed off the edge of the splintered beam.

The ocean's surface rose up to meet it, swallowing the offering before subsiding back down. Froth spread across the surface, obscuring the rocks beneath.

Makayla hadn't surfaced.

Staff members ran toward the water. They carried bodyboards and ropes. They were so, so far away.

Ruth lurched forward. She didn't know what she was doing, only that she had to do *something*. She skittered along her path, further over the water, trying to get near the place Makayla had fallen.

The paths were a maze, designed to confuse contestants, designed to make it difficult to navigate. There was no easy route.

A hand broke the water's surface. Makayla lurched up. Her hair was plastered over her face. Her mouth stretched wide as she tried to gasp in air. She was there for all of a second, then she was gone again, dragged back under before she could make a sound.

Where she'd been, a stain bled through the water. Jewel red mixing through jewel blue.

Ruth reached the edge of the fractured beam. She couldn't get any closer to Makayla without stepping onto it. She pressed one shoe against the wood, testing it, and it tilted. She swore, then swore again.

She looked behind.

Eton had fallen silent. The drone hovered overhead, facing toward Ruth, facing toward the blood spreading through the water, and the images were magnified on the screen.

Most of the other contestants had stopped moving. Only Trigger, sensing an advantage, scrambled toward a box.

Three staff members were forging through the water. The progress was agonizing.

Makayla broke the water's surface a second time. Her fingertips raked through the froth. She was gone again before her face could reach the surface. Before she could draw air.

"No," Ruth whispered.

She scanned the water beneath her. Twelve feet down and with ridges hidden beneath the waves. Nowhere to jump that wouldn't dash her against the rocks.

"Hey! Where is she?"

Ruth snapped back. The three staff members were approaching, straddling the boards as they paddled. The leader looked up at Ruth, her face damp and creased. "Can you see her?"

The waves are obscuring their view.

Ruth threw herself forward and stretched out her arm, pointing at the space she'd last seen Makayla.

The leader had an orange float attached to a rope. She straightened, aimed, and threw.

It landed inside the spreading circle of discoloration.

Ruth felt frozen, her arm still outstretched. The float undulated with the water's swell. Her ears were filled with rushing: the rushing of the water, the rushing of the wind, the rushing whispers from the audience on shore.

A hand broke the ocean's surface.

Its knuckles were stark white as it locked onto the device. A second hand pierced the surf, clawing at nothing, then vanished again.

Then Makayla's face broke out of the depths. Hair plastered her skin, covering her eyes, blocking her nose. Her mouth stretched wide as she tried to gasp in air. She had no clearance; water gushed over her lips.

The staff members pulled at the rope. Their leader yelled, words incoherent. They leaned back, muscles straining. It felt as though the ocean was fighting them, trying to hold her, and each inch was agonizing.

Makayla writhed. Her second hand had latched on to the float, leaving streaks of blood on the plastic. She couldn't keep her head above water.

Ruth bent over, clutching at the beam, willing them to be faster. Foaming waves crashed over Makayla. Ruth couldn't see her face under the veil of hair. But they were closing the gap. Ten feet, then five, then three.

The nearest staff members leaned as far as they could reach.

Hands grasped onto her clothes, pulling her up. A flood of water poured off her as they hauled her onto the bodyboard.

"She's okay!" Eton called, raising both hands. "She's okay!"

His words were met with cheers and shouts of relief from the audience.

He was lucky he was half a beach away. If he'd been any closer, Ruth would have slapped him.

Makayla was not okay.

Blood trailed from a limp arm cast over the bodyboard. More seeped from her back, where holes had been torn through her shirt.

She'd hit the rocks when she'd gone under. And the waves had dragged her over them. Again and again and again.

She was moving, coughing, gluts of water and blood flowing from her open mouth. Except for those erratic jolts, she was limp. If the staff hadn't been holding her on the board, Ruth thought, she would have slipped off and back under.

Ruth straddled her beam, just feet from where Makayla had fallen. She turned, slowly and unsteadily, to look toward the beach.

She was waiting for Eton to call them back to shore. He'd tell them to return to the ground in a safe and cautious manner.

Behind him, the screen changed. The number increased next to Trigger's name, showing that he'd picked up a token while everyone else was distracted.

Makayla's name turned red. Disqualified.

A sound caught in Ruth's throat. The staff members were paddling their boards back to the shore, carrying Makayla with them. She wasn't even out of the water yet, and someone had updated her game status.

Eton hadn't done that, at least. He was announcing; someone else would be in charge of changing the scores. Some employee who didn't know any better.

Surely, they weren't continuing the game.

"Only four contestants remain!" Eton bounced, leaning against the railing as he craned to watch them. "It looks like the slow-and-steady players are being rewarded. With front-runner Makayla out, this could be anyone's game!"

No. How dare you.

Makayla and the staff were almost onto the sand. A fading trail of tinted water marked their journey.

"It seems like now's the time to announce our last-minute twist," Eton called. "There are prizes for the runner-ups. It doesn't matter if you can't catch up to first place, you can still go home with some cash!"

Hot anger pooled in Ruth's stomach.

Trigger, the contestant who had kept moving while Makayla was under the water, had four tokens. Ruth could have sat and waited for him to win, then climbed down the nearest ladder.

But Eton wanted to stretch the game out.

Trigger was moving eagerly, almost gleefully. On the other side of the board, Yu had also reentered the game. He was being more cautious, though. Makayla's drop must have shaken him.

Jessica—the anxious girl who'd started near Ruth—had reached a box and then stopped moving entirely. She sat with her thighs clenching her beam, head pressed against the box, arms wrapped around the post, token dangling from white fingers. Afraid of heights. Even more so now.

If Ruth wanted the game to end, she would have to compete.

She swore, then carefully lifted herself up to regain her feet. She was still poised over the ridge of submerged rocks. Every shift seemed to make the wood sway. The wind was picking up, pulling at her balance.

Her attempt to reach Makayla had brought her close to a box. Ruth moved gingerly, giving each step her full attention, no longer willing to take risks.

"He's nearly there! Trigger's almost at his final stop! Can he make it without succumbing to the beach's curse?"

Her anger was helping mitigate the nerves, but Ruth was at her limit. She disconnected her mind from her ears, refusing to hear another word.

At the box, she lifted the lid and placed her third token around her neck. Then she scouted out her route to the remaining two. The path would take her back over the beach. The shallower half of the game. Small mercies.

The platforms seemed very empty with so many lost players.

She waited until she was over sand and then sped up, desperate to put an end to the experience. Eton's voice was growing frantic, but she ignored it. A burst of roaring applause told her first place had been won.

She stopped at her fourth box, retrieved the prize, and turned toward her final location.

The crowd spread across the sand. It was a disorienting swell of color and movement. Hands shook in the air. Bodies moved as they danced.

We sing, we sing, we sing to you…

It had been a long time since she'd had that song stuck in her head. The celebrating crowd was dredging up memories of another gathering. Equally frantic. Equally euphoric.

You hear, you hear, when we call to you…

She flicked her head, but the tune wouldn't stop looping. Ruth tried to sing a different song under her breath. That was the advice she'd been given: Drown out an unwanted melody by playing something louder.

Only, the modern pop songs never seemed able to completely dislodge the lullaby-like rhymes that had dominated her childhood.

Then, suddenly, she was at her final box. Her head cleared. The sounds from the crowd felt louder, breaking through the numbness.

She took out the token and slung it around her neck. The five rounds of wood rattled.

The board behind Eton had updated. Both Trigger and Yu's names had turned green, but Ruth's was still black.

Isn't the game over?

Then she remembered: the tokens had to be hung on the central post.

Come on. Don't make me do it. Just say the game's finished. Jessica's not moving; I have the tokens. Call it already.

"She looks exhausted!" Eton's voice flooded her ears as she allowed him back in. He thumped his palm on the railing. None of his excitement had faded. "She's drained, she's utterly wrung out, but she's so close to the end! Let's cheer her on!"

I think I actually hate you.

Ruth turned as the audience roared for her. Trigger and Yu were already at the center pole, sitting on the beams as they waited. Their tokens were hung on the hooks nailed high overhead.

The drone hummed above, following her last steps. She could feel the weight of their eyes as the entire beach's focus narrowed in on her. It was agony.

The pole's shadow stretched over her as she pulled her tokens off. The hook really had been placed too high to reach. She wished she'd seen how the other contestants had managed it. Maybe they'd jumped. Maybe they'd shimmied up the pole.

"Hey, we can help," Trigger said, standing. He was a massive person, his short-cropped hair spiked with a thick layer of gel. He crouched, wrapping his arms around Ruth's hips. Yu joined on the other side. Ruth gasped as she was lifted off the platform.

The hook swayed into view. She tilted forward and threw the ribbons over it, then they cautiously lowered her back onto the wood.

"Game over!" Eton yelled.

Booms sounded around the cove's edge as the concealed cannons went off a second time. Roman candle fireworks sent cascades of light through the billowing smoke. The crowd applauded, but the game's end felt like disconnecting a magnet. Those nearest the jungle were already turning back to get more drinks or an early dinner.

Trigger swung himself over the edge of the beam, hanging by his hands for a second before dropping into the sand. Yu crossed to the nearest ladder instead, and Ruth followed in his wake. Two yellow-shirt staff members had climbed up to help Jessica back to the beach.

"Get over here!" Eton's voice was no longer magnified by the microphone. He'd left the announcement tower and held his arms up, ushering the three of them closer. "Come and claim your prizes!"

Trigger and Yu broke into sprints. Ruth, feeling the crashing effects of fading adrenaline, simply walked.

The other two had already accepted their prizes and congratulations and had left by the time Ruth caught up.

"And here you are!" Eton spread his arms wide as though to offer a hug, his smile warm enough to replace the fading sun. "Our third-place champion, Ruth!"

She kept her even pace right up until the end, then raised her hand and hit him.

9.

"Whoa!"

Eton rocked back, his hand over his cheek. The reaction felt exagger-ated. Almost cartoonish. It was as though he was still playing the persona he put on in his videos.

Or maybe there was no persona. Maybe he'd never been acting.

"Makayla was hurt," Ruth said. The anger felt like a molten metal trickling down her throat and burning every scrap of exposed flesh it touched. "Seriously hurt."

"Yeah, damn, that was bad, huh?" Eton lowered his hand. She hadn't hit him hard. Thoughts of how fragile humans really were—full of things that could pop and burst and snap—had been haunting her, even through the anger.

"Why didn't you stop the game?"

Eton blinked, then grimaced. "I guess I should have. I knew she fell, but I couldn't see what was happening, not really. Pet told me how bad it was just a moment ago."

The assistant, Petra, stood at his side. Her icy glare was fixed on Ruth, and Ruth knew she wouldn't get another shot at Eton. Not that she wanted one. The anger was already cooling, turning solid and heavy.

"I wasn't thinking. Like, at all." Eton looked rueful, something Ruth hadn't actually expected. "We've spent the last few weeks trying to make everything flawless, and in the heat of the moment, all I could think about was keeping the game going. You know? It felt so important to put on a good show. That was a mistake. I'm going to be a lot more careful from here on out, I can promise you that."

"Okay." Ruth swallowed. "Makayla. Is she…?"

"I'm about to head over to check on her now. She's with our medical team. They're really good, but we might still need to bring in a helicopter to take her to a mainland hospital. The doctor's going to make that call."

Ruth sensed movement behind her. Zach was there, his body tense. Prepared to step between her and Eton. To back her up.

It wasn't needed. Not anymore.

"Sorry for hitting you," she managed. "Shouldn't have done that."

"No, no, I get it." His smile was back, though sheepish. "Honestly, I'm pretty sure I deserved it. Oh, and here. I owe you this."

He held out a velvet bag tied with a gold cord.

"Your prize," he prompted when she didn't react. "For a strategic and well-earned third place."

Ruth glanced toward the game. The setting sun backlit it, turning the wooden beams dark and skeletal.

"Yeah, it feels gross to be talking about money when someone was hurt," Eton said, his voice soft. "But…I think I'd feel even worse if you turned it down. Besides, if you don't take it, it'll just languish in my bank account, and that's not helping anyone, huh?"

Ruth finally reached out. Eton placed the bag in her palm. It was unexpectedly light for something that looked like a pirate's treasure bag. Which meant it probably held cash.

"Oh, and do you still have your welcome bag rock?" At Ruth's nod, Eton gave her a thumbs-up. "Great. Hold on to that. It might come in handy tomorrow, yeah? Anyway, you guys ask a staff member to show you to your cabin. I'll be back soon, but I want to check in on Makayla real quick."

He waved as he turned away. Ruth felt tingly and uncomfortable as she clutched the velvet bag.

"Hey," Zach said. Hayleigh and Carson stood behind him, watching but hesitant to get nearer. Zach cautiously brushed his fingertips across her arm. "What happened?"

Ruth shook her head. A sinking, miserable sensation was rising through her.

She'd promised Zach that they were just going to have a fun, relaxing week. And on the very first day, within hours of making land, she'd tried to start a fight with the man who'd paid for the whole trip.

Her mouth was open, but she didn't know what to say. Or how to fix any of it.

"I'm sorry." Zach's voice was very soft. "I shouldn't have pressured you to play."

The sinking feeling was growing worse. "You didn't. It's fine. I'm sorry—I'm—I—"

Hayleigh swooped in. She threaded one arm through Ruth's, half comfort, half support. "You've been in the sun for *hours*. And I don't think you ever had lunch. Come on, we're going to get you some shade and something to drink."

Ruth swallowed around a lump in her throat.

Thank you, Hayleigh.

They crossed to the edge of the jungle, and Carson shook out towels for them. Zach offered Ruth his water bottle, and Hayleigh coaxed her to sit down. They seemed determined to pretend the scene with Eton hadn't happened.

"You were amazing up there, Ruthie," Hayleigh said, kicking long, tanned legs out, pink nail polish winking in the sun as she flexed her toes. "You got third place! Honestly, I don't think I would have made it past two minutes if I'd tried."

The gathering on the beach was beginning to thin out. Some guests were climbing onto the game structure, intent on recreating the challenge for themselves. Others had waded into the shallow water to enjoy the last warmth of the afternoon. Most, though, were trailing into the jungle, led by staff members, to find their accommodations.

"How much did you win?" Hayleigh threw her head back, laughing. "Oh my gosh, that was so rude. Don't answer! I'm just so excited for you."

"You know, that second-place guy lost a lot of time," Carson said. "I bet you could have beaten him if you'd tried."

It was the first time he'd spoken to her since arriving on the island. And Ruth didn't know whether to take it as the joke it was phrased as, or the accusation it felt like.

"Hey now," Hayleigh said, elbowing Carson. "She did *great*. I'm pretty sure you'd have ended up in the sand if your places were switched."

A ripple of color-drenched fabrics crossed their view. A group of women were passing, climbing up to the paths. They were young, their clothes flowing around athletic bodies, glossy hair cascading across flawless skin. Posed against the pale sand and ocean horizon, they looked like a snapshot of a magazine ad promising pure luxury and indulgence.

The leader glanced toward Ruth. Foxlike eyes blinked, then she turned back to her entourage in a swirl of amber hair. Ruth caught a single word through the white noise of their conversation.

"Petition."

The air left Ruth's lungs.

"I wonder how far off dinner is?" Hayleigh continued. "I was thinking we could get some snacks from that kiosk, but I don't want to ruin our appetites."

The beautiful women vanished, stepping onto the jungle path. Ruth felt as though the world had tilted at a sharp angle. She clutched the metal bottle, unable to make a sound, unable to breathe or even think.

"Hey," Zach said. He'd noticed. One hand pressed into Ruth's back. "You don't look well."

"Walk." She swallowed, her tongue thick and unresponsive. "I need to take...a walk. Clear my head."

She sent him a pleading glance, and he caught her meaning.

"I'll go with you." He rocked onto his feet, directing the next words to Carson and Hayleigh. "Why don't you guys see if you can find where we're staying? They should have gotten our luggage dropped off by now."

"Oh, yeah." Carson stretched. "Hopefully, they didn't leave it on the boat. I like this outfit, but not enough to wear it for the next five days."

In the distance, the cruise ship had nearly vanished. Sunset bled across the sky behind it, vivid and violent.

Ruth led the way into the jungle. She could sense Zach's concern growing as they left the path behind, but she didn't want to risk being overheard. She'd always had a strong sense of direction. They weren't going to get lost.

When she stopped, the only sounds that intruded were the trill of insects and rush of air through the lush growth.

Ruth reached out and pressed her fingers into a rotting branch. Wood pulped beneath the light pressure. The jungle was overflowing with life, but it was also drenched in death. Mulching leaf litter returning to soil. Dying trees bowed over. Insects that ate and died and were eaten in turn.

Death supported the life. A contradiction.

"Ruth. I'm worried about you."

Zach leaned against a tree. His thick hair was growing heavy in the humidity.

"I know. I'm sorry." She closed her eyes, felt the way her heart galloped. "I need a reality check."

"Sure. Lay it on me."

"Is there a chance that anyone here could know about…Petition?"

She whispered the last word. It didn't matter how secluded they were, it never felt safe to say it too loud.

Zach's eyebrows rose.

"I think I was specifically picked for the game," she rushed on. "And just now, on the beach, I heard someone say its name. And I've got this awful sense of dread—like something bad is coming down on us, and there's no way to escape—"

Zach held out his hands. Ruth, gulping air, took them. He massaged her fingers, his thumb running over her skin tenderly.

"Reality check," he confirmed. "You and I are the only people here who know."

She nodded. It was the right answer, she knew. Even if it didn't *feel* right.

"There was one video," he continued. His voice was gentle and faintly sad. "It was blurry and dark, and you were a child. Nobody could recognize you after all this time."

And she'd been so careful afterward. She'd never let any of the foster parents take photos of her. She'd dyed her hair every time they moved to a new house. To cut any links.

To sever herself from that terrified child as thoroughly as possible.

"I think you were picked for the game through pure luck," Zach continued. "Someone had to get the rock, and sometimes coincidences are just coincidences. And that word—*petition*—has more than one meaning. They might have wanted to petition Eton for a favor, for example."

She kept nodding. His words rang true, and yet, they weren't getting underneath the slick dread.

"You never told anyone?"

She almost couldn't hear her own question over the ringing in her ears.

The sadness in Zach's face grew rawer.

"Never," he confirmed.

She leaned into him, and he hugged her so tightly that it was almost enough to squeeze the fear out.

"Sorry," she whispered into his chest. "I don't want to ruin the holiday. I'm going to do better."

"You're not ruining anything." Hot air ghosted over her scalp as he kissed the top of her head. "I just wish I knew how to help."

She leaned back but didn't entirely let go of Zach. "Everything here reminds me of Petition."

"It does?"

"The stage." She thought back to the moment when she'd recognized the invisible pull of Eton's charisma. "The audience applauded every time he spoke. It didn't matter if they liked what he said; they only liked that he was speaking."

"Oh." Realization washed over Zach's features.

"The foundations are here. *All* of them. The charismatic leader in Eton, the blind adoration of his fans. We're isolated, unable to leave even if we wanted to. And it's an echo chamber. A singular message, repeated over and over: *We love Eton.* We've even been given matching clothing with his logo on it."

Zach was watching her with real concern.

"But—" Ruth sucked in a ragged breath, forcing her lungs to expand even though they didn't want to. "This isn't like Petition. Parts feel similar, but it's not the same."

"Yeah?"

"There's no control." Ruth forced the words into the world, trying to make them feel real. "I could have dropped out of the game if I wanted to. There's a power imbalance between Eton and everyone else, but he's not abusing it."

I hit him. There were no repercussions.

In Petition...

They would have pulled my teeth. One per day, until they decided I'd shown enough repentance.

"That's the key," she finished. "That's the difference between a fan club and a cult. Whether the power is abused."

"I know you try not to talk about it," Zach said. "About Petition, or what you went through there. And with good reason. But..." He rubbed her hands, gently. "You keep everything wrapped up so tight, and sometimes I worry about what it's doing to you. I want you to feel like you can ask for help when you need it."

"Zach…" She didn't know where to look. "Carson's been strange. Have I done something to upset him?"

His frown was back. "I'm sure you haven't. Carson thinks you're great. Just the other day, he told me he likes having you around."

Ruth bit the inside of her cheek.

"Did he say something?" Zach leaned closer, searching her face. "I can talk to him."

Ruth hesitated. Before she had any chance to reply, a sound cut through them.

Loud, harsh, angry, searing the air like a breathless shriek.

The island's emergency siren.

10.

Logan was surprised the alarm still functioned.

He pressed his hands over his ears. Even through the walls of his wooden cabin, it was deafening.

As he staggered out into the heavy dusk, more sounds assaulted him. Shrieks, yelling, indistinct voices. The residents of their temporary village moved past, not caring when they knocked into him.

All the while, the siren rose and fell. It was an eerie sound. An angry noise that ran at the ragged edges of each note, mistuned. Like a whale call, bellowing across their spit of land.

Although Eton's team had tried to play coy about the island's exact location, it wasn't hard to pinpoint if you knew where to inquire. Logan had taken the opportunity to do some digging into its history before the trip.

The island had been owned by a string of investors. Some had simply kept it—a place to park surplus money with the hopes of realizing profits at some future date. Others had plans to develop the land, build resorts. While none of those developments had gotten far enough to leave more than a couple of permanent structures, the emergency sirens stood sentinel as one of those long-forgotten remnants.

The island was prone to taking the brunt of the worst storms that swept the region. That was not only the reason behind the alarm, but also the reason why very little else had been built.

The system was at least twenty years old. A miracle it still worked.

And no surprise that the undulating wails ground and crackled and swung off-tune.

The guests around Logan shouted to be heard, asking one another what was happening, yelling for someone to make the deafening noise stop.

Logan pushed through the crowd, aiming for a trail that led up the mountainside. He seemed to be the only guest in their clearing who knew what the siren was and where it could be found. South side, built into the rising slope of the island's peak.

The thick foliage dampened the noise, but not enough. The trail was steep and narrow. It might have been a proper road during those failed developments, but Eton's crew hadn't put in any effort to reopen it for the festival.

Leaves slapped across Logan's skin. He kept his hands clamped over his ears. The siren dipped into a lull, then rose again, building like an inhuman scream.

And then it cut out.

The silence was somehow even more immense, even more oppressive. Logan cautiously removed his hands just as he found the trail's end.

The space would have once been a clearing. Tropical plants and small trees had spent the prior decade taking advantage of the bare ground; they tangled across one another, filling the clearing but not yet providing a canopy.

Through the midst of them, the tower stood like a monument. Its base was weather-stained concrete, narrow windows implanted at infrequent intervals.

It would have once housed a communication room. Somewhere to send and receive radio messages. Advance warning of incoming storms.

Above, iron grids built up to a peak of four massive loudspeakers, straining above the jungle's reach. The iron was rusted. One loudspeaker hung loose, dangling from its cables. As it drifted, it tapped against the metal. The echoes felt like the island's heartbeat.

Two staff members stood outside the tower, their yellow shirts bright against the green, talking in rushed voices. They seemed on the verge of an argument.

Logan pulled his phone out and snapped a photo, making sure he got the tower in the background.

The clearing was dimmer than he'd realized. The flash went off.

They turned.

Wild eyes fixed on Logan. Lips were clamped into thin lines. Perspiration glimmered on skin.

Then the tension snapped as broad smiles flooded their faces.

"Hello there!" The older staff member—still no older than twenty-five, Logan guessed—strode toward him. She extended her hands at her sides, somehow seeming both happy to see him and apologetic. "Sorry for the disturbance. There's nothing to worry about!"

He would have liked to get closer to the tower, but the staff member's outstretched arms effectively blocked him. "What happened?"

More staff members were spilling out of the structure. The door was rusted and jammed, and they had to squeeze through the thin gap. One person was speaking into his phone. Either Eton or his second-in-command, Logan guessed, wanting answers.

"Just an accident," the woman said, all bright energy. "We were testing the power system, and it set the alarms off."

"Uh-huh."

In the background, the other staff members clustered around the phone. One of them spoke into it, answering questions. His voice was low. Barely a mumble to Logan's ears.

But he could still see the staff member's mouth move.

Lip-reading wasn't a one-to-one replacement for hearing. Media liked to push that myth, but even a proficient lip-reader with a clear and well-lit view of their companion might catch less than half of what was said.

Logan had been practicing the skill for years, and he knew his limitations. But he wasn't relying purely on lip movements. Mumbled sounds stretched across the space between them.

The hard clicks and thumps of consonants. The stretch of vowels. They helped. Not much, but enough.

A guest...got into the tower...all fine...exploring, I'd say, a little drunk...

The woman shifted to fill Logan's view, blocking his eyeline to the other staff, and the traces of conversation vanished.

"I really can't apologize enough," she said. The smile shouldn't have felt so big or genuine. No one could be that happy. "We'll definitely make sure it doesn't happen again."

If they were testing the power, why lie to Eton about it?

If a guest set off the sirens, then why don't I see them here?

The distant conversation ended. Five staff members, all clean-cut, all with full smiles, turned toward Logan.

"I'd be happy to show you the way back, Mr. Lloyd," the woman said.

Years before, at the start of his career, Logan had attended an in-person interview with a retired boxer. They were there to talk about a rigging scandal, but then Logan had started asking questions about the boxer's tumultuous relationship with his model girlfriend. The boxer, a mountain of a human with veins like cables along his arms, had turned sour. His hands flexed. His words became shards of ice. And Logan had felt a deep chill of imminent risk, the kind most people might only experience once or twice in their lives. Later that night, the girlfriend's body was found, crumpled into a dumpster and two days decayed.

That video series—no longer about match rigging but about the boxer and the murder trial—had dragged Logan out of obscurity. It had gained a glut of media attention and netted nearly thirty million views across its five parts.

Sometimes, when Logan couldn't sleep, he remembered that interview and wondered what would have happened if he'd kept prying. If he'd followed his instincts and doubled down with harder questions, like he believed journalists had an obligation to, instead of politely wrapping up the interview and leaving. Would he have been a headline for a very different reason?

There, isolated from the rest of the festival, facing the six eager and smiling staff members, Logan felt that same vivid, nightmarish chill.

"I'll find my way back," he said, his tongue dry.

He felt those six pairs of eyes watching him even long after the jungle had hidden him from their view.

Petra watched Eton from the side of the stage. His energy was flawless. There was no way to tell how few hours he'd been sleeping or how many stimulants he'd taken. He engaged with the audience so warmly that he might as well have been walking between them and clasping their hands.

He was their best friend.

He was *everyone's* best friend.

His greatest skill—and one he wielded perfectly.

The pink mark on his cheekbone was subtle enough to look like a flush. The contestant, Ruth, hadn't hit him hard.

She'd still hit him, though.

And Eton hadn't even faltered. Within seconds, he'd turned himself from an adversary into an ally.

Validating her emotions. Showing vulnerability. Asking for a chance to improve.

Petra herself might have even believed him, if she hadn't been standing beside him on the platform.

If she hadn't learned to identify his lies.

The drone's footage had been playing on their tablet in high definition. He'd seen how bad the fall was. He'd seen the blood rippling through the water. The choice to continue the game was a calculated one.

Continuing the game distracted the guests.

He'd made enough noise to drown out Makayla's aching groans. He'd shifted eyes toward the game board while she was dragged onto shore and carried out of sight.

Preoccupy the audience. Overwrite the unpleasant images before they could be embedded into long-term memory. Make the accident muddy, hazy, forgettable.

Petra chewed the inside of her cheek.

Off to the stage's side, the staff moved quickly, setting up for that night's entertainment. They were efficient. Even after the accidental triggering of the alarm, they were doing better than could have been expected, considering that most were only brought on weeks before the festival's launch date.

Eton's digital empire included an office and a slate of full-time employees, but they'd needed a much larger crew to support the festival. Petra barely knew the new staff, and that made her uncomfortable. But she could put up with that, as long as they continued to do their jobs.

"I know *some* of you have already heard about our island's reputation," Eton said, pacing along the stage, eyes bright. "But have you heard the full story? Do you know the legend…the legend of the *cannibal witch*?"

Ripples of noise rose up in response. Some laughter, some muffled whispers.

"The footnote version wasn't enough for me," Eton continued. "So I spoke to historians. I spoke to local experts. I even saw the original journal—the physical papers, something that has never been released to the public—to find out the full, unnerving truth. As a reward for joining me on this island tonight, I want to share it all with you. The complete story. The dark and sinister history of Prosperity Island."

On cue, the floodlights around the beach changed to a red tint. Shadows thickened. Startled gasps and more laughter rose from the crowd.

"I have to warn you, this is not for the faint of heart," Eton said. He added extra theater to the words, one hand reaching out. "Anyone who feels like they can't endure the squeamish details should return to their accommodations. For the rest of you…I can't promise how much sleep you'll be getting after you learn what happened here."

More excited murmurs. One shout of "Bring it on, man!" from the back of the crowd.

"If you're sure." Eton winked, his grin infectious. "Let's get started."

The screen behind him lit up. Eton neatly sidestepped into the shadows, switching off the microphone and stopping at Petra's side.

"That went okay, huh?" he whispered.

"You were great."

"Okay. Good." Out of sight of the audience, he rubbed his hand across his forehead and throat, clearing sweat. "How about the sirens? Are we safe from being woken in the middle of the night?"

"Should be." She tapped her pad, bringing up the log. "Members of the staff have blocked access. Button-happy guests shouldn't be able to get to the controls any longer."

Eton had turned the alarms into a joke onstage, claiming someone had left the volume stuck on max.

Guests had been agitated after the noise, but most mellowed quickly. An early dinner had helped; the staff members had pushed themselves to get it served ahead of schedule. Now the festivalgoers lounged on towels or in folding chairs scattered around the main beach, half-eaten plates of food in their laps, gazes fixed on the screen above the stage.

Staff moved through the audience like wraiths, passing out blankets to anyone who hadn't thought to change into warmer clothes. They were all keeping busy. Except…

Three of the team, only visible due to their bright shirts, stood at the edge of the lights. They had their heads together. One of them was crying.

Petra had been managing Eton's roster of employees for years. She'd gotten good at picking up on cues; she could tell when someone hit a wall from overwork or stress or even just a bad day.

But this was something more.

The girl wasn't just crying. She looked *terrified*.

"I'll be right back," Petra said to Eton, and climbed off the edge of the stage.

11.

Ruth sat cross-legged on a beach towel. The sand had grown hot through the daylight hours, but its warmth was quickly fading.

The darkness felt immense. A cold and lonely breeze had kicked up. Sounds came from the jungle, though the trees could no longer be seen.

Zach was beside her, but he wasn't looking at her. He stared up at the screen, faint lines forming between his heavy eyebrows.

Around Ruth was an ocean of strangers. She could see their outlines and hear their breathing, the rustle of clothes, their whispers. Everything more distinct had been swallowed by the night. They seemed like wraiths. Low, dimly lit forms, shifting and swaying.

Above, the video played.

A woman narrated. Her voice was low and clear.

And the deeper into her story they went, the more Ruth wished they had never heard any of it.

Prosperity Island.

That's the name given to fifty-eight acres of tropical land situated along the outer edge of the Caribbean.

Uninhabited.

Or is it?

Ownership of the island changes every few years. Developments have been started, canceled, revived, and abandoned in a seemingly never-ending cycle.

In the 1980s, a developer set their sights on an ambitious project: a sprawling resort capable of housing upward of two hundred guests. While clearing land, a worker put his arm into a woodchipper. His companions tried to stop the bleeding. He passed two hours later, on board a ship rushing him to the nearest hospital.

Later that week, a foreman stepped away for his lunch break. He never returned. As afternoon faded to dusk, the island was filled with shouts as search parties crisscrossed the land. They did not find him that night, nor during the following three days of searching. His fate remains unknown.

Within the following month, one of the workers fell into a tide pool and shattered his leg. Another developed an infection that rotted his eye and spread to his spinal cord. The final blow came when an unexpected storm damaged critical early infrastructure, a devastating event that would cost tens of millions to repair. The project was put on hold and ultimately abandoned four years later.

In 1992, a music producer bought the island to be a private oasis. His planned mansion was less ambitious than the resort, but not any luckier. The first construction crew quit before even breaking ground, and the second crew fell far behind schedule as injuries and illnesses mounted. Superstitions bubbled up; some workers claimed the island was cursed. Others said they could hear voices from between the trees: moaning, sobbing, pleading. The voices of every life that had been snuffed out on the island.

The project was canceled less than four months into development when the producer's two business partners cut him out of his own company. The resulting legal battles bankrupted him and ended his career.

Then, in 2006, another attempt was made. These plans were for an extravagant health sabbatical for celebrities and high-profile business moguls: a detox spa that was inaccessible to fans or paparazzi.

Land was cleared. Preliminary infrastructure was built, including some that still stands today. And then, just months into the project, another tragedy struck. Shortly after eight in the morning, workers radioed the mainland. Only pieces of the transcript have been released to the public, but they include a man shouting, over and over, "*Hide me, hide me, hide me. He's coming.*"

The island's terrain made it impossible to land a helicopter. It was only accessible by boat, which took hours. When help finally arrived, they found a massacre. One of the cement layers had taken a knife from the kitchen and systematically hunted down his coworkers. Out of thirty-one contractors staying on the island, eight were found dead and another two later passed at the hospital.

These are just a handful of the tragedies that have haunted Prosperity Island.

Again and again, developers purchased the land with grand plans for development. None ever made it to completion. Accidents, structural faults, embezzlements, and deaths seemed to gather around the island like flies around a carcass.

But was bad luck truly the sole reason that Prosperity Island never became the luxury resort its owners envisioned?

Or was something more sinister at play?

Let's turn the clock further back.

The 1960s ushered in a massive cultural shift. The swing dresses and sport coats of the 1950s were traded for go-go boots and bold prints. Men let their hair grow long; women wore trousers. A counterculture emerged, and it was eager to break free of every tightly wound conservatism that had preceded it.

The hippie movement of the late 1960s and early 1970s embraced music, love, drugs, and peace. Through sit-ins and marches, they cried for an end to the Vietnam War, as well as greater tolerance, civil rights, and harmony.

But not every participant was truly altruistic. This is a dark facet of humanity: Whenever a peaceful flock grows large enough, wolves begin to sneak between the tender bodies.

The best-known photo of the Secret Door Movement shows Stephan Moore and Martha Moore with their arms around one another. Stephan's hair is to his shoulders; Martha's brushes her thighs. They wear loose, flowing clothes covered in ripples of sun-faded pink, yellow, and orange.

Twenty-five followers stand around them. Gerard Lenehan sold insurance before joining the movement; in the photo, leaves are threaded into his headband. Eleanor Beresford left her husband without warning and was listed as a missing person for more than two years. Robbie Fox was the disowned son of a state senator; he smiles as he makes the peace sign, the fringe on his vest a blur of movement.

Not much is known about Stephan Moore's younger years. Police records show an arrest as a teenager for soliciting donations door-to-door on behalf of a hospital that didn't exist, and another arrest in his early twenties for an insurance scam.

After that, he lay low for several years. When he finally reemerged, it was as a self-proclaimed High Priest—the moniker given to spiritual guides and teachers—in the hippie community. His teachings cobbled together a surface knowledge of nearly a dozen religions. Despite his rudimentary sermons, a small but eager following developed around him.

Stephan Moore claimed that everyone had an accessway to a higher dimension inside them, and that once unlocked, it granted powers such as mind reading and prophecy, or even resurrection. This accessway was the *secret door*, and he was willing to show his followers how to pick its lock.

They called themselves a movement. Today, they're considered one of the era's most notorious cults.

The Secret Door Movement's momentum built through the summer of 1970, and as the season crept toward its end, the crowds that came to Stephan's sermons could no longer fit inside a single tent.

And then, without warning, the Secret Door Movement and two dozen of its most committed followers vanished.

On the nineteenth of August, 1970, the twenty-five chosen members failed to show up to their jobs. Their apartments were abandoned, the contents untouched and food left to rot in the fridges.

Concerned friends and family submitted missing person reports. People who had known the group were questioned, but no one could provide answers. Reported sightings failed to bear fruit. It was as though the group had simply ceased to exist.

For nearly fourteen months, their whereabouts remained a mystery. The case grew cold, but, considering Stephan Moore's history, many assumed he would reappear eventually.

And he did. In the worst possible way.

In June of 1971, a fishing ship spotted the burned-out hull of a yacht on the eastern side of Prosperity Island. The island was uninhabited at that time, and the fishermen pulled in for a closer look. What they found unnerved them so severely that they cut their workday short and contacted the authorities.

Signs of human life—and human death—littered the island.

The burned-out yacht belonged to Robbie Fox, the senator's son and one of the missing followers. Several hundred meters inland were the remains of a settlement: a firepit surrounded by five rudimentary buildings in various states of collapse.

Past that was a clearing. Wild plants had begun to retake the empty land, but tilled rows were still visible. A failed attempt at farming.

A major discovery was uncovered in one of the weather-beaten buildings. Tucked inside several blankets was a journal marked with the initials *EB*. It may have belonged to Eleanor Beresford, age twenty-three, who had left her husband nearly two years prior to live with the Secret Door Movement.

Her journal is the only known record of what happened on the island.

The entries began several months before the group vanished. They included revelations delivered during Stephan Moore's sermons, the chores assigned to *EB* as a new member, and her work to unlock her own internal secret door.

Mid-August, she wrote a chilling passage:

> *Eight of us lay down for the Peacekeeping Ceremony. Only seven of us stood up again. Stephan says Addy became stuck at his door but is on a journey to revival. We were told to put him on a bed and to cover him in a blanket.*

A Peacekeeping Ceremony was a trance state induced by high doses of psychedelics and herbs. Stephan claimed that his followers would fight off evil influences during the ceremony and protect the movement's other members.

Addy is believed to refer to Adrian Folek. His body was found in his apartment two days after *EB* made this journal entry. At first, it was viewed as an accidental overdose. That changed when police interviewed neighbors and learned that three men had entered Adrian's home, carrying something large, on the last day he was known to be alive.

It's now believed that Adrian died during the Peacekeeping Ceremony inside Stephan Moore's main tent. Afraid of the possibility of criminal charges, Stephan waited until dark and then moved the body so the death couldn't be linked to him.

On the eighteenth of August, police interviewed both Stephan Moore and Martha Moore. The interviews lasted approximately three hours, and they were both released.

The following night, Stephan rallied his closest supporters and fled the country.

It's happening, EB wrote in their journal. *We are going to Paradise!*

During his sermons, Stephan often spoke about creating a country of his own, outside of any government's control. It seemed he intended to do just that. Making use of Robbie Fox's yacht, they spent two days crossing the ocean to reach the secluded, rarely visited oasis that would become their new home.

Prosperity Island.

The first week after their arrival was filled with euphoria. The journal spoke about the joy of building their homes with their own hands—*as we were supposed to all along, but forgot how*—and of the ceremonies Stephan and Martha led to help cleanse and purify the island.

Their homes were nicknamed *the shipwreck houses*, since the buildings made use of sailcloth and other material taken from the yacht.

They began to clear land for their farm. Every member worked hard; they went out of their way to care for one another. It was a joy to serve the community.

That sense of purpose and connectedness lasted eleven days.

A storm swept in. It was a night without sleep as their shelters toppled. They were forced to rebuild, but four of their community had fallen sick. *EB* worried that the water they drank was tainted, but Stephan said a wicked entity was suppressing them. He held another ceremony. Martha Moore tended to the unwell.

More misfortunes came quickly. Ants invaded one of the shelters and followers developed welts where they were bitten. Water got into bags of grain and caused them to rot. Small mistakes led to squabbles.

Then a member referred to as *H* fell while foraging. Bruises covered his leg and he was unable to stand. Stephan said he would be healed if he could access his secret door. *EB* wrote that she didn't sleep that night because of how loudly *H* cried.

The following morning, a split formed in the community. Six followers demanded they be allowed to bring *H* and the other sick back to the mainland for treatment and to collect fresh supplies. Stephan said that going back would be an act of broken faith and that they would be sacrificing their paradise and everything they had worked toward. The argument lasted for hours, then *EB* wrote:

> *The sky grew heavy with smoke. We knew what it was and began running.*

The yacht was consumed by fire: too far gone to hope to save, and too hot for anyone to get near.

If the group knew who was responsible, *EB* didn't outright name them. But, with emphatically heavy pen strokes, she noted that Martha wasn't involved in the argument. This comment was underlined twice.

Without the yacht, the community was entirely cut off from the rest of the world. They had brought no means of communication. No one knew where they were. They had no choice except to try to survive.

From there, *EB*'s journal becomes less structured and more chaotic. She lost track of the day and drew question marks in its space. Long, rambling, and repetitive entries interspersed brief one-line notes.

> *Another sick; tainted water or bad food?*
> *From now on, we can only have one meal a day until the farm can feed us.*
> *Stephan says we're only facing these hardships because we let doubt creep in.*
> *The canned food is vanishing faster than it should. Someone is stealing.*

Infection set into several of the ant bites. The community had been boiling their drinking water, but they still became sick. There weren't enough able-bodied members to keep up with the work.

Then *H*, the man with the injured leg, died during the night.

EB's entry was disjointed. She seemed to be dancing around the subject, as though afraid to put her thoughts down plainly.

> *He couldn't walk but he wasn't dying. Martha has been tending to him*

all this time. She took a break yesterday to talk to Stephan. They walked to the ocean's edge, away from the rest of us. They talked for so long.

Many experts agree with *EB*'s apparent train of thought: It is very likely that *H*, suffering from a fractured or broken leg, was seen as a drain on their dangerously low resources. It's possible that Martha or Stephan ended his life that night.

The community buried *H* on the beach, where the sand was soft enough to dig. They marked his resting place with a wooden cross. Over the next few pages, two more crosses joined it.

By that point, the island colony's situation was dire. They had eaten the last of the nonperishable food they'd brought with them. Any edible plant life had already been scavenged. There were no mammals or large birds to hunt on the island. They tried fishing but couldn't catch anything.

And their farm was failing. Seeds decayed without sprouting. Those that did sprout were eaten by insects. The few cornstalks that managed to grow refused to form heads.

EB's penultimate journal entry was short and emotionally raw.

Another dead this morning. There is no more food. Martha says we must think about what we do with this one.

From there, records fracture. Several pages start with just a single letter, or a question mark over the space where the date belonged, as though *EB* wanted to write but found herself unable.

A block of empty pages follows. The final entry is on the last leaf of the journal, as though *EB* herself knew there was nothing more to say. It seems symbolic: the end of the journal, the end of her story, of her hope, of her humanity.

Martha was behind it all. She looked after the sick; the sick died. She oversaw the food; the food vanished.

She was the one who wanted to stop burying our brothers and sisters when they passed.

We've all been thinking it…whispering it… We held off…for so long… We let her take…so many…

Robbie started it. He whittled his stick first. The rest only followed.

Help me, I was one of them.

There was no other choice.

We pierced her through again and again.

She would not die.

I am sick remembering. It took…so long…to make her stop moving.

Stephan only watched. But he led us in burying her. Not on the beach. Not with the others. We stuffed her into a hole where she will never be found. It's what she deserves. She was a poison on this island.

Witch.

Even free from her, we're too far gone to be saved.

It's believed the cult survived on the island for somewhere between five and six months.

Examination of the empty cans and grain bags suggest Stephan wildly underestimated how much food they would need to bring. Small shells scattered about the settlement show the cult resorted to picking limpets off the ocean rocks.

There was another discovery in the settlement's center, though. Something that might explain why *EB* stopped writing in her journal. Some experiences are too painful to put into words.

The firepit was built from a ring of stones about five feet across. Worn-down logs created seats around it, and the space was likely the main gathering place for anyone who wasn't working or sleeping.

Scattered around this communal center were bones.

Human bones.

All of them had distinct scrape marks showing where a blunt knife had cut.

Several bore teeth marks.

EB's second to last journal entry seems to be the point where their desperation became overwhelming.

> *Another dead this morning. There is no more food. Martha says we must think about what we do with this one.*

As starvation set in, the group resorted to cannibalism.

By the time the settlement was discovered, many of the group's belongings had decayed. Pieces of stained clothing were found next to stacked bowls and cutlery inside the collapsing shelters. Books were swollen and rotting from the damp. Family photos and mementos—the few personal items the followers had brought—were all but eroded by insects.

But sealed inside a metal box was an Instamatic camera belonging to Stephan Moore. Investigators developed the roll of film and found it only contained a single picture. The iconic last photo, taken the morning after they landed on the island.

The group stands on the beach, just a few hundred meters from your own accommodations, and very near where their teeth-scarred bones were found. They smile, leaning against one another. Robbie Fox, owner of the yacht, makes a peace sign. They seem happy. Excited.

And in the center, arms around one another, are Stephan Moore and Martha Moore.

The Secret Door Movement is a large part of why Prosperity Island has remained vacant for so long. Despite its prime location and size, the island's history is off-putting to both investors and potential guests.

And there is one other aspect to the story.

In the fateful last photo, Martha is smiling. But there's something unsettling about her expression. Her head is tilted down, casting shadows across her eyes and around her teeth. While the others appear happy, she seems cruelly delighted. As though she knew exactly what fate awaited them. As though it was *planned*.

The journal's final entry accused Martha of being the poison that destroyed them. And there may be some truth in those words.

Members of the hippie community who crossed paths with the Secret Door Movement have said Stephan was manipulative, self-serving, and controlling. But many of them refused to speak about Martha at all. Those who did, kept their voices to a whisper. As though afraid she would hear them.

Even before the Secret Door Movement vanished, rumors were circulating. They murmured that the cult was not actually being run by Stephan. They claimed he was only a front man. That Martha Moore herself was pulling the strings in the background.

They claimed she was a witch.

No verifiable information has ever surfaced about her past. Not even her name or her date of birth. She was at Stephan's side when he started the Secret Door Movement. She seems to have adopted his surname, although there are no legal records of them marrying.

Most believed her to be at least fifty—significantly older than Stephan or any of his followers. Her esoteric dances during Stephan's sermons were said to be hypnotic. She hand-mixed the substances members took during their ceremonies, including the one that allegedly killed Adrian Folek and caused the group to flee to Prosperity Island.

Her followers ultimately turned on her, killing her. But perhaps it wasn't enough.

Investors, construction crews, and visitors who stayed at the island have all claimed to see Martha Moore.

They say she stands in the distance, between the trees, watching them.

Her dress is drenched with blood. Dark tangled hair trails down her back. When she opens her mouth, her teeth are rotting.

Fortunes have been poured into developments that never materialized. A string of accidents and deaths plagues any contractors that try to tame the island. Owner after owner, no one has been able to break through Prosperity Island's curse.

Some people believe this is why.

They say, if you're foolish enough to try to spend the night here, you'll see her. The island's true owner.

The cannibal witch, Martha Moore.

Dead for more than fifty years, she'll stand in the trees, watching you with colorless eyes. Her nails are claws. Her dress is heavy with her companions' blood.

She's the true reason no construction crew wants to stay. Her presence is why the island is passed from owner to owner.

She lives here.

And if you try to disturb her peace, she'll come for you next.

The screen faded to black. The lights around the beach's perimeter dimmed into nothing. For a second, they were swallowed by the immense darkness, as heavy as an ocean.

Then a spotlight burst to life as a hiss of static shot through the air. Its beam hit the jungle's edge. A perfect circle of harsh white light sliced into the trees, bleaching their leaves.

In the light's center stood a figure. Filthy hair hung past her waist. Her body was contorted, her hands like talons, her white dress soaked with red.

Her lips peeled back to reveal a grimace of blackened teeth.

12.

Screams broke the silence. People shouted. Someone bumped Ruth from behind.

At the edge of the forest, the red-soaked woman raised one hand, grime caked around her fingernails. Muscles flexed in her arm as she stretched it high overhead. Fingers curled, as though grasping the very atmosphere.

The lights cut out again.

The voices rose. More screams, this time with real panic tinging them.

Ruth felt her breath pass between her lips. She knew it was all theater, and yet, in the dark, it felt both too close and too real.

Something squirmed across her knuckles. Ruth flinched, biting down on a gasp. It was a hand. Zach's. She hoped. The fingers coiled around hers and squeezed.

Her eyes were starting to adjust to the dark. She could see the people around them. Hundreds of figures, shifting. Moving. Twisting. They seemed inhuman.

Then light flooded across them. No longer red, but bright and painful as the floodlights were switched on. She squinted.

"Sorry, sorry, sorry!" Eton was laughing as he leaped onto the stage. He waved a hand, calming the guests. "I couldn't help myself."

At the tree line, the figure was gone. Instead, a row of yellow-shirt staff members stood, beaming at them.

A rush of relief moved through the audience. Laughter—some giddy, some panicky. To Ruth, the scene had seemed pretty obviously staged, but others must have been more sucked into the narrative. Hayleigh had her face in her hands, her shoulders hunched, even though she was starting to laugh. Carson held her, rubbing her back and murmuring softly.

"You okay?" Zach asked. It was his hand that had found hers in the dark, after all. Ruth gave a quick nod.

"Our visitor might not have been real," Eton continued, speaking over the murmurs and laughter. "But the story is. The Secret Door Movement lived and died here, just a few minutes from where you'll be staying. How cool is that?"

An image appeared on the screen behind him: the group photo taken on Prosperity Island's pristine beach. The subjects all wore flowing clothes and sandals; many had headbands and held seashells up to the camera.

Very slowly, the image began to zoom in toward the woman in the group's center. She was older than the rest of them. Cascades of black hair hung on either side of her face. Her head was tilted slightly downward, and the shadows lingered uneasily around her eyes and mouth. The closer the image drew, the harder it became to look away from her glittering eyes.

"Which leads to our next game," Eton said. "It's a game you can *all* participate in."

"Oh!" Hayleigh lifted her head. Her cheeks had splotches of color, but the promise of a game had caught her attention.

"Somewhere on this island is the cannibal witch's grave," Eton said. He spread his hands out, gesturing to the jungle behind them. "Somewhere out here, her companions hid her corpse. Bring me proof that you found her final resting place and you'll be rewarded. In a huge way. *A hundred thousand dollars.*"

An eerie silence fell over the crowd. Bodies near Ruth craned forward.

"It's a treasure hunt," Eton finished, winking.

Someone yelled. Figures moved, leaping out of the crowd and racing up the beach. Ruth felt her heart turn cold as the guests passed the final line of lights and vanished into the jungle.

"You'll probably have better luck looking in the daylight." Eton was laughing. He bent forward, hands on his knees. He still wore ragged shorts, even in the growing cold. "She won't be easy to find, but you have the rest of the festival to look."

Ruth's jaw ached, but she couldn't get it to relax.

Guess you lied about being more careful.

"We have some entertainment to finish off the night." Eton stepped to the side, waving as a group of long-haired, very bony musicians stepped onto the stage. "Berry Red are here to help celebrate. Have some drinks. Enjoy yourselves. I'll see you tomorrow!"

A cold weight sat low in Ruth's stomach.

She'd heard about the Secret Door Movement, but only in brief mentions—she didn't like to stick around when talk turned to cults since Petition was almost always the next word on people's lips. She knew they'd starved on an island and their bones showed signs of cannibalism. But she'd never expected it to be *this* island.

"So." Zach leaned back. "A treasure hunt."

"Want to go look?" Carson reached out and gave Zach's shoulder a friendly bump with his fist. "You were always wicked good at treasure hunts when we were growing up."

Zach looked pleased, but he shook his head. "No point in trying right now, when it's so dark. I mean, good luck to those guys who wanted to get a jump on everyone else, but I don't think it's going to be easy to find."

"No, definitely not." Hayleigh shimmied around onto her knees. She was smiling and eager, but Ruth couldn't help but notice her hands were still shaking. "I mean, we have five days on this island. Eton wouldn't want anyone to get it straightaway."

"He's probably hidden it somewhere impossible to find unless you know where to look," Zach said. "And he'll drip clues out over the next few days, with the biggest clues toward the end. If we want to play this strategically, we should get a sense of the island and its layout and then wait for the hints. They might be given casually, you know, the kind of thing you wouldn't realize was a clue if you weren't watching for one."

"You've given this a lot of thought," Ruth said. She didn't mean it to sound prickly, but the sight of the guests vanishing into the lightless jungle had left her tense.

Zach looked sheepish. "I'm giving away how many of his videos I've watched, I guess. He's hosted a lot of games like this on his channel. The early ones were kind of a mess—the games would end within five minutes, or people would find loopholes, things like that. But he's gotten it down to an art. He makes the challenge nearly impossible, then gives out hints and advantages any time it begins to stall. And I'm fairly sure he'd stick to that formula now, especially with so many players."

"I mean, you basically predicted this," Carson said. "On the ship. You said you thought Eton would set up something like a treasure hunt. Something that anyone could join at any time."

"A passive game," Zach agreed, nodding. "Give people a place to direct their energy during the downtime. If we want a chance at winning, we should learn the island's layout. Especially pay attention to anything that might be a landmark—strangely shaped rocks, uniquely large trees, that sort of thing."

"Let's be in it together," Hayleigh said, lighting up. "Four people are better than one, and if any of us wins, we'll split the prize."

"I'm in," Carson said, and put his hand, palm down, into the space between them.

Zach slapped his on top. "Me too. An equal split, no matter who finds it."

Hayleigh planted her hand on top, but Ruth hesitated.

Not for the first time, she felt as though she was five paces behind everyone else.

She'd never been part of a treasure hunt before. Any activity that felt too close to a moral failing had been forbidden at Petition. Treasure hunts involved the act of hiding something: deception. And they involved an element of luck in the search: gambling. And they were done purely for enjoyment, not betterment: self-indulgence.

All failings that could damn a person.

You're not at Petition.

You're with friends.

And they want to play a game with you.

She placed her hand on top of theirs. Carson glanced at her, and she thought she saw a thin twist to his lips, but it was gone before she could be certain.

"Treasure hunt!" Zach yelled, and they threw their hands into the air.

It wasn't impossible, Ruth thought. There were only six hundred other guests on the island, and not all of them would be playing. Better odds than the lottery.

The band was reeling into the chorus of a song. Ruth didn't recognize them, but they must have been popular with Eton's following, because a crowd had gathered at the stage and everyone was singing along.

"Hey, hey," someone called. "You! Third Place."

A familiar figure was waving to her. Trigger, the maze's winner, his blocky silhouette easy to identify even in the dark. "A bunch of us from the game are getting drinks. You coming?"

"Uh…" Ruth glanced at Zach.

He smiled. "Do you want to? I can meet you back at our cabin."

Ruth could feel Carson's eyes on her. And it suddenly felt like a good idea to get some space.

"Sure," she said. "I won't be long."

He squeezed her hand. "Have fun."

Ruth wrapped her beach towel around her shoulders as she followed Trigger toward the drinks tent. Long tables had been set up outside it, the chair legs digging into the soft sand.

"We got third place!" Trigger yelled. "We got second place! And we got some disqualifieds too!"

Ruth wondered if his volume ever went below a ten.

Cheers rose from the group at the table. She recognized second-place Yu; the mulleted Blake; Vincent, who had wavered during the freeze portion of the game; and Jessica, who had been afraid of heights.

"Drinks," Trigger yelled. "I'm getting us all drinks. Beer? Shots? What are we doing?"

"Champagne," Yu said, beating a fist on the table. "That game just paid off my car!"

"You think this place serves champagne?" Trigger squinted at the tent. There looked to be hundreds of bottles stacked on racks and inside boxes behind the serving table. "Hell, let's give it a try. What about you? Third Place?"

"Ruth," she said. She had so little on this island beyond her name, and it seemed vitally important to cling to it.

"Yeah, yeah, Ruth. What you want? Vodka?"

"Just some juice."

"Vodka and juice, coming up."

Trigger lurched toward the tent, pushing through people waiting to be served.

"He's *exactly* like he is on his channel," Yu said, laughing. "I don't know what I expected."

"Kids' content, right?" Blake asked.

"That's the one." Yu lowered his voice, even though there was no way Trigger could hear them. "Have you seen his social accounts? They're stacked with photos of his mansion and sports cars, but then people found out they were all rentals. I hear rumors that he's in serious debt."

"He was playing *real* hard to win," Blake laughed.

Jessica sat across the table from Ruth. She was already nursing a drink—something clear and full of mint leaves—and seemed like she regretted accepting the invitation. Ruth leaned toward her. "Are you okay?"

"Yeah." She smiled. "Sorry. Bit tired."

"Me too." Ruth hesitated. "That game was...rough."

Jessica chuckled. She seemed both embarrassed and grateful. "I didn't realize it would be so high up. Do you know what happened to Makayla? Is she okay?"

"She's..."

Eton said she would be fine.

But he also said he was taking our safety more seriously, and then he sent people running into a dark forest for a treasure hunt.

"I heard she's getting medical attention," she hedged.

"She was doing so well, too," Jessica said. "She was so fast! I could barely move."

"Hey, at least you didn't face-plant," Blake said, leaning over to cheers his drink against Jessica's, and Ruth remembered the dread she'd felt as she watched him fall.

"The festival's more intense than I would have guessed for Eton," Yu said. He cradled his phone in one hand, its light ghosting over his face as he used his thumb to scroll. "I guess, since guests have to be eighteen and up, he didn't need to keep it as kid friendly as his videos."

"The history's honestly pretty cool," Blake said. "I mean, if it's real."

"Oh, yeah, it definitely is." Yu turned his phone around to show an article he'd been scrolling. The text was too small to see, but part of the Secret Door Movement photo was visible. "I feel like he's playing up the cannibal witch angle, though. I can't find all that much about Martha Moore online."

Audiences love a villain. Tragedies are more cathartic when there's someone to blame.

The area around the drinks tent was crowded. A table next to theirs cleared and was immediately claimed in a rush of flowing fabrics and long hair.

Ruth stared, voiceless.

They were the four women she'd seen after the game. The ones who'd said *Petition.*

Blake snorted. "The *least* believable part of the story is that twenty-some people sailed to an empty island and genuinely thought they could build a town and live there."

Ruth snapped her focus back, trying to collect herself. "I guess it's easy to get caught up in a fantasy. Especially when someone you trust says it'll work."

"You know, I'm pretty sure *Gilligan's Island* was airing around that time," Yu said. "I'm not saying it *gave* them the idea, but I bet it didn't help."

At the table next to them, the women laughed giddily. Ruth caught the phrase, *utterly impossible*, then their voices were drowned out again.

"Drinks!" Trigger yelled, several decibels above anyone nearby. "They did *not* have champagne, but they *did* have sparkling wine."

"Same thing," Yu insisted, taking his glass.

Snatches of conversation crossed the gap between the tables. *"I'm probably going to have nightmares."*

"Cranberry and vodka for Third Place," Trigger said, passing the drink to Ruth. "And a round of shots for all of us!"

"It's just so messed up," another of the women said.

"Thank you," Ruth mumbled, wrapping her hands around the drink.

"Do you think they know about Petition?"

Bile filled the back of her throat, acid and hot.

"Anyone want to guess what the next game's going to be?" Trigger asked, leaning onto the table. "Treasure hunt aside. Eton's got something planned for tomorrow, I bet."

"I... Excuse me." Ruth stood. Her blood was rushing, her limbs turning numb. The beach towel fell away, and she didn't stop to pick it up. Those damning words circled, again and again.

Do you think they know about Petition?

She moved without thinking. The four women looked up as she lurched to a halt at their table.

"I…" Ruth's mouth was parchment dry. Everything vanished in that moment. Every scrap of socialization, every hard-won lesson in how to fit in, how to talk to strangers. She was a child again, confused and frightened and alone. "I…"

The nearest girl, the leader, tilted her head. Vivid red hair draped over her shoulder. "Hey, I know you."

Please. No.

"You were one of the contestants earlier, weren't you?"

"That's right," another girl said. "Third place! Congrats!"

"Thanks." Ruth caught a stuttering breath. "What…what were you talking about?"

They exchanged a glance. Ruth knew she was behaving strangely, was speaking strangely, but she couldn't stop it.

"You said *Petition*," she pressed.

"Oh!" The leader's face shifted into a wicked smile. She beckoned, inviting Ruth closer, as though about to share a secret. "Have you heard about it? You *must* have. We were talking about Petition. The suicide cult."

13.

"Damn it," Petra whispered to herself. She kept her tablet held against her chest and her smile fixed in place like the world's most perfect shields as she wove between the milling guests, trying to get back to the stage. "Damn it, Eton, *damn it.*"

Things were going wrong in ways she couldn't fix.

She'd seen the three staff members huddled together, one of them in tears. Even from a distance, it was clear something was seriously wrong. The girl was shaking, her face stuck in a horrible grimace.

Petra had left Eton and circled around the edge of the lights to reach the staff. They didn't see her until the last second, but when they did, the reaction was immediate.

Hunched postures became straight. Concern melted into competence, control. Even the distressed employee—LISA, her name tag said—smiled. It was a terrible expression, her lips peeled too far back, mucus and tears trailing onto her chin.

Everything was fine, they said. Nothing to worry about.

Petra wasn't Eton. She didn't need people to put on a happy face around her. She didn't need them to pretend they were a big cozy family that loved to get along.

She needed them to tell her when there was a problem so she could *fix it.*

And they'd stood there and lied to her face. *A spider fell into her shirt. Such a fright. She'll be fine.*

Petra could tell when people were hiding something from her. She'd had that sense around Eton for some time.

She'd managed to get Lisa alone, away from the others, in case she felt safer speaking in private. The girl had kept smiling, her eyes glassy and her face wet, even as she insisted she was fine now, she was feeling good, she was eager to go back to her work.

Before Petra could get any further, Eton returned to the stage.

"It's a treasure hunt!"

And at least half a dozen guests bolted into the forest.

She'd been forced to leave Lisa.

Petra moved as quickly as she could without looking agitated, her own fake smile held rigidly in place. Guests were roaming across the beach as the band took to the stage. She couldn't let them see how angry she actually was.

Eton was passing his microphone over to a staff member when Petra caught up to him. She grabbed his arm and pulled him aside, not letting her face shift until she was certain they were hidden behind the stage.

"What in the *hell?*" she hissed.

"What?" He grinned, delighted, as though they were playing a game.

"We agreed you'd announce the treasure hunt tomorrow, at breakfast. When it was *no longer pitch-dark.*"

"I know. But they needed it, Pet. After the accident at the maze and then the sirens, everyone was on edge. It's like you always say—if you need people to move on from something bad, give them a distraction."

"That is exactly why—" Petra caught herself. She was speaking too loud; guests were still nearby. She lowered her voice again, fighting to keep calm. "The injured contestant is exactly why it needed to wait. You cannot, I repeat, *cannot* afford to let anyone else be hurt. That jungle is full of hazards, and I doubt any of those overeager kids thought to bring lights."

"We'll send someone to find them." Eton was still grinning at her. He reached for her hand, but she snatched it back. "Aw, Pet, don't tell me you're seriously mad."

"You were the one who got upset when Logan Lloyd showed up," she shot back. "And yet, you're basically hand-feeding him material."

Eton rubbed at the back of his neck. "Huh, I guess. Sorry. I got up there, and it just struck me: We're talking about the cannibal witch, and we even have her appearing in the trees. Isn't now the right time to announce the grave as well? I didn't think it through, I guess."

Stop lying to me. Just stop.

Eton played dumb when he wanted to get out of something. And it worked, most of the time. But Petra knew him too well. He'd planned to shift the announcement. And he deliberately hadn't told her, because he knew she'd stop him.

She raised her hands, calling a truce. Yelling would be cathartic, but it wouldn't fix anything, and she was only being paid for the latter. "I'll take care of it. I'll send out search parties. We'll hang up beacon lights along the trails, guiding people back. Hopefully, we can get them all before anyone falls into a pit."

"I'd be lost without you, Pet."

"Spare it." She turned and stormed away, making sure to put her smile back in place before any guests could see her.

The staff would already be exhausted after the day, but she'd have to muster at least ten of them to search the jungle in teams.

Now that the treasure hunt was on the table, they would probably have guests venturing out all through the night. The island had a respectable footprint. Not insurmountable. Not large enough for a person to vanish without a trace, unlike what the legends claimed.

But it was still more than enough space to become lost. The trees dampened sounds. And the hazards—natural pits, rocky cliffs, hypothermia—were significant enough that Petra had been against the idea of a treasure hunt to begin with.

It was too late to close that Pandora's box now. She'd have to deal with it.

That, and whatever had terrified the staff member, Lisa.

Prosperity Island was supposed to be a haven. But it was beginning to feel like quicksand, slowly closing around Petra and squeezing the air from her lungs.

"Petition. The suicide cult. You've heard of it, right?"

Ruth was numb. She made a faint, noncommittal noise.

The leader of the group stared up at her for a second, curious, then gestured to an empty chair. Ruth, not knowing what else to do, sank into it.

"I'm Gilly," the leader said. She propped her chin up on her palm, smiling at Ruth. "Are you doing okay? You look a bit…off."

"Just…" She cast around for something that wasn't too far from the truth. "Seasickness. Hasn't fully worn off."

"Aw, that sucks," someone said.

"Here, have my water." One of the girls pushed a glass toward her. "I haven't touched it yet, promise."

They were being kind. Ruth hadn't expected that. They were so beautiful, so flawlessly sleek, that she had somehow forgotten they were human.

"Sorry for interrupting," she managed. "I just heard the word *Petition* and…I was curious."

"You *must* know it," one of the girls said. "It's infamous."

"Take a breath, Sam," Gilly said. "You run a crime podcast. Not everyone's plugged into that world."

Sam gestured, not agreeing and, yet, not conceding.

Gilly turned back to Ruth. Her foxlike eyes sparkled. "Petition was this cult from a while back, run by a man who called himself Barom.

They cut themselves off from society and built a commune in the middle of nowhere. It all hinged around one member: a child. The cult leader's daughter. They claimed she wasn't a normal girl; they believed she had the gift of prophecy."

"There was a council of elders," Sam interjected. "Five of them. They interpreted her dreams, basically twisting them to mean whatever they wanted."

Not five, Ruth thought, miserable. *There were seven elders. The number seven was very important.*

Gilly's voice was low and eager. "The child had a series of dreams. The elders believed they were being given an assignment, that they were being asked to save humanity. And to do that, they had to die. Like a big mass sacrifice. So the commune threw a feast and drank poison that the elders gave them. Not just a regular poison, though, but a nerve toxin. It was some formula they'd made themselves. Apparently, they thought it would give a quick and peaceful death, but it did the opposite. It made them go wild."

The scientists at the trial said it would feel like insects crawling inside your skin. They said it would be excruciating.

Sam leaned forward. "Those cult members, they killed themselves over it. They ran into walls until their heads—"

"Enough." Gilly held up a hand. "She doesn't need the details."

It's okay. I know. They ran into walls until their heads split open. They clawed their eyes out and used glass to remove their tongues. They tore at one another and themselves until their muscles couldn't move anymore.

"Anyway." Gilly took a breath. "Police went to investigate a tip-off a few days later. And they found the whole cult—all four hundred of them—dead. All except one. The child."

"No one knows her name," Sam said. "The courts sealed it. People just call her the Petition Child. She's out there, somewhere, probably our age by now. The only survivor. People keep trying to find her, but without luck."

"Apparently there's a video," Gilly said. "The police recorded themselves searching the compound, and somehow it got leaked. I haven't watched it, but I've heard you can see all the bodies as the police walk through the buildings, and right at the end, they find the child, crouched in the dark. Hosting sites delete it as soon as it's uploaded, so you can only get it in really bad parts of the internet. I'm talking dark-web stuff."

"Wow," Ruth said, and she hoped they wouldn't hear the way her voice broke.

"Yep. And you want to know the creepy bit?" Gilly took a sharp breath. "It's the anniversary this weekend. Twenty years."

"Twenty…" Ruth caught herself.

"To the day," Gilly said. "That's what we were talking about. Whether Eton picked this weekend on purpose. I mean, he must have, right? The internet's buzzing about Petition. I'm not even connected to the true crime sphere, but I'm being inundated with recaps about it."

"And Eton picked an island where an entirely different cult died," Sam added. "It's not a coincidence."

"It can't be. We think Eton must have something planned."

14.

"Come on, come on, come on!"

"Shh! Slow down!"

Dylan couldn't stop laughing. He felt giddy and warm and strange as he tumbled through the jungle. Anything was possible. *Everything* was possible.

"Quick, before they beat us to it." It came out very loud. He stumbled against a tree and had to grab the trunk to stay upright.

"Yes, hug the tree," Erika mumbled. She raised her hands toward the canopy, her layered bracelets like wind chimes as they cascaded down her arms. "I told you you'd love nature if you gave it a chance."

"I love...I love *everything*."

"You're so drunk," Jace called, laughing.

Drunk and high.

The beach bar was stacked deep with crates of alcohol. They gave you anything you wanted, as often as you wanted, and it was all free.

Dylan had gone back again and again, wanting to see how drunk he needed to get before they cut him off, but if there was a limit, he hadn't reached it. Even his sloppy request for *whatever makes your taste good* got him a smile and a plastic cup filled with a mix of soda and liquor that made his tongue curl.

Eton was the best. The *island* was the best.

He'd never felt so good.

The alcohol was from Eton, but the mushrooms were from Jace. Dylan hadn't had as many of those, but Erika had. Her pupils were blown out, enormous, like a cat that had spotted a bird, and her smile was filled with intense wonder as she ran her hands through the leaves and across the bark of every tree she liked the look of.

She joined Dylan at his unsteady perch, folding her arms around the trunk so they overlapped his, and pressed her cheek into the moss and ridges with a dreamy sigh.

"Can't stop," Dylan mumbled, even though it felt very nice to rest his face against something cool. "Treasure hunt."

"We're not going to find it." Jace was laughing. He hadn't been shy with his drinks or his mushrooms, but he always seemed to slip into a paternal babysitting role when they got high together. Something that Dylan found annoying, unless he'd taken enough to not care.

And he really didn't care that night.

"No, we'll find it," he promised, and pushed away from the tree. Erika squirmed, giggling uncontrollably as Dylan poked her cheek. "A hundred…a hundred thousand… We'll find it, all right."

"Sure thing," Jace said, indulgent but content.

"This way!" Dylan had thought it would be harder to see at night, but the moon was big, and his eyes felt wide open. He reached his arms out as he scrambled, laughing, up a slope.

Erika shrieked and ran after him, slipping in fallen leaves coated in dew.

They needed to climb the mountain, go toward the peak. Maybe not right *at* the peak, that would be cheesy, but somewhere high up. Somewhere with a view of the rest of the island. That felt like the right place to find the treasure.

And Dylan, in that moment, had no doubt that his gut feelings were correct.

"Quick, quick, quick," Erika shouted, breathless. Behind her, Jace yelled something, but it was drowned out by their crashing footsteps.

Dylan grabbed a branch for support as he reached the slope's top. His vision swam, glimpses of star-splashed sky and jungle and distant ocean blurring like they'd been put in a blender.

"Ahh," Erika said. She was still grinning, but her voice had changed. Quieter, less gleeful. "Dyl, what's that?"

"Hm?" He was still trying to make sense of the horizon. It felt like it was turned the wrong way, like both he and the world were upside down.

"That." She reached an arm out, the bracelets rattling. "What is it? It looks…bad."

It took him a moment to see what had caught her attention. A row of shapes hung from a tree. Too bright, too rigid to be natural. One twisted lightly, and moonlight shimmered off a metal edge.

"Huh…"

Dylan shambled closer, one hand outstretched. He bumped the nearest shape. It clattered against its neighbors, like wind chimes, like Erika's bracelets.

Metal. Wood. Rope.

Strange objects, hand-built and then hung from the trees like fruit waiting to be picked.

"This…" he threw his arms out wide as incredulous triumph crashed through him. "This is it! The treasure hunt! We found the treasure!"

He whooped so loudly that his voice seemed to travel for miles. Echoes answered him, bouncing out of every crevice and corner of the island.

Erika wasn't celebrating. She stood behind him, her pupils enormous, her lips peeled back from her teeth. No longer a cat with a bird. Now a cat that felt threatened, frightened. "This doesn't feel good."

"No, this is great! We found it! We get the prize! It's great!"

He tapped the object again, sending it twirling on its rope.

Erika shook her head, not taking her eyes off it. "This doesn't look like a treasure hunt to me."

The twirling object was a meat cleaver.

Dylan stared. Confusion seeped in around the edges of his good mood. "No, it's… I mean, look at it. This was set up by Eton. It's part of the game."

The next item looked like a hacksaw with screws fastened along its edge, pointed tips outward. Another seemed to be a pair of enormous shears, modified, the blunt side of the blades ground into a sharp edge.

Dylan took a half step back, laughing, but with less confidence. "What do you think, Jace? It's got to be part of the game, right? Maybe a clue, or…"

No answer.

Moonlight splashed over the dirt path they'd been following. It twisted away within a dozen feet, swallowed by jungle. Empty.

"Jace?" Dylan swayed. He couldn't make sense of it. Jace had been *right there*.

"I guess he went back to the beach," Erika said, too fast and too loud. She waved her hands at the jungle, a riot of singing metal. "He got tired. We'll go back and we'll find him."

"We're going to find the *treasure*," Dylan insisted. He could feel his good mood shrinking, like a balloon with a hole in it, and he hated that he couldn't make it stop.

And then a voice floated out from between the trees.

"Hey."

It hadn't come from behind, but from farther up the mountain. The word was half whispered, eerie and hollow.

"Jace?" Dylan narrowed his eyes, willing the images to hold still. "Is that you?"

He thought he heard a faint chuckle. The modified metal tools turned on their ropes.

And the voice came again. Whisper-soft, almost teasing. *"Hey."*

Dylan let out a beleaguered sigh. He stumbled forward, past the row of hanging implements. "What are you doing? We thought we'd lost you."

He didn't get an answer.

The voice had come from somewhere off the path. It was a steeper climb. Dylan was only half-aware of Erika's quick, unsteady steps behind him. Her trip was going bad, and he wasn't in any kind of place to help.

"Did you see these things back here?" he called. "Think it's part of the game? I don't want to leave them in case someone else claims 'em."

"Hey," Jace called again.

His voice sounded fainter, farther away. Dylan grimaced, annoyed, as he had to use his hands to clamber up the slope. He rocked, nearly tipping backward, and caught a branch to steady himself. "This isn't cool. You really upset Erika."

And not only Erika.

The voice sounded so vague, so distorted and untethered. So very much not like the way Jace spoke, even when high out of his mind.

And how had Jace passed them without either Dylan or Erika noticing? It was hard to move quietly in the jungle, and there hadn't been much time for him to sneak around them.

It didn't make sense, and the alcohol was starting to turn sour in the pit of Dylan's stomach. Every step made his vision swim. The slope leveled out. He stumbled a few steps forward, toward where he'd heard the voice.

Small stones, disturbed by his shoe, tumbled over the edge of a precipice. They spun and clicked against the bare rock wall on their way down.

"Whoa." Dylan staggered back, grabbing another tree for security as he stared at the drop.

The plunge looked enormous. At the cliff's base was a pile of mossy boulders. It was growing harder to see as the night deepened, and Dylan's shoe had scraped over the cliff's edge before he even noticed it.

Gold lights shimmered in the far distance, just short of the horizon. The beach, he realized. He could see the stage and the drinks tent that had been so accommodating. The crowd moved, tiny dark dots casting long shadows. He hadn't realized they'd climbed so far up.

"Careful," he said to Erika, belatedly realizing he should warn her. "There's a…a cliff…"

The path behind him was empty.

He couldn't remember the last time he'd heard the rattle of her bracelets or the quick shuffle of her flip-flops.

A shudder passed through Dylan, starting in his scalp and traveling down into his fingertips.

Erika wasn't the type of person who'd leave without saying anything.

Neither was Jace.

"*Hey,*" the voice whispered.

It sounded so much closer. Just behind his shoulder.

Dylan turned, staggering. The drinks in his stomach were no longer sour; they were poison.

The jungle formed a wall ahead of him, an impenetrable line of plants and darkness. His gaze darted, stabbing into each gap, searching for movement.

A jingling metal sound rose from between the trees.

Familiar, but wrong.

Dylan needed to breathe. His lungs wouldn't move.

Something small glittered against the dark earth. It rolled out of the shadows, spilling into the narrow strip of bare ground.

Dylan took half a step back, staring.

It was a bracelet. Thick and silver, with little hearts dotting its surface.

One of the dozen Erika had donned for the evening party.

It rolled toward Dylan, making a full four rotations before losing momentum and tumbling to the side. Another followed after it, thinner and less steady. And then another: the one with little gems along its edge. The gift Dylan had bought her at the airport.

They rolled out of the jungle, spilling out from the gaps between the trees. Twirling and clicking against one another before dropping to the ground.

He couldn't tear his gaze from the thick bracelet, the one with the hearts. It had a spot of liquid on it. Bright red. Like blood.

Jace took a shuffling step back from it. Cold wind grazed the nape of his neck.

The jangling sound started again. No longer light like wind chimes, though. Not bracelets, but a different kind of metal. Deeper and louder and harsher.

Dylan knew, with horrible conviction, that the hand-fashioned implements no longer hung from their trees.

Something was coming closer. Blurred shapes began to emerge from the shadows.

Dylan took a raspy breath, his heart flopping. His shoes scuffed back another pace.

Right up to the edge of the cliff.

15.

The village was a sprawling cluster of cabins, too small to be called houses. The moss-stained wood looked older than any of the other infrastructure. Eton said the island had gone through multiple owners, so the cabins had likely been added at some point during a previous development and then cleaned and repaired for their visit.

Ruth noted all of that in a detached fog as a staff member led her to her room. Lamps were dotted around the clearing, lighting up the paths and signposts, but unable to touch the ocean of jungle outside.

"Here we are, this one's yours," her guide chirped, then stepped aside with a little bow. Ruth shoved the door open.

Zach was inside, sorting through his luggage. The cabin was tiny and left little space for furniture. Two bunk beds were pressed into the walls. At the room's end, a dresser sat beneath a curtained window. They'd need to shove their suitcases under the beds to keep the walkway clear.

"Hey," Zach called. He had his case open on a mattress and was moving shirts into the dresser. "Welcome to paradise! I heard rumors that the VIP guests get actual houses, but..."

"Zach." She couldn't play along with his cheerfulness. "We need to talk."

He straightened. "Hm?"

Ruth shut the door. The cabin had no electricity, only a battery-powered lamp set on top of the dresser. It lit Zach from below, putting uncanny shadows over his gentle face.

"Did you know?" she asked.

Zach still held a shirt. It was one of his nice ones, and he'd packed it carefully, but now it crumpled in his hands. She couldn't get a good read on his emotions. "Know…?"

She leaned her back against the door. "It's the anniversary."

Very slowly, he unclenched his grip and placed the shirt on top of the dresser. His voice was soft. "Oh."

"Did you know?"

She didn't need to ask. He couldn't meet her eyes.

Ruth had filters on her phone and laptop. Petition was notorious enough that people still referenced it, still joked about it, and stray comments could feel like a bludgeon when they came unexpectedly. She was healthier if she never saw them.

Zach didn't have those same filters. If the friends on the beach had been seeing posts about the milestone, then he would have, as well.

Hot emotions burned at the back of her throat, stung like sand in her eyes. "Why didn't you warn me?"

"I…" He took a slow breath. "I'm sorry. I thought you must have already known." He grimaced. "Sorry."

The implication was that she *should* have known. It was her tragedy. Her twenty-year anniversary.

She dug her hands into the wood at her back, felt splinters peel up beneath her nails, and pushed harder. "I would have said something if I had."

"I didn't want to put a cloud over the trip." Zach folded his arms and then, with obvious effort, unfolded them again. He was trying not to put up a wall. "I thought if you knew, you didn't want to talk about it. And if you didn't know…I thought that might have been for the best."

"I need to be able to trust you." Ruth was fighting to keep the hurt from spilling into her voice. "I need to know you won't lie to me."

For a long moment, he watched her, deep pain etched over his expression. "I thought I was protecting you. But...that was the wrong thing, wasn't it?"

"Is there anything else?" She thought of Carson's abrupt shift toward her. "Anything you've kept from me?"

He reached out a hand. Ruth hesitated, then pushed off from the door to meet him halfway. His skin was warm and dry as he ran his thumb across her palm.

"I'm going to try to be more honest," he said. "Even if I'm worried it will hurt you."

She nodded. He understood. The pain of bad news was nothing compared to the pain of being deceived.

"And, being honest, I don't think you need to hide so much." He took a slow breath, watching for her reaction. "I might be wrong. I hope you'll forgive me if I am. But sometimes it feels as though you put so much effort into hiding from Petition that...well, Petition ends up consuming you."

She hated it, but on some level, she sensed he was right. When her life was calm, she could go months without thinking about it. But when stress was applied, as it had been in the lead-up to the festival...

"I don't know what the alternative is," she whispered.

His hands moved over hers, calming. "You keep your past a secret because you're afraid of how people will react. But I don't think many of them would care. It's been twenty years."

She thought of the friends on the beach, sharing her story like it was salacious gossip. *The only survivor. People keep trying to find her, but without luck.*

"People would care," she said.

"I don't." His eyes were dark, sad, beautiful. "I never did."

She hadn't meant for Zach to find out. He'd uncovered the truth by accident, months after they'd moved in together. He'd come to her, looking confused and uncertain, holding a letter from her caseworker that contained updates on the latest round of court hearings.

He'd opened it by accident. And Ruth had felt her world begin to crumble.

After so many years, after so much care, she'd slipped up.

She'd expected Zach to feel disgusted, repulsed. Betrayed.

Instead, all he wanted was to talk. They sat in their tiny living room, knees bumping, as they fought to bare their emotions to one another in ways they never had before.

Zach had told her he didn't care. He'd said that she was still Ruth, and that was all that mattered to him.

And he'd kept her secret.

He could have sold it. Tabloids would have paid him unimaginable sums. Ruth could have been his ticket out of debt.

But he hadn't. And Ruth, very slowly and in unsteady increments, was starting to learn to trust.

"I never cared," he said, and he kissed her forehead. "You're right, some others probably will. But not as many as you think. Maybe you don't need to hide anymore."

Ruth closed her eyes. She felt herself tearing in half: the part of her that believed she would only be safe if she was never, ever associated with Petition, and the half that wanted to believe in the world Zach saw.

Their door shoved open. Hayleigh, gasping with breathless laughter, stumbled in. Carson followed her, making clawing motions. "Watch out, the cannibal witch is going to ge-e-e-t you!"

"No!" Hayleigh shrieked. Ruth staggered and a bunk bed rocked as Hayleigh hurtled into them. Then she and Carson caught themselves, panting and laughing.

"Sorry, man," Carson said, gripping the bunk's upper rail. "Did we interrupt something?"

Zach glanced down at Ruth, smiling. "We're okay?"

"We're okay," she confirmed.

Not entirely the truth.

But, maybe, if she willed it into existence hard enough, it would be.

You have to die, Josanna.

It doesn't work if you don't die.

Salt water lapped at a sandy beach.

The water was turning red.

She reeled back and saw the bodies.

Dozens of them, rocking in the currents. Their hair moved like seaweed. Their limbs drifted, undulating, the skin torn to shreds.

Lifeless eyes stared vacantly. Gaping mouths let streams of blood mix into the brine.

There were so many of them, more bodies than ocean.

She moved closer, keening softly in her chest, and stopped at the edge of the ocean, blood and salt lapping over her toes.

His shattered limbs drifted in the current. His bleached eyes were vacant. His face was swelling, the skin beginning to peel.

Zach.

Ruth clawed at her throat. She was awake, but she couldn't breathe.

Another sighting. There have been so many.

She was in the lower bunk, and it felt like a coffin. She pulled her mouth open and dragged a breath through a trachea swollen by panic.

Not a sighting. There is no such thing as sightings.

Even with the curtain open, their cabin was dark. Her clothes were damp and clinging. Ruth coiled her hands into the blankets around her neck, squeezing them as hard as she could as she waited for the sensations to fade.

They never lasted more than a few seconds after a dream. But those few seconds were brutal.

The upper bed felt uncomfortably close. Slowly, Ruth turned her head, trying to escape the sensation of being trapped.

Across the narrow walkway was the second bunk. Hayleigh had claimed the top, leaving Carson on the lower level, opposite Ruth.

He was awake. And he was staring at her.

Ruth's throat closed over again.

Carson's eyes were wide, almost perfect circles beneath his heavy forehead. The thin light glinted off them.

Ruth squeezed the blankets harder.

He wasn't blinking. He wasn't looking away. A muscle twitched in his jaw, and she couldn't believe she'd once thought he had a rounded face, because it wasn't—it was rigid and blocky and harsh.

"What?" Through the terror, through the squeeze of her throat, she forced herself to whisper. "Why are you angry? What did I do?"

That was the wrong thing to ask. His mouth twisted: raw disgust, a sliver of teeth.

Panic pressed her. She couldn't endure his stare for even a second longer.

She lurched out of bed. The cabin was small, and she was at the exit in two paces, snatching up her jacket from the hooks. As she slipped through the door, she looked back.

Zach was asleep in the bed above Ruth's, his arm drooping over the side of the mattress. He didn't move. A scrap of Hayleigh's blond hair was visible in her upper bunk.

And Carson...

He continued to watch her, his head tilted to keep her in view. Heavy shadows obscured his face, leaving just the eyes. Two pinpricks of light, shining out of the dark.

She pushed the door closed, breathing hard. She kept her hands planted against it even after the latch clicked.

Why? Why? Why?

Hot tears on her cold cheeks. She stepped back from the door.

The village was silent. The other cabins were dark.

Guests had continued partying well after Ruth had gone to bed, so she suspected it was closer to dawn than midnight. And it was bitingly cold. Her feet were bare.

But she wasn't going back into that cabin.

Ruth tugged her jacket on. Her limbs were unsteady: part sinking adrenaline, part lingering effects of sleep.

Zach had left his shoes outside the cabin door. She took them, tugging the laces tight so they'd stay in place.

Then she stepped off the small porch and onto the path.

There were places to sit scattered around the village. Tree stumps off the side of paths, picnic tables in the center. She could huddle up on one of those and wait for dawn.

But she had a quiet, creeping fear that Carson could still be watching her. That he'd pressed his face up against the cabin's walls, his eyes following her through the cracks in the wood.

Irrational. Paranoia.

Impossible to excise from her head once it was there.

Ruth hunched, wrapping her arms around herself. There were pathways cut into the jungle. She wouldn't get lost if she stayed on the trails, and a walk would help. It was a place to put the anxiety. And it would keep her warmer.

One of the other cabins had left a battery-powered lamp hanging outside their door. She took it, switching it on as she left the village and picked a trail at random.

For a long while, she just walked. It was a relief. There had been a constant onslaught of noise since boarding the ocean liner. This was the first time she'd been really, truly alone.

The dream had rattled her. When she closed her eyes, she could still see Zach, bleached and rotting beneath the ocean's surface.

Petition had believed in the gift of prophecy. They'd called it *sighting*.

But they'd also believed the world was ending, and that hadn't exactly come to fruition.

After being found in Petition's compound, Ruth had become a ward of the state. A string of people had stepped in to help her, some better equipped than others. Foster parents, counselors, psychologists, caseworkers, behavioral specialists.

A lot of her struggles had centered around the sightings. Ruth had believed she'd prophesied her community's death.

She'd been having dreams for the week leading up to it. She'd seen the mothers convulsing on the floor, bleeding as they clawed ribbons of flesh off their faces. She'd seen her sibling running into a wall, reeling back, and then running into it again. She'd seen her family's bodies piling up against doors, crushed as they tried to escape the compound.

And it had all come true.

That was the bite. The piece of it all that had jammed up the gears in her head for years afterward.

Her dreams had manifested into reality.

It had taken several years and an especially skilled counselor to finally put a crack in that unmovable belief. That crack had started with a question: *Did you see the future? Or did they create the future to match what you saw?*

The jungle was damp from recent rain. Drops fell on her hair and back. The cuffs of her pants were saturated. She felt miles away from the festival, and she leaned back against a tree, relishing it.

Ruth still had dreams. Sometimes, when they were especially vivid and especially violent, her mind defaulted to calling them sightings.

She'd been having a lot of them in the week leading up to the festival. Stress, manifesting in the only way it could. Unspoken fears made real.

A distant, guttural sound rattled through the jungle. An animal... though, she remembered, Eton's video had said there were no mammals on Prosperity Island. Maybe some had been introduced later. More likely, it was a bird.

The noise repeated. It hung in the air, intrusive in the quiet of night. Eerie.

Cold was beginning to creep in again. Ruth set off, hoping the trail might eventually lead to a beach. She wanted to see the horizon. It would give her an idea how far off dawn might be.

Sounds came again, in the distance somewhere to her right. They were different. Pulsing, almost, the pitch rising with every repetition.

Ruth's mind tried to match a word to the noise. *Help, help, help, help—*

She turned her head, cutting through the unnerving thought. The sounds faded.

Her trail rose upward, which meant she was heading inward, toward the island's peak. Ruth idled. She could backtrack and pick a different direction, but the last fork in the road had been a while ago…

"Help me! Help, please, help!"

Ruth turned rigid.

There was no uncertainty. That was a human voice. A woman's.

And it was frantic, ragged and broken at the edges.

The sound was coming from her right, but that would take her off the trail, and it sounded a long way into the wilderness. She could turn back, try to find some of the staff, but how long would that take—

No words. Only a sharp, jagged scream.

Pain, manifested.

Ruth ran, cutting into the jungle. The lantern swung wildly as she held it ahead of herself. Her other arm came up to shield her eyes from leaves and jagged branches.

The scream cut out. Ruth tried to aim toward it, but sound distorted in the jungle. She could be off the mark.

"Hello?" she yelled. *"Hello?"*

No answer.

She thought of the figures she'd seen bolting into the trees the night before, delirious at the thought of finding the witch's grave. She thought of all the things that could happen to a person who was alone in the dark.

Broken legs. Fractured spines. Anaphylaxis. Concussions, lacerations.

Memories of one of the mothers rhythmically stabbing the kitchen knife into her open mouth.

"Hello!" Ruth shouted.

There was a thin gap in the trees. A path, running crossways to her trajectory. She staggered to a standstill, lantern held high, searching for any sign that another person had come that way.

Eerie silence.

Ruth counted her heartbeats. *One, two, three, four—*

Whispers of noise to her left. Leaves crushed. Something large moving in her direction. Ruth took a step toward it, but then her legs refused to carry her further.

Whatever was coming through the trees, it didn't sound human.

No mammals, unless the explorers introduced them. That was a thing they sometimes did, wasn't it? Wild goats, wild boars.

"Hello!" Ruth's voice broke. Clammy sweat and dew trickled off her forehead and into her eyes. She swiped across them with her sleeve.

The uneasy rustles of movement fell still. It wasn't far from her. Just out of sight, buried in the darkness.

What could make sounds like that?

The cannibal witch. Creeping on all fours, blood staining her teeth.

Ruth eased forward, lantern stretched out, pushing back the night an inch at a time.

And then another sound. From behind, this time.

A clotted, choking gurgle.

Ruth twisted. Her lantern lit trees, leaves, moss. And then something else. Something pale and moving.

Fingers stretched out of the dark. An arm, then a body, staggering into the path. And Ruth opened her mouth to make a noise that never escaped.

The witch. It's the witch, after all, her dress soaked in blood.

The figure's eyes locked on Ruth. Her reaching hand curled. Blood trailed over the fingertips. More spilled from her gaping mouth.

Not a witch.

Something far worse.

16.

Ruth gaped. There was no air left in the jungle. Only stifling, incredible terror.

"*Gilly.*"

The word tasted like a crime.

Muscles around Gilly's mouth twitched. Her red hair hung loose, curtaining her face. It was damp, tacky, tangled.

Her open mouth trembled, as though she was trying to form a sound. Blood dribbled from her lower lip.

A flowing dress was cinched around her waist. It was torn. The cream fabric soaked up blooms of her blood.

Sharpened sticks protruded from her. Three in her chest. Two in her abdomen. Another in her thigh. Each was no wider than a finger, but long. They went right through her, bloodied tips shining in the lamplight.

One ran through her throat. Cutting off her voice.

She had one hand gripped around it, trying to hold it still.

"Gilly." Ruth felt numb. The world seemed very dim.

The woman took a wavering step closer. Her feet were bare, the soles cut through by the forest floor. Her fox eyes were wild, bloodshot.

The inertia rooting Ruth in place snapped. She moved forward, reaching for Gilly but afraid to touch her in case she made it worse. "I'm here. I'm going to help. Don't move—"

Gilly's eyes flicked to the side. Raw terror flashed through them.

Ruth tried to grasp her hand. Too late.

Gilly bolted.

"No!"

The trees closed in around the woman as she vanished between them. Something had scared her.

Ruth swung, searching the jungle at her back, but if anything lurked between the thick leaves, she couldn't see it.

She swore and turned, giving chase.

Gilly shouldn't have been able to move so fast. Not when she was cut through like that. Not when she was *dying*.

Because that was the truth, Ruth knew. The sharpened sticks ran through her lungs, through her throat. She was going to die.

That was always how it happened, wasn't it? The disobedient ones. They fought the hardest right before the elders killed them.

She ran, the lantern held high, straining to follow Gilly's trail. She glimpsed flashes of fresh blood on the leaves. Heard the reckless crash of the woman breaking through branches. But following the trail was slowing her down. With every second, Gilly drew farther away.

Ruth couldn't lose her. No one would be able to find her again in time. She had to keep running, keep focused. Gilly would collapse eventually.

And then?

Her phone was back in the cabin. She didn't know which path she'd been on. But she was certain they were nowhere near any kind of help.

Ruth clenched her teeth. She ran harder, faster, pure fear driving her.

She could no longer hear Gilly.

A toppled tree cut around her path, waist-height. Ruth caught herself on it, her hip burning from the impact. She lifted the lantern, frantic, as she searched for the telltale specks of blood.

None on the fallen tree. None on the plants to either side.

No sounds.

"*Gilly!*"

Ruth spun, hunting. For anything. Blood. Broken branches. Gilly's path had been erratic; she could have tilted in any direction.

As far as Ruth could see, no one else had been that way.

"No. No." She backtracked, trying to pick up the trail. It felt like an impossible task. The jungle was so dense, so full of lush decay. The trees were damp with condensation. In the lamplight, it all looked like blood.

She was losing time.

"Gilly!"

Ruth screamed it, the sound tearing from her lungs.

That word hung in the air. Echoing.

And a fresh kind of dread encroached on Ruth, like hands slowly wrapping over her shoulders and then squeezing tight.

The sticks cutting into Gilly had been purposeful. She'd seen their tips; they'd been whittled into points with deft strokes of a knife.

No accident.

Man-made weapons.

Ruth hesitated for just a beat, then pulled the lantern close and turned off its light.

A haze of predawn light spread across the sky. It wasn't much to see by, but the lamp made her into a target. She began to move again. Cautiously, carefully. Every few steps she slowed, still hunting for any trace of Gilly, ears and eyes straining.

She had a strong sense of direction, but the blind dash through the trees had left her off-kilter. She judged her angle the best she could and was rewarded when she hit a trail.

Ruth pulled off her jacket and tied it around a branch. It was a heavy brown color that blended into the jungle, but it was the best she could do in that moment. She broke into a run, following the path downhill, knowing it would lead to either the beach or the village.

They'd been deep in the island. A long way from any of Eton's established zones. Ruth could picture the hand-drawn map in her mind's eye;

if she wasn't wrong, she'd circled most of the way around the island's peak by the time she lost Gilly.

Wet tears threatened. Ruth, gasping, forced them back down. Tears would use energy, block her nose, make her slow. She could have emotions later. At that moment, all that mattered was survival. Hers. And Gilly's.

She hit the village, her legs shaking. Ruth slowed only long enough to mentally mark the path she'd come from, then sprinted toward her cabin.

Dawn had barely arrived. With the amount of partying she'd heard the night before, she was surprised that so many people were already awake. Eton's guests must have included fitness enthusiasts. Tight leggings, loose singlets. One man was doing a yoga routine at the edge of the jungle, his hair shaggy and his beard neat, an expensive camera on a tripod filming.

There were no staff members that she could see. Ruth didn't stop moving until she hit her cabin, then she beat her fist on the door, hard, before shoving in.

"What—"

Zach sat up in bed, squinting, his hair in his eyes. Hayleigh rolled over, craning to see Ruth over the edge of her bed.

"Someone's hurt." Ruth's skin felt hot, prickly, painful. "I need you to come with me. We have to find some staff."

"Hurt?" Hayleigh's eyebrows rose in immediate worry. "Ruthie, are you okay?"

"There was a woman in the jungle. She's…" Ruth pictured the sticks piercing her, the blooms of blood through her dress. "It's serious."

"Wait, slow down." Zach dropped over the edge of the bunk, not wasting time on the ladder, and staggered as he hit the floor. "Where in the jungle? What happened to her? How bad is it?"

"She's bleeding out." Ruth slapped her hand against the door's frame, urgency making her frantic. "Please, I don't know who to speak to. I need you to help me."

"It's okay. You're okay." Hayleigh slipped out of bed, long legs bare below her shorts, and shivered as she took Ruth's arm. "We're here. Don't be afraid."

Carson sat on the edge of his bed. His forearms were braced on his knees, his expression unreadable.

Zach blinked hard as he crossed to Ruth. "Slow down. We need to think this through. She was in the jungle, right? What was she wearing?"

"A dress."

"Was it covered in blood?"

"Yes!" She didn't know why it mattered. But Zach drew a deep breath, then let it out in shaky laughter. He reached for her hand.

"Ruth, I think this must have been an Eton prank. Remember last night? The cannibal witch watching us from the jungle?"

"Ohh," Hayleigh sighed. She kept rubbing Ruth's arm, comforting. "What a mean thing to do to you."

"No." Ruth pulled away from them both, stepping back until her shoulder hit the doorframe. "This wasn't a prank. She...she was full of spears."

For a second, they glanced between themselves. Carson spoke first.

"*We pierced her through again and again. She would not die.* That was part of the movie."

"I should have seen this coming," Zach said. "Eton announced the treasure hunt to send people into the jungle. *Of course* he'd also have an actor out there to scare anyone who was looking for the grave. It's a classic Eton twist."

"Zach."

He reached for her again, but she shook her head, refusing to let him touch her.

"I'm so sorry." His voice grew softer. "I didn't realize the show last night had rattled you this much. You looked so calm afterward—if I'd guessed—"

"No." Anger was overtaking fear. "You're not listening to me. This wasn't some actor dressed up as the witch. She's one of us—a guest. I met her yesterday."

A hint of uncertainty passed through them. Hayleigh fidgeted, toes squirming on the cold floor.

"Could be a plant?" Carson suggested. "Maybe they wanted to make it more realistic, so they had the actor pretend to be a guest for the first day?"

"Eton's channel had a prank phase a few years back," Zach added. "They got increasingly convoluted toward the end."

Ruth felt like she was suffocating.

It hadn't been a prank.

An actor couldn't scream like that.

An actor couldn't choke on their own blood like that.

"Ruth. We're on your side here." Zach watched her intently. "If you think we need to speak to the staff, we will. It's just…it's Occam's razor. Most of the time, the simplest solution is the most likely. And this feels like such an Eton move."

Hayleigh's eyes had narrowed. She reached out a finger, stopping just short of Ruth's collarbone. "What's that?"

She was pointing to a narrow smear of red on Ruth's skin. "She left blood on the plants as she ran. I chased her. Some of it must have gotten on me."

Zach's face shifted, losing the softness. He licked his fingertip, then dabbed it against the mark, pulling some off. He squinted at it, trying to see the texture, as he rubbed it between his fingers.

His eyebrows drew low over his eyes as the confidence drained out of him.

"I think it might actually be blood," he said.

They all stared at Ruth as though they were seeing her for the first time. She stood, framed by the doorway, her clothes wet, her hair snarled, her face hot with strangled emotion.

"You really think she was hurt," Zach said.

"Not just hurt. She was dying."

Zach took a shallow breath. He reached for his coat.

"Okay. Let's find someone."

17.

They moved quickly.

Ruth gave Zach his sneakers back and pulled on her own. Hayleigh and Carson dragged clothes over their pajamas. They were out of the cabin in less than thirty seconds.

"Staff..." Zach muttered, scanning the village as they crossed it. "Staff might not know what to do. But they can get us to Eton. Maybe Petra."

"There," Hayleigh said, pointing to a yellow shirt at the noticeboard.

A young woman was pinning up a schedule for that day, her hair fastened back into a neat ponytail. She turned her smile on them as they jogged to her.

"We think a person's hurt," Zach said, skipping any preamble. "We need to speak to someone in charge."

"Oh no!" Her voice was chirpy. The smile didn't move. "I can send one of our excellent medical team to check in on them. Could I have the guest's name and location?"

"They're in the jungle." Zach glanced at Ruth.

"Off-trail," she filled in. "Other side of the peak. I can show you the area, but she ran, and I lost her." She took a tight breath and added, "It's serious. I don't know if she's still alive."

"Wow, that sounds bad!" She was so chipper. It was uncomfortable. Ruth fought the impulse to pull back. "I'm going to see about getting them some help right away."

Zach glanced at Ruth. He held a question in his expression: *This doesn't feel right to you, does it?*

She gave her head a small, barely perceptible shake.

"Where's Eton?" he asked.

"Oh." The staff member tilted her head, suddenly apologetic. "I'm so sorry, we're not allowed to disclose that kind of information about management. It's for security reasons."

Ruth clenched her hands, the desperation turning her fingers numb.

"Listen…" Zach paused, then adjusted his tone, burying his frustration. "I completely get that. No problem. But is there any way we could speak to someone involved in management? It's an urgent situation."

"Oh, for sure." The woman pulled a device out of her belt. "I can get one of my team leaders to meet with you. They're all occupied right now, but they'll be able to stop by your cabin a little later this morning."

Zach grimaced. "No. We don't have that much time."

"Oh, I'm sorry! If you think it's something concierge could help with, they're available around the clock at Sunset Beach. I'd be happy to show you the way!"

Zach looked at Ruth, then Carson and Hayleigh. Ruth could only meet his eyes, equally lost.

"No," he said at last. "Don't bother."

"Okay, thank you so much!"

She pinned the last poster onto the board, then was gone in a flick of her ponytail.

Zach rubbed at the back of his neck, his thick eyebrows creasing the skin around his eyes. "Okay. She was young. She's probably inexperienced and running on a script. We'll find another staff member. Or, actually, we might have more luck if we can find one of the technicians at the stage—"

"Hey. Sorry for interrupting."

A man stood at the noticeboard behind them, long fingers lightly pressing on a sheet of paper. Shoulder-length hair was tied into a bun at the back of his head, and he dressed casually, but something about the way his eyes darted over them made Ruth think the relaxed posture only went skin-deep.

"I overheard part of that," he said. "You can try the medical clinic. Eton's visiting the injured contestant from yesterday."

"Oh!" Zach clapped a hand to his chest, relief bleeding through him. "Thank you. That's exactly what we need."

"Do you know the way?" The man hooked a thumb toward the trails. "I can show you."

"Yes. Please. We've only been to the beach and the village so far."

The man's steel eyes flicked toward Ruth before fixing back on Zach. "Logan, by the way."

"Zach."

Logan's pace was smooth and quick as he led them out of the village. He seemed to know the island well, cutting corners and taking turns without needing to check the signs.

Ruth barely had time to feel the simmering anxiety before they hit an oval clearing with several banks of buildings, larger and less aesthetic than the cabins. Glimpses of a beach came through the trees. Sunset Beach, their main location, if her sense of direction hadn't failed her.

"These are the admin buildings," Logan said, weaving between them. Like the cabins, the staff area seemed to be repurposed from an older development. Water-stained metal and concrete dominated. "Staff accommodation, logistics, kitchen prep. Medical is right up here."

"Hey there," another staff member said, moving to intercept them just as they reached the building, smile in place. "Can I help you?"

"No, we're good." Logan didn't break stride as he sidestepped and shoved through the double doors. Ruth rushed to follow him before the staff could react, her friends close on her heels.

The room wasn't small, but it felt crowded. Six beds were lined up along the wall, divided by movable curtains, two desks opposite them.

Every other spare space had been filled with locked cabinets and rows of basket shelving, stocked with plastic-wrapped medical supplies.

Only one bed was occupied. Makayla sat in it, her legs hanging over its side.

Ruth faltered. Makayla's right arm was in a sling. Bruises ran along her legs, her arms, and her jaw. More would be hidden under the cotton T-shirt. It was like her skin had been turned into a canvas.

Eton sat in a chair beside the bed. One knee had been pulled up to his chest and he leaned over it. They could have been friends at a sleepover, they seemed that casual.

Then Makayla saw them, and she sucked in a breath. "Hey, it's you! Ruth."

Eton swiveled, his eyebrows raised. "Ruth…and friends! How're you all doing this morning?"

Ruth fought to tear her eyes off Makayla's bruises. Bandages had been taped across the tapestry, sealing off areas where the rocks had punctured her skin.

"We just got some good news," Eton said. He reached out and lightly squeezed Makayla's shoulder. "She's okay to stay. Dr. Coleman says she can return to the main festival this afternoon, as long as she takes it easy."

"That's…good. Really good." Ruth's mouth was dry. The others were hanging back, letting her take the lead. She didn't know how. "Someone's been attacked."

Eton started to chuckle, but it died out when no one else joined in. He shook his head, smiling but dazed. "Sorry, what's that?"

"I saw a woman in the forest. She'd been hurt." Ruth's hand fluttered up to her chest, gesturing to where the sticks had pierced Gilly. "She was frightened. Running. I couldn't catch up to her. I…I don't think we have much time. We might already be too late."

"Oh!" Eton's confusion faded into delight. "You saw her! You saw the witch!"

Ruth's mouth was dry. She could feel her friends at her back. She knew what they must be thinking. "Is...?"

"Scary stuff, huh?" Eton winked.

Ugly emotions began to bubble up. Shame. Disbelief. "Is...she an actor?"

No one in her group made a sound, but Ruth felt them shifting.

"Let me put it this way..." Eton continued to smirk, and it was meant to be the kind of smile a person gave a close friend, but they weren't friends, and she hated the way it made her feel. "Prosperity Island is full of secrets and surprises."

"No. I'm not trying to play games. She was screaming—there was blood everywhere—" Ruth caught herself right on the edge of shouting and brought her voice back down. "I need you to tell me. If this was an actor, you need to say it outright. Because, if not, someone's going to die out there."

Eton's smile had faded. A beat of silence hung between them. She felt him scanning her, reading her. The scrutiny turned her skin hot and itchy.

"No one's been hurt," Eton said, and even though he pushed some joy into his voice, it no longer sounded genuine. "We have staged reenactments of the cultists. I guess I took this one too far."

"Oh."

It felt like having cold water poured over her. Humiliation crept up.

She didn't want to turn around. She didn't want to see her friends' faces and what they held. Embarrassment. Annoyance. Or, worst of all, pity.

Then Makayla spoke. "Hey, Ruth? I'm glad you're here. I wanted to find you once I was let out."

"Oh."

"I know this isn't the time." Makayla, perched on the edge of her bed, leaned forward. She was cutting through the awkward silence, saving Ruth from herself. "But I wanted to thank you."

"Right." Ruth rubbed damp hands on her legs. "It's okay."

"They told me you helped after I fell into the water. And…I feel bad. I was so aggressive in that game. I nearly ran you off a beam."

Ruth had almost forgotten. She managed a wonky smile. "But you didn't."

"Yeah. Well." Makayla grinned, and it felt genuine. "I owe you one."

"Thanks. I'm glad you're okay." Ruth slowly turned. Zach rested a hand on her shoulder, voiceless but warm, as he guided her out of the tent.

Her throat still ached. She couldn't bring herself to look at any of them. The others trailed alongside her for a few feet, then Zach spoke.

"Hey. You okay?"

She nodded.

He must have sensed the lie, because his hand squeezed. "This was the *good* outcome, right? No one was hurt. That's what matters."

She nodded again.

"You did the right thing by checking. I'm proud of you, Ruth."

No one was hurt.

Her footsteps faltered.

She'd trusted Eton before, when he'd sent them up onto the maze of boards.

She'd trusted it was okay, that he knew what he was doing, that he wouldn't take risks with his guests.

And Makayla had paid for it.

How many chances was Ruth supposed to give someone? How much faith could she put in a person who'd let them be hurt, then promised to do better, then sent them into the jungle to be hurt again?

"I want to talk to someone else," she said.

Behind them, Carson groaned. She tried to act like she hadn't heard it.

"Ruth…" Zach started, concern spreading across his face. "Eton said—"

"I know what I saw. I want to talk to someone else. A woman's dying, maybe already dead, and I can't just leave her out there."

A cool voice cut over them. "What was that?"

Petra had appeared through the crowd of staff members, digital pad held to her chest, pen in one hand. Her hair was immaculate, her eyes cold as ice. One slim, perfect eyebrow rose as she scanned the group. "Did I hear you say there's been an injury?"

Ruth stepped forward before the others could stop her. Words rushed out, desperate. "Yes. A woman, Gilly, in the jungle. It looked like she'd been attacked."

Petra's eyes were inscrutable. Ruth held still, the tension in her chest feeling so taut that, if it were to snap, it would tear her apart.

Petra raised her tablet and tapped the screen rapidly, then poised a digital pen over it.

"I need you to tell me everything, as clearly and accurately as you can manage," she said. "Don't leave anything out."

18.

Logan hung back, largely forgotten.

He'd been keeping tabs on key figures that morning. He'd seen Eton headed to the medical tent, working on damage control. An injured player was less likely to file a lawsuit against a friend, after all.

Logan had also tracked Petra for a bit, but her speed made it challenging to trail her without being obvious, so he'd switched his focus. He'd been trying to learn more about the staff—their numbers, their jobs, their internal structure—when he saw Zach's group.

They were rushing, half-dressed, and anxious.

Logan had sauntered up to the noticeboard under the guise of reading the schedule. And he'd listened.

Just as he listened now.

The witness, Ruth, recounted what she'd seen. The details were more visceral than Logan had expected. Sticks, whittled down to sharpened points, stabbed through a woman. The witness balled her hands up at her throat as she showed how the victim had tried to hold one in place.

Allegedly.

Logan had learned to handle extraordinary stories with some doubt. That didn't mean they were never true. Sometimes, events really were as shocking as described.

And sometimes you were on an island filled with people who aspired to fame and craved attention, and who were given access to more liquor than was strictly wise.

Logan suspected he was being generous by reserving judgment.

Though…the witness genuinely did seem shaken. And her skin was shiny with dried sweat from running along the trails.

There were no vagaries about the directions either. She told Petra exactly which path she'd been on and described a jacket tied to a tree near where she'd last seen the alleged victim.

He'd play it safe. Reserve judgment.

He suspected Petra shared his hesitations. But, to her credit, she listened intently. Her pen raced across the pad, and she wasn't just scribbling. He got a look at the screen as he idly circled. Her notes were thorough and bullet-pointed.

Eton may have blown them off, but his assistant was doing both of their jobs.

Ruth hit the end of her account, and Petra clipped the pen back onto the tablet.

"Leave this with me." Her tone was cool. Not alarmed, but not dismissive either. "This is very likely a misunderstanding—it sounds like one of our actors may have gotten too into their role. But I'm still giving it the same attention I'd give to any other crisis report. I'm going to start by getting search parties with EMTs canvassing the area you indicated, and then I'll be attempting to track down Gilly or the group she arrived with. We're going to account for her, one way or another."

"Thank you," Ruth said. She looked smaller, as though telling the story had opened a valve and allowed all the energy to drain out of her.

"This was a distressing event," Petra said, softening a fraction. "We have counselors available if you think it would help."

"No." A slightly bitter laugh from Ruth. She had some experience with counselors, then. Enough that she either didn't trust them, or, more likely, didn't expect to gain much from a company-sponsored session. "Thanks, though."

"I'm going to ask you to stay close at hand for a while." Petra gave the group a once-over. "That means all of you. Get some rest at your cabin. Or join in the activities. But I'd like to avoid having anyone wander too deep into the jungle for the time being, until we know more. Understood?"

She was moving again before they could respond. The tablet flashed back to life as she danced her pen over the surface, setting up tasks, delegating.

"You did great," Zach whispered, lightly touching Ruth's back. She seemed uneasy even as she nodded.

The whole group was interesting to him, but Logan found himself watching Zach again.

They already knew each other. Though Zachary Waldon was oblivious to that.

Logan had sent his email from an anonymous address, after all.

Zachary Waldon had aged more than the intermittent year should have cost him. His face was less animated, the angles slightly harder. He seemed more cautious.

People could change, Logan knew.

But *real* change was hard, and it took time. More commonly, he saw the store-brand version of it: superficial, transient, inadequate. Put in five dollars' worth of effort, get five dollars' worth of results.

He'd reserve judgment. Again.

Logan recognized two of the companions, though he hadn't learned their names. The girl—blond, slim, graceful—and the guy—meaty, muscled, his hands large. He'd seen them both associated with Zach back then.

But...

The other one, dark-haired and with intense eyes, she was new.

And there were a lot of things about her that were making him curious.

Her story seemed calculated to draw attention, but her body language was trying to repel it. She didn't want people looking at her.

She was trying to hide something. Or hide *from* something.

"Hey, you look familiar. Where do I know you from?" Logan asked. He kept his voice light and his smile disarming, but Ruth still pulled back from him, her face closing in.

"I'm no one," she said. A reflex, he thought. She caught herself and added, "I was in the game yesterday."

"Yeah, that must be it." It definitely wasn't.

Zach reached out a hand. "Thanks again. You really helped us out. Let's get a drink later, yeah?"

"Sounds good," Logan lied as he shook the offered hand. "You guys stay safe."

They split up, Zach and his group turning toward the beach and breakfast.

Logan slipped his phone out before they could get too far. He pressed his thumb over the speaker to muffle the shutter effect and snapped a photo. It caught just a sliver of Ruth's face behind her dark hair.

He was probably wrong.

Probably.

He opened the caption on Ruth's photo and typed:

PETITION CHILD?

19.

"You're going to kill me."

"Come on. A bit more. You almost have it."

Maya arched her back, one hand raking through her hair. Foamy surf washed over her calves as she knelt in the wet sand.

Peyton crouched, satchel slung over his shoulder. The camera whirred as it focused, then clicked with each photo. Maya stretched, lips parted, stomach sucked in, twisting as far as her spine would allow.

"Focus on the camera," Peyton said, and he sounded irritated.

She gave him an ugly grimace, teeth bared, then fixed her face back into a sultry invitation.

He had no room to be getting snippy with her. At least he was fully clothed and dry; she was freezing.

Peyton had wanted to get the sunrise in the photo shoot, but they were going to have to digitally erase gooseflesh off her legs and put color back into her face. And the bikini was made of cheap fabric, and her lower back itched from the stitching, and she couldn't scratch it because that would get sand on it—

"Focus. On. The. Lens!" Peyton lowered the camera. "It shows in the photos when you don't make eye contact. Come on!"

Maya scrunched her face up, trying to pull herself together. It didn't matter how cold or tired or crampy she felt. Lara-Mee Swimwear had sponsored them for a post she was contractually obligated to deliver.

And she would. They were professionals. Peyton had his fitness brand.

She, her modeling. Both only mid-tier, but just enough to live off the sponsorships if they hustled hard and weren't too picky.

And they couldn't squander the opportunity the trip offered them. They weren't VIP—nowhere near big enough for that—but they'd won the lucky dip. Completely by chance, she'd been assured, though Maya had a high school classmate interning on Eton's team who she suspected might have nudged their luck a little.

And it was perfect. Pristine beaches, lush jungle, and the most stunning sunsets she'd ever seen. They had to make the most of it. Any minute they weren't networking, they were using to bank photos. Even if it meant freezing in a tiny bikini at dawn.

"Let's try a different angle," she said, gingerly turning so her back was to the camera. A quick breath in, a second to elongate her posture, then she raised one hand over her head and tilted to give the camera a come-here look over her shoulder.

"Good," Peyton said, frustration fading. "That looks good. Yeah. Turn a bit further. Push your right leg out. Okay—okay—suck it in—okay—"

Keeping her face both serene and engaged was near impossible when the pose hurt her hips and her hair was getting blown into her mouth. But she did. Right up until she saw them.

"Maya, face," Peyton said.

She blinked, then focused back on the camera. "We have an audience."

They stood at the jungle's edge, staring. Not uncommon. A lot of her photo shoots were in public areas and sometimes people liked to stop and watch. That was why they'd trekked to one of Prosperity Island's smaller beaches that morning: it saved a lot of time when they didn't have to wait for people to wander out of the shot.

"Just ignore them," Peyton said. "One more set. We're nearly done."

Her toes curled in the icy water. She flipped around again, facing Peyton, and mimed crawling out of the surf, head tilted back to show off her long neck.

"Oh!" she broke into shocked laughter. Peyton lowered the camera, confused, and Maya shook her head. "They're naked."

It hadn't been easy to see before. They'd been too far away and too deep in the shadows. But, while she'd adjusted her pose, they'd moved into the open. The bare skin looked greasy and pallid in the light.

"Ugh," Peyton muttered, squinting up at them. "Want me to chase them off?"

Public perception was everything for a model. Getting a reputation for having an entitled attitude or for being icy to fans could kill brand sponsorships faster than anything else.

"I don't care," Maya said. "Maybe they wanted to go skinny-dipping and thought this beach would be empty. I'm basically naked anyway, so..."

"Well, we only need a couple more minutes." Peyton focused back in on her. "Can you get deeper into the water? I want some with the surf breaking on you."

She gave him a look to tell him just how cruel he was being, then shimmied backward.

As she moved, she found it hard to ignore the bare flesh in the distance.

Nudity didn't faze her. Having an audience didn't faze her.

What bothered her was the way they just...stood there. They weren't trying to come onto the beach, but they weren't leaving for a more secluded location either.

And the way they were staring...

"Maya, all good?" Peyton asked. He crouched low, blocking their new shot.

"Fine."

She couldn't tear her eyes away. They stood, evenly spaced, ten feet between them. And that was the worst part. They hadn't trailed in as a group. They weren't talking or even looking at each other. But they formed a line at the jungle's edge, eight of them, their faces too far away to see, their arms held slightly out from their sides. Stiff.

"Maya? Ready?"

"Yep." She adjusted her body again, stacking each part to best play to the angle. Two years, four hundred photo sessions, upward of a hundred thousand pictures, arranging herself in ways that pleased the camera had become second nature.

She shivered as a wave beat across her back, then focused in. Relaxed face, parted lips. Eyes on the lens. Tense the abs. A slight inhale. The shutter began to click.

In the distance, she sensed movement.

She snapped her eyes to the figures. They were motionless, but they were nearer than before, she was sure. She could see them more clearly. Skin, washed-out and sagging. Genitals, puckered and shriveled in the dawn chill. Bodies, motionless except for a slight sway as they balanced on the sand. Their arms were held tightly out from their bodies, and they carried...

"Maya, focus!" Peyton's frustration seeped into his voice again. The camera was still held to his face, his finger poised over the button. "Come on, stick the landing."

"I think...I think we should leave."

It emerged as a whisper, tiny and trembling, utterly unlike her.

He couldn't hear. The ocean crashed over her back; the breeze cut between them.

And he was facing away from the figures. He didn't see as they took another step nearer. He couldn't see the things they held.

A hook, rusted, like something torn off an anchor.

A line of barbed wire, trailing through the sand.

A machete.

"I want to go," she said again, afraid to raise her voice too much, afraid to let them hear.

He lowered the camera. "I'll get you something warm to drink once we're done, but we don't have a solid shot in this pose yet." His voice softened. "C'mon, show Lara-Mee why they should sponsor us again. One last round."

The figures moved.

Tilting forward, breaking into a sprint, arms pumping at their sides. Flesh gray, metal rusty red.

"Peyton!" she shrieked.

He rested the camera on one knee, his expression concerned.

They leaned forward, growing faster. Half the distance gone. No expression on their terrible faces.

"Peyton! Peyton!" She was screaming. Thrashing through the water to get to him. "Move, get out!"

He turned. He saw them. Shock passed over his face.

The machete got him first. Blunt metal buried into his back, between his shoulder blades.

He convulsed. His mouth opened. There was no pain in his face; the signals from his nerves hadn't gotten there yet. There was only shock.

The hook caught on his shoulder, sinking into his shirt and then his flesh. It dragged him around, twisting his legs out from under him. A splatter of blood landed on the sand.

Maya no longer scrambled to reach him; she clawed her way back, deeper into the water. They advanced on her: two men and a woman. Surf crashed over their legs, and if they felt the cold, they didn't show it. Their faces were locked into a singular expression. Focused. Hungry.

"No, no." Maya clawed her way back, fighting to stay out of their reach.

On the shore, Peyton writhed. He still held the camera. He reached up, trying to beat it against the nearest figure.

They pulled the machete free in a sickening wash of blood. The camera fell from his grip as a thick slab of wood came down onto his face.

More of the figures were turning away from Peyton as his struggles weakened. They waded into the water, lifeless eyes on Maya.

"Please. Don't. I have family. My…my mother."

She wasn't sure if they could even hear her. There was no flicker of reaction in their faces. They didn't even blink.

The water was up to her chest. Painfully cold. Each step back became more fraught as she scrambled to keep contact with the ocean floor.

She wasn't a strong swimmer. All they had to do was get her out far enough and then wait.

On shore, three of them still stood over Peyton. Their naked bodies were painted in flecks of blood. They moved rhythmically, their weapons rising and falling in a brutal pattern, even though he'd long since stopped moving.

The water was up to Maya's shoulders. She glanced to her side. The beach curved around, a sandbar level with her. It wasn't too far. If she could just get to it—just get to solid land—then she had a chance.

She wasn't a good swimmer, but she could run.

One of the figures raised something. The barbed wire, Maya realized. A long coil, studded through with shiny silver points.

She threw herself away from them and toward the sandbar. Hands sliced into the water. Her feet kicked, froth gushing behind her.

Metal whistled through the air. She saw the shadow on her outstretched hand.

The line of tarnished metal landed across her back, its end splashing into the water ahead of her.

And then another. And another.

Three lines, flying across her body, hitting her as they dropped.

It didn't hurt at first; it just felt like a weight, pressing her down into the ocean.

She thrashed, trying to get away from them, trying to slip them off her.

But they were heavy. Sinking into the ocean in front of her, more like a net than a line.

Then the strangers pulled.

The barbs cut into her. A dozen vicious bites across her body; tiny clouds of blood flooding the azure blue.

And they pulled again. Reeling her back toward them.

Maya screamed into the ocean.

20.

"A game!" Eton yelled. "It's time for a game!"

I wanted to let you know.

"Everyone gets to join this one."

We located Gillian Davies.

"Everyone is in the running for the prizes."

I met with her myself.

"Find me at Endurance Cove, ten minutes!"

She's fine.

Someone touched Ruth's shoulder. She flinched. Zach was there, his smile fading. "Ruth. Did you hear me?"

"Sorry, what?"

"Did you want to play? Everyone's leaving."

She blinked. The trestle tables spread across the beach were emptying out. The remains of breakfast were scattered over them, and staff members were already rushing through, bagging disposable plates and cups.

Most of the guests were trailing toward the path leading to their second beach. Hayleigh and Carson stood by their table, waiting.

Again.

It felt like they'd spent half the trip waiting on her.

"Yes. Right." She'd been worrying a napkin between her fingers but threw it back on her half-eaten food.

"You don't have to." Zach gave her a small smile. "We can just take the morning off, maybe nap a bit, if you think that would help."

"No. A game's going to be good. Help us shake everything off." She wasn't sure if that was actually true. She just knew that she'd ruined her group's morning and embarrassed them in front of their host, apparently for nothing.

Because she couldn't tell the difference between a dying woman and an actress.

But I can.

I know what I saw.

That was Gilly.

She shook her head. Petra had stopped by their table during breakfast. The message had been brief, but crisply clear. Gilly was accounted for.

What if she's lying?

Ruth hadn't seen Gilly at breakfast. But the space was crowded, and even Gilly's vivid red hair would have been difficult to spot through the mass of bodies and their colorful beachy clothes.

"You can stay close to me," Hayleigh offered. She looked nervous, fidgeting, twisting her gemstone ring around her finger. "If it helps."

"Thanks. Yeah." Ruth grabbed her tote. She had to do better. She had to stop pushing her baggage onto the people around her. "Let's go. Let's have fun."

The audience trailed through the jungle. As they emerged into the second cove, Ruth found herself staring up at the raised platform from the day before.

The broken board had been removed, leaving a gap on its far side. None of the ladders had been blocked, though. The suspended maze seemed to be open to anyone who wanted to take a turn on it.

There was another change. A line of small red flags. Stabbed into the sand, they created a kind of border that stretched the width of the beach, into the ocean, and vanished into the jungle behind.

Debris had been scattered inside the arena. Driftwood, large rocks, palm leaves. It gave the impression that a hurricane had swept through overnight.

And, in its center, between the raised maze and the announcer's platform, was something like a house.

It was made from what seemed like scrap material, pieced together haphazardly. Old metal sheets, gnarled wooden boards, crooked doors that barely filled their openings. It might have had three, possibly four, rooms inside—none even remotely weatherproof. Unlike the other structures, it had been built to look as derelict as possible.

Music played. Tracks from the band they'd heard the night before, Ruth thought: upbeat, excited, like the promise of an adventure.

Eton was already on the announcer's tower, hands braced on the rail as he watched his audience arrive. By his side, Petra held her digital pad at the ready.

Ruth found herself staring at the woman.

She's not the kind of person who would lie, is she?

Petra glanced at her digital pad, then tapped rapidly. Frustration tightened her face.

The music faded. A hiss of feedback came through the microphone.

"Welcome, welcome, welcome," Eton called. The speakers felt too loud. The cheers that answered his greeting, even louder. He waved, beaming, then raised his eyebrows. "Look what the ocean washed up last night. Pretty cool, huh? But it would be a shame to just look at it. How about a game?"

"Yeah!" Hayleigh yelled as the audience broke into applause. Even Zach was clapping, his eyes bright. Ruth made herself join in. Her hands didn't feel like her own as they smacked together.

"Are we ready to *win some cash?*"

More cheers, more shouting. Ruth still hadn't looked in her prize bag from the day before. Something about the island made money feel distant, unreal.

"Okay, okay, okay!" Eton laughed, hands fanned out as he tried to calm the crowd. "Let me tell you exactly how this is going to go down!

In a moment, you're going to break into teams. Four people per group! If you already have your team worked out, you're going to head to the right, over there."

He gestured toward the jungle.

"Or, if you're on your own or have half a group, head over to the left, thataway. Team members will come through and get you paired up."

He pointed toward the ocean.

"Four to a team, no more, no less. If there's an incomplete group at the end, then some of our staff will fill in. Once we have that sorted, I'll tell you the rules of the game. Okay? Get going!"

"Together, right?" Hayleigh asked, reaching out to grab both Carson and Ruth's arms. "The four of us?"

"Of course," Zach said, beaming. "We're sticking together."

Around them was chaos. People yelled and shoved through the crowd. "One more! We need one more!" a man shouted.

The more athletic men were in demand, with some teams fighting over them. There seemed to be a prevailing belief that they'd need to carry or move the debris.

Some lone guests were already trailing toward the other side of the beach. The ones who didn't have a group and weren't confident about being invited to one. Ruth watched them with a pang. She knew what it felt like. She'd been one of them through all of school: never picked for teams, never invited to games.

Not now.

She looked down. Hayleigh held her forearm, babbling eagerly. Zach was on her other side, craning as he tried to get a read on the board, the other contestants.

She was part of a group. For the first time.

"One minute!" Eton yelled. The screen behind him was a digital clock, counting down. "If you have a group, head to the starting spot!"

"Let's go," Carson called. He was grinning, his hand in Hayleigh's. The four of them ran up the soft sand, toward the space where other teams were already buzzing.

Staff began sifting through the partial groups, piecing them together and directing them up the beach. Eton seemed acutely focused on not letting the process drag out. Ruth understood. The crowd was hyped, eager, raucous. Too much energy with nowhere to direct it. He had to get the game moving fast.

"Okay! Okay! Okay!" he shouted, music nearly drowning out his voice.

The last teams were spliced together. Ruth looked around. The groups were clustered on the upper half of the beach, no longer mingling as a crowd but standing in tight bunches.

Six hundred guests, one hundred fifty teams. Ruth suspected nearly everyone who had attended the festival had chosen to play.

More staff members moved through them, fingers tapping on digital pads as they checked that each group had exactly four members.

A young man stopped in front of Ruth's group. "Team name?"

"Oh—" Zach glanced toward the others.

"Tans and Plans!" Hayleigh shouted.

Carson pumped his fists. "Yeah! Tans and Plans!"

The staff member chuckled as he wrote it down, then moved on.

Ruth nodded, smiling, as her group talked. She could barely hear what they were saying. Her eyes kept being drawn to the beach that stretched out ahead of them, scattered with debris.

"Okay!" Eton yelled again, and the music faded to make room for his voice. "You need to know how to play! It's a fun one. Remember these?"

He held up a small rock. The screen behind the stage zoomed in on it, showing the red mark in its center.

"Hidden through this area are red circle rocks," Eton said, still holding it high for everyone to see. "It's our own island-style Easter egg hunt. The team that finds the most wins! Ah—no—hold on!"

Two teams had dashed forward. They halted at Eton's call, but reluctantly. Staff members circled around them, ushering them back to the starting line.

"I'll tell you when to begin," Eton said, laughing. "We've got to have the rules first. This is a game, and games have rules, yeah? First—the rocks can be found anywhere *inside* the flags, and only inside."

The crowd around Ruth strained to reassess the game's border. The flags cut straight lines, creating a field that encompassed the debris, Eton's tower, the previous day's raised platform, part of the ocean, and part of the jungle.

"Oh!" Someone in the group beside them pointed, whispering to her companions. Ruth followed the gesture. The derelict shack had open windows. A small stone with just a hint of red sat on one of the window-sills, clearly visible.

"If you think I'm going to be sneaky by hiding some outside the flags, I'm sorry, you're only going to be disappointed," Eton said. "But anywhere inside the flags is fair game."

He flipped the rock to his other hand.

"The ten contestants from yesterday should still have their lucky dip stones. Those count for this game! They're an extra little reward for taking part yesterday, an early leg up on everyone else. Congrats!"

"Ruth?" Hayleigh whispered, grasping her arm, breathless.

"I have it." Ruth lifted her tote bag.

"You can search for stones anywhere you like, but you are *not* allowed to steal from other teams. We're going to be watching closely. Any team caught stealing will be immediately disqualified. Yeah?"

Ruth was grateful for that rule. Looking around, so many of the teams appeared frighteningly eager. They weren't just competitive. They'd spent years watching Eton's games, each time imagining how it would have gone if they'd been on the field. And those fantasies were, for the first time, coming to life.

There would be no hesitance. No caution. They were playing to win, whatever the cost.

"The game will last exactly one hour," Eton said. "Once it ends, you'll have an extra sixty seconds to return to the tower and pool your team's rocks together. The teams with the highest totals win. Twenty thousand dollars for first place. Ten thousand dollars for second. And then five thousand for third, fourth, and fifth place."

He paused just long enough to let the teams perform the mental calculations. Then he added, "That's per person, by the way."

Eager ripples moved through the groups. Even Ruth, worn down and wary, felt it. The prizes were significant.

"There's a drink station, so stay hydrated," Eton said, pointing toward tents set at the back of the beach, outside the flags. "And remember: no cheating, no fighting, no stealing. Okay? Those are the rules!"

"Here," Zach whispered, beckoning his teammates in. They put their heads close, and strands of Hayleigh's hair tickled Ruth's cheek.

"Most teams will go for the house," he whispered, quick and quiet, not wanting the groups around them to overhear. "That's the obvious bait. There'll be rocks in there, probably lots of them, but it'll be too crowded to do anything. Aim for the driftwood and wreckage on the beach instead. Places with fewer people."

"With that, I think we're ready," Eton called. He was bouncing, his eyes bright, like a child at the gates of an amusement park.

"The first few minutes will be a feeding frenzy." Zach spoke as fast as he could. "The easiest finds will be snatched up fast, and we want to get as many of them as we can. Don't spend any more than a second on each location, okay? We can go back and search more carefully once the easy rocks are gone."

They all nodded, Ruth included. An incredible, urgent desire was growing in her. She wanted to do well. She had a team, for the first time in her life.

She wanted—needed—to prove she belonged there.

"On your marks." Eton raised one hand. Zach broke the huddle.

Other teams tilted forward, muscles taut, feet digging into the sand for purchase.

Eton let the pause stretch, and stretch, and stretch.

And then he threw his hand down.

"*Go!*"

21.

Ruth dashed forward.

It was like a stampede. Contestants ran, pushing, stumbling.

Someone shoved Ruth's shoulder. She staggered, then caught her balance again. She turned just in time to see Carson passing her. *Did he—*

She swiped that thought out of her mind. It didn't matter.

Zach had been right. Easily two-thirds of the teams had aimed for the derelict house. The fastest contestant snatched the rock off the window-sill. The structure creaked as others forced their way through the leaning doorways. More on their heels. There wouldn't be any room to breathe inside.

Ruth swerved away from it. Other players, the ones ignoring the house, had stopped to search the nearest debris. She passed them, aiming for further along the map, where there was no competition at all.

A piece of driftwood lay up ahead. Ruth skidded to a halt and pushed it over. A painted stone fell out from between the branches. The thrill was immediate, powerful. She grabbed the stone and dropped it into her satchel.

Ahead, a heavy piece of volcanic rock. She tried to get her fingers under it, but it was too large to move alone. The stone was pockmarked with hollows, though. And inside one of those was a hint of red.

Ruth squirmed her fingers into the opening. Rough stone scraped at her skin. She could touch the pebble, but she couldn't get it out. She'd need to use something else—a stick, maybe.

She turned to scan the debris for something that might work, then caught herself. Zach had said not to spend more than a second at each location. By the time she fetched a stick and wormed the rock out, she could have time to find three other stones.

Ruth swore under her breath and kept moving. Nothing under the nearest branch. But one had been tucked in a palm frond, and she lucked out by thinking to pick up a seashell and finding a pebble under it.

She was at the shoreline. Behind, teams were flooding out of the shack. Pieces of debris were being flipped over, tugged at, kicked. Someone had descended on the volcanic rock and was working at the stone Ruth had left behind.

She moved sideways, following the edge of the water, hunting for items that hadn't already been searched.

The raised beam structure loomed overhead. Ruth felt a twist of discomfort at the sight of it.

But it was inside the flags. Which meant it was part of the game.

Other teams had already started climbing it. Some aimed for the ladders, others shimmied straight up the posts.

Ruth didn't bother trying to get onto the beams. Instead, she circled the posts.

A pebble had been balanced on one of the ladder rungs. Just a few paces on, she found another stone, nearly invisible, half buried in the sand at the base of a post.

She slipped both into her bag. With each second, more contestants joined her at the structure, climbing it, searching every surface. She turned away.

In the distance, Eton leaned over the edge of his platform, watching the game with unashamed delight. The screen behind him was a timer, counting down. They'd already spent three minutes.

Where else?

The game's field extended into the jungle. Plenty of players were already there, but it would have an abundance of hiding spaces as well.

She jogged up the beach, pausing to check debris, but everything had already been turned over multiple times. She was near the temporary house when she saw a familiar form jog into the forest.

Carson. He'd had the same idea as her.

Ruth balked, suddenly squeamish about working alongside him. She turned into the house instead.

They were past the first frenzy. About a dozen people were still inside the structure. It was claustrophobic, but at least there was room to move.

Inside was dim and full of the scent of raw wood and dust. Planks had been laid as flooring, but they were irregular and buckled, leaving her off-balance.

It had been decorated as a mock house. Cupboards, built out of weathered planks and haphazardly crooked, hung open. A discarded tablecloth and six crates would have been a dining room before the contestants tore through. The length of cloth—sails, she thought—were being shaken out by two men.

The theming clicked into place for Ruth. Eton had styled the house to look like something a shipwrecked crew might build.

Or maybe something the Secret Door cult might have built.

The easy rocks would all be gone. Instead, Ruth moved methodically, trying to think about where *she'd* hide something if she was trying to be clever.

Nothing in the cupboards. Nothing in the broken dining furniture. Ruth dragged a piece of crate over to the bench and stepped onto it.

There—on top of the cupboards, in the narrow gap between them and the ceiling. A stone. She craned, splinters catching in her sleeve, and snatched it up.

Then she turned her gaze to the ceiling. There were holes in it, allowing dappled sunlight to splash over the floor. She reached her hand through one of the larger openings, fingers feeling around the house's roof, but if there had been anything there, someone had already found it.

Though…

She glanced down. The floor was just as irregular as the ceiling. Ruth hopped off her crate and then was forced back into the wall as three contestants rushed past. As soon as they were gone, she crouched and began peeling up pieces of the flooring.

The boards weren't even nailed in place, simply resting on the sand. Beneath the second one she found a rock.

Someone yelled: "Over here!"

They'd noticed. Ruth tugged up a third board, but that was all she could manage. More contestants descended on the room, pulling up the flooring and throwing pieces through the open windows.

Ruth muttered under her breath. She slipped past them, into the pseudo-bedroom and its swaths of sails. The men who had been searching it were gone, and tears along the hem told her they'd found at least one rock stitched inside. The room didn't even have flooring: just bare sand beneath her feet.

She was about to leave when a patch of shadows caught her eye. The doorway had a gap in it. About knee-height, six inches wide, and barely any taller. Hard to see, especially when rushing. Ruth crouched.

Something like spiderwebs filled the space. Beyond, the glint of a painted stone.

The house wasn't old enough to attract insects. Ruth reached in, cautious, and felt synthetic strands.

A net?

That would align with the theming.

She reached her arm in, sliding her fingers between the mesh. The rock was deep in the cavity, and once her hand was in, she could no longer see it. She'd have to find it by touch.

Something cold brushed Ruth's fingers. Metal, she thought.

She kept reaching.

A second sliver of metal grazed her wrist.

Nets had weights, she knew. Little balls fastened around their edges to help them drop through the water. That had to be what she was feeling.

Her fingertips stretched farther and touched stone. Ruth sucked a breath in through her teeth, squirming her hand an inch farther, fastening her fist around the trinket.

The metal at her knuckle pinched as she pressed against it.

Net weights weren't supposed to be sharp.

Ruth began to pull her hand back. The metal pressed harder into her, no longer just pinching but fully painful, and Ruth bit the inside of her cheek.

Nails? Surely, they wouldn't leave exposed nails when they knew players would be crawling over the building.

She adjusted her hold on the rock gingerly. She could make her hand smaller if she let it go, maybe small enough to slide it out entirely, but that risked letting the rock tumble down the gap between the walls.

Instead, she tried turning her hand to see if she could twist it away from whatever was cutting her.

The sharp sensation moved, following her hand. Not a nail, then. Not fixed in place. It hit resistance and pressed into the back of her hand, and she felt a trickle of blood run down her finger.

"Ah." She was finding it hard to breathe. Contestants raced through the house. None of them paid her any attention.

Ruth shifted again, slower, testing each millimeter. She tried to turn her hand again. The pain pinched, hard. A new sliver of metal pressed into her thumb.

"Hey, get out of the way."

Ruth looked up. Two women stood over her, trying to get into the bedroom. And Ruth was blocking the doorway.

She grimaced. Her muscles were starting to ache from how still she was holding them. "Give me a minute. I'm stuck."

The nearest woman's mouth curled. She thought Ruth was lying. "Well, we're coming through."

And then, before Ruth could stop her, before she could do anything more than draw a breath, the woman planted her hands on Ruth's shoulders and pushed.

22.

Her hand was wrenched out of the gap. Ruth choked on the pain. She coiled back, her fingers on fire.

And the woman stepped over her, into the bedroom that had already been ransacked.

Ruth curled over her hand. She blinked furiously, trying to keep moisture from flooding her eyes.

There had been a net inside the wall after all. Several feet of delicate interlocking threads trailed from her hand.

But she hadn't felt weights when she reached through it.

The net had been filled with fishing hooks.

Tiny, horribly sharp, they'd been tied to the threads every few inches. Each hook had three prongs at its end, layered with multiple wicked barbs.

Four of those hooks had embedded themselves into Ruth's hand.

Her breathing was shallow. Using her spare hand, she brought her tote around, then gingerly relaxed her fist. The painted rock fell into the bag.

Wood cracked behind her. The women were tearing at the barely functioning wall, breaking the beams apart.

Ruth's fingers were shaking. Carefully, she pinched one of the hooks between her index and her thumb and began to ease it out.

The barbs dragged, catching in her skin. Ruth didn't stop. A gasp caught in her throat as the hook tore free.

The spines were tiny, but they'd gone deep. A trickle of blood seeped from the raw hole as Ruth turned her focus to the second hook. Pinch. Gritted teeth. Pull.

Something crashed in the dining room. Players cheered.

The second hook came free.

Ruth's hands were shaking so badly that she could barely hold the third. Blood was on her fingers, slippery and tacky.

"Whoa, whoa, whoa!" someone yelled. Another crash. It sounded like part of the roof collapsing in.

Third hook out. Blood trailed along the heel of her hand, dripping onto her shoes.

More guests rushed into the bedroom, barely glancing at Ruth, who was hunched on the floor. They joined the women grabbing at the boards, tearing into the structure.

That had been intended all along, Ruth realized. Stones must have been hidden inside the shipwreck house while it was being constructed. Eton wanted them to tear the building down.

She fixed her stained fingers on the final hook. The barbs peeled out of her in aching increments. Farther, farther. The skin clung to it, raising up into a peak, then broke free.

Her hand burned, skin red. But the metal was out.

The net lay on the floor, crumpled, dozens of barbs peeking out of the gray threads.

If she left the net there, someone would step on it.

Or, worse, grab at it as they searched for stones.

Ruth shuffled to her feet. Moving gingerly, she used her good hand to get hold of the material without touching any of the hooks.

The tiny pieces of metal clicked together. She held the net away from her body as she left the house. She didn't need to use either of the doors; enough walls had been torn down that she could just step through the gaps.

She turned toward the raised platform, toward Eton. He was facing

Petra as they discussed something, his hands flicking animatedly. He looked so happy.

The clock on the screen showed twenty minutes had passed.

People ran up and down the beach, moving between the jungle and the raised beams. She couldn't see Zach.

Yellow-shirted staff members stood along the game's perimeter, just inside the flags, watching. Ruth picked the nearest one: a middle-aged woman with sandy hair that was beginning to show gray streaks. A smile started to form when she saw Ruth approaching, but it vanished as her eyes spotted Ruth's bloody hand, then the net. She left her post, jogging to meet Ruth.

"Sweetheart, what happened?"

One of Ruth's foster parents had called her *sweetheart*. It had been the first time anyone used a term of endearment on her, and she'd loved the woman for it. Still loved her, even though she'd only kept Ruth for eight months.

"It was in the walls," she said, holding out the net. Her voice seemed strange and stilted. "Thought someone should know."

"I'm going to get you to the first aid tent." The woman eased the net out of Ruth's hand. "We'll have a doctor look at that."

Ruth let herself be guided away from the game, but she stopped just past the flags. She looked back.

Forty minutes left on the clock. Her three friends were still out there, searching as hard as they could. They believed they had a chance at winning one of the prizes.

Their odds would vanish along with Ruth.

"It doesn't hurt much." That was mostly the truth. The sting was already fading into an ache. She knew it would fade further with more time. "Can I go to the first aid tent after the game?"

The staff member turned to face Ruth, her eyes pulled tight with concern. "Sweetheart, are you sure that's what you want?"

"Yeah. It is." She paused. Her hand was still bleeding, but slowly. "But do you have, maybe, a bandage or something?"

The woman set the net down next to her post. Then she pulled a small towel out of her pocket.

"It's clean," she said as she wrapped it around Ruth's hand. She took care—not tugging, not pulling too tight—then tied it off at the end. "Don't use that hand much until the doctor can look at it, okay? And come and see me or one of my team if it starts to hurt too much."

"Thanks." Ruth ran her fingers along the edge of the cloth as she turned away.

"Sweetheart?" The staff member was smiling, but she looked achingly sad. "I'm truly so sorry about what happened. I wish I could give you something to make up for it. But I'm not allowed to tell contestants where the stones are; the organizers were very clear about that."

Ruth nodded.

The woman tilted her head, eyebrows raised, words laden with meaning. "But there are no rules against contestants asking around."

It took Ruth a second, then she inhaled. *The rocks can be hidden anywhere inside the flags.* "Uh—do *you* have a stone?"

The staff member smiled as she reached into her pocket. She passed Ruth one of the red-painted pebbles. "Good luck."

"Thank you," Ruth managed. She tucked it into her bag, hiding it before any of the other players could see. Then she craned, searching the field.

Ten staff members stood around the perimeter, watching for rule violations. Ten that she could see, at least. There could be more in the jungle.

And…

Someone was jogging toward her. Zach. His eyes fixed on the cloth around her hand, fear widening his eyes.

"Ruth?" He reached for her. "What happened? That's blood. Are you hurt?"

"I'm okay. Just an accident." She'd tell him the truth later. "Listen, I have something."

"Ruth…" He reached for her hand but fell short of touching it. "That looks bad."

"Don't worry about it." At the other end of the beach, the clock was ticking down. She dropped her voice to a whisper. "The staff has rocks. They'll give them to you if you ask. But be discreet. We should try to get as many as we can before the other contestants notice."

"Oh," Zach said, his eyebrows rising. "Ruth, you're amazing."

Warmth bloomed through her. "Let's split up. If you see Hayleigh or Carson, pass it on."

"Got it." He ducked in and pressed a kiss to her cheek, then smiled as he split away from her.

Ruth's face felt warm where his lips had touched. Her breath shuddered through her lungs as she turned back to the game.

She needed to stay calm. As soon as contestants realized there were stones under the house's flooring, they'd descended on it like a swarm. It was tempting to run to the nearest staff member, but that would only draw attention.

Instead, she jogged along the beach, pretending to be scouring the sand, and only veered to a staff member at the last second. "Hi. Do you by any chance have a stone?"

They smiled and wordlessly passed Ruth her prize.

She tried to look casual as she walked away. She made it to one more staff member before the secret broke.

Shouts rang through the beach as contestants rushed toward the yellow shirts. Ruth couldn't tell if she'd given it away, or Zach, or whether someone else had figured it out on their own.

Three rocks wasn't bad. She knew she wasn't going to get a fourth. Groups crowded around every available staff member.

"Yes," Eton called from his perch, earning a whisper of a smile from

Petra. "We were quite sneaky, weren't we? And it doesn't stop there. If you think you've exhausted all points, there are still plenty more to find."

Ruth turned in a circle to survey the field. It was hard to imagine what was left.

Driftwood had been cracked open, rocks overturned. The shipwreck shelter had been fully dismantled, fragments of it scattered around the scene like bones picked over by vultures. A handful of guests still sifted through its remains. More walked up and down the suspended beams, tracing paths that had already been searched. Many more had vanished into the jungle.

Then she saw it. A man was digging in the sand.

Within seconds, a dozen others had dropped to their knees, clawing with bare hands. There was a shout as the first rock was found.

Ruth joined them and plunged her fingers into the sun-warmed sand. Her injured hand ached as she tried to scrape with it, so she gave preference to her good hand instead.

How many were buried? How deep? How far apart?

She kept one eye on the teams around her. Every few seconds, someone rocked back, a small pebble held up as they verified its red circle.

Ruth shuffled as she dug, forming a trench. She made it three feet, then a small gray shape rolled out of the golden sand. She snatched it up, saw the red, and shoved it into her bag.

Only having one hand made her slow. A lot of contestants were using tools they'd scavenged—fragments of the broken shelter, pieces of driftwood. Ruth crawled to grab a scrap of wood herself. It hurt less than using her hands, but she felt the extra strain in her shoulders.

The sun was hot. The sand was hot. Sweat ran down Ruth's face, pooled between her shoulder blades.

More and more contestants poured out of the jungle as they abandoned it in favor of the sand. The beach had been nothing but gold-white peaks when they'd arrived, hot and dry. That pristine surface was being churned over; darker, damper sand from layers below was taking over.

A second stone rolled out of the sand. Ruth caught it up and added it to her trove.

Fifteen minutes remained on the clock. She couldn't keep digging that long. Her body ached and the heat was becoming overwhelming.

The jungle would give her some respite. She doubted there would be much left to find there. But she'd be more effective than if she stayed on the sand.

As she crossed the field, she spotted Zach. His face was tight, sweat dripping from his chin.

"I'm trying the jungle," she called as she passed him.

"Sure. But be careful. We only have sixty seconds to turn in our points when the timer ends."

"Got it. I won't be late." Ruth checked the countdown as she climbed the beach. Fourteen minutes. She pulled her mobile out and set a timer for twelve.

Most likely, there would be some kind of alarm or signal when time was up. But she wasn't going to rely on that alone. She checked that her volume was on high and tucked the phone away as she stepped under the cover of the trees.

The shade was euphoric. Ruth stretched, arms fanned out at her side. The humidity was high, and it did nothing to dry the perspiration dripping down her sides. But at least she could let the heat discharge off her, like an overcooked radiator.

More contestants had opted for the jungle than she'd suspected. Figures moved between the trees, but after the crowds on the shore, it felt very close to solitude.

The players had been about as gentle toward the island's plant life as they'd been to the beach. Branches were torn down, vines ripped free and left dragging over exposed roots. Their paradise was growing a little less idyllic with every hour they spent in it.

She moved deeper, scanning. The game's bounds went farther into the jungle than she'd expected. Flags were visible to one side, but the ending line was still out of sight.

Where's the best place to search? Where would I hide points if I didn't want them found in the first forty minutes of the game?

There were a multitude of obvious places: hollows in trunks, nooks in splitting branches, concealed pockets in the exposed roots. All checked a dozen times already, she suspected.

Some would be hidden in the canopy. Two men were already above her, clinging to branches, trunks swaying under their weight. She hadn't climbed a tree since she was a child, and it wasn't a skill she felt confident in revisiting.

Where else? If I were Eton, where—

The answer came immediately. In the ground.

He'd buried stones in the sand. He'd do the same in the jungle.

Only, the sand was easy to turn over; a contestant only had to keep scraping it back until they found something. The forest floor was dense, hard, damp. It would take too long to search at random. So what did that leave?

Recently turned soil. If the rocks had been buried within the previous day, the earth would look different.

Ruth began kicking leaf litter out of the way as she scoured the silty earth. It took a moment, but she was rewarded with a circle of darker earth, not much larger than her hand.

She sank to her knees and used a torn-off branch to dig. The recently disturbed earth was easy to burrow into.

The stone was only a couple inches under the surface. It came up beautifully, damp earth stuck to the red circle.

She checked her phone's clock. Six minutes until game over. Barely any time at all. She sent Zach a quick text, letting him know what she'd found, but she knew he might decide it was a more efficient use of time to stay on the beach.

Her hand throbbed. Her head ached from too much sun and not enough water. But she kept moving, scraping leaves out of the way, determined to use every second.

Ruth found another patch of churned earth with just two minutes to go. She dug with her good hand, dirt clumping under her nails as she peeled her prize free.

She'd made it to the end of the map. The final row of flags cut off her progress just feet away.

Ruth turned, intending to try for one more stone as she made her way back to the beach.

Three women stood close by. They weren't searching. Based on their body language, Ruth guessed they might have given up within the first few minutes.

Their arms were crossed, their shoulders hunched. They faced one another, but even without hearing what was being said, Ruth knew it had to be an unpleasant conversation. One of them looked close to tears. The other two were angry.

Ruth gripped the strap on her tote bag, her damp clothes clinging against her body, her throat suddenly tight.

They were Gilly's friends.

23.

Ruth took a step toward them.

The one with the podcast, Sam, saw Ruth first. She cut herself off, ending the conversation before Ruth could hear what she was saying.

"Hey." Ruth's mouth was dry. She tugged at the cloth tied around her hand. "Sorry for interrupting. I wanted to ask… Have you heard from Gilly this morning?"

The three friends shifted, sharing a look Ruth couldn't quite read. She felt certain she'd touched a nerve.

"Unfortunately," the tallest one said.

They were trying to push Ruth out, angling their bodies away from her. She took a step nearer, refusing to be excluded. "What do you mean?"

"Honestly? This is kind of a private chat." Sam's expression had turned sour.

Ruth hesitated.

Everything about the scene felt *wrong*. Petra had told her that it was fine, that Gilly was accounted for, but now she was missing from her group, and her group had turned hostile.

"I don't know if Petra has told you about this, but I saw Gilly last night," Ruth said. "On the trails near the island's peak. She… I think she might have been hurt."

"Why would Gilly be on the trails?" The tall one stared at her. "She hates hiking."

"You *think* she was hurt? Was she, or wasn't she?"

"Is this some kind of joke?" Sam asked.

An alarm trilled, sharp and sudden. Ruth grasped for her mobile and switched it off. Two minutes until game over.

"Look, I just need to know she's okay. You said you've spoken to Gilly today. Is she all right?"

They were silent for a beat. Then Sam grimaced. "She's been texting."

"And?" Ruth pressed.

"She's being a—" The tall one caught herself. "She's mad. Because I told her about how her boyfriend had been messaging me. She should be angry with *him*. But she's not. So she stormed out and is refusing to come back."

"But you've definitely spoken to her since then?"

The podcaster's phone chirped. She glanced at it, her mouth twitching, then angled it toward Ruth. "Like I said. She's been texting."

Ruth reached for the phone, knowing she was being rude but past the point of caring. She scrolled back through the conversation. The screen displayed what, at first glance, looked like a one-sided conversation. Sam's messages were green bubbles on the right-hand side. Variations on: Just talk to us already. Why are you being like this?

And on the left-hand side were Gilly's replies in gray.

Each one identical.

A small, round bubble holding a single emoji. Line after line of them. Skulls.

A whistle shot through the air. They all turned toward it, toward the beach.

Game over.

Joel trailed deeper into the jungle.

It hadn't been a full day on the island, but it had been so much, so fast, so loud, and there was nowhere to hide from it.

Joel had never been good with noise. Hearing it, as well as making it. He had memories of his family coaxing him to speak. His aunt had held him in her lap once, pinching him over and over as she tried to get him to make a sound.

He'll never talk if you don't force it out of him, she'd said.

He shouldn't be on the island, not really. People had been fighting over the tickets, and it felt wrong for him to have taken one when he so badly wished he could have stayed at home.

But he couldn't. Not with the rest of the team there.

Camping Quest was a video series based around three friends who explored unknown locations. Their slogan was *an adventure in your own backyard,* and they visited areas that no one really knew about. They'd camped on cliff edges, in dry riverbeds, in abandoned warehouses.

Joel was their cameraman. He carried the equipment. He set up their shots. And he did the editing.

Or he had. In the early days. Before the channel had gotten more attention than any of them were ready for.

They'd never planned for Joel to be in the videos. But sometimes there was no way around it. If they filmed clips while driving, Joel was always in the back seat, headphones on as he monitored the sound.

He'd tried to keep his head down. To not make noise, not move too much, not interrupt the hosts as they ran through their scripts about the location they were visiting.

But, for some reason he still didn't understand, people had noticed him.

@realanna8961 3 days ago

Joel!!!

@thehonestnorris 15 hours ago

1:06 joel looks at the camera

@MisaMoon 17 hours ago

I only saw three hotdogs? Did Joel get something to eat??

@sophiamendoza6225 2 days ago

Obsessed with Joel trying to fix the cables in the background at 12:44

@minty-choc 3 days ago

i wanna have his babies

@httmlp 1 day ago

We love you Joel, shine on you beautiful diamond

Joel had gone from being the quiet one, the forgotten one, to being a fan favorite.

And no one knew what to do about it.

The hosts didn't want him there. Sometimes they'd try to goad him into saying a word or two on camera, just as his family had tried to tease him into speaking when he was a child. But they didn't talk to him much outside of that, when the cameras were off. He wasn't one of them. And he understood.

He saw himself in the videos. He heard himself.

Weak as a whisper. Thin, and not in a way that was nice to look at. Even his beard seemed hazy and pale, though it covered a lot of his face. His clothes were loose, and his hair was long. All that was really left of him were his eyes. Too big, too round.

He saw himself in those videos and he saw someone who looked scared and lost.

And he wondered if that was why the viewers spent so much energy on him.

He wondered if it was all a big joke. An ironic thing.

If the adoring messages were making fun of him.

And the worst part—the really bad, uncomfortable part—was that he stayed. The team didn't like him. The viewer comments were strange and confusing. But it was the closest thing to kindness he'd felt in a long time.

Joel stepped over fallen branches. He'd left the flag markers behind a while before. He knew his team would be frustrated with him when he returned with only three stones. But for that moment, it was worth it. Just to be alone.

He let his feet move where they wanted. Let his shoulders unclench. His face fall slack. Easy, gentle. Soft and quiet. Just for a moment.

There was a sound ahead. Distant and reedy.

Not an insect, though. Not a bird. A human.

Joel stopped, then slowly, carefully turned away. He didn't want to have to meet another person. They were very far from the game. Whoever was out there, he hoped they wouldn't want to meet him either.

The sound came again before he could get more than a few steps. It was low and strained. Like a person trying to say *nuh-uh* through closed lips.

And it was coming from a different direction.

Joel turned again, trying to move away. The sound made him uncomfortable. It wasn't a word. It was almost like…a warning. A warning through a sealed mouth.

"Nuh-uh."

Again, this time from his right. Joel faced the trees. It was hard to separate shapes in there. The longer he looked, the more he began to imagine eyes were staring back.

He pulled his shoulders in. Lowered his head. Shuffled away, hoping that, whatever it was, *whoever* it was, they would let him leave.

And then he heard the hum.

Like the drone Eton had flown over the beach. Like a beehive. Like a hundred people, all whispering under their breath.

And there was a smell. It was…

It was like the smell from his father's trailer that one weekend.

Death.

Joel began to back away. Outside was calm and quiet, but inside was a cacophony and he didn't know how to make it stop.

Then, from right behind him: *"Nuh-uh."*

He jolted forward. Past the last trees. Into the humming, into the smell, into death.

A cliff rose ahead. It was sharp, at least two houses tall. In front of Joel, at the cliff's base, were uneven rocks. And on top of the rocks was a man.

He lay on his back. His limbs were spread. Too far. One arm wasn't attached anymore.

The man's face looked toward the sky. His mouth was open, just like Joel's father. And the back of his head was missing. Like Joel's father.

Insects sang. They moved in clouds, landing on his body and taking flight again. Thousands of them, reveling in a feast.

The man's blood soaked over the rocks. Most of his body still looked like a person on the top, but it was all crumpled and strange where it had hit the rocks.

Joel opened his mouth. He never made much sound. And the sound that came out then was a whisper, a soft rush of air. He wasn't sure he would ever make sounds again.

And then, one final time, right behind his back, whispered as gently as a human could: *"Nuh-uh."*

24.

Ruth swore and shoved the phone back into the podcaster's hands. The whistle lingered in the air as she clutched her tote to her chest and ran.

Sixty seconds to get back to the beach.

And she'd strayed a long way.

She could hear distant noise from the crowd, but it seemed she and the three friends were the only players left in the jungle.

She burst out through the foliage's edge. The sun was harsh after the gloom, nearly enough to blind her. Ahead was Eton's tower. The teams clustered around it, filling large wooden bowls with their finds.

"Ten," Eton shouted from the podium. "Nine, eight—"

She saw her team and tore across the beach to reach them. As she skidded onto her knees beside Zach, he gave her a huge smile. "Cutting it close."

"Still on time," she retorted, and upended her tote over their bowl. A small cascade of pebbles fell into their pile, along with Ruth's map, sunglasses, and empty water bottle. She fished those back out.

"Two, one, *done*!" Eton called. "Game over! Take a step back, everyone!"

Voices rose. Some cheers, some exhausted laughter. One irritated shout: "Joel, come on, man!"

Ruth glanced through the crowd to see a team of three young men, arms stretched out in exasperation. Apparently, she hadn't been the last one back, after all.

The bowls had small signs stuck in the sand behind them, each one bearing a team name written in black pen. Staff began to move through, asking teams to confirm their bowls before they were lifted away to be counted.

Ruth rocked back on her heels, feeling giddy and a little sick.

And with a pit of quiet dread lingering inside her stomach.

The race back to the beach hadn't been enough to dislodge the images from her mind.

Text messages from Gilly's phone. Each one just a skull.

She glanced up at the podium. Petra was watching the crowd. Sleek hair, cool eyes. A calculated gaze.

"I think we did well," Carson said. He'd slumped next to Zach. They were both ruddy-faced and breathing hard. "I had a look at some of those other buckets. We got more than a lot of them."

Hayleigh had tied her hair up on the top of her head. Her clothes were dripping. She must have waded into the water in search of stones. "I bet it'll be close. Hopefully, not too close. This one girl snatched a rock right out from under me. I'll be so upset if we lose because of it."

"You killed it, babe," Carson said.

She laughed, using a knuckle to wipe sand from his jawline.

Despite everything, Ruth felt herself smile at the gesture. Zach had told her that Hayleigh and Carson started calling each other *babe* as a joke. At some point, it had just stuck.

Team members moved through the groups, passing out bottles of chilled water and wet towels. Ruth took one, grateful, and blotted her face.

The screen behind the stage changed.

Team names were listed in two rows, an empty box next to each.

"Results are beginning to filter in!" Eton called, turning to stare up at the names along with them. "Take a look!"

"Hey," someone behind Ruth said. "Our teammate's still not back."

On the board, scores began to appear. *31, 40, 29, 15...*

"I'm worried. His name's Joel. He has asthma."

Ruth shot a glance over her shoulder. Three men—the men who had exclaimed when their teammate didn't make it back—were speaking to a staff member. One was running his hands through his hair. Another was on his phone, apparently trying to reach their missing companion.

Hayleigh gasped; Carson whistled. Ruth turned back to the board. Tans and Plans's number had come up. *48.*

It was high. Really high, actually.

She scanned the others. There was a *51* and a *54*, but many were in the twenties and thirties.

But Ruth couldn't block out the voices behind her. The staff members were trying to calm the men, but they were only growing tenser, more frustrated.

"We can't leave him out there. You don't understand; he has a medical condition. He's not supposed to be on his own."

<hr />

They surged into the jungle. Six staff members, two EMTs.

No one had noticed when Logan joined in.

Something's wrong with him.

A guest led them, earnest and sunburned. He'd gotten turned around when trying to find his way back to the beach, he said. And instead of finding the beach, he'd found a man.

Logan had heard the news by pure luck. He hadn't wanted to play the Easter egg game, but he *had* wanted to watch. Not so much the contestants, but the staff. There were a lot of them, and from what he could surmise, they were split into at least three divisions. Most other details about them were a black box: the hierarchy, whether they were all paid or if some were volunteer positions, where they'd worked before joining the staff.

He'd been at the edge of the jungle as the game wrapped up, trying to pry information from a smiling but unmovable assistant, when the guest had come crashing out from between the trees, yelling that he needed help. That someone was hurt.

Logan had been entirely forgotten in the scramble that followed, and he slipped in behind the EMTs as they raced through the jungle.

Their guide came to a halt.

Ahead, a cliff wall blocked their path.

"There," the guest said, pointing.

Off to the side was a cluster of umbrella-shaped ferns. And beneath the curling green fronds, Logan caught glimpses of brown fabric and pale flesh.

He craned, trying to see over the staff as they crowded the hunched figure.

"I heard him whispering," the guest said, arms folded, hanging back. His face was twisted in polite concern, but underneath was just a hint of the same dark curiosity that consumed Logan. "He was saying something about a person being dead."

EMTs moved about the figure. Voices overlapped as they tried to tease out a response. "What's your name? Can you tell us what happened?"

The staff members shuffled, and there was just enough of a gap between them that Logan finally got a clear look at the hunched figure.

He'd buried himself in the ferns, his back pressed to a tree. His legs were pulled up against his chest, the legs slightly akimbo, as though he'd scrambled into that position and then froze.

A pale, stretched face stared over his knees. Shaggy hair clung to dots of perspiration.

Logan knew him. Joel, from the unexpectedly popular *Camping Quest* series. A background character who always looked like he was afraid to be seen and yet managed to be the show's greatest asset.

He seemed even thinner and even paler in reality, if such a thing was possible. Hollowed-out eyes fixated on a spot beyond any of them. Parts of his body seemed slack, as though the life had been sucked out of him, but the skin around his eyes quivered.

And he was staring at the base of the cliff, as though consumed by it.

Logan stepped back, giving the area a second look. The cliffs formed one face of the island's peak: multiple levels of sharp, exposed rocks, rising like steps. Clusters of plant life interrupted the cliffs, ferns and layers of moss marking the natural channels water followed after rain.

Joel's mouth opened, a tacky sound catching in his throat.

Logan shifted forward, straining to hear.

"He fell," Joel muttered, staring at the rocks. "There was…blood."

Murmurs spread like fire between the staff members. Several broke off from the cluster to approach the cliff base, pacing as they searched between the boulders. Others pulled phones out of their pockets and began sending messages, presumably to the higher-ups.

Logan knew, through his research, that one of the island's trails led to the cliff's top and a view of the ocean. It could be an attractive photo opportunity for the guests.

There were no rails. Anyone hiking the peak and not paying attention could easily find themselves on the edge of a precipice.

And if they were running…

His mind lingered on the story he'd overheard that morning. A woman, attacked and bleeding, fleeing through the jungle in the dark. It was the obvious connection.

But Joel had used a male pronoun for the body. Not the woman Ruth had seen the previous night, then. Not unless there had been a misidentification.

"Hey, careful there," an EMT said.

They were trying to pry Joel from his hole. His knees dropped away from his jaw, and that was when Logan saw it.

Scratch marks ran up and down his neck. Whatever he'd experienced had been bad enough to make him claw at himself. Some scratches deep enough to leave thin trails of blood.

And…

More blood. At the nape of his neck. In his hair.

The EMTs moved around Joel, searching, pressing areas of his scalp with cotton pads. Reality hit Logan harder than he would have liked.

Joel had pulled out clumps of his own hair.

Logan's eyes flicked down, where Joel's limp hands rested on the layers of dead bracken. They were long and bony. Dirt had gotten under the fingernails, and it only made the skin seem more pallid.

Dirt. Not blood. At least, none that Logan could see.

Clumps of his hair were pulled out…

Logan's gaze moved from the cliff to the hunched, shivering man.

But not by him?

It didn't make sense.

One of the EMTs gestured to the staff. They hunched together, sharing a whispered conversation, then the staff leader stood. "We're going to take our guest back to the medical tent. You two"—he gestured to Logan and the man who had led them there—"please accompany us back to the festival. The rest of you, search the area thoroughly. Radio me if you find anything."

The EMTs threaded their arms under Joel's and carefully lifted him. His steps were faltering, but he put up no resistance as he was shepherded toward the trees.

The remaining staff gave each other a brief, bemused look, and then began shuffling around the area, staring at each rock they passed. It was a pantomime of a search. Logan couldn't blame them. There was nothing to find.

Logan made as if to turn away, then hesitated.

He tilted his head, staring at the cluster of rocks Joel had been facing. They were damp. That was true for all the stones on that side of the cliff; moisture leaked down them, leaving trails of algae and small, bare-root ferns.

But that cluster of rocks in particular…

He raised his phone and took a photo.

They were damp in a different way. A shiny kind of way.

No algae.

Logan could almost convince himself that they'd been cleaned.

Sixth place.

They'd been four rocks shy of claiming a winning spot.

Carson had groaned dramatically, and Hayleigh had thrown herself back on the sand, arms spread in defeat. Zach had shaken his head ruefully, though he still looked pleased. Sixth place was a great result, all agreed.

Ruth had found herself content with the outcome. They could have all done with the extra money. But there had been a big ceremony, the teams invited up to the announcer's platform, one at a time, while music played and Eton handed them their prizes.

And Ruth had felt pure relief at escaping the attention. She'd already had more than she wanted. More than she could cope with. She would call herself lucky if no one on the island looked at her for the remainder of the trip.

The game's temporary medical tent had been set up next to the water station. High cloth walls rippled against the poles holding them in place. Inside, it was cool, with fans running off generators. Folding beds and several chairs had been set up. Ruth sat in one of the chairs while a young but pleasant doctor disinfected her hand.

Zach sat with her, holding Ruth's other hand for comfort as he watched the doctor work.

She wasn't the only patient. On the other side of the tent, one young woman was having a sprained ankle strapped. A man had tripped in the driftwood house, and a doctor worked on removing an inch-long splinter from his forearm.

Two men and a woman lay in the folding beds, clothes stripped back and ice packs stacked around their necks. A doctor moved between them, monitoring their vitals and offering iced water. Suspected heatstroke.

The sun had been high as the game ended. Ruth had felt brutally hot while digging in the sand. If anything, she was surprised those were the only casualties.

"You really shouldn't have kept playing," the doctor said as she applied cream over the growing bruises where Ruth had removed the hooks.

"You're probably right." She was still glad she'd continued. She hadn't let her team down. A good feeling. One she wanted more of.

"Well, your hand will be sore for a bit. Keep watch for any spreading redness, inflammation, or itching. I wouldn't be too concerned about the results, but you should have them by the time you arrive home."

They were screening for blood-borne diseases. Ruth thought it was overkill, but the doctor had deemed the situation strange enough to warrant it. That, and a tetanus booster.

All paid for by Eton's company.

Ruth didn't know how to feel about that. As soon as a guest was hurt, he seemed to throw every possible form of help their way, no cost spared.

But, again and again, they were *allowed* to be hurt.

The cloth doorway flapped open. A staff member brought another man inside and guided him toward an empty chair.

"Is any doctor free?" The staff member glanced about the tent. "We have some scalp injuries. I'm concerned about a concussion and potential heatstroke."

"Excuse me a minute." Ruth's doctor put her bandages aside. "I need to screen this patient quickly."

Ruth watched them move around the man. He was tall, thin, pale.

And his eyes looked horrendous. Wide but hollow. He stared at the floor without seeming to see it.

The doctor asked his name, but he didn't answer.

"We can go," Ruth said to Zach.

"You sure?"

"Yeah." The doctor hadn't finished applying the bandages, but Ruth slipped two off the desk and stuck them on herself. "All good."

As they crossed the tent, Ruth caught snatches of conversation from the group gathered around the new patient.

"He's had a shock," the staff member said. "We're trying to find out what happened, but it might have been a hallucination."

Ruth faltered. The hollowed-out man was staring at her. Not much of his face was visible behind his wispy beard, but there was a torrent of emotions in his eyes.

Zach held the tent flap open for her, and, as she slipped through, she caught one last phrase before the scene faded away.

"He says he saw someone die."

25.

The bundle of fishing net rattled as it was placed on the table.

Petra stared at the three-pronged hooks sewn through the material. They were tiny, but the points were like needles.

Heather looked tired, heavy circles under her eyes. "A contestant found it inside the shipwreck house and brought it to me. I'm still trying to figure out how it got there."

Petra had never seen a net made like that before. She carefully plucked up one of the hooks to see how it was attached. Several loops of thread had been used to tie it to the mesh. Hand-knotted. Considering how many there were, not an easy or quick project. "What do you know so far?"

"I've spoken to three of the staff who were constructing the shelter." Heather braced her hands on the plastic table, staring at the net between them. "They say they didn't see anything unusual, and I'm inclined to believe them. I still want to talk to the rest of the game design team, especially the ones who were on-site when the arena was being built."

Heather was a long-term employee at Eton's company and one of the few who had been able to come to the island. Something Petra was immensely grateful for. The new staff had proven themselves to be hard workers, but she *trusted* Heather.

Petra let the net drop back to the table. "Is it possible any guests had access to the shipwreck house before the game started?"

"I'm trying to find that out too." Heather's gray-streaked hair was tidy, but strands were coming loose where she'd raked fingers through it. "Team members were supposed to be on-site to prevent tampering ahead of the game, but the generator failure meant not everyone was at their assigned places."

Shortly before seven, a generator behind the kitchen had burned out. A minor avalanche of catastrophes was to be expected when hosting an event on a remote island, but it still meant the morning had been a frantic scramble to save perishables and repair the machine.

The net represented an entirely new category of problem, though. Someone had placed it inside the house. And there was nothing ambiguous about its purpose.

It was designed to hurt.

Petra needed to find out who had created it. Or at least determine whether it had been planted there by a staff member or a guest. And that had to happen fast.

There was the possibility that other traps had been left around the island.

"I want you checking in with me once an hour," Petra said. "Update me on who's been interviewed and what you've found. This is a red task, understand?"

Red tasks were urgent. They could not be bumped or neglected for anything short of an emergency.

"I'll do that," Heather said.

"Good. Give me a second." She tapped at her tablet, adding the net to the list of open jobs and processing recently closed tasks. The search teams had finished canvassing the area around the cliffs; nothing had been found. The broken generator was back online without any food spoilage. The updated weather report predicted moderate rain in the evening—a daily expectation for the region—but no significant weather warnings.

She stopped at a low-priority task. The staff member who had been crying. The one who wouldn't tell Petra why.

"Do you know Lisa?" she asked. "I want to check in with her."

"Lisa?" Heather's eyebrows pulled together.

"One of the team. Young, sandy hair, small chin."

"We don't have anyone on the team named Lisa." Heather hesitated. "Unless that's a nickname?"

"It was on her name tag." Those were issued by management and, as a security precaution, they had to match the employee's registered name.

"Are you absolutely sure?" Heather's frown deepened. "I know every person on our team. I've spent one-on-one time with all of them during training. We don't have anyone called Lisa."

Petra's pen hovered over the open task. It had been dark and loud and chaotic when she'd spoken to the crying girl. But Petra knew she had the right name. That wasn't the kind of error she would ever make.

She opened their list of employees with a few quick taps. Names passed beneath her pen as she scrolled. They were grouped into teams: game development, catering, guest assistance, technicians…

There were more than eighty names in total. She reached the end of the list. Heather was right.

Lisa simply didn't exist.

She let her pen hover as she churned it through her mind.

"We need to account for every person on this island," she said at last.

Heather had been staring at the hook-riddled net, her mouth fixed into a thin line. She seemed to have been thinking along the same lines as Petra, and she gave a sharp nod.

"Check their photo IDs and cross-reference them against the guest and staffing lists. I want to be sure every person who boarded that ship is still accounted for. And I want to be certain there are no unapproved visitors."

"It'll need to be thorough," Heather said. "If I can offer a suggestion?"

"Of course."

"Sort through the guests during lunch. That gets them all together in one place; it'll be easier to see if anyone is trying to slip away without being checked. While that's happening, send a separate team to the search the cabins and surrounding areas to make sure no one's left behind."

"Yes, let's do that." It would be less disruptive to the guests' routines. She paused, thinking. "We also have cameras for the live streaming event Eton planned. Can we convert those into a surveillance system?"

"I'm sure it's possible."

"Get that set up. They might give us a way to see who's in the vicinity if there are any more incidents. Lunch is in forty minutes. Do you have enough time for it all?"

A tired smile. "I'll get it done."

Petra waited until Heather stepped out, then slowly sank into her chair.

She'd need to tell Eton what was happening. That thought filled her with exhaustion. She knew how he'd react. Jokes, dismissals, glib comments about her needing to worry less.

In Eton's world, everyone was a friend. There were no problems that couldn't be solved with a few jokes.

Petra knew better.

And she felt very alone as she stared down at the tangled net and its ugly barbed hooks.

He says he saw someone die.

The words clung to Ruth as they left the medical tent behind.

A second person on the island thought they'd witnessed death.

A second person, also being dismissed.

She'd wanted to stay. She'd wanted to ask the hollowed-out man what he saw. But between the two doctors and the staff crowding over him, she doubted she'd be allowed to finish her question.

Instead, she followed Zach, fighting not to let the anxiety take over.

Maybe it really was as the staff member said. Maybe it really was a mistake, a misunderstanding.

Maybe.

"Hey!"

She'd been staring at the leaf-filled sand beneath her feet and jolted. Carson ran toward them, hand raised. "Hey, hey!"

His face was pink and eager. Hayleigh sprinted after him, clutching her sun hat to her head, wearing a giddy smile. She'd had time to change; a flowing dress rippled behind her.

"Hey." Carson staggered to a stop next to them, breathless. "Fifth place."

Zach stared. "What?"

"A team was disqualified." He couldn't stop grinning. "We just made fifth place."

Zach's face lit up, then he and Carson were hugging, slapping the others' backs, laughing.

"Ruthie," Hayleigh trilled, gripping her arm, moving in little hops that made her hair bounce. "Ruthie, Ruthie!"

Ruth found herself laughing. The joy was intoxicating. "How'd they get disqualified?"

"Cheating," Hayleigh said. She didn't seem able to stay still. "It was the third-place team. They collected a bunch of normal rocks and used red nail polish to paint circles on them."

"Wow." Ruth shook her head. "That's actually really smart."

"I thought so too. Eton couldn't stop laughing as he made the announcement. What a shame you missed it; it was so funny!"

Carson and Zach leaned on one another, arms around shoulders, and for a second Ruth saw them as the children they'd been when they first became friends.

"Can't believe they didn't shoot for first place," Carson said. "Imagine cheating and still only getting third."

"They probably thought it would be less obvious that way," Zach said. His eyes were unfocused, and she knew his mind was racing as he processed the ramifications. "Fifth place is fantastic. Hays, that should be enough to get that car you've been saving up for, right?"

Hayleigh squealed, burying her face in Ruth's shoulder, too excited to speak.

"I'm going to splurge like the bad boy I am," Carson said, slapping Zach's back. "My share's going straight into *debt reduction*."

Zach laughed. "Look at us, actual adults. Nothing gets the blood pumping like paying off a loan early."

"Drinks," Carson said suddenly. He swiveled, pointing to Ruth. "You allowed to drink?"

"Uh—" It was such a shock to hear him speak to her that she faltered for a second. "The doctor didn't say I couldn't."

"Then we're all getting smashed. We deserve it. Plus, they're free, so…"

"It's the financially responsible choice," Zach agreed. He reached his hand out to Ruth while Hayleigh skipped ahead.

The trestle tables from breakfast were still spaced around Sunset Beach, arranged to leave a large section of clear sand in the center for guests who wanted to lounge on their towels. Ruth caught the scent of lunch cooking as they passed the staff area, though they were still a while from anything being served. A band had taken up position onstage, and the stands serving refreshments were being swarmed.

They split up: Zach and Carson to get drinks while Hayleigh and Ruth went in search of snacks. As they joined the booth's queue, they stared at the options displayed on the board above it: packets of chips and pretzels, fruit cups, popcorn, small cakes.

Not for the first time, Ruth was struck by how much the festival must have cost Eton and his company. No one there had paid anything to attend. Even their travel costs were being covered.

The festival had sponsors—the branded goods in their tote bags—but

Ruth couldn't believe those sponsorships even touched the festival's actual cost.

Eton's videos followed the same trend. Huge amounts of money seemed to flow out of him like a fountain that never ran dry. Hundreds of thousands of dollars in prize money when he hosted games. Thick blocks of cash given to strangers in the streets. In one video, Eton spent a day walking through a destination theme park, stopping families to ask how much it had cost them to get there between flights and hotels, and then paying for all of it.

Zach had tried to explain it to her. "It's the reason Eton became famous in the first place," he'd said. "There's something addictive about watching a person being given a life-changing amount of money. The more he gives away, the more people watch him, and the more he makes."

Ruth could understand the practice in theory, but it still felt contrary to everything she knew about humans. Actually experiencing Eton's generosity left her uneasy.

Or maybe it was tied to Petition. The commune's structure had been the opposite of Eton's style.

Their leader had called himself Barom. He'd made promises: safety, absolution, a path out of the corruption of the world.

All his followers had to do was give him everything they had.

Barom talked about it as though it was a vital part of redemption: the shedding of the earth's rot. Only by carrying nothing could a person be light enough to rise out of the mire.

And every promise turned hollow.

There was no redemption, only death.

For all the talk of shedding earthly temptations, Barom was worth millions by the time the commune collapsed. His private quarters—spaces never seen by the followers—were filled with the trappings he'd told them to cut out of their lives. Movies, luxury rugs, imported trinkets and trivialities.

Barom's body was found draped across his silk bedsheets. There had been no poison for him, no agony. Just a single bullet hole through his head.

For Ruth, the greatest shock had come when she learned his real name during the inquest. Peter Donoghue. An incredibly normal name for someone who had, at the end of it, been nothing more than a normal man.

The word was echoed from behind her, as though plucked straight out of her mind. *"Petition."*

"Don't want to ruin our appetites," Hayleigh was saying. "But it looks so *good*. Should I just get a bunch of stuff? No, that's wasteful…"

Ruth's body had gone rigid. She turned, moving carefully, not wanting to draw attention by reacting too suddenly.

A group of friends lounged on towels nearby. They wore swimsuits and their hair was wet from the ocean. One man held his phone in the center of the towel, where they could all see it.

A video played. It was hard to tell from the angle, but Ruth thought she recognized the face. One of the big creators Zach sometimes watched.

"It doesn't stop there," the tinny voice said, words bleeding in and out as Ruth fought to hear it through the crowd. "Yesterday, an account tagged nearly two hundred of the world's top journalists in a photo. It was an image of Petition's logo, nothing more. That's strange enough on its own, but…"

"Ruth?" Hayleigh lightly touched her arm. "They're ready for us. What did you want? Chips or—"

"I don't care." Ruth couldn't keep the terseness, the panic, out of her voice.

Hayleigh's smile vanished, hurt clouding her face.

"Sorry. Get whatever you want." Ruth stepped away, moving closer to the group and their video.

"—only post the account had ever made. Which leaves the question: How does an account that's never published anything gain nearly five thousand followers?"

Ruth took another step nearer. The friends hadn't noticed her, even though her shadow was encroaching on the edge of the towel. They seemed captivated by the video.

On the screen was an image Ruth knew intimately. A black-and-white rendition of a lamb, collapsed on the ground, its head tilted upward to face the sky.

The video creator was wrong. That wasn't Petition's logo—they'd never had one. Logos were a form of idolatry.

But it was an image she was uncomfortably familiar with. It had been painted above every doorframe in the commune. Both a blessing and a curse on anyone who walked beneath it.

Sacrificial blood will wash you clean.

"Were the followers bought? Why? And for what purpose? And why did this account—an account that was created years ago and remained dormant until this week—choose to make its first and only post be about Petition, so close to the anniversary?"

The rest of the world had faded out. Ruth couldn't feel the heat on her skin any longer. She couldn't hear the crowds around them. There was only her…and the phone in the center of the towel.

The image had changed. It showed the commune. Not the version Ruth had known, when the inhabitants had scrubbed its white walls clean every week.

This version was stained, decayed, crumbling. This was the commune years after it had been emptied, before the buildings had been demolished entirely.

"I have a pet theory. Just a hunch. We know Petition died out exactly twenty years ago." The image flashed back to the presenter, who leaned over a desk, a coffee mug in one hand. "The cult eradicated itself…but not completely. It left a single member behind. A girl. The Petition Child."

Ruth felt as though her body was on fire, and she could do nothing to put it out.

"We know almost nothing about the Petition Child, but the few details that have leaked are concerning. We know Petition relied on the child's prophecies to guide them. And we know one of those prophecies sparked the mass murder—the death of every single member of the cult. Everyone *except* her. And here's the really creepy part…"

A slice of sharp panic bored into Ruth. *Stop. Please.*

"According to a senior police officer, when they led the child away from the bodies, she began laughing. And she didn't stop for hours."

The pressure squeezing Ruth's heart felt overwhelming.

Shortly after Petition's collapse, an anonymous blogger had posted an interview with a police investigator who was part of the first team at Petition.

The interview included a string of salacious quotes, including the one that stuck the hardest: that the Petition Child had been laughing as she was led away.

It spread like wildfire.

Very few people seemed to realize the blog was fiction. The police investigator didn't exist; his name and rank were inventions, just like his quotes.

The blog had been deleted, but its influence still permeated accounts of Petition. Not everyone put enough effort into their research to separate rumors from facts.

She'd never laughed. But, for a certain portion of the population, Ruth wasn't just the Petition Child. She was a monster.

Audiences love a villain.

The screen flicked to an image of the commune posted in a newspaper shortly after the collapse.

"Here's what I think," the voice whispered. "I think that child's back. I think they're tired of staying silent. I think they're trying to tell us something. And maybe, just maybe, they're ready to make good on their final prophecy."

The silence hung for a terrible, impossible stretch.

"That's all I have for now." The presenter gave the camera a smile. "Watch this space."

The screen went black, then filled with recommended videos. Ruth couldn't read the titles, but the image of the lamb had been used in two of the thumbnails.

More videos, all churning Petition back to the surface.

One member of the group looked up at Ruth, finally noticing her.

She turned, afraid they would see the panic in her eyes or the sweat on her face.

It had been getting better. Slowly, in increments, people had started to forget about Petition. But now it was all crawling out of the earth again, a monster that would not stay dead.

She stared across the crowd. How many of them had talked about Petition that weekend? How many had watched videos, messaged friends about it?

And then her eyes landed on Hayleigh.

She stood, her arms full of snacks. She watched Ruth anxiously, her bare feet squirming in the sand. Ruth had no idea how long she'd been standing there.

"I'm sorry," Ruth said. The words came out stilted and uncomfortable. She felt as though her body had been rattled until it forgot how it was supposed to work.

"Um." Hayleigh took a small step forward. She tentatively held out a plastic container, a fork taped to its side. "I got you a fruit cup. I hope… that's okay?"

"Yeah." Ruth took it, swallowing, hating the way Hayleigh was watching her. "Sorry. I didn't mean to snap at you. I'm…I'm not feeling well. You didn't do anything wrong."

A smile flickered back over Hayleigh's face. "It's okay. You've had a bad few days. Let's find our table, yeah? Some food might help."

A bad few days.

As Ruth forced numb legs to carry her across the sand, she swore she could hear the word repeated from every mouth she passed.

Petition...

Petition...

Petition...

And that was when the sightings started.

26.

Logan followed his marks at a distance.

Two staff members struggled along the trail leading to the village, a suitcase carried between them. They staggered under the weight but seemed unwilling to let it touch the ground.

One of the staff was the man with the unusual teeth.

Logan couldn't shake the creeping sense of familiarity. Or the sense of wrongness, for that matter.

The luggage was a metal shell painted steel-blue, a black zipper holding it closed. It was large, but no different from any of the other suitcases the guests had boarded with.

Seeing two staff members moving luggage shouldn't have caught Logan's notice under normal circumstances. The toothy staff member had.

And so he trailed them, hanging just far enough back to not draw attention. They weren't alone on the trail. The lunch whistle would sound soon, and the path held a flow of guests traversing the path between the main beach and their cabins. No one paid any attention to the staff or to Logan.

The men paused as they stepped into the village clearing. They shuffled their grip on the case, panting, as they spoke. The toothy one gestured with his chin, then they set off again, passing between the blocks of accommodations.

Logan circled around, keeping them in sight but following a different path to make himself less obvious.

They struggled to lift the case onto a cabin porch and shuffled awkwardly as they set it down. The toothy staff member took a cloth from his pocket and used it to wipe around the case, giving extra care to the underside and wheels.

It would have felt comical if Logan hadn't been so unnerved. The VIP guests were staying in a different area. Everyone in the village was a standard Eton fan who had won the entry lottery, and Logan doubted any of them would be so high-maintenance to notice—let alone complain—if some dirt got onto their luggage wheels while they were staying on an island.

The staff member knocked, and, when the door failed to open, he used a key from his belt to unlock it. They then carefully rolled the luggage through the door, one on each end, treating it as though it were made of glass instead of metal.

They remained inside for a full minute, and when they stepped back out, the toothy one was tucking the cloth back into his pocket.

Logan watched as they shared a few brief words and split up. He stayed where he was—leaning against a cabin, covered by its shadow—until he was certain they weren't returning; then he crossed to the cabin and climbed its steps.

The door was locked again. He rattled the handle to be sure.

Windows were built into the back wall of every cabin. Logan circled the building and rose onto his toes to look through.

The curtain had been left open. It was dark inside. He slid his phone out and turned on the flashlight, then pressed it up against the glass.

Inside, the beds were rumpled. Clothes were strewn about: bathing suits hanging on the end of the beds to dry, skincare products lined up on the dresser beneath the window.

The blue metal suitcase had been left in the center of the room. It looked almost too perfect among the disarray; it had been left upright, perfectly centered, facing the door.

Mystery solved, and with about as little excitement as most mysteries contained. The staff had been returning a guest's luggage. Maybe it had gotten lost when they disembarked the cruise liner.

Or…

Maybe it was part of an upcoming game.

A card tag had been tied to the luggage. It sat neatly on top, placed at a slight but deliberate angle, the string loop circling the handle. A message had been written in black ink, though Logan couldn't read it from his vantage point.

It looked very much like something Eton would do to kick-start his next competition. A mysterious suitcase waiting for the unaware recipient to find it. Inside would be clues to the game, tools, or, for all Logan knew, a giant jigsaw puzzle.

No. Not a jigsaw. Something heavy and possibly fragile. That would explain why the staff had been so delicate with it.

Logan switched to the phone's camera and then held it to the very top of the window, trying to get the highest angle he could to photograph the tag. The shutter clicked.

"Can I help you, Mr. Lloyd?"

Logan's shoulder hit the windowsill as he flinched.

He liked to think his career had left him stoic, had hardened his nerves. But any pretense at composure vanished with the voice whispering behind his ear.

The toothy staff member stood right there, inches from him. Hands clasped together at his waist. The wide, easy smile contrasted with something very unsettling in his eyes.

"Just looking for a friend." Logan scrambled to regain control. He slipped his phone back into his pocket.

"Ha." A single syllable. Not quite mocking, but…

Logan tried to read the man's expression.

He might have expected mistrust or full hostility. Logan was, for all appearances, creeping. Not only looking into a cabin occupied by four women, but taking photos of the contents.

Instead, the toothy staff member seemed pleased.

Not happy. That was a subtle but important distinction.

He was *pleased*. As though they were sharing a secret.

"Who are you?" Logan asked. He didn't like the way the cabin hid them from sight of the rest of the village. He didn't like how isolated it made him feel.

"I'm Barry, of course." The assistant used the tip of his finger to lift his name tag, reflecting light off it. That secretive, delighted smile grew a little wider.

That wasn't any kind of answer Logan could use. "And where do I know you from?"

"Ha." Barry's eyes seemed to pop wider with the sound. "You don't know me. And that's okay. Because I know you, Mr. Lloyd."

A fan. Or, at least, someone who had seen his videos.

And still, that distant familiarity itched at Logan. Wherever their paths had crossed, it had been brief. A few seconds at a convention? A brief glimpse in a video? Not something good, though, not any common kind of encounter—

"I'm so very glad you could be here, Mr. Lloyd," Barry said. He stepped forward. Logan froze as the man's arms reached around Logan's chest. They tightened, pinning him in place. Barry rested his head against Logan's shoulder. Squeezed.

A hug. A terrible, unfriendly, hostile kind of hug.

"So glad." His fingertips dug into the spaces beneath Logan's shoulder blades like screws into his skin. "I am very much looking forward to seeing how you are at the end of it, Mr. Lloyd."

———

You have to die, Josanna.

Ruth staggered.

Images were pushing in. Screams. Blood on teeth. Her head throbbed and swelled and rocked.

"Ruthie?"

She held something cool in her hands, but she squeezed it too hard and it cracked, juices spilling over her palms.

"Ruth! Can you hear me?"

You know it only works if you die.

"What happened?"

"I don't know! She said she wasn't feeling well."

"Over here." Zach's voice in her head. Zach's hands on her arm, guiding her. She saw him drifting in the ocean of corpses, drained of blood, eyes open, limbs broken. "Sit down, careful now. Carson, see if you can find some shade. An umbrella or something."

She crumpled down onto a bench. Someone prised the broken fruit cup from her hands, and she slumped forward, resting her arms on the table, her head hovering above the wood.

"I'm going to find a doctor," Zach said.

"No. I'm okay. Just…dizzy."

The images were blurring in and out. She focused on her breathing, trying to claw back control over her mind.

The island's peak, sharp as a knife against blue sky. Blood pouring down its sides. You have to die, Josanna.

A carcass writhing. Alive with a swarm of maggots, their white bulging bodies moving in vulgar undulations against the raw red flesh. Another look, and they were no longer maggots but humans, naked, their mouths stretched into screams as they coiled and writhed in their bloody mire.

It only works if you die.

The hot sun vanished from her back. Sand scraped as a beach umbrella was forced into it.

"Water," Zach said, putting his bottle into her hands. "See if you can swallow a bit."

Pushing back against the sightings was like trying to break free from a deep sleep. She had to fight for every inch she gained, but gain them she did. The images swelled to become larger and brighter, then slowly faded back down.

The real world was becoming clearer again.

Zach leaned over her, his brow deeply creased. Behind, Hayleigh and Carson lingered, not quite wanting to look at her.

"Sorry." Her tongue flopped, loose. "Sorry. I'm fine. Vertigo."

"You've lost your color." Zach pressed the back of his fingers against her throat, testing her temperature. "I really want you to see the doctor."

There was nothing any man or woman could do to fix her. So many had already spent years trying.

"I'm…I'm going to go back to the cabin." Every conscious thought was a struggle—not just to form, but to translate into words. "I'll feel better if I can lie down."

Dark. Quiet. To be alone. That would help.

"Okay, I'll come with you." Zach gently moved his arm under Ruth's and helped her stand.

Carson and Hayleigh lingered beside the table. Its surface was filled with snacks and icy drinks.

She shook her head. Images of blood trailing down a delicate nose spread across her mind, and she forced them back. "Stay. We came in fifth. Celebrate for the both of us, okay?"

"Absolutely not." His smile was small but tender. "I'm not going to be having fun if you're somewhere else, feeling sick. Here, lean on me."

A whistle sounded. It was followed by a woman's voice, amplified through the loudspeakers.

"Lunch is served. All guests, gather at Sunset Beach for lunch."

"Let's get out of here," Zach said. "If you're feeling better after some rest, we can always come back and catch the tail end of the meal."

Prongs, stabbing into the earth. And then prongs, stabbing into screaming bodies as they tried to crawl away.

Ruth didn't trust herself to speak. She just nodded.

They climbed toward the jungle. Platters of food were being ferried to the serving tables, their foil tops peeled off to reveal endless lines of triangle-cut sandwiches and stacks of grilled meats and roasted vegetables. The smell should have been enticing, but Ruth had to hold her breath as they passed.

They were nearly at the trail when two staff members came in, one from either side, to intercept them.

"Lunch is ready," the man said, beaming.

"We're not feeling well, so we're going to take a rain check," Zach said.

"Thanks for letting me know! Guests are requested to stay on Sunset Beach for now." The woman's voice was bright, happy. She made it sound as though she was delivering the best news they'd ever heard. "We'd love to invite you to help yourself to a plate and then find a table."

Ruth was struggling to keep up. Zach had his arm around her, and she could feel his muscles growing a fraction tighter.

"We want to leave," he said, speaking slowly and clearly. "Are you telling me we…can't?"

"That's exactly right!" The man nodded, teeth too bright. "Guests are requested to stay on Sunset Beach for lunch."

"Requested, or required?"

The two staff guys seemed to smile a little more. They replied in unison. "Required."

Zach paused, waiting. The men stood, alert and pleasant and with their hands clasped at their waists, blocking the path to the village. Slowly, Zach began to back away, easing Ruth back down the slope with him.

"I'm okay," Ruth said. She didn't feel it. Not at all. But she didn't know if they had any choice. "I can sit in the shade until lunch is over."

"No, this is ridiculous. Eton probably wants to make an announcement or something, but it's overkill to refuse to let anyone out." Zach lowered his voice as they moved out of the staff's hearing range. "We're going to keep moving until they stop watching us, then we'll get into the jungle via some other route."

"Can we go back to the others?" More than anything, Ruth just wanted to be able to sit. "The umbrella's shade was good. I can rest on the table."

"You're not well. I don't care what they say, we're going to leave."

Ruth blinked against the harsh sun. Flashes of yellow had appeared all along the tree line. As she watched, two women were blocked from taking another of the routes out of the beach.

There were more than just a few lookouts. There was a wall of them.

Smiling. Their calculating eyes searching the crowd.

Ruth squeezed Zach's hand as very real fear rose in her throat. "I don't think they'll let us."

27.

"We won't take long."

Petra's silky voice floated from the stage.

Ruth leaned over their table, her head pulsing. Her body felt slick and hot, and not even the shade did much to dampen the rising temperature.

"I'll let you know as soon as we're finished."

"Ridiculous," Zach muttered.

"At least the drinks are free." Carson raised his glass. It was nearly empty. His eyelids seemed heavier than before.

Staff members roved through the tables like sharks. They each had a digital pad, identical to Petra's.

She'd said something about verifying guest details. Maybe someone had gone missing. Or maybe the hollow man's story had spooked them into action. Privately, Ruth hoped they were looking for Gilly.

"I bet it's for the next game," Hayleigh said. Her hands were clasped around her own glass. Her thumb fidgeted along its plastic seam, the nail clicking off it again and again like a heartbeat. "Like, they need to set something up and don't want anyone stumbling on it. What do you think, Zach?"

His jaw twitched. "I think there would have been easier ways to distract us."

The table's mood felt off-key, sour. They'd been so happy to get fifth place. So eager to celebrate and relax. And then Ruth had started to get the sightings—*not sightings; there's no such thing as sightings*—and everything had crumbled in a matter of minutes.

Carson drained the last of his cup and tossed it back onto the table. "I'm going to get another," he said.

"Freedom!" someone yelled farther down the beach. "You'll never take me alive!"

Trigger. His arms were raised above his head as he sprinted through the sand. It was a comedy routine, and a few tables nearby cheered but no one actually laughed.

"They can't take us *all* down!" he shouted.

He was coming toward Ruth's table. Staff was beginning to move in, drawing a circle around him. He leaped away, windmilling his arms and legs theatrically. He hit Ruth as he stumbled. It jammed her against the table, and she gasped.

"Hey!" Zach yelled, on his feet. He put one arm out, a barrier between Trigger and Ruth.

"Aw, my bad, Third Place," Trigger said.

Her ribs felt tender where they'd hit the table. Her mind rocked. The unsteady walls she'd put up against the sightings were crumbling. She clutched for them, trying to block the gaps again.

Behind her, the staff had tightened their circle around Trigger.

"Can we help you back to your table?" one asked, all deferential cheer.

"I'm sorry to see that you're upset, sir," another said. "We'd be happy to assist in any way we can."

Ruth clamped a hand over her mouth, afraid she was going to be sick. The images swelled up again, and she couldn't force them all down in time.

"Can't catch me!" Trigger bolted again. The staff didn't try to stop him as he slipped between them, fists pumping into the air.

The island's peak, turning red.

Maggots, writhing.

You have to die, Josanna...

She keeled forward, her head resting on the tabletop, as the images buried her.

Logan sat at one of the tables farthest from the stage. No one tried to talk to him.

He tapped his phone, opening apps, scrolling a second, and then closing them again. A way to look busy.

No. He wouldn't lie to himself. It was an anxious habit. He was trying to distract himself and nothing was working.

He'd thought he'd left the anxiety, the uncertainty, behind in college. *You have to be the most controlled person in the room,* one of his teachers had said. *Being the apex predator is the only way to keep yourself from being eaten alive.*

And he'd lived by that mantra.

People responded to confidence. To certainty.

And here he was, robbed of it in a single afternoon.

His thumb landed on the photo app again. It was the third time he'd been there, but the first time he actually paid attention to the image that filled his screen.

The most recent photo: grainy, poor lighting, odd angle. Taken through the cabin window. Looking down toward the suitcase, trying to capture the tag.

He pinched his fingers and zoomed the image larger. It was too dark, too muddy. He tapped the settings and worked on increasing the contrast.

Dark writing on a neutral paper tag. The kind someone might tie to a gift box.

He turned his phone, zooming larger and then smaller as he struggled with the poor image data.

It took a second. Then a word appeared.

SURPRISE!

Not a guest's luggage after all. Part of a game, most likely. But he'd already suspected that.

He zoomed the image out, preparing to exit the app, then caught himself.

There was a mark on the suitcase's side. That shouldn't have been unusual. Things didn't stay clean on an island for long.

But it stood out, specifically because the assistants had put so much effort into wiping the case down. Multiple times. As though they were having trouble keeping it clean.

And that mark?

It looked very much like a trail of dark liquid.

Leaking out from between the zipper teeth.

Bleeding.

It doesn't work if you don't die.

Ruth bit the inside of her cheek until she tasted blood.

Forked implements, stabbing into the earth.

Stabbing into flesh.

"Name and date of birth, please?"

One of the staff members stood over Ruth, smiling, a digital pad held at the ready.

"She's not well. Can you come back later?"

That was Zach. He'd half risen from his seat.

"I'm so sorry. I just need to check you off. Name and date of birth, please?"

Running along thin boards. Running toward the ocean. Toward the rocks.

"Her name's Ruth Phillips," Zach said.

"I'm sorry, sir, I really need to hear it from her."

"She's not well! Don't hassle her!"

A woman, her skin made of rot. Arms reaching out. An invitation.

The man bent closer, filling Ruth's vision. That awful smile overwhelming everything else. "Name and date of birth, please?"

"Ruth," she mumbled. "Phillips."

She was a child, crawling through the dark, searching for a way out. Her fingers landed on cold flesh. Mouth gaping open; eyes gouged out.

The staff member tapped at his digital pad. "Mm-hm. And date of birth?"

It took her a beat to remember. Her real date of birth had been lost; Petition didn't allow its members to celebrate or even remember them. The courts had assigned her a new one. She gave it to the smiling man as he compared it to the details on his pad.

"Are you done?" Zach asked. Ruth couldn't remember ever hearing him that angry before.

"All good." The staff member turned the pad around to show Ruth the screen. A scan of her ID—provided when they accepted the tickets—stared out at her. "Thank you for helping me today."

A man, standing at a cliff, staring down into the water.

Staring down at a corpse.

Petra stood onstage, watching as staff progressed through the crowd.

The guests were growing restless, unhappy. They could tell something was wrong. They didn't like being told that they couldn't leave.

Eton would have smoothed it all over. He could spin it into a joke, make it feel like a game, keep them entertained through the remainder of lunch.

Only, Eton was missing.

Petra had messaged him four times over the prior hour, with increasing levels of urgency. He hadn't replied. And no one on the staffing team could tell her where to find him.

That wasn't out of character. Even the overly gregarious Eton would be facing exhaustion after living in close quarters with several hundred guests who all wanted to meet him, all craving a piece of his attention.

But the timing was frustrating. She needed him to be present and in control now more than ever.

A few guests had tried to cause trouble. She suspected Trigger, the kids' content creator, had been pretty close to inspiring a rebellion before he'd settled down.

The messages tab was open on her tablet. Heather had been sending a steady stream of updates.

All the staff had been verified and accounted for. Heather had attached a list of every employee in each department, each one checked off. She'd been thorough; even the medical team and the bands providing live entertainment had been checked against their photo IDs.

The inventory was being counted. They were ensuring the staff uniforms were all accounted for: either being worn by someone on the list or in storage. Petra thought it was unlikely someone would try to impersonate a staff member, but she wasn't leaving anything to chance.

Finally, the cameras had been set up. Heather had included a note that the setups were all piecemeal and would need to be redone with better weatherproofing and cabling before the end of day, but for a temporary stopgap, it worked fine.

Petra had pinned the link on her tablet. It allowed her to click through each live video feed: two angles for the main beach, two for Endurance Cove, three for the village, and two for the staff area.

The beaches were large; even with two cameras, clear footage would be limited. And the accommodations were riddled with blind spots.

But at least now they would have some way to track unusual activity.

The staff had nearly finished checking the crowd. They were moving quickly. Hopefully, fast enough to outrun the guests' waning patience.

Petra checked the time on her tablet. Nearly two full hours since she, or any of the staff, had heard from Eton.

It was no longer just frustrating. It was starting to become alarming.

She created a new message.

PLEASE RESPOND ASAP.

28.

"You have to die, Josanna."

She knew the compound's layout. She could creep along it, even in the dark.

And she knew all the ways out. She was only seven. Small enough to squirm through narrow gaps. The little holes, the windows that didn't lock properly, the loose boards.

They'd sealed so many of them. But they couldn't have found them all.

"Don't you want to fix this? Don't you want to save them?"

There was no one left except for her and Mother Aama. The one who was always watching. The one who scared Josanna the most.

Barom's favorite wife.

The halls were full of bodies. She'd seen them dying before the lights cut out. They'd bitten and clawed and smashed their faces into the white walls they'd always scrubbed so dutifully.

Josanna shuffled forward, reaching into the dark. She couldn't make a sound. Not even when crawling across the soft and bleeding bodies in her path.

Mother Aama wanted her.

And Mother Aama carried a jar of the sweet nectar that had made the others so wild.

Josanna had watched her feed it to the others—the ones who hadn't consumed during the supplicant feast. As the commune fell to screams and violence, Mother Aama had found the abstainers and held them down and prised their lips apart and poured the honey into them.

Josanna was the only one left.

And she didn't want to die.

It was wrong. She knew that. None of them would be reborn unless all of them perished that day. It had to be together, or not at all.

That was what Barom had said.

Josanna's dream, her sighting, had shown the commune full of screams, full of death.

No rebirth. Just suffering.

She'd tried to whisper that warning to one of the mothers, but Aama had overheard.

And now Aama was hunting her.

"Don't you want to save your family?" Her voice was sweet, but hidden under the sugar was a knife. "Don't you want to save us, dear Josanna?"

She wanted more.

She wanted to live.

And so she crawled.

Across bodies she couldn't see. Across a maze of tangled, cold limbs.

"Josanna…" Mother Aama sang her name, full of fury. "Josanna…"

She was nearly there. The concealed door. The elders had blockaded the commune before the feast to make sure none of them broke out when their minds turned rotten, but they wouldn't have thought to cover their hidden door, surely. They didn't think anyone knew about it.

Around the corner. Grit stuck to her palms. She wore a coat, taken from a body she couldn't even see, but she still felt so cold. The heating had shut off at the same time as the lights, and Josanna didn't know how many hours had passed since then. But she knew her mouth was dry and her stomach was empty and the winter had seeped into their home.

"You can still fix this, Josanna. Come back to me and we'll fix it together."

The concealed door was at the end of a hallway. It was the closest way out. The best way out. And so, Josanna crept over someone's legs, her breathing shallow and aching, and entered the passage.

Forward. Forward. She could hear Mother Aama's footsteps. The compound was a maze, but Mother Aama knew it better than anyone. Better even than Josanna.

Metal scraped against the wall. Josanna moved faster.

Her hand landed in something damp and slimy. A stomach, torn out. She opened her mouth but didn't make any sound. She couldn't. Because she wanted to live.

Over that body, there was another. And another.

They were piled up.

She crawled across them. Limbs slipped under her hands. Hair stuck to her skin. Still more bodies. So many.

They'd staggered into that hallway, into that dead end, as they'd tried to escape.

And they'd filled it.

Blocking the hidden door.

The footsteps were very near.

Josanna turned. For the first time since the power had gone out, she could see.

Candlelight. Golden and warm and sweet. It bloomed over the wall at the opposite end of the hallway. A wall covered in bloodied handprints.

"Josanna…" Mother Aama sang the word again.

So very near.

Josanna clawed at the bodies stacked up against the door. There were so many of them. Heavy. Limp. They wouldn't move.

"Josanna…"

She looked down at her own hands. They were covered in blood. The long jacket hung heavy over her shoulders.

Josanna pressed her hands over her face, covering the skin with crimson, then plunged her hands into the bodies again and dragged freshly wet fingers through her hair.

Sacrificial blood will wash you clean.

The lamb hung over every doorway, reminding them that their salvation had to be bought with death.

Their own death.

"Josanna…"

The light was growing brighter.

Josanna flattened herself into the pile of bodies. She couldn't move them without making noise, but she squirmed between them as much as she could, dragging one leg over her back, pulling a hand across her head. The hand had lost its fingernails from clawing at the wall.

"You have to die, Josanna."

Mother Aama entered the hallway.

Her long dress swung about her bare feet. It had soaked up the blood of her family as she walked the halls, turning the pale linen red up to her knees.

She held a candle in one hand. Wax dripped over her fingers.

Her satchel was fastened around her waist. In it was the jar of honey, thick and sweet and made of nightmares.

Her other hand carried a screwdriver. As she walked, she stretched it out, letting the tip trail across the walls.

"Sweet Josanna. Don't you love us? Don't you want us to be saved?"

Her eyes were white as curdled cream. They stared into the pile of bodies, searching.

They were the reason she was Barom's favorite wife.

She'd been blind, he said, until he healed her. The milk had never left her eyes, but after his gift, she saw more clearly than any of the others.

And Josanna was terrified that Mother Aama would see her again now.

Every shallow breath, every beat of her heart, seemed designed to give her away.

Mother Aama tilted her head toward the ceiling. Her skin was crepey and creased. Her pinched lips pale.

"You saw this, child. This was your sighting. You must be afraid, but if you come to me, we can still make this right. We can save our family. Together."

Tears leaked from the corners of Josanna's eyes. She was petrified they would reflect the light and give her away.

Aama stood, swaying lightly. The hand holding the screwdriver touched her hip, where the bottle of honey was fastened. Checking it. Reassuring herself.

Then she turned.

Her bare feet stepped onto chests and arms and faces as she walked over her family. Her skirts trailed through the blood like a paintbrush, dragging color across the floor.

And then she turned the corner, her voice losing some of its sweetness to anger.

"If you do not come out quick, I will take the feast myself, and then you will be all alone, Josanna, all alone in the dark, with no one to love you and no one to protect you, and you will wish you had listened to your mother."

29.

Ruth trickled back into herself.

She was slumped on the table, arms around her head. Her back ached from the angle. Her body was slow and sluggish as she raised herself. Wetness on her face.

Across the table, Carson stared at her. He didn't even try to hide his disgust. The corners of his mouth twisted as his lip curled.

Slowly, as though picking herself up out of a car crash, Ruth pressed her hands over her face. Wiping away tears and sweat.

"You okay?" Zach rested a hand on her back. "I think you fell asleep."

His voice was thicker than normal. Empty cups were stacked in the center of the table. A lot of them.

"Sorry." She scrubbed the back of her hands over her face again, embarrassed and shaking. "I'm good now. Sorry."

Carson grunted, glaring into his drink.

"Hey." Zach leaned an elbow on the table. "Hey, what was that?"

Carson opened his mouth, then turned away. "Doesn't matter."

"I think it does." Zach kept one hand on Ruth's back, and she could feel it twitch. "Ruth said you've been acting strange. Is there a problem?"

"Hey," Ruth whispered. She patted Zach's leg, trying to get him to calm down.

Carson was flushed from the alcohol, but his ruddy complexion intensified as anger bled into him. "Oh, I love that question. *Great* thing to ask, buddy. Who's got a problem? And how many?"

Seated next to Carson, Hayleigh was staring at her hands on the table. She hadn't moved at all since Ruth had woken up. At first, Ruth had assumed she was dozing, or maybe bored, but now she realized that behind Hayleigh's curly hair, her eyes were vacant disks.

A deer in headlights.

The three of them had been friends since they were children. She knew that much. Whenever she'd spent time with them, they'd seemed so happy and comfortable together.

This was something different.

"Zach…" Ruth kept her voice a whisper, afraid to make it worse.

His hand twitched again. He and Carson were locked in an unblinking stare, a challenge neither was willing to back down from.

"This is messed up," Carson muttered.

"I really expected better from you. Especially after your mother—"

"*Don't.*" Carson lurched up, his face contorted. He pointed a finger at Zach, and it was shaking. "Don't you dare bring her into this."

Hayleigh didn't move, didn't make a sound, didn't blink. Fear-glazed eyes stared into nothing.

With effort, Carson coiled his finger back into a fist, pulling away from Zach. He gave Ruth a final, icy glare, then pushed away from the table. His shoulder muscles strained against his shirt as he stormed across the beach.

Zach didn't move for a moment. Then he took a shaking breath, the rigidity in his face melting, and pressed a hand over his mouth.

"I shouldn't have said that," he mumbled.

Hayleigh's glassy eyes glanced up, then fixed back on her unmoving hands.

"I…I'm sorry," Zach said. Ruth didn't know if he was apologizing to her, or to Hayleigh, or if he wished he could say it to Carson. "That was a mistake."

Ruth rubbed his leg. She didn't know what else she could do. She was the new one to the friend group. The interloper. And she felt it more acutely than ever before.

Zach looked at her, and his eyes were full of shame. "I messed up. I shouldn't have… His mother had problems when we were growing up. He spent a lot of time at my house because of it. I never should have brought that into an argument."

"I should go check on him," Hayleigh whispered. She was out of her seat before anyone could respond, her feet light and quick on the sand.

Zach sighed. He looked exhausted. The cup next to him was half full and he picked it up, then grimaced and shoved it away again.

"Sorry, Ruth. You shouldn't have had to hear any of that."

"Do you think you can talk it out with him?" she asked. It was a genuine question. She was acutely aware of how little she understood the group's history.

"Maybe. Yeah." Zach rubbed his hands over his face. "Maybe I should—no. Later. You're not well. They said we're allowed to leave the beach. We should stop by the medical clinic and get you checked out."

"I'm okay." And she was. The sightings—the hallucinations, dreams, whatever she chose to call them—had run their course. At least for that moment. "Catch up to Carson. See if you can make things right."

<hr />

All guests checked.

Petra stood behind the stage, scrolling through Heather's message.

516 standard guests, 30 VIP guests, and 53 entourage were verified using their photo ID and confirming their date of birth.
Details all match the original guest list and ship's boarding manifest.
No guests were missing. No discrepancies found. Final file attached.

Petra tapped the attachment. It opened into a spreadsheet; each line held a guest's name, date of birth, link to the scan of their photo ID stored on the company's server, and the time stamp and staff ID from when they were checked. Each line was coded green: no issues.

She breathed deeply and leaned back against the stage.

It was a relief.

Especially considering how many attendees had come up to her that morning to say they couldn't find a friend.

Behind her, guests milled about. The beach restrictions had been lifted forty minutes before, as soon as the final table was checked, but many of the guests still chose to stay. Including some who had sent up the loudest complaints, such as Trigger.

Eton was still missing.

Petra had messaged one of their bands, asking if they could play a set to fill the dead space. They were setting up on the stage behind her, somehow both hungover and drunk.

Petra filtered through her open tasks, tagging and filing away the ones she could. The injured contestant, Makayla Wells, had been released from the medical clinic but would receive ongoing check-ins from the lead doctor.

Preliminary checks of the employees had been carried out by team leaders, with a more thorough review planned for that night. Heather had been asking staff if they knew anyone who went by the name Lisa or had been spotted wearing a LISA name tag. So far, nothing.

Petra hovered her pen over an open task marked urgent. It had gone out to all staff, asking them to notify her as soon as they saw Eton.

No replies.

She was growing increasingly worried. He had a habit of taking vacations without warning, but he *never* missed prescheduled events.

It had been his job to do the announcements during lunch, a task that had fallen to Petra in his absence.

Then there was the game. It was scheduled to start in an hour. Even if he turned up right then, they would be cutting it close. And Eton lived for his games.

In the distance, clouds were beginning to form against the harsh sky, ushering in that day's shower.

Rain could be expected nearly every day on Prosperity Island. It was unavoidable. Petra would count them lucky if they could finish the festival without any of the storms the region was known for. They were getting updated forecasts every hour, and so far, it looked promising.

A message flashed on the screen, and Petra took a sharp breath.

Eton.

He'd finally replied to her, right when she was seriously considering search parties.

She opened the message. Her relief curdled.

PET.

FIND ME AT SHIPWRECK BAY.

IT'S BAD.

30.

Ruth sank down to the damp jungle floor.

She'd left the beach shortly after Zach. It was too busy, too bright. It made her feel exposed and raw, as though her secrets were peeled open and put on display for anyone to see.

She dreamed of Petition often. Those dreams usually ended before Mother Aama grew too near. She hadn't relived those final moments in a long time.

Mother Aama was not a woman who made empty promises. She'd roamed the compound for hours while Ruth hid, too afraid to move. When Ruth did not appear, Mother Aama uncorked the bottle of neuro-toxins and drank what was left.

Ruth, surrounded by the cold flesh of her family, had covered her ears. It wasn't enough to block out the sounds of Mother Aama stabbing the screwdriver into her face over, and over, and over.

And then, just as Mother Aama had threatened, Ruth was left terribly, horribly alone.

She never found an exit.

The police broke into the compound while responding to missing person reports and a tip from a nearby farmer who had noticed the commune's unusual lack of activity.

Ruth had lived in the dark and the cold, surrounded by the dead, for two full days.

She'd been dehydrated and incoherent. The staff at the hospital had been forced to sedate her. Any sleep had been broken by screaming night-mares. Wakefulness was filled with confusion and terror.

She'd never been outside of the commune before. Especially not to a hospital.

Barom had taught the commune to fear medicine; he said that every treatment and every medication carved away a part of their humanity. It was a cruel bargain, he said. A balm to take away pain, in exchange for a piece of a person's soul. Anyone who spent too long under medicine's control would lose their humanity entirely and become a beast in human skin.

Ruth descended into panic any time the hospital staff entered her room.

It had taken a lot of time and a lot of patience to reach her. A series of people who gave more than they were being paid for, people whose kindness surpassed what should have been expected. Ruth believed she owed her life to them.

Her original caseworker, Leslie, was one of those. She'd never been affectionate or sweet, but she viciously guarded Ruth as the courts tried to figure out what to do with her. She'd fought for every protection possible: the name change, the relocations, the media bans and record seals. New foster families when the previous ones grew exhausted. New psychiatrists when the original ones weren't up to the job.

The name change was one of the best gifts she could have given Ruth.

It let her put a chasm between herself and her childhood.

She could look at Josanna, the Petition Child, with grief. The girl who had slavishly absorbed Barom's teachings. The girl who believed the world was corruptive and desolate and evil, and that their family alone was safe and good. The girl who had hidden as every person she'd ever known died.

She was no longer Josanna. She was Ruth.

And Ruth could choose her destiny.

Ruth was in control of herself.

Ruth could, against all odds, even in defiance of what some of the foster parents had believed…

She could live a normal life.

Ruth breathed slowly and carefully as she lifted her head to see flecks of blue sky through the canopy.

Petition felt closer than it had in years. The memories, the dreams, and the anniversary were reviving it in a horrifying way. But it would seep back underground with enough time. She just had to refuse to give it any power.

Premonitions weren't real. *Sightings* weren't real.

She was certain of that.

She had to be.

Because, if she wasn't…

Then the sightings were warning her that they were all going to die.

<hr />

Logan scrolled through his photos.

Comments appeared beneath each one, vanishing again with a swipe of his thumb.

ROCKS TOO CLEAN?

PETITION CHILD?

STORM ALARM

He stopped at that last image. It captured the derelict communications tower, two of the staff standing outside as they spoke in urgent whispers.

He zoomed. And zoomed again. And then scrolled over to the tower, its clouded window and open door…

Footsteps crunched just behind his shoulder. Logan slid his hand over his phone to hide the image.

The afternoon was hot despite the gathering rain clouds, but the man who'd approached his table still wore a sweater that draped from his too-thin frame.

The camera man from Camping Quest. The one they'd found hiding at the cliff base.

Joel's face was hidden by his beard. He couldn't look at Logan directly, but his large eyes traveled from the tabletop to the sand to the horizon and back without blinking.

"Hey. You doing okay?" Logan asked, because the answer was clearly *no*.

Joel picked at his sweater sleeves. His eyes kept traveling. He took a shallow breath and then said, so softly that Logan very nearly missed it:

"Don't leave the beach. I think they want you next."

Shipwreck Bay was a small section on the island's western side, past Endurance Cove. It was allegedly where the burned-out yacht was found. A peninsula ran out on one side, holding a slim stretch of sand. Tide pools rose into rocky ledges, creating a shelf thirty feet above the water.

Petra picked her way across it. She could see Eton ahead, sitting on the ledge with his knees drawn up to his chest, staring at the water below. His beanie was pulled low.

When they'd made plans for the festival, Shipwreck Bay had been discounted for any of the key locations. It was too small, too rocky, too dangerous.

Waves crashed against the tide pools and flecks of spray kissed Petra's cheeks.

"Where have you been?" she called.

Eton flicked a hand out, a vague gesture. He didn't lift his head.

Petra chewed the inside of her cheek. The path to Eton was uneven and damp. Her sneakers struggled to find solid purchase.

"Lunch is over," she said, her voice clipped. "Have you been seeing my updates?"

"You're always so angry, Pet."

She stopped short. Small dots of ocean spray were beading on her skin.

"Maybe," she said, "I'd seem a little less angry if I didn't feel like I was the only one trying to put out a forest full of spot fires. And maybe I'd seem a little less angry if you weren't running ahead of me and *starting* those fires."

He finally turned to look at her, forearm resting on his knees. His face was damp. The hair that poked out from beneath his beanie held droplets that trembled every time he moved.

"Is that really how you see it?" he asked. "I'm creating fires for you to put out?"

She stretched her arms wide, gesturing to the island. To *everything*.

For a moment, Eton did nothing but stare at her. His normal joviality was gone. There was none of the teasing, none of the energy, none of the joy she associated with him. He seemed…broken, somehow.

"Why do you hate me?" he asked. "And, if you hate me, why do you stay?"

Below, a wave broke on the rocks. It was a hollow, lonely sound.

"I don't hate you." She moved forward again, closing the gap between them. Then, very carefully, she lowered herself to sit on the rocks next to him. "I'm…tired. I feel like I've spent my life cleaning up after other people. Everyone else has fun, and then I follow behind, picking up their toys and putting them away."

"Then why don't you stop?"

Oh, Pet. What's wrong with me? Why aren't I good enough? That was her mother, crying hot tears into Petra's shoulder after her fiancée left. Petra, holding her, stroking her hair, telling her it would be okay.

I'm a horrible mother. It's no wonder people hate me, as Petra brought her a plate of dinner when she was too tired to lift herself off the couch.

My sweet girl. You're the only one who's never given up on me, as Petra emptied her savings jar onto the coffee table when her mother lost her job.

She was only twelve.

"I don't know how," Petra said at last. "I don't think I can."

Eton watched her, eyes gentle. He reached out a hand.

Petra hesitated, then took it.

They sat close, damp fingers clasped together, and for a moment, Petra saw an alternate world where they were even just a little bit more compatible. Where their brief relationship hadn't been destined to sink.

"I've made a very big mistake," Eton said. His voice was small, barely an echo of how he usually sounded, and Petra knew the words were costing him. "I don't want to tell you, but I think I have to."

"You've been hiding something for a while," she noted.

"You know me too well." He released a breath and let the salty air snatch it away. Above, the sky was growing dimmer, heavier, as clouds moved in. "You said I was running ahead and starting spot fires. And you weren't wrong."

She waited.

"Do you remember, not long after you started working with me, you taught me how to handle a PR crisis?"

"If bad news is about to break, create a distraction," Petra said.

She remembered the event that had precipitated that strategy. People had found one of Eton's old videos back from when he'd tried sketch comedy.

The video hadn't been considered shocking at the time it was released. Not when compared to what some other major creators were putting out.

But it was tasteless, and it grew less and less acceptable with each passing year.

Eton deleted the video. But people had made copies. Clips were being shared on other platforms. The sketch was like poison to Eton's wholesome reputation.

He'd been in a panic, trying to figure out how to explain himself in an apology video, when Petra had swiveled the strategy.

The next morning, they announced a countrywide treasure hunt. A million dollars was buried somewhere in the U.S., and the first person to decipher the clues and race to the location could claim it.

Over the following twenty-two days, Eton dripped out hints across his social accounts: a blurry photo of a tree, the corner of a street sign, an anagram.

It worked. The buzz was enormous. By the time someone dug up the faux treasure chest on the outskirts of Las Vegas, the scandal was all but forgotten.

It cost them close to a million and a half between the prize money and the logistics.

Both Eton and Petra had agreed it was worth it.

"Exactly." Eton squeezed her hand. His skin was cold. "I made a mistake, Pet, and I thought…I needed to make sure it never hurt anyone. I needed to create a distraction."

"Why didn't you tell me this at the start?" He never hid things from her. Petra's job revolved around knowing everything, being able to account for everything.

"I wanted to take care of it myself. We were already looking at the island. And I realized *it* could be the distraction. Obviously, it's not the only reason I bought it. It's an investment. There's a lot we can do here. But…"

"It's why you rushed us through the planning phase."

"Right. Yeah." He stared at the crashing waves below them. "And here's why you're chasing spot fires. I thought we needed something dramatic to go down at the festival to really seal it. I didn't do anything bad. I just… let things happen. I ignored you when you said we needed a safety officer. I announced the witch's grave when it was dark out. I told the bar staff not to cut guests off even if they were drunk."

"You wanted someone to get hurt."

Eton didn't respond. And he didn't try to stop her when Petra extracted her hand from his.

"Okay." She shuffled her sneakers on the pockmarked rocks. Thirty feet below, the ocean groaned. "Nothing too bad has happened yet. Nothing we can't come back from. We can patch this, repair it." A thought occurred to her. "Was the fishhook net yours?"

The confusion was clear in his face. "Net?"

Petra shook her head.

She felt he was being honest with her, at last. He hadn't done anything to directly cause harm. He could be accused of negligence—no question there—but she thought she could get them out of it relatively unscathed.

But the fact that Eton, a man who had relied on her to order his groceries and to organize his friend's rehab, hadn't entrusted this to her? That was concerning.

"You said the festival was a distraction," she said. "What from?"

He hesitated. "A mistake."

She kept her voice neutral. "What was the mistake, Eton?"

His elastic face shifted, a montage of emotions moving through his eyebrows, his mouth, his cheeks. He started to look at her and then turned away again before he could. "You remember I told you I was seeing a girl?"

"Amy." She remembered. Eton rarely dated and he'd been excited about this new match. He'd said she was a fan; he didn't give Petra any other details. They broke up after just a few months.

"It's bad, Pet." His face was still moving, growing pained. "I didn't know when we started. I swear, I didn't know. But she wasn't legal."

The cold began to move out of Petra's hands and legs and into her stomach, thick and uncomfortable. "How young?"

"I had no idea. She looked so much older. And she never said anything about—"

"Eton." She spoke the words very carefully, very clearly. "How young was she?"

His tongue darted out over wet lips. "Nearly fifteen."

Spasmodic shudders crawled up her back. They felt like they were eating her alive.

"We never met up! It was all online. And I swear, she seemed so mature—" He caught himself. "She didn't look that young. At all."

"Eton…" Her voice sounded distant, strange. "You're thirty."

"I know. I know." He ran his hands over his face and then into his hair. The beanie fell off, landing on the wet stone. "You must hate me."

"You dated…a fourteen-year-old child."

"She was nearly fifteen—"

"*Fourteen*," Petra screamed. It exploded out of her, shockingly loud.

Eton stared at her, his eyes bulging, as the echoes faded. And then, his voice raspy and raw: "She never told me. I didn't know. She looked so much older." A choking breath. "You hate me, and I deserve it."

"Don't." She held her hands against either side of her head, trying to block his words out. "Do *not* play the pity game with me. Not over this."

He shuffled, pulling his legs up, turning away from her.

A wave crashed. Flecks of icy spray spit on her face. In her eyes.

Petra reached for her internal voice. The part of her that was always churning through problems, poking at angles, figuring out what to do next.

It was silent. A machine broken down, gears spinning against thin air.

"How did it end?" she asked.

"Her parents found out." Eton was hunched. "They were angry. Obviously. Her father said he was going to go to the media. I…I offered to send them money."

A noise rose in Petra's throat.

"I didn't know what else to do." He was growing frustrated. "I told them it could be for her college. To make up for…anyway. It came out of my own bank account, not the business's. In case you're worried about that."

She didn't let herself react. He was trying to lead her into a tangential argument about bank accounts, about keeping personal expenses out of business funds, and she refused to take the bait.

"They went away," Eton said, his voice dropping again. "But...I didn't know if they were completely gone. So I thought I'd do what you do. I'd put out a distraction. A big one. Just in case I needed some noise to drown out any rumors."

Petra knew why he hadn't told her. She'd used the distraction technique to mask old mistakes, to blot over poorly considered blunders.

She never would have agreed to use it as cover for an actual crime. Especially not involving a child.

Petra remembered his reaction to seeing Logan Lloyd, a man whose career was built on unearthing secrets and ending careers. The sudden panic, quickly hidden.

"What are you going to do?" Eton asked. He sounded very small.

She didn't trust herself to speak straight away.

She wanted to leave, right then.

But the festival wasn't over. They had hundreds of people under their care, and that didn't end until the cruise ship docked back onto the mainland.

Eton had already taken risks with the guests' safety in the interest of misdirection. Would he push those limits if he felt cornered?

She settled on, "I don't know yet. I need time."

"Yeah," he said. "Yeah, of course. Absolutely. And you have to believe me, I never would have messaged her if I'd guessed—"

"No more," Petra said. She flexed her hands on top of her knees.

"Right. Sorry." He cleared his throat.

"We're going to play the safest version of events possible for the remainder of the trip," Petra said. She could do this. She could reel the festival back under her control. "No more risky games. You can host trivia this evening. And, at breakfast tomorrow morning, you'll give away the location of the witch's grave."

Eton stared at her.

"We can't encourage guests to rove across the island," she shot back. "Make sure the prize is found before midday tomorrow. Remove the temptation. We're lucky that none of the accidents so far have caused permanent injuries. We need to keep it that way."

"That's the thing, Pet." His voice was weak, raspy. "That's why I called you here. I messed up. And now it's too late for either of us to fix."

"What?" Her hands were numb. Her face was turning numb too.

Eton didn't answer, but he stretched out an arm, finger pointing toward the rocks and water below them.

Petra craned forward.

Her mouth opened, a thin gasp, as she saw the thing Eton had been staring at the whole time they'd been there.

Thirty feet below, a shelf of tide pools created a basin. Waves broke on the walls, tipping soft cascades of fresh water and foam over the lip to replenish the bowl.

Inside was a shape.

A body.

Loose and sodden, drifting with every wave that swept over it.

31.

Ruth felt sticky, clammy. The village's showers would get busier as evening set in; if she took hers early, before sundown, she might not need to line up.

She slipped through the village, aiming for their cabin.

Around her, the buildings were starting to feel lived in. Clothes hung on the porch railings to dry. Crafts made from vines and palm leaves had been strung outside doors. People had taken chairs from around the firepit and sat in informal clusters, talking or playing music.

The energy would rise again as the late-night party crowd came to life, but she was grateful for the temporary lull.

Ruth jogged up the steps to their cabin and raised her key to the latch. The door, already unlocked, swung open as she bumped it.

Carson and Hayleigh were inside. They stood in the narrow space between the bunk beds, and Ruth knew she'd interrupted a private conversation.

"Sorry." She considered backing out, then forced herself to step inside instead. "Just came to collect my towel."

"Hey, Ruthie." Hayleigh's smile was shaky. "I hope you're feeling better."

"I am. Thanks." Ruth crossed to her bed and dragged the suitcase out from underneath. She could feel their eyes on her as she unzipped it.

She couldn't tell if Zach had already spoken to them.

If he had, it hadn't helped.

Carson didn't smile, and he didn't speak. He only stared.

Ruth shoved her case back under the bed, towel clutched to her chest. She strode to the door, then stopped.

She was Ruth.

She got to decide how her life was shaped.

And she wasn't going to spend five days in close quarters with someone who hated her and didn't even have the courtesy to hide it.

"What?" she asked, turning.

Hayleigh's eyebrows rose, but Carson's expression didn't shift.

It was flat. Cold.

Disgusted.

"What did I do?" Ruth spread her arms, towel flicking. "Why do you hate me?"

"Babe." Hayleigh pressed her hand into Carson's chest and tapped rapidly. "Babe, I don't think…"

His jaw twitched. He whispered: "It isn't right."

The cabin felt too small. The air was too dense, too hard to take in.

And Ruth was noticing just how huge Carson really was.

He'd seemed a gentle giant when she first met him, bouncing and loose and flexible. But all that softness had turned rigid. He towered over Ruth, crowding the narrow space. Hands the size of her head flexed at his side.

"Babe," Hayleigh whispered again. "You know what'll happen."

He shook his head. Color was spreading up his throat, into his face. "No. I'm done with this. We've got to tell her."

Hayleigh closed her eyes, squeezing them until creases spread across her forehead and nose. Then she nodded.

"Tell me what?" Ruth had backed up against the door. The air was no longer thick—it was suffocating.

Carson turned toward her. He held one hand around Hayleigh, gripping her shoulder. She still hadn't opened her eyes.

"You need to know," he said.

She felt her pulse in her throat, in her skull, in her bones. "Know what?"

"He told us." Carson's lips peeled back. The corners curled, disgusted. Teeth flashed in the faint light. "Zach told us you're the Petition Child."

"Eton." Petra dug her fingers into the wet stone. She leaned forward, over the edge of the precipice. "Eton, Eton, *no.*"

Below, the body rocked in the tide pools. She was face down, limbs spread. Shoulder-length brown hair fanned about her head, drifting like algae.

"I came out here to have a break," Eton whispered. "When I saw her, I tried to get to her, but I couldn't. It's too steep."

A wave crashed over the rock wall. The overflow swept about the body. Flecks of spray kissed Petra's skin.

"Do you know who it is?" she asked.

"No." He'd hunched again, knees up to his chest, arms around them. "There's a phone down there."

She caught a glint of metal. The phone, broken, lay half submerged on the rocks. Its screen had shattered on impact.

The unknown woman might have tried to stand at the edge of the cliffs to take selfies against the sky. But there was no railing. No flat surfaces. And the rocks were very wet.

"Back from the edge." Petra crawled away, still on her hands and knees. "Eton, move back."

He continued to stare down at the water. "What do we do, Pet?"

"We contact the local authorities." Eton hadn't been involved in any of the disaster preparation meetings. Petra had. "It's a private island, but we're still under their jurisdiction. They'll need to retrieve the body and transport it to a morgue. While that's happening, we'll want to…"

Identify the body and determine next of kin.

"Eton." The clouds were growing thick across the horizon, bruised blues and grays. "Eton, how long have you been here?"

"I don't know exactly. A while. I needed to think."

"Longer than an hour? This is important. You've been uncontactable since well before lunch. How much of that time did you spend up here?"

"Most of it, I guess." He rested his chin on his knees, frowning. "Does it matter?"

A low moan reverberated through her chest.

She'd left her digital pad near the edge of the jungle, afraid the ocean spray would damage it.

And on her digital pad was a spreadsheet, compiled barely more than an hour before, verifying that every guest on the island was accounted for and safe.

Every single one of them.

Including, presumably, the woman in the water.

Someone was lying.

———

"Zach told us you're the Petition Child."

The invisible strings holding Ruth together were severed. Her legs went boneless. Her heart ceased moving. She slid, crumpling, until she hit the floor.

"I'm sorry," Hayleigh whispered. Tears slipped over her lids, trailed down to her chin. She clung to Carson, who refused to look at either of them.

Years of guarding her secret.

Years of avoiding school photos, of watching every word she said, of burying any link that could tie her back to Petition.

A fragile shield she'd built one piece at a time, one day at a time, engulfed in flames before her eyes.

She opened her mouth. Searched for an excuse, for a lie, for anything that might put the fire out.

But her body no longer responded. She couldn't feel anything. She would burn to death there on the cabin floor and couldn't do a thing to stop it.

"We're not upset with you," Hayleigh whispered.

Carson's jaw twitched. His eyes were thunder and ice.

"We couldn't agree on whether we should tell you." Hayleigh squeezed at Carson's jacket. "Car wanted to. He said you deserved to know."

Through the numbing shock, through the screaming fear, one question managed to escape. "When?"

"On the ship." Carson's mouth twitched again. "You were sick. In the cabin. The rest of us got drunk and…Zach asked if we wanted to know how he'd *really* gotten the tickets."

No. No. No. No. No. No.

"We all entered the contest." Hayleigh's voice was small. "Three chances to be picked, instead of just one. The form had a comments section. I wrote about how I'd watched every video since I was fifteen. Carson wrote about how much of Eton's merch he owned."

"And Zach told them about you," Carson finished.

Ruth's hands rose, covering her mouth, wrapping across the lower half of her face. Trying to keep the keening, aching sounds inside.

"I'm sorry! I'm sorry." Hayleigh crossed the cabin and dropped down beside Ruth. She moved very slowly, very carefully, as she touched Ruth's shoulder. "It's going to be okay."

It wasn't.

Eton knew.

People on his team knew.

And she had no doubt it would begin to spread quickly. If it hadn't already.

She could move. Change her name again.

But the drone had recorded film of her during the first game. The team had a scan of her photo ID. She would appear in the background of countless candid pictures taken over the festival.

Her face was going to be known.

And there was no way to ever truly hide once that happened.

She'd watched how the world treated other infamous men and women. They tried to start fresh lives; they changed their hair and clothes, found new friends, a new community. It never lasted more than a couple of years.

Strangers would recognize her.

People would take photos of her in public.

She'd be found, every single time. And Ruth would spend the rest of her life under scrutiny from an audience that believed she did not deserve mercy.

"I'm sorry," Hayleigh said again.

Carson was backlit by the window. His arms were folded, his eyes on the worn floor.

He wasn't trying to hide his disgust any longer. She'd been catching flashes of it for days, but this was the first time she saw it plainly.

It wasn't directed at her. It never had been.

It was disgust…with himself.

With *Zach*.

Every time he'd stared at her, he'd been warring with himself: betray his closest friend's secret or live with the guilt of what they were doing?

The friendship had lost.

"There's more," Carson said, fingers digging into his arms. "It's…ugly stuff. I don't know if you want to hear it."

Ruth eased her hands away from her mouth, let them fall into her lap.

Her world was consumed in fire—it wasn't like it could burn any worse.

"Tell me."

32.

A suitcase filled the aisle in Lia's cabin.

She stopped in the doorway, a pair of sand-crusted platform shoes dangling from one hand. The suitcase was big and looked like it was made of metal.

She, her two sisters, and her cousin had bought matching luggage for the trip. All silvery-lilac, one wheel on Lia's suitcase broke when she dropped it while boarding the ship. The luggage in the center of her room was steel-blue.

And it meant someone had been inside their cabin.

Lia put her sandals down beside the door, not moving her eyes from the case. It had a tag tied to the handle.

SURPRISE!

A present? From her sisters? No. They couldn't have gotten it onto the ship without her noticing, and the kiosk on the beach only sold small things like hats and sunscreen.

From the guy she'd been chatting with? He was sweet and she hoped they'd get a chance to spend more time together, but they'd literally only met the previous night, and it would be a field of red flags if he'd broken into her cabin to leave some big romantic gesture.

She crossed to the case and flipped its card over. There was nothing written on the other side.

No words to indicate who it was from. Nothing to say who it was intended for either. There were four of them staying in the cabin; if it was meant for one person in particular, surely it would say that?

Lia bit her lip to smother a growing smile.

It had to be part of a game.

The staff would have backup keys; that was how they'd gotten the case in and still left the door locked behind them.

She hadn't heard any whispers from other groups. Which meant, if cases like this had been left in any other cabins, they hadn't been found yet.

Lia reached into her shorts for her phone and sent a rushed text to her sisters and cousin, telling them to come fast.

They were still at the beach. It would take them a few minutes to catch up, even if they ran.

She couldn't wait that long.

The zippers had been sealed so that both tabs were at the top of the case. She took the left-hand one and pulled it, feeling the vibration of metal on metal, until it hit the end of its tracks.

A slim gap opened at the parted zipper. She could smell something. Lia leaned away from it, her throat closing over. It wasn't a good smell.

She reached for the second zipper. Something tacky had gotten onto the tips of her fingers. Something rust-brown.

A little part of her no longer wanted to open the case.

But she was already moving, carried by momentum and excitement, and she didn't have long enough to question whether she should listen to that little part or not.

The zipper hummed along its track, the teeth peeling back, and with each inch, the gap bulged wider as the case's contents put pressure on it.

Lia dragged the zipper right down to the ground, and suddenly her fingers no longer had a *trace* of the dark sticky liquid, they were drenched in it, and more was dripping out onto the floor, staining the wood, spreading.

The gap bulged, zippers like fangs on either side.

And in the shadowy interior Lia saw…

Hair, wet and sticky.

Skin, gray.

A mouth wide-open, trapped in an endless scream.

The lights in the medical clinic vanished with a soft whine.

Dr. Coleman looked up from his laptop. Three bulbs had been set into the ceiling. They'd been neither bright enough nor warm enough to make the room a pleasant environment, but that wasn't unusual when working in remote locations.

Without them, the room vanished into a gloom. The three narrow skylights were too small and too dirty to do much more than give a whisper of light.

Across the room, Dr. Young, his arms full of electrolyte replenishment bottles, sighed. "Seems like it's time for my break."

"Seems like it." Dr. Coleman, his body washed in blue light from his laptop screen, stretched.

The six medical beds were empty. Their overnight patient, Makayla Wells, had been discharged. Guests had filtered through their clinic throughout the day: some complaining of headaches, some seeking sunburn relief, some with sprained joints and pulled muscles, and a not-insignificant number requesting relief from hangovers.

But the last few hours had been quiet. Their colleagues were getting rest, Dr. Young was restocking, and Dr. Coleman was using the window to catch up on paperwork from the day. Or he had been. The battery symbol was active in his laptop's bar.

Two quick knocks on the door announced a smiling team member.

"Afternoon, doctors," he said, holding the door open. The light bled around him, pressing into the medical clinic's gloom. "I'm very sorry about this. It seems we're having some trouble with the power, but we're going to get it fixed up right away for you."

"Well, as you can see, it's an extremely inconvenient time," Dr. Coleman said, gesturing to the patientless room.

The staff member broke into laughter. It was very loud, very eager. And it lasted too long. Dr. Coleman felt like he was a CEO with an intern who was desperate to keep his job.

"All right," he said, shuffling back to his laptop. "No harm with the lights. I'll let you get to it."

"Sure, sure, sure. It won't take a moment."

The staff member stepped into the room.

Four others came with him.

Dr. Coleman hadn't even seen them standing outside the clinic. They all smiled, their eyes bright as they followed behind the leader.

Dr. Young, nearly finished restocking the electrolyte bottles, frowned. "The generator's outside."

"You're absolutely right, for sure."

One of the staff members closed the door behind them. There was a heavy clunk that sounded like a lock being engaged.

"We just need to take care of some stuff in here first," the leader said, all politeness, all smiles. "It won't take a moment."

A heavy *thud* reverberated as a roll of barbed wire hit the floor.

Ruth sat on the edge of her bunk bed, feet pulled together, hands clasped over her knees.

Opposite, Carson and Hayleigh were on Carson's mattress, Hayleigh with her hands wrapped around Carson's arm, either to hold herself steady, or him steady, or maybe both.

"Zach's deleted a lot of this stuff from the internet now, so you probably wouldn't find it unless you knew how to search for it," Carson said.

He kept trying to make eye contact but couldn't manage to maintain it for more than a second.

Ruth, her skin clammy, her body hot, waited.

"He took a shot at being a creator a couple of years back. First a video channel, then, when that didn't really work, he started a podcast. He's always been...smart. Really smart. More than I ever was. And we all knew he could make it work, as long as he had the right angle."

"*Unmasking the Cult*," Hayleigh said. "That was the name of the podcast."

"He talked about Petition, didn't he?" Ruth asked. It would almost be stranger if he didn't. Petition was such a deeply embedded part of the public's consciousness that anyone who talked about cults brought it up sooner or later.

"Yeah." Hayleigh swallowed.

Carson ground his heel into the floor. "He didn't just mention it. That was the whole podcast. Petition. I guess he planned to go on to others later, but for the year the podcast was running, that was his only topic."

She looked for the lie in Carson's face. There was shame and frustration and anger. But no deception.

A little delicate part of her broke.

The part that loved Zach.

"It was such a big news story when we were growing up," Carson said. "The inquest was happening when we were all teens, but Hays and I stopped listening to it pretty quickly, and he just...didn't. Maybe he felt like he needed to understand it? I don't know."

Ruth had seen that effect in a lot of people. She'd heard the phrase *cultural trauma*. Atrocities had happened close to home, and it wasn't something they could move on from. They needed to know the *why* and the *how* and the *who*. Timelines, personal backgrounds, layouts. They couldn't accept Petition without first understanding it.

"He didn't want to just recycle the known stuff," Carson said. "He talked about that a lot. Every podcast and blog just borrowed from one another."

They did. She'd seen that. Half the facts weren't even true but had been echoed so often that no one questioned them.

"He wanted his podcast to be...I don't know, like a definitive version or something," Carson said. "He put in applications for inquest transcripts to be unsealed. He tried to track down lawyers who had worked on the case, though most wouldn't speak to him. The three of us even took a trip to the compound."

"Ah," Ruth whispered, sick to her stomach.

"It had been all torn down about two years before." Hayleigh squirmed. She still held on to Carson. "There wasn't much left, but you could see some concrete pads and the outlines where a few buildings had been. He spent hours taking photos."

She pictured Zach, tracing his fingertips up her thigh. Zach, bent over the stove as he poured every ounce of concentration into making the perfect blueberry pancakes. Zach, sleepily stroking her hair to help calm her after she had a nightmare.

"The biggest thing, though?" Carson's jaw was tight again, muscles in his neck standing out like cables. "He wanted to find the Petition Child."

Ruth closed her eyes, her fractured insides aching so badly that she thought she might never feel whole again.

"And that's where it went bad," Carson said. "All the stuff until then? That was whatever. But he wouldn't leave this alone. The requests to have transcripts unsealed were all being rejected. And I'm not sure if he even knew he was crossing a line, but he did."

"He found a caseworker," Hayleigh said. "Their identities were supposed to be kept private, but he managed to narrow it down by comparing the inquest dates to some kind of employment register. Someone called... Les?"

"Leslie," Ruth whispered.

Carson took a deep breath, and it seemed to drain the oxygen from the room. "We were out one day, and he asked me if I wanted to stop and visit a friend. And he took me to a long-term care facility. And we went into a room where a little white-haired lady was curled up in bed. Zach told me she had Alzheimer's, and he'd been going there to spend time with her."

"No." Ruth's memories of Leslie were crystal clear. The woman had been a bear. She'd shouted at their legal team. She'd stared down the judge as she listed exactly what protections Ruth needed. She'd thrown her phone at the wall after spending three hours bouncing through government departments trying to untangle Ruth's situation, and then she'd picked up her phone again and made another call.

She'd never been loving or sweet or gentle, but she'd fought for Ruth like she was fighting for her own child.

Ruth's last contact with her had been at age sixteen, when she was placed with her final foster family. Leslie had seemed a little smaller and a little less brash, but Ruth believed that was only because she herself had grown bigger.

"She wasn't really there," Carson said. "She didn't know who Zach was, but he just kept telling her he was her friend, and she seemed to accept that. The doctors and nurses too. They all knew him, and they seemed happy he visited. Zach's good at making people like him."

"He didn't…" Ruth let her voice fade out, afraid to ask.

"At first he just chatted with her, gave her some snacks, told her stories." Carson grimaced. "But after about ten minutes, he started pressuring her for your name. Not, like, really bad. It was stuff like, *Hey, remember that child from Petition? What happened to her, again?*"

No.

"She wasn't all there, but I don't think she was fully gone either. She went very quiet when Zach started fishing and became kind of suspicious, like she knew that was something she shouldn't talk about."

Ruth clenched her hands on top of her knees. Leslie, the guard dog.

Fierce, protective. Left without anyone to protect *her* when she most needed it.

"We spent about an hour there," Carson said. "Zach toed the line the whole time. When Leslie started to get agitated, he'd back off and talk about nice things again. And when she calmed, he'd try another angle." He paused. "That was the only time he brought me along. I think he was hoping that having two people in the room would put more pressure on her. But he kept going back after that. I don't know how many times."

Ruth had squeezed her hands so hard that they started to shake.

Hayleigh said, "Zach did other things too. Things he didn't even tell us about until later. He found the court transcriber who'd worked on the inquest and called their home. And he'd pretend to be a lawyer or say he was law enforcement to try to get the records."

"I don't think he knew how bad it looked," Carson said. "Because he talked about the stuff he was doing on his podcast. I didn't listen—I didn't want to hear any of it—but he must have shared a lot."

Hayleigh added, "The podcast wasn't *big*, but it started getting more attention."

"And then someone sent an email." Carson's heavy shoulders hunched. "Don't know who. But it seemed like someone powerful. Zach showed it to me to get my advice. They said they were giving him one chance to do the right thing, and if he didn't, they would report him to the police. I don't think it was an empty threat, because they included a list of exactly what crimes he could be charged under, with the codes and everything."

"Impersonation of a government employee, elder abuse, coercion." Hayleigh swallowed. "He quit the podcast. He deleted the whole year's worth of episodes and deactivated the social accounts connected to it."

"We thought that was it," Carson added. "He said he was done. And I mostly believed him. But...sometimes, when we were talking about our weeks, he'd mention that he was visiting a friend. He never said who. And even though he'd given up on the podcast...I think he was still going to see that caseworker. I think he was still trying to find the Petition Child."

Carson looked at Ruth, seeming to really, fully take her in, and suddenly the anger was gone and all that was left was exhaustion.

"Guess that was true."

"I'm really sorry." Hayleigh squirmed again, her knees rubbing together. "We didn't know what to do after he told us. And we didn't know how you'd react."

She didn't know either.

The fire inside Ruth was no longer the raging inferno of destruction.

Everything had burned down during Carson's story. Every structure, every safeguard, every hope for her future. It was gone, crumbled, and now the flames simmered over the coals.

But coals were the hottest part of the fire. So hot, Ruth could barely stand them.

A key scraped into the cabin lock. Turned.

Carson and Hayleigh jolted to their feet, stepping back from the door, alarm on their faces.

Ruth stayed where she was, sat on the edge of her bed, her coals all-consuming as Zach stepped into the room.

33.

The door let in a flood of dying daylight around Zach's shoulders. He paused, halfway inside, taking in the group.

"Hey," he said, eyes flicking from Ruth to Carson. "I've been looking for you, buddy. You're not answering your phone."

"Oh." Carson offered no excuse. No explanation. Just that single word.

Hayleigh had gone very still. Her eyes were fixed on the floor. A deer in headlights.

She hadn't reacted that way around Carson, Ruth realized. Not even when anger had pulsed through him.

She only froze when Zach was involved.

"Everything okay?" His eyes were back on Ruth. He seemed to be holding himself very carefully. "The atmosphere in here is giving me a weird feeling. Carson, I came to apologize."

Ruth stared up at him, and she saw a face that she'd loved. His thick eyebrows. His nose. The warmth in his smile. She'd adored them. She watched as those feelings plunged into the coals, consumed by a heat so immense that they barely had time to fizzle and spark before they were gone.

She kept her gaze on him as she asked, "It wasn't an accident that you opened that letter about the inquest, was it?"

There was a flicker of shock in his expression. Shock, and guilt, and... grief. The same emotion she'd caught just before he'd sworn that he'd never shared her secret with anyone.

"You must have been waiting for something like it," she continued, not giving him a chance to collect himself. "You must have been searching the mail every day, looking for anything that would link me to Petition. It took months. You must have been so happy when it arrived. When you finally had an excuse to ask about it."

A shaky laugh stuttered, and then faded. "Ruth. I think…I think there's been a mistake…"

She waited. A small faint, pathetic part of her still hoped he might be able to fix it all. Explain it all. But even though his mouth was open, even though his lips made twitching movements, no sound came out. And he glanced at Carson, and that tiny hope died, plunging into the coals along with everything else.

He didn't have any answers.

He was trying to guess how much of the truth Carson had given away.

Ruth stood. She moved carefully, as though controlling her body for the first time. Everything hurt.

"Ruth." Zach swallowed. "I know you don't want to hear this right now. But I never meant to hurt you."

He was blocking the doorway. Ruth swayed as she crossed the room. She stopped, just inches from him, close enough to feel the warmth from his body.

And she gazed up at him, at his panicky, searching eyes. And she spat, with every ounce of hatred and fury, "*You snake.*"

Then she shoved past him. Her strides lengthened. She was moving, rushing, as she crossed between the scattered cabins and turned toward the jungle.

Behind her, Zach swore. His footsteps pounded on the compact dirt as he gave chase.

"Ruth!"

Her throat felt as though she'd swallowed knives. Her insides ached. She didn't shift her eyes from the distant trees.

"Ruth, damn it! Stop a moment." He'd nearly caught up. "I love you."

He'd never said those words before. She hated him even more for using them in that moment.

"No. Ruth. Stop and talk to me a moment." He jogged alongside her, one arm reached out, trying to get her to slow. "I shouldn't have kept secrets. I was wrong for that. But I swear I never meant to hurt you."

She ground to a halt and stared at him. He was breathing heavily.

"What secrets did you keep?" she asked. "I want to hear them from you. Every single one. What secrets?"

His tongue darted over his lips. She could see his mind racing. He didn't know how much Carson had told her; he was trying to judge what he could get away with.

She forged on toward the jungle.

"Ruth!"

He grabbed her wrist.

She saw red. She swung, her fingers digging into the soft flesh on the inside of his forearm. He winced, but he didn't let go.

"I was never bothered by your past," he said, the words fast and sharp. "You were right the other day. A lot of people would look at you differently if they knew. But I never did. It never upset me. I didn't care."

"No." She squeezed harder, her nails digging into him, and was finally able to break free as his hand spasmed. "Not being upset and not caring are two different things. You cared. So, so much."

"Is that a crime?" His panic was turning to anger. Guests who had been trailing along the path or sitting outside their cabins stopped to stare at them. "If anyone tells you they *don't* care about what happened back then, they're lying. That's just your reality, Ruth. I'm sorry. I know you don't like it. But it's your reality, and it always will be."

She leaned toward him, closing the gap, so she could whisper words only he would hear.

"I had a sighting today."

There was a small rush of breath through his parted lips. So subtle, she wouldn't have noticed if she hadn't been watching.

"In that sighting, you were dead, Zach. Your body was broken, and your blood had drained into the water." She leaned even closer, so close that their breaths were intermingling. "I hope it comes true."

Then she turned and crossed into the trees.

"Ruth!" He stood at the edge of the village, his arms spread out, as he shouted. "I'm on your team! I have been, always, from the very beginning! Don't sacrifice that just because you're hurt."

The shadows swallowed her, but they weren't enough to block out his final words.

"You're not going to find many allies in this world."

Petra tapped out rapid-fire messages on her pad as she walked, calling for an urgent meeting with the staff management team. She'd need to inform them that a guest had passed away and begin preparations for everything that entailed.

Simultaneously, she sent out a message to the full team that all nonessential trails were to be restricted. Guests would be allowed in the village and Sunset Beach, and they could traverse the path that connected the two, but every other route had to be cordoned off. A staff member was to stand at each entrance, making sure no one tried to slip past the ropes.

They couldn't afford to let guests wander unsupervised any longer. At best, it could be considered negligence. And she didn't need any unsuspecting festivalgoers stumbling on the body before it could be retrieved.

Somewhere, in the midst of all that, she would need to broach the topic of the guest verification spreadsheet to her management team. Heather had overseen it, and Heather would have the most insight into what part of the process could have gone wrong.

Because something had gone *very* wrong. Every guest and every member of staff had been checked and marked against the ocean liner's manifesto.

There were two possible explanations. Either the woman in the water had never been on their list to begin with—something that shouldn't have been physically possible—or someone had gone out of their way to falsely mark her as present.

Petra didn't know which would be worse.

"You'll have to control the crowd," she said. "I'd recommend not saying anything about the deceased guest; we need time to retrieve the body and notify next of kin. There'll likely be a postmortem, and we might be advised not to make public announcements until after that."

Eton walked beside her. They were moving fast, and they were both breathing hard. His eyes were fixed ahead, but he nodded, showing he was listening.

"Guests might get unruly once they realize they're being restricted for the second time today. You've got to defuse that the best you can."

"I can do the trivia game," Eton said. "Like you suggested earlier. It was scheduled for tomorrow, but it won't be much work to move it up. I can stretch it to fill the rest of the night. They'll be ready for bed by the time I'm done."

"Good. Excellent. We'll do that."

The trivia event—where guests could win prizes by identifying jokes and props from Eton's videos—would be a crowd-pleaser.

"I'll tell the bar staff to start cutting guests off if they seem intoxicated." Eton scratched fingers through his hair as he ran through his own list. "And before trivia, I'll announce that the witch's grave has been found. I'll say the winner wanted to remain anonymous. But I'll also tell everyone to stay close by, because I'm about to announce a new game with a huge prize. That should, I hope, cut down the temptation to wander."

"I like that. Any plans for what the new game will be?"

"No idea yet. It can be anything, even something silly, as long as the prize is big. Best sandcastle wins a million dollars. We'll figure it out; right now, we just need to give them something to look forward to so they're not upset about the grave. Unhappy guests make bad decisions."

For that moment, they felt like a team again, no longer frustrating one another but working in tandem to resolve a crisis.

Petra just wished it hadn't been tainted. Because she doubted Eton would have been so determined to help, so eagerly proactive, if he wasn't trying to win back her favor.

They entered the village. The staff center was on its other side, just a few minutes away. They could raise the alert about the body from the communications hub and begin to fix things before they spiraled any further.

"Pet?"

Eton touched her arm, and Petra had to repress a shiver at the contact. He wasn't watching her, though. He was staring across the clearing.

A crowd had gathered near one of the cabins.

This wasn't the type of cluster that formed around a musician or a VIP guest who'd offered to put on a performance. This group's energy was hushed and urgent. Unhappy.

Yellow shirts were visible at the edge. They were speaking to guests as they made pacifying hand motions.

The staff had instructions to notify Petra about any guest discontentment. They'd update her on whatever this situation was as soon as they had the chance.

Petra glanced at her digital pad. Her messages to the team were on her screen, but there were no responses. That was unusual. Even the low-priority tasks accumulated a string of received replies within seconds.

In fact, she'd had absolutely no incoming communication in nearly twenty minutes.

She looked back at the crowd. Several girls were huddled together, crying.

Something wasn't right.

"Quick," she said to Eton, striking across the clearing.

"Oh my gosh, I'm so glad you're here," one of the staff said as she saw Petra. She looked exhausted; her hair was in a ponytail, but strands had come loose and frizzed around her face. "I have no idea what I'm supposed to do."

Petra didn't stop. There was a clear center to the scene: a nexus that held the guests transfixed.

A cabin, its door open.

"Is this part of a game?" a man asked. His voice wavered, somewhere between distress and outrage. "You could have given us a warning."

Petra pushed past him and climbed onto the porch. The open door invited her in, the room beyond dim and cool. Something large was positioned in the room's center.

The wood creaked as Eton climbed up behind her. Petra took another step forward. The cabin's peaked roof blocked the dying light and made it possible to take in the shadowed scene.

An upright suitcase hung open.

And a body spilled halfway out of it.

Its bloodstained arm was extended, fingers trailing over the wood floor. A face loomed out of the gap in the seam. Lines of red crisscrossed the pale skin, like roads across a map, showing where her blood had flowed.

The eyes stared downward, the lips slightly parted, jaw loose.

Petra held a hand over her mouth.

"Oh," Eton whispered, and he made a choking noise as he turned away. "What—what is—how—"

"I know her." Petra forced the words out as every nerve in her body turned cold. "I know that girl. That's Lisa."

34.

Ruth ran.

She didn't follow a path. She didn't have a goal.

She just needed to move.

Her mind kept churning up desperate options. *We could beg Eton to make his team sign NDAs. We could break into the equipment rooms and destroy the footage. We could negotiate with Zach...*

She recognized what was happening. She was in the bargaining stage of grief.

No amount of begging or coercion or bribery could keep this contained. There were too many parties involved. Too many disconnected people with differing motivations.

For all she knew, it might have already spread beyond Prosperity Island. She hadn't been online to check.

With containment out of the question, her only option left was acceptance. And she wasn't even close to ready for that.

So she ran.

He swore he would keep my secret.

And he'd sold her out. In exchange for four tickets to an island festival.

Did the promise mean anything *to him? It must have. Surely, he'd meant it when he made it, or he would have told people sooner.*

But...was she sure about that?

Zach was smart, thoughtful, strategic. He'd anticipated Eton's games well ahead of time. His plan had gotten them fifth place in the hunt.

An impulsive person might have exposed Ruth on day one. Tabloids and newspapers would have paid him for his story. He might even have been able to get a book deal out of it.

But Zach had always played the long game, in every part of his life.

If what Carson said was true, Zach had spent months visiting Leslie to pry the truth out of her.

And then he'd spent further months dating Ruth, growing closer to her, moving in with her. He'd waited patiently for a letter that let him pretend he'd discovered her past by accident.

She pushed herself, lengthening her strides, even though the ground was leading upward.

If Zach was always playing the long game, then what *was* his goal? What had he been steering them toward?

It only took her a moment to find the answer.

He hadn't sought Ruth out for fame. He didn't care about the money he could get for interviews.

He wanted to know about Petition.

The truth. All of it.

A lot of details had been revealed to the public, but there were still large swaths, especially from the final day, that the courts had kept sealed.

She'd watched true crime enthusiasts squirm with curiosity over what had really happened. She'd heard the wild speculations, driven by the need to understand.

Ruth was the only survivor. The one witness.

The only person who could fully answer every question.

That was what Zach wanted from her. What he'd been trying to get.

And he'd been oh-so gentle about it.

Because he knew, Ruth was sure. He knew that if she'd sensed even a hint of morbid curiosity, she would have clammed up and never relaxed around him again.

So he'd stroked her hair after the nightmares, but never asked what was in them. He'd let her speak about Petition when she wanted to, but he kept the follow-up questions minimal.

He worked on building her trust. Making her feel secure, safe.

He wanted her to give her story voluntarily.

The ultimate gift.

But then…Eton's festival had been announced.

And Zach, the man who always had a strategy, was tempted so deeply that he sacrificed all of his work to get a ticket.

No. That didn't ring true.

That wasn't Zach.

So why?

Because, Ruth realized, it had been a strategic play.

She'd given Zach almost nothing over the months they'd been together. And Eton's festival had appeared as a rare opportunity to quicken the process.

So he'd given away her identity in the comments field of the submission form.

There was a chance that they weren't even being read, and it would remain buried in the pile of unselected entries.

But if they won, then Zach could force Ruth's secret out in a way that hid his involvement. It was the twenty-year anniversary of Petition. They were on an island surrounded by social media personalities, including several who focused on true crime.

If rumors began to spread about Ruth…

Ruth would believe she'd slipped up somewhere. Said the wrong thing to the wrong person while Petition was at the front of everyone's minds.

And, as the truth rushed out, Zach would be there to support her, to shield her, to fight off anyone who invaded her space. He would be the one person she could trust.

Ruth would tell him everything then. It would be a relief to have someone she could be that close to, someone who could share the burden.

And that was exactly what would have happened.

Except Zach had made one very small mistake. He'd told his friends.

They'd been together for so long. They listened when he gave instructions. They didn't argue or question him because, if Hayleigh's frozen stare was anything to go by, they'd learned *not* to.

He hadn't realized how close they were to snapping.

Ruth staggered to a halt, her lungs strained and her body shaking. She was somewhere near the peak's eastern side. Its shadow covered her, but she wasn't cold.

She didn't think she would ever be cold again, not with the heat burning her up from the inside.

Her hands hit the soft dirt as she dropped to her knees.

She'd tried to escape Petition.

She'd guarded her secrets, hidden her scars, severed any ties to her past.

All that effort had only been enough to delay it.

Petition had come to claim her at last.

Ruth screamed.

Burning tears trailed down her face. Her fingers pressed into the dirt as she wailed and ached and shrieked. She poured her anger and her pain into the damp earth until she had nothing left. And then, shivering, her ears ringing, she slumped onto her side.

Ruth stared up at the canopy. Time flowed strangely, and she didn't try to fight it. Small insects crept over her limbs. Leaves fell around her, one settling onto her shirt.

Dusk began to change the world from vivid green to gray. She didn't want to ever move again.

The jungle sounds seemed magnified. Leaf against leaf, branch against branch. Insects chewed. Small birds called, delicate wings flittering.

And then a new noise joined the others.

Ruth felt its presence the moment it started. A slow, uneasy emotion passed through her. She couldn't identify what caused the sound, or where it came from.

It was like...a heartbeat.

Rhythmic, steady.

But not comforting.

And it didn't feel like it belonged on the island. Not like the birds, not like the insects. The new sound seemed wrong, somehow. Unkind.

Ruth, aching, sat up. Her eyes were blurred from how hard she'd cried. She turned, trying to pinpoint the noise, and it took her a moment to realize why that was so difficult.

There were two of them.

One coming from straight ahead. One to her right. They overlapped, blending together.

And they seemed to be growing closer.

Louder.

Building with each repetition.

Plants crowded around her in every direction. The low light made it hard to see.

No animal or bird could call like that. It wasn't mechanical. The sounds felt jagged, unnatural.

A third repetition set up. This time from behind. And as Ruth turned toward it, she was finally able to identify it.

Chanting.

Her skin rose into gooseflesh. The voices barely sounded human. Single syllables snapped out from between teeth, sharp and hoarse and building.

It's one of the games.

They would have announced it at dinner. Maybe it was a puzzle where guests were supposed to decipher scrambled words. Or maybe they were role-playing a Secret Door Movement ritual.

Whatever the theme, Ruth wanted nothing to do with it.

The voices were converging toward her, though. There were five of them now, and it was becoming hard to keep track as the chants overlapped.

She'd have to move before they saw her and tried to rope her in. Ruth got to her feet, every muscle aching. It felt deeply unfair that the game was set on the one small part of the island where she'd taken refuge.

An uneasy, crawling sensation prickled through her.

The earlier games had been centered on the beaches, where Eton and his staff could easily oversee the activities. This part of the jungle was too dense, too dark. Nowhere close to their accommodations. No clear, wide paths leading to it.

It was a strange place to have a game.

And where were the guests?

There were no other voices. No laughter or shouts.

The chanting continued to build. If they were speaking words, it was nothing Ruth could recognize. She could no longer tell how many of them there were.

A spit of rain broke through the canopy and hit her cheek.

She turned, slowly, the tip of her tongue between her teeth. She needed to get out of there, but she didn't know which way to move.

The voices had formed a circle. With Ruth at the center.

Growing louder. Closer. Rising syllables and hard, snapping consonants. Aggressive. Angry.

Breath caught in Ruth's throat. Through the hazy dusk, through the blur of foliage, she saw skin.

Eyes caught the dull light, round and fixated on Ruth.

Unblinking.

Panic thumped with every pulse of her heart, but a part of her still wanted it to be a game, a joke, a prank.

A man was moving closer. Leaves dragged across bare skin as he pressed through them. She saw ribs and knees and hip bones and pubic hair.

Not a game. Not any kind of entertainment that had been promised at the festival.

His jaw moved, rigid, as he spat out the stream of jagged sounds. Unblinking, rounded eyes seemed to bore into her soul.

Ruth shifted back, her hands rising.

Movement to her left. A second figure, creeping out from between the trees.

Her hair hung shaggy around her face. Her breasts and stomach quivered with each frantic chant.

Ripples of light caught on metal as she twisted something in her hand.

A hook the size of Ruth's head. The kind butchers used to hoist up slabs of meat for storage.

Voices came from every direction. So close and so loud that she could no longer hear her own thoughts.

Another spit of rain hit Ruth's arm. The drop was heavy, hard. Promising not just a sprinkle, but a downpour.

Ruth dragged a shuddering breath into tight lungs.

And she found there was still something of the girl from Petition living in her.

The girl who did not want to die.

The girl who would crawl, the girl who would scramble, the girl who would do whatever it took to survive.

The stranger lifted the hook, and fading light snapped over the metal like a ghost.

Ruth bolted.

A bare arm reached out to snatch at her. She ducked it. Bodies moved in, their eyes staring, their hands reaching.

Ruth skidded, scrambling. Fingers grazed through her hair as she leaped through them.

Out through the net of strangers that had been tightening around her. Past them and into the jungle.

The chanting hit a crescendo, then cut into silence.

And in that silence, Ruth heard their bare feet pounding over the ground as they gave chase.

"Get the guests away from here," Petra yelled, pointing at each of the four visible staff members to make sure she had their attention. "All of you, get them moved back to Sunset Beach and set a perimeter around this cabin. No one goes near it. No one goes *into* it. Understand?"

They stared at her for a second, their eyes large and frightened, and then her words seemed to register and they broke into action. It was fumbled and confused; they grabbed at guests and tried to physically turn them away from the cabin, stammering instructions. But at least it was something.

Petra stood on the edge of the cabin's porch, her back to the scene.

Two bodies. Two deaths.

At least one of them violent.

Her mind shrank away from the word *murder*, and she hated herself for it. Petra was not an impractical person. She knew what she was looking at.

Behind her, Eton still stood in the doorway, facing into the cabin. He didn't seem able to move. His breathing whistled, tinged with panic.

"Is anyone's phone working?" a woman yelled.

Many of the crowd had their mobiles out. Some were texting, some were trying to make calls.

They wanted to contact the people they'd arrived with, or maybe call family at home.

Petra's focus moved from figure to figure. Some guests held their phones straight up to the sky, straining to see the screens.

She looked at her own digital pad. Twenty-five minutes with no messages.

Petra swore.

"Eton, we need to find the team leaders." She grabbed his arm, tugged him away from the corpse in the luggage. "This is urgent."

Two bodies.

A spreadsheet that said everyone was accounted for.

Communications cutting out right when she most needed them.

She was not enough of a fool to believe those things were unrelated.

Which meant...

Her mind balked at the idea, but she forced herself to face it anyway, because it was her *job* to face the ugly stuff.

Someone on the island was dangerous.

They appeared to be planning their attacks. Not spur-of-the-moment violence, but calculated moves.

And, when the spreadsheet was taken into consideration, that person was most likely one of the staff.

Petra shot glances at the four harried employees as she passed them. They were young, barely more than teenagers, and they seemed confused and distressed as they tried to make the crowd listen.

She didn't know anything about them. Almost the entire staff team had been brought on mere weeks before the festival. The people Petra genuinely knew and trusted could be counted on the fingers of one hand.

She didn't like the idea of leaving *any* staff member to watch over a cabin that was now a crime scene, but she didn't have much choice.

Eton couldn't stay. He staggered in her wake, his breathing still panicked, his eyes wide but not seeing much.

It was Eton's island. Eton's festival. Eton's guest list. Eton's employees.

He was the obvious target. The most at-risk of any of them.

Petra couldn't let him out of her sight.

She dragged him through the jungle, no longer walking but running. They broke into the staff clearing. Petra stopped short, still holding on to Eton's arm.

The area had never seen a quiet moment since they'd arrived.

It was where the bulk of their supplies were stored; it held the staff accommodations, the medical clinic, the communications hub. Even in the middle of the night, there were always at least a few of the team moving through it.

Now, it was deserted.

35.

Petra's tongue darted out to wet her lips. Lights were on in multiple buildings, but there was no sign of movement through the narrow windows.

It felt like a ghost town.

Maybe they're scattered over the island, trying to solve problems. Working on the communications system or blocking off the paths like I asked. Trying to fix things in my absence.

She was losing her emotional detachment. She couldn't tell if those thoughts were pragmatic or born from desperation.

Cold drops of rain hit her back, her hair. The promised evening shower.

Petra moved quickly, even though her instincts were yelling at her to slow down, back away, get out of there.

"Pet?" Eton was twisting as he watched the buildings around them.

She approached the medical clinic. No light came from beneath its doors. Someone had taken chains and looped them through the door handles, locking it.

Petra beat her fist on the metal doors. She didn't receive a response. She kept moving.

The communications room was at the clearing's opposite end. Its door hung open. Lights danced across the metal, dull and flickering, like the glow from a television.

Petra used her foot to shove on the door, nudging it inward until it hit the wall.

Papers were strewn across the floor. The room had felt bright every other time she'd been there, but now it had a sickly pall. The light bulbs in the ceiling had been broken; glass shards glittered across the floor.

Even in the dying afternoon, the air in the communications room felt humid and heavy. Pressurized from the pending rain.

The systems were still running. Five screens glowed, providing the room's only light.

Chairs had been pulled out from the desks. A coffee mug lay on its side. As Petra watched, a drop of spilled liquid fell from the edge of the desk, landing on damp papers on the floor.

The people working there had left fast.

And they'd left very recently.

"Pet," Eton whispered.

He was staring at the wall next to the door. A red handprint pressed into the metal, then smeared away.

"Pet," he said again. "I think we need to get back to the beach."

"Thirty seconds," she whispered.

Their main internet coverage for the festival came from a specially built receiving tower. It handled not only traffic from the guests, but also the staff's private network. The system was well beyond Petra's abilities to fix.

But they had a backup.

Two satellite phones had been packed into their equipment.

Those phones didn't rely on a network or modem. They only needed clear access to the sky to make a call.

Petra crossed quickly and quietly to the metal cabinet on the far wall. Her key scraped as it turned in the lock. She wrenched the doors open and stared down at the space on the lower shelf.

The empty space, where the satellite phones and their waterproof box belonged.

The growing sense of danger, of vulnerability, crawled up her throat. Only a few people on her team had keys to the cabinet. Most of the staff didn't even know the phones existed.

Petra turned. Eton stood in the center of the room, his arms wrapped around his chest as the screens washed him out into a pale, distorted version of himself. He was staring at the row of monitors.

Feeds from the temporary security cameras played.

Petra crept closer, straining to make out scenes. The cameras had been designed for up-close interviews in well-lit rooms; that translated poorly to a broad-view security feed at dusk. The images were muddy from lack of contrast.

She saw the angle overlooking the staff camp. Empty paths, lifeless buildings. Only the wind catching in the branches gave any evidence that the feed was live.

At the village, the staff seemed to have gotten a perimeter around the cabin that held Lisa. Guests still moved about, some trying their phones, one even climbing onto a cabin roof to reach his mobile up to the sky.

The feed for Sunset Beach was alive with activity. Guests milled about, carrying drinks and food. Word hadn't reached them yet.

Then, at the edge of the screen, a row of figures moved into view. Their yellow shirts were tinted a shade of brown in the dying light.

Petra leaned closer, resting a hand on the desk's clutter.

The crawling panic was beginning to choke her.

On-screen, a procession walked onto the beach. At least twenty forms. Most of the figures bore torches, held high, to light their way. Several carried tall upright objects covered with cloths.

Guests parted for them, some clapping, some craning to see the objects. They thought it was the start of a new game. Of course, they would—an Eton festival wouldn't be complete without evening entertainment.

Petra was still scrambling to make sense of it all, to reel it back into some kind of rational explanation. She couldn't find one. But she knew, with horrible certainty, that the longer she hesitated, the worse it was going to get.

"We need to get down there," Petra said.

Eton's eyes were glassy in the screens' light, his pupils constricted. He gave a very small nod.

As Petra moved, two tiny pieces of shiny metal on the desk caught her eye.

Earrings. Familiar.

They were Heather's. And the studs were stained with dried blood.

Leaves slapped across Ruth's skin as she ran.

Footsteps beat into the earth behind her. Chants, thick and guttural, rose in staccato bursts.

Her lungs were empty. Her body ached.

She couldn't stop picturing Gilly, her flesh pierced through, her eyes frenzied as they searched the depths of the jungle.

If Ruth could get to the village, she could get help.

But the village was to her back, and the figures pursuing her weren't allowing Ruth any room to turn around.

Her mind clawed for options. She had a lead but only a slim one. Not enough for her to hide in any effective way. Not enough to lose them between the trees.

Ruth's foot snagged on a low branch. She fell, hitting the ground hard, dirt grinding into her palms and elbows, but she was back on her feet and moving again before she could even feel the pain.

She needed to live.

And to live, she had to run.

She couldn't get back to the village. But if she veered slightly left, her route would carry her to Endurance Cove.

Both of the previous games had taken place at the beach. She held out a slim hope that there might be staff there, working on preparations for some future activity.

No guarantees. But it was a better chance than she'd have if she kept running deeper into the island.

Ruth adjusted her trajectory. Tacky froth gummed around her lips. A cramp was bleeding across her abdomen.

The chanting voices sounded closer, louder. Excited.

But the ground was leading down. The air was growing cooler. Ruth blinked through tears as she burst from the jungle and onto sand.

The remnants from the collapsed shipwreck house had been cleared off the beach. Only sparsely scattered debris betrayed that it had ever been there in the first place. To the side, Eton's observation tower stretched high.

Ahead, the raised platforms looked like the skeleton of a great beast, silhouetted against an aching and bruised sunset.

The beach was barren of life. No staff, no guests, no one to see Ruth as she staggered down the sandy slope.

The chanting had fallen silent.

Ruth took a chance and turned.

Four figures stood at the edge of the jungle.

Two men, two women. Naked. Their chests rose in heaving gasps.

They carried weapons.

A spear, long and thin and whittled at one end. A massive butcher's hook.

An object that looked like a machete—metal, ground down to have a sharpened edge, fabric wrapped around one end to create a handle.

A slab of wood, nails driven through its end so that a dozen sharpened points protruded.

They stared down at her. Their bodies rocked with each breath, but their faces were unmoving.

One of them already had splatters of red blood across his bare torso, and Ruth didn't let herself question where it had come from.

She stared up at them as they stared back. Twenty feet of bare sand stretched between them. Thick drops of rain hit Ruth's back.

They lurched forward, breaking into a sprint.

And Ruth was forced to race for the one option she had left.

The ocean.

36.

Don't leave the beach.

Joel hadn't said much, and pulling information from the man was near impossible.

I think they want you next.

That was the last phrase Joel had uttered before clamming up. But he'd stared, trying to convey sincerity without words, and his eyes had been haunted, frightened pits.

Logan, his phone full of photos he didn't understand, could have been persuaded with much less.

A procession of staff emerged from the jungle path. It wasn't quite dark, but they carried torches made with raw ingredients: cloths wrapped around wood batons. The scent of burning gasoline floated across the crowd.

"Looks like the entertainment's started," Brent said.

The Camping Quest team had made uncomfortable small talk when Joel brought Logan back to the group, but they shared precious little common ground.

Logan had watched a couple of Camping Quest videos. The hosts were excitable, eager, friendly. They had cartoonishly exaggerated reactions whenever things went wrong: screaming when water got into their tents, shouting as the car became bogged. But, all the while, maintaining a sense of camaraderie and joy that classified them as a "comfort watch." It wasn't really his scene.

Logan suspected their exposure to him was similarly limited. They hadn't needed an introduction to know his name, but their familiarity likely didn't extend beyond his reputation for killing careers.

Which helped explain why the small talk was so stilted.

Logan didn't care. He was just grateful to have a group to stand with.

The staff's procession continued down the beach. Five of them held tall posts. Heavy cloths had been draped over them, covering objects, and tied to the poles with ropes. Still more carried cloth bundles in their arms, as though nursing babies.

"What do we think it is?" Mitchell asked. "Hopefully, nothing that involves running. I overdid dinner."

Mitchell was the one who, at least in the videos, was most likely to goof off and have a fun time. Brent was the planner, the logistics person.

The third host was the support, setting the others up and laughing at every joke. Logan had no idea what his name was.

Joel hung behind them, silent. But not calm.

His breathing was fast, shallow.

Terrified.

"Joel?" Logan tilted just far enough to see the man without losing sight of the procession. "Do you know what this is?"

Joel's thin beard shifted as he swallowed. He seemed to be fighting to put words together, but no sound escaped.

"He's been kind of off today," Brent said, motioning with one hand. "Don't worry. He'll feel better after some sleep."

The procession stopped near the shore and turned to face the crowd, standing in a rigid line. The staff was all beaming, heads tall, proud to be part of the show.

It was odd that Eton wasn't leading them.

No sign of him near the stage either.

He'd been missing all afternoon, a fact that hadn't escaped Logan.

It was hard to imagine Eton green-lighting a game without being able to oversee it. He took too much vicarious delight in watching players compete.

"Hey, I want a closer look," Brent said.

The crowd was shuffling toward the staff, forming a loose circle around them. The Camping Quest hosts joined in.

Logan just barely caught Joel's gesture. A small grasping motion, as though he wanted to grab them all and pull them back.

He knew something.

And Logan's sense of unease, his sense of discomfort, was screaming at him to listen.

"Can you tell me what happened?" Logan dipped his voice into a whisper.

Joel's tongue made wet sounds as he fought with it. His breathing was still too fast, too thin. Logan leaned toward him and lowered his voice even further.

"I want to know."

"No one…" Joel swallowed again, his beard quivering. The words were like ghosts, thinner than air. "Believed…before."

Before. The body at the base of the cliffs.

"I believe you," Logan said.

The staff holding the posts stabbed their bases into the sand, grinding them in so they would stand on their own.

"They were…picking people," Joel managed. Each word seemed to cost him dearly. "I saw it. Couldn't…tell anyone. I didn't know how to… make people believe."

"Couldn't tell anyone *what*?" Logan took Joel's arm, not tearing his eyes off the staff as they impaled their torches into the beach, creating a ring of light around the taller posts. "What did you see?"

Joel shook his head in quick, panicked flicks.

The crowd was murmuring, shuffling. Growing hungry.

Most of the staff paced backward, leaving the ring of lights. Five stayed, one by each post. They undid the ropes tying the cloth in place.

"What did you *see*?" Logan pressed, but Joel was shrinking back into himself.

The five staff each reached up a hand. Took hold of a corner of the cloth. And then they pulled, dragging the fabric away, unveiling the shapes underneath.

Ruth's shoes snagged in the sand. She couldn't afford the few seconds it would cost her to take them off.

She pushed herself hard, aiming for the raised platforms.

Guttural, excited noises burst out of the four pursuing figures. She heard the whisk of metal swooping through air. They were barefoot. Faster.

Ruth reached for the nearest ladder. Grasped the rungs. Hauled herself up.

She'd had her turn on the platforms the previous day. She knew how to balance on them; she knew their layout. She hoped it might give her an advantage, even a small one.

The sounds rose into eager shouts. They were delighted with Ruth's choice.

She didn't stop to think, didn't stop to check how close they were. She just threw herself upward, grasping for the raised beams, lifting her legs out of reach as fast she could.

Over the top of the ladder. Onto the platform. She staggered as she tried to find her feet. She needed to rest. She needed to *breathe*. But that would kill her.

The wood vibrated. The others had started to climb.

Ruth stepped off the platform and onto one of the boards.

She'd been cautious the first time she'd played the game. She'd picked her routes carefully, moved slowly.

But that was when money had been on the line. This time, she was gambling for *everything*.

She fixed her eyes on the beam as she ran. She couldn't look to see how far away the ground was; she couldn't check on the others' progress. If she wanted to keep her balance, she had to fix her eyes on her feet and nowhere else.

She could feel the others through the wood; it shivered with every pounding step. Someone had started to laugh, and it was a ragged, angry, gasping noise.

Ruth passed one of the token boxes. Her memory of the maze was hazy in places, but she could visualize most of it. She knew which paths to take to avoid dead ends, how to get across to the other side.

And, she thought, the others knew the maze too. She could feel the vibrations spreading out. They weren't following her in a line but were choosing different routes. Trying to get ahead of her. Trying to cut her off.

She pushed herself faster. Her foot threatened to slip off the side of the board; she recovered at the last second, arms spinning.

Past another token box. The sand beneath gave way to ocean, tinged red as the sunset began to fade. She was impossibly high above it.

The laughter was growing closer. Their balance was good; they could have bested any of the game's players.

But she was nearly there. Ruth took a corner, staggering, and then faced the horizon.

She'd been shown where to go.

In her sighting.

She'd seen herself racing along this very wood beam, its color distorted by the sunset.

And she knew what she had to do when she reached its end.

The path was straight. Ruth lengthened her strides. She was running toward the section that had broken. Toward the spot where she'd stood and watched Makayla fight against the waves.

The others had converged behind her, their pounding footsteps matching her own.

Ruth ran faster…and faster…and faster.

And then she reached the end of the maze.

And she leaped.

37.

Ripples of noise pulsed out of the beach.

Petra followed the sound, weaving through the jungle, Eton close on her heels.

The industrial lights washed over them as they stepped onto the sand. They were sharp, bright, designed to keep the beach visible and safe through the night.

In the distance, a different kind of light took over. Torches, flickering. The sunset, dying. Organic and earthy and primal.

The crowd had gathered around the newly erected display. They moved like a current, some flowing forward, others flowing back, churning.

And the sounds they made…

There was laughter. Some of it shocked, some of it genuine. One man was shouting. And underneath, the low murmur of a hundred voices whispering all at once.

Petra pushed forward, into the gathering, trying to get a clear view. She held Eton's sleeve as she moved, afraid of losing him.

Voices pressed in from all sides.

"I don't get it. What is this? Is it a joke?"

"It's not real. Come on. Obviously."

"They didn't even give us any warning."

"First the witch, now this? It's not fun. It's not what I thought we were getting."

Deeper and deeper. Petra held her spare hand out, shoving bodies aside as she forged toward the center.

Guests shouted to Eton as they saw him, trying to ask questions, seeking reassurance. He'd fixed a smile on his face, but it was rigid and unnatural.

One voice rose above the others, unhappy and cracking. "What's the *game*? If we're supposed to be doing something, you need to give us the rules. What's the damn *game*?"

Petra broke through and stepped into the torches' light.

At least twenty staff stood in a line, their backs to the ocean, their faces to the crowd. They had their hands clasped at their waists, their smiles broad and comfortable as they surveyed the guests.

Ahead of them, the torches encircled five tall stakes that had been driven into the sand. The flickering flames lit the display from below, giving it an uncanny sheen.

And on those stakes…

Body parts. On either end, legs, bent at the knee and run through like meat on a skewer. Between those, two arms, arranged similarly, limp fingers hanging toward the sand.

And in the center, a head. The post entered through the neck cavity. Its sharp tip exited the top of the skull. The mouth hung open, pearly teeth and a sliver of wood on display. The whites of the eyes were barely visible beneath heavy lids.

"That—" Eton grabbed Petra's arm, and his fingers dug in hard enough to leave bruises. "Pet, that's—"

She knew.

The face was slack and drained of color. The torches gave it a strange pall. But it was still recognizable.

Ryan Sherman. The content creator who called himself Trigger.

"It's fake, right?" a woman asked.

"Obviously," her friend answered. "It's a game. Don't freak out."

"I don't want this." That came from their other side. A man, disgruntled, repulsed. "No one warned me there'd be a horror theme. I thought we were having a fun week on a tropical island."

"Calm down, it doesn't even look that realistic."

A globule of congealed blood clung to the center pole, oozing from Trigger's neck.

"What're the rules?" someone called. They were looking at Eton. "What are we supposed to be doing?"

He stared at Petra, eyes glassy with fear.

He wanted her to solve this. To take charge. To give him a role, a script. To fix the crisis, the way she'd fixed every one of his crises for the past six years.

But Petra could only stare at the separated limbs, arranged like flags in the sand. Her digital pad was heavy and useless in her satchel. The emergency preparedness briefings had been given to a team she no longer had control over.

Rain came down, not threatening but beginning in earnest, heavy drops that clung to her face.

She felt powerless in a way she'd never, ever experienced before.

One of the staff stepped forward. Her hair was tied back in a ponytail, her yellow uniform clean and crease-free. Her name tag read *Glenda*.

"Anything I can help with, Petra?" she asked, and Petra realized the girl had given her the same question no less than a dozen times over the previous days. Always eager to assist, always excited to learn new skills. She stood next to Trigger's limp arm and beamed at Petra with the same joy she'd had when they crossed paths at breakfast that morning.

"What…?" Petra was aware that the crowd's focus had turned toward her and Eton, waiting for their reassurances, waiting for Eton to break out into giddy laughter and apologize for his prank. She wet her lips, her voice raspy. "What is this?"

"What we've been working on all this time," Glenda said, and her teeth looked too large and too red in the fire's light. "We're very close to the end, so it's fine to share it with you now. It's too late for any of it to be stopped."

Behind them, guests flowed out of the jungle, shepherded by staff. They seemed to be gathering all the attendees onto the beach.

Eton shifted, his grip still painful on Petra's arm. "Hey, Glenda. Things have obviously gone wrong somewhere, but I want you to know I'm here and determined to work with you and everyone else on the staff team. I want to know how I can make things right. Can we have a chat, do you think? Somewhere a bit quieter?"

He still thought that any problem could be solved with a conversation. That it was possible to make the world his friend.

"You know I'd love to chat, sir, anytime!" Glenda unclasped and then refolded her hands. "That sounds like so much fun. Maybe after the game? The guests are expecting it, and I don't want to make them wait any longer."

Whispers were passing through the parts of the crowd that could hear them. Jags of nervous laughter. One woman had started crying.

"Please…" Petra didn't even know what she was begging for. She felt as though she was on a cliff, tilting over the edge, grasping at anything that might stop the plunge.

"Don't feel bad. You haven't done anything wrong." Glenda reached out, palms up, as though offering Petra all the warmth and love in the world. "None of what's about to happen is your fault. I want you to remember that, okay?"

A rush of noise burst across the beach. The stage lights came on in a series of heavy clunks. Static from the microphone infused the air—powerful, inescapable—and the crowd turned toward the noise.

Another row of staff members stood on the stage, their postures perfect, their smiles flawless.

One man stepped toward the microphone. The yellow shirt turned white in the harsh light. His teeth were uneven and large, an inch of red gum visible above them. He dipped his head, a deferential nod, and then rested one hand on the microphone.

"Apologies for the confusion," he said. "Our much-loved host, Eton, is not in a position to make the announcements tonight, so I hope you'll bear with me as I step in to take his place."

Parts of the crowd began to break away from Trigger's remains. They shuffled toward the stage. They wanted this. They wanted someone to take charge, to explain, to defuse the horror.

"Pet," Eton whispered, shaking her slightly. "Pet, what should I do?"

She didn't know.

The staff behind the posts were staring at her, smiling at her. Guests were being drawn toward the stage like moths to a flame.

If she tried to rush the man at the microphone, she'd be stopped. If she tried to lead the guests away, her voice would be drowned out.

Petra was skilled at planning. She was good at crisis management.

But she was only one person.

Petra tugged on Eton's arm, pulling him toward the jungle. The guests were so fixated on the figure onstage that they didn't seem to notice.

The man spread his hands out, bouncing slightly, mimicking the same infectious enthusiasm that Eton radiated. "We do, in fact, have a game for you tonight! And it's a good one!"

Thin, scattered applause answered him.

"Everyone will be able to participate," he said. "It's a beautifully easy game; don't worry. No complex rules to remember, just pure fun. As you can see, we've already given you a pretty big hint about the game's theme!"

He gestured to Trigger's severed limbs.

Rain tapped across Petra's back as she crept across the beach. It was a warm rain. Stifling.

Behind the row of torches and up onstage, the staff began to move. Yellow shirts were tugged over their heads and discarded. They undid the buttons on their pants. Unclasped bras.

The simmering sounds rising out of the crowd swelled. Anxious questions, shocked exclamations. One drunk, raucous cheer that triggered a series of guttural whoops and applause from a band of young men.

The staff stepped out of the last of their clothes. They displayed no embarrassment, nor did they react to the wolf whistles. They simply stood, postures straight, arms at their sides, wearing those awful customer service smiles.

"It's very simple, dear guests," the man at the microphone said. His skin seemed both ghostly white and angry pink under the stage lights. "It's a game of hide-and-seek."

The staff all crouched. Cloth-wrapped parcels had been left on the ground beside them. They rummaged inside and lifted out implements.

Petra saw metal. She saw spikes. She saw rust and sharp edges and hooks.

The man's smile widened as he grazed his lips across the microphone, sending shrieking static across the beach.

"You hide. We seek."

38.

Brine-laced air rushed past Ruth.

Her legs stretched out. Her arms swung.

The foam-flecked ocean was so enormously far below her.

She thought she'd done enough. She'd gotten as much momentum as she could; she'd leaped with every remaining scrap of energy. All with a single goal: to strike down as far from the game board as possible.

The line of volcanic rocks that had chewed up Makayla stretched beneath Ruth.

Past that was open ocean.

It was going to be close. Ruth reached her legs out and took one last gasp of air.

The impact was brutal. It jarred up Ruth's legs and through her back and into her skull. She plunged deep, the ocean closing over her head, blotting out the light.

She could sense that her pursuers had followed her over the game's edge.

They hadn't realized how far she was trying to jump. They hadn't been focusing on the band of rocks. They had leaped after her, eagerly, unhesitatingly, without thinking about where they were trying to land.

Enveloped by the deep ocean, Ruth heard their bones splinter. Heard their screams.

"You hide. We seek."

Clammy chills gripped Logan as he gazed up at Barry. The staff member with the unique teeth, the one he'd recognized on the first day.

"The game will last until dawn," Barry said. He smiled, eyes feverish and bright as he stared down at the crowd. The rain was seeping through his hair, dripping from his chin, but he didn't seem to feel it. "You win by surviving the night. No other rules. No restrictions. You just have to survive until sunrise."

Behind him, the wall of staff held their weapons. Blades, poles, an auger. Most seemed hand-fashioned. And, if Logan wasn't mistaken, they had been built from materials scavenged off the island.

"What the hell," Mitchell whispered. A queasy smile split his face. "What *is* this?"

Behind them, Joel shook his head, his lips pressed together, his eyes glassy as he stared at the sand.

He saw, Logan knew. *He saw them kill Trigger. But who could he tell? Not his teammates; they wouldn't believe him. Not the staff; he didn't know how many of them were involved.*

There was movement near the trails. Eton and Petra, their hosts, vanished into the jungle.

"To keep things fair, you'll all have a head start," Barry said. He bobbed his head, mimicking Eton's bouncing movements. "Three minutes! You'll hear a whistle once time's up, okay? Make the most of it! Three minutes! Your countdown starts *now*."

The rows of staff members placed their weapons back at their feet. Then they straightened and brought their hands together. A sharp, snapping crack, cutting through the static hanging in the air. Repeated. Again. And again.

One every second. Counting down.

"Seriously, what the hell?" Mitchell broke into uneasy chuckles as he looked at his group.

No one in the crowd seemed to know how to react.

They shuffled uneasily. A few—those closest to the trees—backed away from the beach.

Voices bled over one another, asking questions without answers. Most of the crowd was craning, turning, trying to gauge the mood, seeing what their neighbors were doing.

Herd mentality. *When in doubt, follow the majority.*

The clapping continued. Sharp punctuations, tracking the time trickling out from under them.

"Go," Joel whispered. "We need to *go.*"

"It's a joke," Brent said. He looked as though he didn't entirely believe himself. "It's messed up, but—"

"Where'd Eton go?" the third one, the one whose name Logan couldn't remember, tapped Mitchell's shoulder. "Why's he not onstage?"

The sharp, rhythmic claps seemed to be growing louder.

Then Logan saw him. Through the crowd, near the water's edge. Zach. He stared up at the stage, his eyebrows tight, his jaw clenched.

And pieces fell into place.

Logan finally knew why he recognized Barry.

"Get moving," he said, giving the Camping Quest hosts a shove each to get their attention. "This is real. You need to get off the beach."

"One minute to go," Barry called, full of cheer. The clapping increased in volume again.

A few of the guests jogged toward the jungle. Not many, though. Not nearly enough.

Logan did not like to invite attention. Being loud was an antithesis to his work; he was most comfortable when he could blend in, sink to the back of a group, observe.

But no one else was saying anything.

No one was *doing* anything.

"Run!" he yelled, grabbing at the nearest guests, pushing them toward the trees. "Run, and hide, and be prepared to defend yourselves! This is real! You have to move!"

His shouts earned uneasy laughter and one mocking *boo*.

Heat rose over Logan's neck and onto his face. He raised his voice again, fighting to be heard over the deafening claps, trying not to squirm at the way the staff's smiling gazes had fixed on him.

"This isn't a joke; this isn't a prank! Move, run, fight!"

A few guests started breaking away, no longer jogging but outright sprinting for the cover of the trees.

Logan shoved, harder and harder, trying to get groups to break up. "Run!" He yelled. "Run, run!"

A second voice joined in. Raspy, half his volume, but full of all the desperate urgency Logan felt.

"Run," Joel pleaded, grabbing at his companions' arms. "Please, run!"

An unseen switched flipped. Suddenly, the beach was emptying, a flood of guests racing for the trees.

Herd mentality. *If everyone else was running, you better run too.*

Logan finally let himself join the fleeing crowd. He made it to the jungle's edge, then turned.

Call it journalistic curiosity. Call it bad judgment. He needed to see.

The clapping built into a crescendo, then abruptly cut to silence.

Horrible, eerie quiet enveloped the beach.

Three minutes, gone.

The staff raised their arms, hands stretching overhead, as though praising the sky.

Then they crouched, retrieving their weapons.

Guest groups still lingered, many of them close to the stage. Some laughed; some seemed incredulous. They stared up at the staff as though they were watching a confusing stage play.

One woman had her back to them, phone held at arm's length as she recorded herself and the unfolding events.

Out of the six hundred guests, maybe eighty had stayed. Including Joel's group. He was tugging at them, cheeks puffing as he tried to speak. They were talking over him, making *calm down* motions with their hands, telling him to stop panicking.

Then the whistle sounded.

Sharp, painful, and shooting from every speaker. Loud enough to be heard across the island.

And the staff lurched into motion.

They flew from the stage, leaping from its edge, pouring into the groups that had lingered.

A hand-sharpened machete sliced into the woman who had been filming the events, burying itself halfway through her skull.

A pole impaled a man who had been grinning at the bare breasts, cutting in between his ribs and striking out the other side in a shower of blood.

Two staffers descended on a group as it tried to scatter, a hook and a spiked wooden bat stabbing out indiscriminately, cutting them down before they could make it more than five paces.

Laughter transformed into screams.

The Camping Quest team made choked noises, then began running, Joel among them. Other groups—ones who hadn't been lingering so close to the stage—began racing for cover.

But the staff was moving fast, and the row that had stood behind Trigger's remains swept in from the other side to cut them off. They were just as focused and every bit as efficient as they had been throughout the festival.

Barbed wire around a throat, cinched tight.

A paring knife stabbing into a shoulder and then shearing down, carving a long line across the victim's back.

An axe through a leg, carving it off just below the knee.

Shrieks rose, cutting out into gurgles.

Blood splashed into sand; sand ground into open wounds. Rain poured over them, filling mouths and drenching writhing bodies.

Some ran into the ocean, leaving froth in their frenzied wakes. The staff followed without hesitation. The slowest disappeared into the water, and the water turned red.

Logan watched in frozen horror. Bodies fell…and fought…and died.

The staff member with the unique teeth crouched over a body, using a sharpened stone to pound his victim's face concave. He keeled back, his face and torso drenched in blood and bone fragments, and he looked toward the trees.

His eyes locked with Logan's. His smile grew.

And Logan knew he'd stayed too long.

39.

They ran.

Petra's heart slammed against her ribs. She could hear the clapping on the beach, the terrible countdown, and it wasn't a question of whether she would be too late to stop it, but a question of *how* late.

The woman, Glenda, had said there was nothing she could do.

And Glenda had been right. Petra, on her own, was powerless.

But what if she wasn't on her own?

She'd counted the staff on the beach. They accounted for a very large part of her crew.

But not all of them.

There had been blood in the communications room. Locked doors on the medical clinic.

She could only hope that at least some of her team had gotten away, managed to hide.

Into the staff clearing. Eton was gasping; Petra had to fight to see through the rain. The compact ground was already turning to mud. The forecast had predicted a light downpour. This was a true storm.

The medical clinic was closest. She tugged at the chains, checking for any sign of give. None. Petra slammed her open palm into the door, shouting, asking if anyone was inside.

No response.

"Pet," Eton called, but a distant whistle cut across his voice.

She didn't slow but crossed to the accommodations.

The doors hung open. Petra moved through the rooms, one after another, not even bothering to touch the lights.

Every single bunk had been made. Crisp corners, flat pillows. Suitcases stacked neatly at their ends.

The sight left Petra feeling chilled, uneasy. Those perfectly made beds weren't just habit. They were a message. The staff didn't intend to sleep in them ever again.

She skirted past the storage rooms: All had their doors open; all echoed her shouts back to her.

"No one's here, Pet," Eton called. He was no longer chasing after her. He stood in the center of the clearing, watching her frantic search with sunken eyes.

He was wrong. They couldn't be alone.

She circled the clearing to reach the kitchens.

Scents reached her at the door. Raw onion, cooking bread. And something queasy, foul.

She reached for the light switches. A dozen overhead globes flickered as the power came on.

The kitchens were designed to hold eight cooks and industrial-sized equipment. Steam billowed from pots and flat-top griddles, spiraling around the lights, filling the space with stifling humidity.

Petra felt herself sway as she stepped inside. Her eyes moved from one station to another as she passed between them.

The knives had all been taken. Even the tiny paring blades.

Slabs of meat lay across the cooktop, each piece six inches thick. They were gray, steaming, the undersides burned to charcoal.

The pots were full. A simmering, roiling mirage of meat and half-cut onions and disintegrating potato.

More meat was lined up on the chopping boards, raw fluids dribbling over the counter's edge and onto the floor.

Most was indistinguishable: lumps of muscle and fat, cut thick.

But among those were little bits of familiarity.

A hand.

A jawbone.

Teeth laid out in a row.

Eton stepped up to the open door. She didn't have a chance to warn him. He turned and was sick into the mud.

Petra felt her mind floundering, disintegrating like the chunks of potato in the vats. She rotated, unable to look away from the laden prep areas and overflowing cooktops. She wondered how many of the dead she'd known by name.

The steam was thick. It was sticking to her skin, plastering itself to her, and a heaving, choking cry bubbled up, filling her throat, her mouth—and then she was running past Eton, gagging but unable to get any relief.

She dropped onto her knees, one hand pressed into the mud to hold herself steady, as she let the rain wash the scent off her.

Eton had been right.

They were alone.

Logan tried to control his breathing as he ran.

He needed oxygen to think.

And he needed to think if he was going to stay alive.

Barry had said the game would last until dawn. That was a long time to avoid being caught. He estimated there had been approximately forty staff members on the beach.

What were his options?

Band up with other guests? Find weapons, try to rally into a defensible corner, hold out until dawn?

It wasn't feasible with a group of three or four. Not against the numbers they were facing. A small group might hold out for ten minutes, fifteen max, before they were overwhelmed.

What about a larger group? What if he could collect enough people to outnumber the staff?

Weapons were their weak point. The guests were unarmed, and they didn't have enough time to change that in a meaningful way. They could grab glass bottles, maybe tear the rails off one of the village buildings, but the staff had implements designed to kill. Machetes, spears. Metal and sharp edges.

Historically, the army with the better weapons always held the advantage.

What if he could rally enough bodies, not just to defend their position, but to fight back? It would be a bloodbath, but the guests outnumbered the staff by a significant factor. Could they actually turn the game and kill their hunters if they worked together?

No, he decided, pausing to catch his breath. Figures raced past him, confused and frightened. Too many of the guests were young, shy, squeamish. Most would try to fight if they realized it was their only chance at surviving, but not enough of them would have the conviction necessary to kill.

Unlike the staff, who had seemed ready for it, hungry for it. He'd watched how quickly they launched off the stage at the whistle's sound. It would be a bloodbath indeed.

What options were left?

He could hide, as the theme of the game indicated he was supposed to. Try to pick a good spot. Hope not too many other people tried to hide there, too, because each additional body was an additional liability.

And, of course, hope that the location was clever enough for him to escape being found.

The staff was familiar with the island. They'd been planning for this, preparing for this. Logan had just minutes to choose a hiding place.

Inside one of the buildings? No chance; those would be searched first. Up in the canopy? Possibly, and his chances would get better the farther into the island he ran. It encompassed more than fifty acres. The staff wouldn't have the time or motivation to search every tree thoroughly. Once he got far enough from the settlements, he could rely on the sheer scope of the wilderness to give him an advantage.

No. That was relying on luck. And luck was a poor protector.

He squeezed his eyes closed, regulating his breathing, getting as much oxygen into his body as possible.

What about into the ocean? The guests on the beach hadn't fared well, but a person became hard to see once they were far enough out. If he could find something to keep him afloat—a sturdy piece of wood, an inflatable mattress—then he could hang on to it and drift off from shore until dawn.

No. Still too many risks, too many variables. Ten hours was a long time to spend in the water. The currents could pull him out to ocean. A wave could break his hold on the flotation device.

Logan opened his eyes and turned off the trail.

If he couldn't hide, and if he couldn't win through brute force, then he had one option left. He could try to outwit them.

Historically, the army with the better weapons had the advantage.

Unless their opponent had a stronger strategy.

It was reckless, dangerous. Probably even more so than hiding. But at least it would be an active choice. A risk taken for a purpose, rather than being cornered into it.

He aimed for the staff clearing.

When he'd seen Eton and Petra slip into the jungle, he felt certain that was where they were headed.

A figure jolted through the trees ahead of Logan. A man, blood dripping from his stubble, holding on to his left arm. It had been partially severed and flopped, limp, as he tried to pin it in place.

Logan reeled back as the man vanished into the jungle.

A second figure, bare skin drenched in blood and rain, followed. Focused on his quarry, he didn't notice Logan frozen against a tree.

There was a whack of metal against flesh. Too far away for Logan to see, too close for him to escape hearing.

He sucked a thin breath between clenched teeth, then bolted away from the scene. The sound repeated, again and again: metal sinking into skin, then pulling free with a wet sucking noise.

Logan didn't stop moving until he hit the staff clearing.

All attempts to keep his thinking clear and his body calm had shattered. His vision was hazy. His hands shook. He stared at the clustered buildings but couldn't properly see them.

But—

Petra. She was there. Crouched in the middle of the pathway, staring at nothing.

He'd been clinging to the idea that she had a plan. If she did, it hadn't survived the intermediate few minutes.

And Petra herself wasn't going to survive much longer, slumped in the open like that.

"Get up," he hissed, jogging toward her. "Quick. How do we make this stop?"

She stared at him, eyes blank, face slack.

Not far away, Eton pressed against a wall, dry heaving.

Guests sprinted through the village but none stopped. A scream rang from the jungle behind them.

Logan grabbed Petra's shoulders, shaking her.

"What's next?" he pressed. "What's your plan?"

"Plan…" Her mouth worked, creating strange shapes. "There is no plan."

"Come on; you organized this." Logan fought to keep his frustration under control. "There's always a contingency plan. What is it?"

"You're Logan Lloyd." Petra's eyelids were heavy as a chuckle escaped her. "The journalist. I sent your invite. You know, it's funny; Eton doesn't want you here."

She was in shock.

Logan clawed through his options in a matter of seconds. The longer he stayed there, exposed, the greater the danger. The safe choice would be to move on, figure it out on his own.

But Petra and Eton had organized the festival. Of anyone, they'd have the best knowledge of the infrastructure and the logistics, now that the staff had turned.

He couldn't give up on that kind of advantage.

"I'm going to help you figure this out," he said, squeezing Petra's shoulders, one eye on the tree line. "But we can't stay here. We're going to... we're going to..."

He thought of the photos he'd taken. So many of them now felt like warnings.

Especially one in particular.

A shiver moved through his bones.

"The tower," he said. "Remember yesterday? The sirens went off. That means its system is still functional."

Petra blinked. "From the old development."

"That's the one. It had a communications system. How much do you know about it? If we can get in there, would you be able to use it?"

Eton staggered up to them. He'd lost his beanie. Red blotches colored his cheeks. "We had a survey done of the old buildings when I bought the island."

"To see what could be repurposed for the festival." Petra shook off Logan's hands as she stood. Focus was returning to her eyes. "The communications tower was written off. Too hazardous to bother repairing."

Eton said, "But it might still be working—if we can send out a distress signal—"

"Stop and think for a moment." Petra shook her head. "When the siren went off, the staff deactivated it. The same staff who is now holding us hostage. Do you really think they'd leave the system intact?"

"Maybe," Eton snapped. "If they didn't know what it was."

"They're not that naive."

"It's the best shot we have." The color on Eton's cheeks was growing brighter. "It's a chance to *fix* this. Maybe the only one we have."

A howling scream rang from the jungle.

Logan ran his hand through his drenched hair, pushing a trickle of water down the back of his neck. He didn't want to say it out loud, but he suspected Petra was landing closest to reality.

He'd taken a photo of the tower. It had been meant as a simple memento, a time stamp for the siren in case the events found their way into a video. He'd only taken a closer look at it much later.

It showed the two staff members standing outside, speaking in a huddle. It had captured the tower itself, its partially open door, and the lowest window.

And inside the window…

More staff. Unclothed, their bare skin distorted by the glass. Standing shoulder to shoulder. Facing the window. Facing Logan. Their faces blank, their lips twisted into thin, angry lines.

Yes. He agreed with Petra. The staff would have very readily realized the tower's significance.

But, perversely, he also sided with Eton.

They were facing death either way.

At least the tower would get them moving, get them farther from the massacre.

And on the small chance the systems could be salvaged?

He would take a small chance over zero chance, any day.

"We're going to the tower," he said, cutting over them, leaving no room for arguments. "I want a weapon first. We'll try the kitchens."

"No." Petra's face contorted, a reaction she didn't seem to have control over. She smoothed it out with effort. "No, they took the knives from the kitchen. And most other easy options, I suspect."

"Then we'll make do." Logan scanned the staff clearing as he moved through it.

The flags used to create the boundary during the Easter egg hunt had been left bundled against the storage building, waiting to be cleaned and put away. Logan wrenched some free. The poles were thin, flexible plastic, but their bases had spikes used to anchor them in the ground. Dull, but enough to do some damage.

He tossed one each to Eton and Petra, then turned toward the jungle, aiming for the overgrown trail that would lead toward the tower. "Make sure you're prepared to use those. You'll likely have to."

40.

Thunder broke, and it sounded like mountains crumbling from the sky.

Rain above. Ocean below. Darkness all around.

Ruth latched her hand onto a rock and pulled. Inch by agonizing inch, she wrenched herself from the sea and onto the island's peninsula.

For a moment she lay there, one cheek on the algae-slick stone, feeling her heart pound.

Distant noises began to seep into her awareness.

Shouts.

Screams.

Ruth crawled onto her knees.

The peninsula separated Endurance Cove from Sunset Beach. If she followed it, it would lead her to sand and, eventually, the food stalls and stage.

The floodlights were on. The storm massaged the beach's details into a hazy blur.

But she could see flames.

Until then, all of Ruth's energy had gone into pure survival. First the chase, then the maze, and then the swim through the inky ocean.

This was the first time she'd had even a second to ask what was happening. To think about the implications.

To question whether hers was an isolated situation.

Thunder crackled through the sky, and beneath it, Ruth heard a voice rising into a powerful, shattering scream.

She'd heard sounds like that before, many years prior, at Petition.
It was a scream that heralded death.

The tower seemed immense.

Far above, the sirens dripped water. Vines and plant life crowded in
and choked the structure. One massive siren was loose, hanging by its
cords, rocking as the rain weighed it down. Even through the storm, Petra
could hear it creak.

Lightning cut across the sky, and for a second, the grime-clouded
windows turned into blocks of pure white.

She released a shuddering breath. They hadn't been able to use any
lights for fear of drawing attention, and her knowledge of the old developments was sparse. She'd been lucky that Logan Lloyd had known the way.

Now that they were here, though, he faltered, staring up at the structure as though unwilling to get any closer.

Eton pushed forward instead. He was breathing hard, his clothes clinging to his skin.

The tower's door was closed. Yellow tape had been pasted in an X-shape
across it, marking it as off-limits, and a padlock sealed the latch.

The door's handle was as rusty as the rest of the building, though, and
it already hung crooked, two of its screws undone.

Eton jabbed at it with his stick. Then, when that didn't help, he lifted
a foot to kick at the door.

The handle rattled, but didn't break.

Logan snapped out of his stupor. He picked up a rock off the ground,
then moved in beside Eton.

Three sharp blows snapped the handle off entirely. The lock fell to the
ground, and Logan used the tip of his pole to cut through the plastic tape.

The door screamed as it opened. They couldn't move it far, only about a foot and a half. Just wide enough to get through if they turned sideways.

The jungle was already dark. But the space beyond the door was pitch-black.

Logan, standing at the opening, switched on his phone's flashlight and held it up to the gap. He became very still.

"What?" Petra stepped closer, trying to see past him, but he blocked the view. "What is it?"

Logan took half a step back, turning to her, his expression strange.

Petra had her own phone out and its light on before he could form any words. She held the beam up as she stepped inside the tower and tasted acid at the back of her throat.

Inside was a rough hexagonal shape. The walls were concrete, the floors too coated in grime to distinguish, the ceiling high.

Storage, long forgotten, crowded the space: boxes, metal tins, crates. Most decayed and rusted beyond recognition. Some were being enveloped by the vines that had invaded even the tower's insides.

Along two of the walls was an angular console table.

And in the room's center…

Petra's light glazed over their sneakers first. They were at head height, discolored with mud and other fluids. One had fallen off, leaving just a white gym sock in its place.

She raised her light. Above the sneakers were jeans. And above those, yellow shirts. And above those…

Ropes, cinched around necks.

A strange sound gurgled in the back of Petra's mouth.

The ropes had been fastened to metal beams crisscrossing the ceiling. One of the ropes creaked as its body slowly rotated.

She stared up at their faces, wanting to recognize them, to identify them. Their cheeks and jaws were swollen and bloated. One of their lips had split, yellow liquid oozing out of it.

Petra sucked in a shallow breath and the smell hit her. Rot. She hadn't been able to detect it outside, but in the tower, it was powerfully overwhelming. For a second time, her stomach twisted, threatening to upend itself.

Their eyes were a pearlescent white under sagging lids. Liquid stained their clothes and dripped out of the toe section of the sneakers, where it had pooled. Their hands were mottled, bruised, from settling blood.

The tower, made of concrete and metal, would get hot in the tropical afternoons. It had sped up the decay. Cooking them.

"They were putting out clues from day one." Logan's voice was muffled. He had his arm up, the sleeve pressed over his mouth and nose. "They just left the bodies here to be found. Almost like they *wanted* to be caught."

The hooked net hidden in the shipwreck house. The eyewitness accounts of people dying in the jungle. And Petra had dismissed them all. Just like she'd dismissed...

Her heart was in her throat, fury and frustration like a vise.

Guests had reported their friends missing. At least five of them. And those were only the ones that had made it to her ears.

It was a busy festival. People were drinking. People were mingling, making new friends. It seemed expected that some guests might take a few hours' break from their group. She'd delegated the work of following up on them to the staff, and all those tasks had been marked as resolved within the hour.

How many of those guests had been dead before they were even reported missing?

Behind her, Eton and Logan stared up at the bodies, phone lights bringing them into uncomfortable relief.

Petra turned her own phone toward the opposite wall.

Behind the bodies was an angular desk, ten feet long. It held a jumble of equipment as old and rusted as the rest of the structure. Cables, switches, dials. Screens, blank and dusty.

The communications system.

Tines into dirt, tines into flesh.

Ruth staggered as she hit the sand. Her head was swimming. The screams seemed deafening, and they seemed to be coming from every direction.

Blood dripping over the bridge of a nose.

A flurry of limbs. Pounding footsteps. A man ran from the trees ahead. A woman, unclothed, pursued him. Her pitchfork extended. Stabbed out. Cutting into his leg, tearing a jagged line down the back of his calf. Toppling him.

"No," Ruth whispered, staggering forward, one hand reached out.

Too late. The hayfork was raised and then brought down again, this time into the man's back. He arched. A sharp, gasping inhale. The hayfork withdrew. Then stabbed again. And again. Spritzes of blood burst over the woman's skin.

Ruth snatched up a rock from the shore. It was heavy, the size of her fist. She threw it.

The rock hit the naked woman's hip. She turned, her huge eyes staring into Ruth, and her mouth split into an enormous smile. Without moving her gaze, she brought the tines down again, stabbing through the man's torso, pinning him into the sand.

He wasn't dead, but he was close, the bubbling undercurrent to his breaths telling Ruth that his lungs were filling with fluids.

She backed away. The wide-eyed staff member held her gaze on Ruth until the sheets of thundering rain blurred the space between them like a curtain.

And then Ruth turned and ran.

The island had devolved. When she'd last seen Zach, the village had felt placid. Music played, guests lounged in chairs, people hung out wet bathing suits to dry. Not much more than an hour had passed, and now a storm was filled with screams and the scent of blood.

So familiar. So horribly, terribly familiar.

The final feast. We had it at midday.

She could see the tables, stacked with all their favorite foods.

Barom had given a sermon. He'd told them they had been noble and had held their heads upright against the world's wickedness.

And he'd said they were ready.

Ready to shed their corrupted bodies and be recreated, fresh and pure and spotless.

One by one, they'd knelt at Barom's feet as he poured the honey into their mouths.

He'd said they would all lie down together and rise together, their new bodies at last free from the world's corruption.

They had all been so happy.

Ruth staggered. Ahead, a body lay crumpled in the mud, face down. The skin had been stripped off its back. Vertebrae poked through, starkly white, washed clean by the storm.

Teeth, biting into flesh. Teeth, biting into glass.

The night before Petition's feast, the sightings had built like a storm in Ruth's head. She'd whispered the visions to one of the mothers. The mother had only smiled and stroked Ruth's hair as she told her not to worry; Barom wouldn't let them come to harm.

But the images had seemed so real. So vivid.

And so Ruth didn't eat any of the feast.

And she hadn't swallowed the honey.

She'd climbed onto the stage and let Barom pour it into her mouth, like everyone else. The amber liquid had been so incredibly sweet, but with a trace of burning bitterness.

But she'd held it on her tongue.

And as soon as she thought no one was watching, she went to a corner. And spat, and spat, and spat, and then she took some of the field flower wine and rinsed her mouth and spat again.

She hadn't known that Mother Aama had overheard her whispered confession.

Mother Aama had watched her through the feast. Mother Aama had seen her spit the honey.

Mother Aama knew.

Howling laughter broke through Ruth's fog. Three figures raced past, close enough to clip her. A guest, wild-eyed, her jewel-toned dress clinging to her body. And her hunters, naked, frighteningly excited, carrying shears and the blade of a circular saw.

They were gone before Ruth could even move.

She clutched at her head.

She'd watched her sightings become reality once before.

Her family had feasted. They'd sung. They'd drunk the honey. And then they'd turned, and the joy soured, and they'd begun to scratch at their skin and pull at their hair and dig their fingernails around their teeth.

Ruth stumbled, choking. She clutched at trees as she moved through them, half blind.

More sightings poured into her, overwhelming.

Bodies, swaying in the ocean.

A low wail built in Ruth's chest, a screaming protest against the visions that clouded her eyes. She dug her fingernails into her scalp, but not even pain could force the images away.

Fingers, cut off.

She moved faster, as though she could get away from the sightings if she only ran hard enough, far enough. She could barely see what was around her.

A woman stood in Ruth's path, one hand held above her head as though waving.

No, not waving. And not standing. Pinned to a tree, wrapped there with wire, her throat cut down to the vertebrae and her head nearly falling free.

Ruth staggered past her.

The jungle was overwhelmingly loud. Brutal distress verbalized. So many screams. So many voices.

Ahead, a fight. Two women on the ground. One pinned, hair covering her face, her jaw stretched as she wailed. Palms beating, hands clawing.

And the woman on top of her. Naked. Seemingly not feeling the wounds being dug into her skin. Smiling, so pleasantly, so calmly. Using a paring knife to gouge open her victim's face.

Shock snapped through Ruth. Her vision became clearer, sharper.

Even with her hair across her face, Ruth knew the woman on the ground.

Hayleigh.

41.

The tower's room wasn't large, and the clutter of storage made it cramped. Petra had to crouch to get around the hanging bodies without brushing against their legs.

Dust coated the desk like a blanket. Dead insects lay over the controls, their stick legs poking into the air. Two swivel chairs had been unceremoniously shoved aside, their padded seats rotted to nothing in the humid air.

Only one part of the console had been recently disturbed. Smudges in the dust showed where fingers had pressed.

Petra didn't recognize the system. Labels were stuck beneath buttons, but many had flaked away with time, and others had unfamiliar abbreviations and acronyms.

Papers were attached to the wall above the system, bordered by one of the narrow windows. Petra leaned her pole against a chair and raised her phone, shining its light over the posters.

They seemed to be memos interspersed with pages from instruction manuals. Some were laminated. Petra used the back of her hand to wipe grime from them. Instructions for activating the storm warning system, instructions for reading the barometric system, instructions for using floppy disks…

"Here," Logan said. He tapped on one of the signs. "Communications."

They clustered around, shoulders bumping. There was a microphone, dust-clogged. Two speakers built into the desk. And a screen.

"To initiate system…" Eton read.

Logan was already ahead of them. He pressed his thumb into a switch and pushed.

The screen stayed dead. The row of lights next to it were blank.

"It needs time," Eton said. "It's an old system. It'll take a minute to start up."

But Petra was already shaking her head. She remembered old systems at the library she'd visited growing up, back when computers were a luxury not every home had. They'd needed time to wake, but they always showed *some* kind of life. A light. The angry roar of a fan. Rattles and clicks as power surged through the components.

This was dead.

Logan swore under his breath, turning the switch off and then back on. Petra crouched to see underneath the desk.

Her light glazed over tangled cables.

"No," she said, feeling numb. "They disabled it, after all."

Logan and Eton bent down as well.

The cables had all been severed. Not neatly either. It seemed as though someone had taken a pair of shears to them, hacking recklessly. Scraps littered the floor.

"Can we...reconnect them?" Eton's voice betrayed how little he believed in his own suggestion.

Petra stood. Ahead of her, the age-fogged window was streaked with falling rain. Her own face was reflected back at her, twisted as in a fun house mirror. Behind that, the reflection of the three hanging bodies. And behind them...

Movement.

She turned, slamming into the desk.

A figure rose out of the gloom.

They'd been so focused on the hung corpses that they hadn't noticed the folding seat tucked behind a wall of storage boxes. And they hadn't seen the woman waiting in it.

Folds of bare flesh shifted under Petra's shaky light. Bare breasts, sloping stomach, thighs—each playing eerie games with the shadows as the figure stepped forward.

"I was hoping to see you again," Heather said.

Hayleigh fought, her nails scratching across skin. Blood trailed through her hair, seeped between her teeth.

The woman on top of her, pinning her, smiled. She tilted her head, admiring, as she dragged her paring knife across Hayleigh's face.

Ruth slammed into her.

Skin, wet from rain, wet from blood, slipped and squirmed under her palms.

Maggots, coiling. Flesh, writhing.

The paring knife sliced across Ruth's hip. Then, again, just below her ribs. They tumbled through damp ferns, grappling, both trying to gain the upper hand.

Ruth slammed her elbow into the other woman's stomach, but the woman barely reacted. That delighted smile filled Ruth's vision; Ruth was certain she knew it, and as they hit a crop of mossy rocks, Ruth became convinced it was the staff member who had chirpily declined to help when they had tried to report the attack on Gilly.

No time to examine that. No time to even breathe. The paring knife was wickedly sharp, and it kept moving: across Ruth's forearm, across her shoulder. Lines of fire spreading with every swipe.

They were crowded into a ridge of rocks. Ruth grabbed the woman's head between her hands, pulled it toward herself, and then slammed it back.

She heard the sound of her skull hitting stone. A wet crack. It was terrifying, horrific. The woman's eyelids twitched, but the smile was still there.

And so was the knife. Across the tip of Ruth's ear. She felt blood on her throat and saw a sliver of her own flesh land on the woman's stomach.

She pulled on her attacker's head again. Slammed it back. Forward. Back. Each time the cracking sound was denser, wetter. The knife stopped biting. But the smile was still there, enormous, as the woman's bloodshot eyes stared into Ruth with unbridled delight.

Ruth wanted to look away, wanted to close her eyes, but she knew she couldn't. Crack. Her hands were growing warm from the liquids seeping over them. Crack. The woman stopped resisting, the tension flooding out of her muscles. Crack. The eyes still stared, but they no longer seemed to see Ruth. Crack.

Crack.

Crack.

And then Ruth crawled back, shaking. Blood covered her hands. Blood covered the rocks. The woman lay across them, like a sculpture in a museum, staring toward the sky.

The back of her head was gone.

Slowly, Ruth turned.

Hayleigh lay on her side, her knees pulled up to her chest. Both of her hands were across her face, across her torn skin. She watched Ruth from between those fingers: wide, glistening eyes, the pupils tight with terror and pain.

Ruth shuffled toward her. The phrase *are you okay* died on her tongue. "Can you stand?" she asked instead.

"Ruthie," Hayleigh whispered. "They're going to hurt Carson. Ruthie, Ruthie, they went after him. They're going to hurt him."

"Okay. We...we're going to figure this out." Ruth swallowed. Tasted blood. Tried not to focus on it. "Do you know what's happening?"

"The staff. They said...a game. Hide-and-seek." Hayleigh's breathing was shallow, fluttering. She refused to move her hands. As though she was holding her face in place. "We tried to get away. They found us. And Carson…Carson…"

"Shh," Ruth whispered. The screams echoed all around them. She heard running footsteps, the whisk of disturbed foliage.

"Carson charged at them. He tried to lead them away." Hayleigh's body pulled taut, convulsing. "They're going to hurt him, Ruthie, they're going to hurt him."

She wished she could make promises. *We're going to help him*, or *He'll be okay*, or any similar gentle lie. Instead, she reached her arms under Hayleigh. "You're going to stand now. Lean on me as much as you need to."

"Ruthie—"

"You have to stand."

A howling shout, cut short. It sounded no more than twenty steps from them.

"Quick," Ruth hissed.

And Hayleigh moved. Shaking, struggling to find any kind of balance, her hands an inch from her face. As if prepared to catch it if it fell off.

"Okay," Ruth whispered as they made it to their feet. The places where the knife had caught her burned. She didn't think she'd be able to run again, even if her life depended on it.

But then, Gilly had run. And Gilly had been filled with spears.

"This way," Ruth whispered. She didn't know where she was leading them. She just knew they had to get out. They were pinned between Sunset Beach and the village, and it seemed to be a nexus for the violence.

Back to the ocean, her mind whispered. When she'd climbed out of the swell and onto the rocks, she'd been alone. All the noise—all the death— had seemed miles away. It was cold and exposed, but the jumbled rocks would hide them. At least for a moment.

The beach's floodlights stretched through the trees. Ruth hesitated at the jungle's fringe, trying to see whether they were safer taking the more direct line across the sand or sticking to the jungle's shelter.

Bodies littered the beach. As she watched, more were dragged onto it. Staff brought their kills in, either hauling them by their wrists or working in teams to carry them. The bodies were dropped in the sand, forming loose rows.

And near the shore...

A structure had been built. Two sets of braces with a long pole running between them, about ten feet high. Beneath the pole was a large wooden tub.

Pure, sickening fear bolted through Ruth's stomach. She lost the will to move.

"Ruthie?" Hayleigh whispered. She still had her hands over her face, only her wild blue eyes shining through. "Ruthie, can we go back? Carson isn't here."

Ruth's mouth moved, but she didn't have an answer to give. The raw fear in her chest was so immense, so all-consuming, that she felt as though she was drowning in it.

A staff member threw a rope over the pole. Three others took its end and began to pull.

The rope was lashed around one of their victims' feet. His body scraped over the sand, then began to rise, as slack as a doll.

Please, no. Please.

They didn't stop pulling until the body hung high above the ground, slowly rocking. One of them slid the tub beneath his body. Another approached with a knife.

Not again.

A careful, slow slice across his throat. They stepped back. And they watched as his blood drained into the tub.

"You recognize this, don't you?"

A hand grasped her forearm. She flinched away, half wild with fear.

Zach.

His thick eyebrows were twisted, a thin trail of blood leaking from his hair and blending into the rain. His voice was raspy, hoarse. His eyes bored into her, desperate, demanding confirmation.

"You know what this is."

She did.

She had seen this before.

It was Petition.

42.

"Heather."

Petra felt shock, disgust, shame.

Heather had been her greatest support. One of the few long-term employees who had come with them to the island. One of the only faces from the temporary staff team that Petra not only knew but trusted.

"I wasn't sure I'd have the chance to say goodbye," Heather said. She sounded worn down, tired. And she moved gingerly as she stood from her chair, her bare toes flinching against the cold floor. "I'm glad I got to see you again. It's been a joy working with you both."

Eton didn't seem to know where to look. It was one thing to see the new staff—the unfamiliar staff—naked, but he'd worked with Heather for months, sat opposite her in meetings. "Heather? What's happening?"

She inhaled, then released it in a deep, aching sigh. "A lot."

Behind them, the bodies creaked on their ropes.

"Can you at least tell me the truth?" Petra asked. "Or are you just going to give me cryptic answers?"

"No, no. It's fine to tell you now. You won't hurt anything by knowing." Heather took a slow breath, shifting her weight. The floor had to be hurting her feet. "I've been working with you for, what is it, about three years?"

"About that."

Heather had been one of Petra's hires. An older woman, not a conventional choice for a digital media company. But Petra had liked her resumé—office admin, payroll, and project management, going back decades.

"You don't know much about my personal life," Heather said. "That was deliberate. There's a lot of pain hidden there, things I wanted to keep private. Without going into too many details, my daughter died about eight years ago."

"I'm sorry," Eton said, a reflexive response.

"Thank you. I didn't understand how I was supposed to continue living after that, so I started meeting with a grief support group. One of the women there introduced me to an online community. And they showed me...miracles. *Real* miracles. Amazing things. For the first time in my life, I began to actually understand this world."

Logan, lingering near the wall, spoke. "And that community called themselves Petition."

———

"Ruth?" Zach's voice was a hoarse whisper. "Talk to me. You don't know how many risks I took to find you again."

The body was empty. Ruth watched as the cult lowered it, dropping into the sand and then dragging it away, like a husk to be discarded.

In Petition, a dead body remained sacred as long as its blood was liquid. Once the blood curdled, the body was considered *truly* dead, and it became no more special than vegetable scraps thrown to the animals.

While the blood was wet, though? It had power.

A fresh rope went over the bar. Hands pulled. A new body was raised.

"I know you hate me," Zach said. He leaned close to her, speaking in rapid whispers, but not tearing his eyes from the scene playing out below them. "And I get it. You don't have to forgive me. But I'm right, aren't I? This is a Petition ritual."

"It is," she said, and that admission felt like it was shattering her very essence.

"You were supposed to be the last of them."

She could only stare, unable to tear her eyes away as the knife was dragged over another throat. Thick trails of red dripped into the basin below.

She was the only one found by the police. That statement had been drilled into her so often—the last, the only one found, the sole survivor—that she had never questioned it.

And yet.

Petition was here, on the beach.

And they were performing a cleansing ceremony.

A dozen of them crouched in the sand, carving channels, and as the lines connected, Ruth could make out a too-familiar shape.

The bound lamb, its head tilted upward, as though to stare toward the crashing waves.

Someone had lied.

Petition hadn't ended that day at the commune. Ruth wasn't the final survivor.

Her family had endured.

And they had come for her.

Focus swiveled to Logan.

He tried to hold himself steady, keep at least a veneer of control.

"What's Petition?" Eton asked.

He seemed sincerely confused.

The cult had become such a cultural touchstone that it was hard to believe an adult wouldn't be at least passingly familiar. But then, Eton seemed to avoid darker topics. His channel revolved around games and comedy. Like a child who refused to grow up.

"I never went far down the research hole for your community," Logan said, holding Heather's gaze. "So, forgive me if I get the nuances wrong. But you believe in a prophecy that can only be fulfilled by the death of the Petition Child, correct?"

"Contrary to what you say, it seems you went *quite* far down the research hole," Heather said. She sounded pleased.

Logan had never been especially interested in cults or in Petition. But he'd taken a detour into the topic a year before.

There'd been a podcaster: Zachary Waldon. And he waged obsessive hunt for an individual who clearly wanted to remain unidentified.

Logan had come close to making a video on him. There was plenty of fodder there. Zach had admitted, on his podcast, to trying to convince an unwell caseworker that she should give him access to her files. He'd talked about trying to gain access to groups that were equally obsessed with Petition, hoping they would help him.

That was where Logan had seen that unsettling smile, with its oddly spaced teeth.

Zach had posted a photo of himself meeting Barry at a true crime convention. Zach's caption hadn't said much, but he apparently stopped trying to join those groups shortly afterward. Logan's best guess was that their interests tended in very different directions, to the point that even Zach had grown uncomfortable.

But not uncomfortable enough to give up on his project. He'd started impersonating registered officials to try to get records. He talked about offering money to court transcribers who had been there during the inquest. He'd even gone as far as discovering an unsavory detail about a retired solicitor that he could use as leverage.

Altogether, it was a frightening package that would have given Logan's subscribers plenty to churn through.

Especially considering how many of Zachary's actions were illegal.

And that, at its end, was the only thing that kept the episode as a bundle of notes, nothing more.

Logan couldn't truly take the moral high ground without putting those same morals into practice. Zachary's case was barely borderline—the man's judgment so clearly clouded by an obsession—that Logan felt he deserved one warning.

One anonymous email.

He never received a reply. But, two days later, Zachary's channel was deleted, and his social accounts were purged. The project seemed dead.

He'd kept Zachary Waldon's name on his notification list in case the man ever resurfaced, but he hadn't heard a whisper from him in the intermediate year. Until the festival.

Logan had never thought to delve any deeper into Petition itself. Cults weren't his arena.

But it seemed he'd underestimated the significance of Zachary's photo. To a catastrophic degree.

"Petition was founded by a prophet," Heather said. "He saw how the world was sinking into corruption, and he asked if there was any way to save it. And the answer was a sacrifice. A willing, wholehearted sacrifice from the last remaining pure beings. And his family gave up their lives to cleanse the world."

Petition had called everyone in their gathering *family*. Any woman who was old enough to bear children became *mother*. Their leader alone had been *father*. And the children had been raised communally, cared for by all the older women, never knowing who their actual birth parents were. It was one of the cult's tactics to reduce individualism.

"Only, the sacrifice failed at the last second," Heather said. "One of the family revoked her promise and refused to lay down her life. Without her, the family's bodies withered away, and the pact remained unfulfilled."

Logan bit his tongue. In his peripherals, he saw Petra shift, and he knew she was thinking the same thing. *She was a child.*

Heather's hand twitched, and Logan realized she was holding something. A weapon? No. It was small. She swayed, and as she moved in the light from their phones, speckles of perspiration glittered across her face.

"The world has been trapped in a limbo since then," Heather said. "Unable to save itself, it spirals, and we become more corrupted and broken with every passing year."

The words flowed out of her, but they didn't sound like they belonged to her. Logan had the uncanny sense that he was listening to fragments of a sermon.

A sermon that had been repeated so often and so vehemently that the phrases had become entangled with the woman's very identity.

"But we've been given another chance," Heather said. "A chance to complete the pact, to fulfill Barom's prophecy. We are ready. And so is she."

"She?" Eton asked, voice weak.

"The Petition Child." Heather shifted, and Logan got a glimpse of the object she carried. Something made of glass, slim enough to hide inside her palm. "She is ready to atone for her broken promise. We know this. Because she has offered herself to us."

Petition is here. Does that mean…?

Ruth couldn't tear her eyes from the figures spread across the beach.

Barom was dead. He was found in his private quarters, a gunshot wound through his head.

At least…that was what they'd told Ruth.

She'd never seen his body. Not while she was trapped in the commune, and not afterward either. Leslie had shielded her from the postmortem photos presented at the inquest.

Did they make a mistake?

Could Barom still be alive?

Is he here, on Prosperity Island?

Twenty years had passed. He would be in his sixties. Would she even recognize him?

"Ruth," Zach said.

Yes. She was sure she *would* know him. No matter how much he might have changed, she could never forget his face. His eyes. His slim, calculated smile.

"Ruth." Zach touched her arm. "You have to realize how much danger you're in right now."

Ruth tore her eyes away from the blood dripping from the slowly swaying body. Beside her, Hayleigh leaned against a tree, shuddering and unresponsive.

"I have a place we can hide," Zach said. "You can be angry at me. You can be as angry as you want. But let me help you."

Waves crashed over the distant peninsula. It had only ever been a temporary option.

"Is there any chance we can find Carson?"

"He was hurt." Pain pulled at Zach's expression. "He tried to lead them away. I don't think we're going to find him tonight."

She searched his face. She'd known every crease, every slope, almost better than her own. She'd believed she was safe with him. And she'd lost everything because of it.

"How can I trust you?" Ruth swallowed. Shouts radiated through the trees, raw and ragged and frighteningly close. "You're obsessed with Petition. You could be one of them."

Blood seeped from the edge of his hairline, fading to pink as it dripped over his chin. He nodded, slowly, his heavy eyebrows shifting as her words sank in. "That's fair. I'm not going to lie to you again. I met one of them last year."

Ruth let his words hang. The shouts were growing louder, more frantic, closer.

"His name was Barry. We caught up at a convention. He said he was researching Petition, but something felt wrong, so I didn't contact him again. Then I saw him here, at the festival, and I thought it had to be a coincidence. I…I don't believe it is, any longer."

Ruth's eyes burned. In the distance, lit by flame and distorted by the downpour, a fresh body swung as it was raised over the basin. Hayleigh's breathing seemed thinner, shakier.

"I found a place that can keep the three of us safe." His hands flexed. "I could have stayed there. But I came out again—I risked everything—because I want to help you. Please, let me."

She looked up at Zach, and saw his frustration, and fear, and desperation.

"Okay," she said. "Show me."

43.

"It's going to be enough this time," Heather said. She shifted, a pained grimace flashing over her lips as her feet arched. Spots of blood beaded between the toes. "All of our family, plus the one who faltered, plus however many guests join us in this final stage."

"So you're the one who created this all," Petra said. She sounded shattered.

"No. Not me, no. We all have parts to play, ways to be useful. And my part was quite small. I was the messenger." Heather's face relaxed back into a smile. "I reviewed the festival entries. I saw the child reaching out. I made sure she was chosen."

Eton's grimace deepened. "It was supposed to be randomized—"

Petra hissed to make him go quiet.

"I shared the news with the elders. They saw it, just as clearly as I did. This is the twenty-year mark from when the pledge was originally made. This was our call to fix what was broken so long ago."

"And you made sure your family was part of the staff," Logan guessed.

"Yes." Heather's breathing was growing shaky, irregular. She fidgeted with the item in her hand. "I whittled down anyone on the core team who would cause difficulties: HR, team leads, IT. The family used their connections to offer some of them higher-paying and more prestigious jobs elsewhere. Others were removed by terminating them for misconduct."

Logan had heard whispers that there was a high turnover in Eton's team before the festival. He'd assumed it was just burnout finally catching up to the juggernaut of a company. Judging by the way Petra's face turned rigid and white, the turnover had been a source of significant pain for her.

"You trusted me to help interview the replacements, Petra," Heather said. "And *I* brought the people *I* trusted."

"So I see." Petra's jaw was tight, a pulse jumping in her throat.

"It was easier once my family was able to help. We filled the festival staff spaces. You delegated so much to us: background checks, employment checks, ID checks. It made it possible to edit the results as needed."

"Just like the ID checks at lunch today?" Petra shifted her bag. "When you told me all the guests and staff were accounted for, when there were already bodies littered across the island?"

Heather gave a gentle nod. It was cold in the tower, but her perspiration was growing denser, dripping off her jaw and nose.

"But..." Petra frowned. "Gillian Davies. She was the first one reported, and I checked her myself. I saw her photo ID."

"One of the staff." Heather sounded almost apologetic. "When they put on civilian clothes, they looked similar enough to be convincing. The deaths were not planned to start so early. And the hooked fishing net—that was never supposed to be added to the game. Some of the family grew too eager, too soon. They wanted to escalate before we were ready." Heather took a shuddering breath. "And some lost their strength when they needed it most."

Her eyes turned toward the three hanging bodies.

"Here."

Ruth stared up at the building looming over them. "No. This is too obvious."

Zach supported Hayleigh. She swayed, no longer holding her hands over her face, but with bloody palms extended in front of her. She was in shock. In the low light it was hard for Ruth to tell how much of her face was left.

"Trust me, this is our best chance." Zach nodded to the building. "We're going onto the roof. Use the boards to get a leg up."

They were in the staff clearing. The buildings were mostly old structures and shipping containers from prior developments, repaired and refurbished. The boards Zach indicated had been used to seal up rusted metal in the side of the building.

Thunder crackled overhead. Ruth turned, trying to gauge their options, and saw an arm lying in the mud between two of the buildings.

Just an arm.

Ruth planted her sneaker on the boards and grasped at the metal. The roof was sloped and slippery in the rain. Moss and decades of decayed leaf litter compacted under her hand. The cuts in Ruth's side screamed as she hauled herself up.

Small rivers of water trailed around her as she clung to the roof. Skylights had been built between overlapping metal sheets. They creaked as she shuffled around.

"Ready?" Zach asked. He kept his voice to barely above a whisper, his head turned to watch the jungle's edge.

Ruth reached her arms over the roof. Zach crouched to hold Hayleigh around her hips and, gasping, lifted her up.

A broken, gurgling shriek broke out of Hayleigh as Ruth tried to pull her up. Her limbs twitched, her face bumped into Ruth, and Ruth felt the heat of her blood left behind.

"Shh, shh," Ruth begged.

Keening cries filled the air. Hayleigh clawed at her back. Zach pushed up as Ruth leaned back, and Hayleigh collapsed onto the metal. Her voice cracked as she tried to swallow her cries.

Zach hauled himself up in a few quick movements. His nostrils flared and his mouth pressed into a tight line as he hunched, trying to minimize how much of his body would be visible from the ground.

"Here," he said, easing the sobbing Hayleigh out of Ruth's arms. "Over here."

Zach used his shoe to push on the edge of a piece of metal roofing. It was loose; under pressure, it peeled up. Ruth drew a breath.

New roofing had been laid on top of old. A temporary fix to waterproof the structure without committing to a full renovation.

Between those metal sheets was a cavity. Narrow, just barely enough space for a person to lie flat, but wide enough to hold all three of them.

They eased Hayleigh into the gap first. She was slipping in and out of consciousness, her hands rising and then dropping back. Ruth did what she could to arrange her, turning her body so Hayleigh's face wouldn't touch the metal.

"Quickly," Zach whispered, and Ruth shuffled into the gap, pressing herself against Hayleigh's side. Zach slipped in behind her.

The metal sheet dropped down, blocking out the light.

To Ruth, it felt very much like a coffin lid closing over them.

It was impossible not to follow Heather's gaze. Logan found himself looking upward, toward the bodies that filled the room's center.

"They lost their strength," Heather said, melancholy seeping into her voice. "They came to the tower and tried to contact the mainland, to betray us. They didn't know the system. They activated the weather siren instead."

Logan remembered arriving at the tower just after the alarm had been cut off. How the staff had told him the power had been connected during a test, while simultaneously telling Petra a guest was responsible.

He wondered if the three bodies hanging over him were still alive when he turned to leave the clearing.

"There was a fourth, Lisa." Heather groaned, her face contorting, then relaxed it again as she shuffled. Bloody footprints outlined where she'd stood. "She was a new follower. Her faith was weak. But she found her courage at the last second and came to warn us."

"Lisa…" Petra's tension was keyed to breaking. Her hands quivered at her side. "The same one you stuffed into a suitcase?"

"Not my choice." Heather shook her head. "But she was frightened, and it risked focusing the enemy's attention on us. It's okay, though. We're all offering up our lives this weekend. Some just needed to do it a little sooner."

The ropes creaked as the bodies slowly turned.

"I'm afraid that's going to include me," Heather said. A drop of perspiration fell from her jaw. She fidgeted with the small glass object, turning it over and over in her palm. "Does anyone have the time? I've lost my watch."

Neither Petra nor Logan moved. After a second, Eton lowered his phone, which he'd been using as a light, and tapped the screen. "Nearly ten thirty."

"I was hoping to hold out until dawn, but I think I need to accept that's not going to happen." Heather chuckled. She lifted the object. Even that little effort made her breathing labored.

"What are you doing?" Petra asked. She reached one hand toward Eton. "What is that?"

"Just my final duty." Heather gazed at the small glass bottle. She undid the cap. Raised it to her mouth. Swallowed, then tilted forward, coughing. Her feet scuffed over the floor, leaving more red prints.

Logan felt his hands turn numb with silent panic. He reached out, past the hanging bodies, to catch Petra's sleeve without drawing Heather's attention.

"I think Lisa was skipping her restorations." She swiped her thumb across her lips, clearing spilled liquid. "We were taking them to help with…well, everything. Energy, focus…fear. It's only human to feel afraid, this close to the end. Nothing wrong or bad about it. As long as we don't lose power to the doubts."

Restorations? Petition had held a pathological fear of medication. A hubristic choice, since they had died from what was essentially home-brewed nerve toxins.

Logan thought of the uncanny smiles, the eagerness, the upbeat enthusiasm. He would not have been surprised if the crew had been taking some strong drugs, rebranded to more palatable *restorations*.

"I skipped my last dose too," Heather said. "Too busy to go and get it. And I've sure noticed the difference." She inhaled, then groaned. "Makes everything harder. Makes it hurt so much more. Well. I have done my part, and I've done it well. I'm allowed to rest now."

Logan tugged Petra's sleeve again. The anger was bleeding out of her, being replaced with the same stark panic Logan felt.

"Eton?" she whispered.

"Thanks for being here." The glass bottle fell from Heather's hand. It shattered as it hit the floor, tiny shards of glass spreading out in a halo, some still holding drops of a golden liquid. Heather's breathing was becoming faster, erratic. She shuffled, and as her feet passed over the glass shards, she didn't so much as flinch.

"Thank you," she said again, though the words were growing lost, her breaths coming one a second, bellow-loud. "I didn't…didn't want to… die alone."

44.

Carson pulled his torn shirt off and pressed the cotton against the open gash to stanch the bleeding.

He didn't dare slow his pace. The others were behind him. Four of them, hunting in a pack. They'd painted a streak of blood across their faces, running from ear to ear, and their eyes glowed in the center of that hellish red tint.

He'd managed to lead them away from Hayleigh, at least. Smashing a sharp rock into the tallest one's back had gotten their attention. And held it.

They weren't giving him even an inch. He clutched his shirt against his bleeding shoulder as he hurtled through the jungle, following one of the neglected trails.

He had to get back to Hayleigh. *Somehow.* She wasn't weak, but she froze. He couldn't leave her out there. But first, he had to lose the pack hunting him.

If there was just one, he was sure he could take them. Maybe two, depending how big they were. But four? Carrying ugly metal tools and a machete that had already clipped his shoulder?

He had to shake them. Somehow.

They gasped out queasy laughter as their bare feet slammed into the earth.

Bare feet.

Carson inhaled, then swerved off the path. He leaped across a fallen tree, barely catching his balance as he landed, and followed the slope uphill.

The jungle was a mass of exposed roots and prickly vines and rocks. He should have thought of it sooner. Carson had his sneakers, but the terrain would chew up his hunters' feet.

The ground was growing rockier as the slope led toward the peak. Carson fought for air. His torn shirt wasn't stopping the blood. His pursuers were still just a second or two behind him, so close that he had no room for mistakes.

He hoped Hayleigh could hold out for a few more minutes.

And he hoped Zach...

Rain trickled into Carson's eyes.

He had no idea what he wanted for Zach.

Carson ducked under a mesh of vines, gasping, his shirt smearing blood across his torso. The hunters laughed, frighteningly close.

Zach had looked out for him when they were kids. He'd been a good friend. But how far was friendship supposed to stretch?

And how much of this was Zach responsible for?

"Damn it," Carson whispered.

The hunters hadn't stopped. They hadn't even slowed down. The ground had to be slicing up their feet, but it was like they didn't even notice.

Every second carried him farther from Hayleigh.

And he didn't think he could keep running much longer.

A cliff face rose to Carson's left. The sharp side of the mountain: the one part of the island where bare rock poked through the plants. Moss-choked boulders clustered around its base. Ferns trailed up the wall, shivering as the storm flowed over them.

Carson made his choice. He veered toward the cliff, dropping the torn shirt, and threw himself over the boulders.

The cut in his shoulder bled freely, but it didn't go deep. If he could push the pain aside, the muscles would still work fine.

And he'd been doing rock climbing for nearly two years.

The four hunters could run, but that didn't mean they'd be strong enough to scale the cliff.

And if they did?

He doubted he'd feel any guilt about kicking them loose and watching them plummet to the boulders below.

Carson clutched at the wall and dragged himself upward.

The rocks were slippery. Not just from the rain but from algae. He was used to climbing man-made walls with chalk to help his grip.

But the surface was also full of crevices. Plenty of places to hook his fingers and jam his sneaker tips.

Four feet above ground, then six. He moved fast, arm over arm, kicking for extra momentum.

Not fast enough.

Something stabbed the back of his thigh. The pain was so sharp and sudden that Carson's muscles convulsed, nearly dropping him back down.

Raspy shouts of glee came from the hunters. They scrambled over the boulders on all fours. The streak of red painted across their faces was weeping in the rain, dribbling over their noses and into their open mouths.

A fishing spear was stuck in the back of Carson's leg. It had a rope tied around its end, and the closest woman grinned as she tugged it.

Carson yelled. The fishing spear was barbed. It wouldn't come out—not without tearing his leg open.

Panic burned as his fingers scrambled at the slimy ridges. The hunters rocked from side to side, swinging their weapons, like vultures waiting for him to fall.

Carson buried his fingers as deep as he could into a crevice. He had a strong grip. Strong enough for this, he hoped.

He hauled himself higher and yanked both of his legs up, knees to his chest. The rope put horrific pressure on the spear, and his vision flashed white.

The hunters clambered nearer, refusing to let him slip away.

Just close enough...

All at once, Carson let his body drop, plunging down until he hung from his fingertips. In the same motion he stabbed both legs downward.

His heel connected with the woman holding the rope. Her face made a fantastically satisfying crunching noise as her nose collapsed. Blood spurted as she crumpled backward, arms outstretched. The rope swung free.

Carson hauled himself up again as the others screamed with shock and laughter. He kicked his leg and managed to hook the loose rope, lifting it out of their reach. Then he scrambled another few feet up the rock wall, where none of their weapons could touch him, and stuffed the rope's slack into the waistband of his shorts.

His limbs shook and his skull throbbed. He leaned into the rock wall, stone and cold moss against his bare stomach, as he looked down.

The woman who'd held the fishing spear was already back on her feet.

They had to be on drugs. Her nose was distorted, crushed so badly that she could only breathe through her mouth. Five of her front teeth had been knocked out and blood oozed over her parted lips. She bobbed, swaying eagerly, as she stared up at him.

Carson sucked in a thin breath. The cliffside extended up for another thirty feet at least. He'd have to climb it, and he'd have to do that with a leg that felt like it was on fire.

He reached up, choosing a new handhold, and began to move.

Arm over arm. The spear shuddered with each movement, but there was no way he could get it out on his own. He moved carefully, testing his holds before committing to them, trying to keep pressure off his bad leg. Dirt filled the gaps under his fingernails and rotted plant matter plastered his chest.

Then he heard the sound of rattling stones beneath him.

Carson risked another look down.

The hunters were climbing.

They moved in ugly, jerking motions, scrambling and crawling, unafraid of the drop. And they were faster than he'd expected.

Carson swore. He picked up his pace, bringing the injured leg in for small amounts of support. He was horrifyingly aware of how easily one small mistake could send him tumbling down to the ragged rocks beneath.

Only fifteen feet left. He didn't know what he'd do once he got to the top. He didn't think he'd be able to run any longer. But he'd have to, somehow.

"*Ha, ha, ha, ha!*"

One of the hunters snatched at his foot. Carson clutched the rocks and pulled his legs out of reach.

There was a dark gap in the cliff to his right. A crevice, he thought, just wide enough for a person to comfortably crawl into. It hadn't been visible from the ground, but it looked like it would be a good spot to stop, to take the pressure off his aching arm muscles. Maybe he could get inside and defend it, maybe try to knock the hunters off the cliff as they came near him.

But that would be as good as giving up. If he went into the crevice, he'd be cornered. The hunters might decide to wait him out.

And he didn't have that kind of time. Hayleigh was still out there, somewhere.

Another hand snatched at his foot. And this time, fingers hooked into the sneaker's heel. He kicked and managed to dislodge their grip, but his shoe came off with it. There was no time to think about that. He fixed his eyes upward, on the remaining stretch of rock wall and the flat ground at its top.

And up there…

Staring eyes.

Rows of them.

Staff, drenched in rain and blood, stood waiting for him at the cliff's top. Some crouched; others stood, their toes curling over the edge, metal held taut in their quivering grips.

"No," Carson gasped.

Something sharp stabbed at his exposed foot. He shouted, kicking, but met air.

The crevice was his only option.

He scrambled sideways to get to it. Rocks tumbled from under his grip. He fought to hold his perch with his injured leg and felt muscles tear.

But he reached the opening.

Carson crawled inside, blinking water out of his eyes.

It was a cave. Not large—only about six feet deep—but big enough for a person to sit.

There was something near its back.

A queasy lump filled Carson's throat. Blood flowed from his chest and his leg, and he could feel his strength draining out with it.

But he couldn't tear his eyes away from the cave's small shrine.

A cross, made of aged wood and rope, leaned against the cave's back wall.

And in front of the cross was a human skull.

Carson shook his head. The throbbing in his head was growing worse.

The cross looked ancient, except…It was a little too perfect.

It reminded Carson of the stage props his school had created for their theater productions. Pockmarks added in strategic places. Stain applied to give it a weathered look.

A name had been carved into the wood in angry, slashing lines. *The Cannibal Witch.*

The skull seemed to grin up at him. Stain deepened the eye hollows and pooled around the teeth, but he was fairly sure it was made of plaster.

He'd found the grave.

Eton's treasure hunt. A hundred thousand dollars. The skull was supposed to be the proof Eton had asked for; you brought it to him to claim your prize.

Zach guessed it would have been impossible to find without clues. The cave opening, three-quarters of the way up the cliff wall, was nearly invisible from the ground.

It was dangerous to get to, though. Maybe one of the clues would involve discovering a harness to rappel down the cliff face.

That would be a very Eton-style twist. A heroic deed to win the treasure hunt.

"Guess today's my lucky day," Carson muttered.

He'd always wanted to play an Eton game. Those videos had been one of the few things that gave him joy back when everything else in his life was going wrong. And here he was…he'd played, and he'd won.

"*Ha,*" a voice whispered.

Carson turned.

The hunters clustered in the cave opening. Lightning broke overhead, and it transformed them into an inhuman silhouette, a creature born from overlapping limbs and too many heads.

Carson reached for the wooden cross. It felt just as light as the stage props had. His heart had picked up an unsteady rhythm and he knew he didn't have much juice left in him.

But there was enough. Just enough.

The silhouette monster scuttled toward him.

Carson stabbed out with the grave marker, jabbing it into the hunters. Screaming laughter burst from them. Something sharp hit his arm, cutting deep into the muscles, and Carson grunted. He pushed harder and heard a shout as one hunter slipped out of the cave, arms pinwheeling as she plummeted down.

The three remaining hunters watched the body drop with glinting eyes, then turned back to Carson as a smacking, crunching sound echoed from below.

Carson shoved the grave marker forward again. A machete swung through the darkness. The wood shattered into fragments.

The cave was full of their panting, gasping breaths. Fingertips plucked at stone. Metal scraped the cave's walls.

The machete rose up again.

Carson couldn't stop it. He lifted his hands.

The blade cut through his palms first, severing the fingers. Then the metal edge continued and sank deep into his throat.

Again, and again, and again, and again.

45.

Zach's shoulder pressed against Ruth.

The sheet of metal lay heavy over them, blocking out light. The rain, magnified and echoing, drummed off it.

In the far distance, someone screamed, then begged, then became abruptly quiet.

"I'm sorry about what I said." Ruth's voice was a ghost, a breath, barely more than a thought.

She couldn't see him, but she could feel him turn an inch to stare at her in the dark.

"About hoping you die. I'm not going to be able to forgive you, but…" She paused. Swallowed. Focused on holding still, on not letting the metal shift. "I wish I hadn't said I wanted you to die."

Through the rain, she could hear his breathing, her heartbeat.

"Did you really see it?" he asked, and his voice was raspy.

She knew what he meant. Did she see the ocean. See it full of bodies, undulating in the waves.

He shifted again, only a tiny bit, damp skin brushing against hers. "Did you really have a sighting?"

"I don't know." Except she did. She wanted to deny, she wanted to hide, she wanted to insist that it wasn't possible, but she knew.

She'd started having sightings on the day they won their tickets to the festival.

On Ruth's other side, Hayleigh made a faint sound, then faded out again.

At least the metal was protecting her from the rain. But Ruth hadn't had time to see how serious the cuts were, how deep they went. How badly they were still bleeding.

How much blood Hayleigh had already lost.

"Do you have a plan?" she whispered. "Are we hoping someone comes to rescue us?"

"How much of the announcement did you hear?"

"None. I was in the jungle. Some of them came after me."

He shifted again. "They said the game—if we can call it that—would end at dawn. Anyone who can stay hidden until then gets to live. At least, that's what they promised."

Ruth nodded, even though Zach wouldn't be able to see. Barom had hated duplicity. If he said something was going to happen, they always had to make it so.

"You know their mindsets better than anyone else," Zach said. He was speaking carefully, moving around Ruth's sore emotions. "Is there anything we can do? I've been racking my brain. What if we were able to stage a miracle or a sign from heaven? Would they stop?"

Ruth's smile was grimacing and wide enough to be painful. "No. They don't care about any higher power. They listen to no one except themselves."

There had been so many misconceptions about Petition. Its religious fervor was one of the largest.

And with reason. Petition's communal language borrowed countless religious phrases. And its imagery—the bound lamb—only strengthened that perception.

But Petition had been no more religion-based than an organic farm co-op.

Barom had loved the language; it made him feel powerful, wise. And he'd created his own set of rules for how they lived their lives, his own list of what constituted an evil and what meant salvation.

The regular world was evil. It had grown corrupt, poisonous. The only way to remain clean was to separate yourself from it—sacrifice every old possession, every earthly relationship. Desires were remnants from the corrupt world, trying to take root in you again. You had to refuse them to stay clean.

But an evil world hated being shown its own reflection in the mirror of a pure person. At every turn it would try to tarnish them, persecute them, seduce them.

Medication was evil. Grief was a deception, a lie created by the world to keep people focused on its trappings. Technology, books, learning—all things designed to entertain, distract, rot.

A person found redemption through self-denial. By following instructions dutifully and wholeheartedly.

The only religion inside Petition was Barom. The family followed his will, his teachings. They sang to him, and he gave them sermons. His was the final voice on every subject, the ultimate authority. A god of his own creation.

And he had preemptively hardened his followers against anyone who said otherwise.

"Then we'll wait it out," Zach said. "We should be safe until dawn if we stay quiet. No one else found this spot."

That was a terrible proposition: survive, but at the expense of others who were less calculated.

"Do you know if anyone's nearby? Other guests, I mean?"

"Yes. I saw some go into the staff bunks and supply sheds. A lot of them are just hiding under beds or inside crates." A hint of frustration entered Zach's voice. "These are the same people who were treating Eton's games like life-and-death challenges, and yet they're picking the most obvious places possible."

"Panic can do awful things to us." Ruth tried to shift, to take some pressure off her hip, without letting the metal cover move.

"There's a surveillance room on the other side of the clearing. That's how I found you and Hayleigh, incidentally; I caught a glimpse of you in a video feed. They have cameras across the major areas. I thought, if I could find a way to hide inside that building, we could watch the feeds and have a warning when the staff got near. But it just wasn't practical. The best I could manage was space inside a storage closet, and that's almost as obvious as under a bed."

"Which building is this?"

"The medical clinic. The door's locked; I already tried to get in."

That was a bitter piece of irony. There would be painkillers, bandages, and coagulants just feet from them—and still out of reach. Ruth could barely hear Hayleigh's breathing beneath the drumming rain.

She began to ask if there might be another way in—*could they dig through the roof?*—but Zach cut her off with a sharp inhale.

Ruth became aware of distant footsteps.

She fell very still, not letting her chest rise more than a few millimeters with each inhale.

Just like at Petition.

Crowded into a pile of bodies, pretending to be one of them.

Only, this time the bodies next to her were still alive.

But for how much longer?

Ruth's wide eyes stared into the darkness. She could feel how tense Zach had grown. She could no longer hear him breathing.

The footsteps passed right under her, and Ruth knew they were circling the building. Bare feet, sucking out of the mud with each step.

The sounds moved on, then gradually faded, blending back into the environment.

Ruth gave herself no quarter, refused to relax. All it would take was one shift, one sound. Survival was more important than the pain in her hip, or the growing claustrophobia, or the itch running down her lower back as water trickled through her clothes.

She didn't even flinch when a scream broke the silence.

Ruth slowly flexed her hands into fists, holding them tight to keep herself still as she listened to the whack of metal into flesh, into bone.

The screams turned to a gurgle.

She heard people churning through the mud. The slam of a hand grasping at a door. The crack of bones breaking. Three more sharp, fast blows, growing increasingly wet.

And the gurgles finally fell silent.

Tears leaked out of the corners of Ruth's eyes. Her mind wanted to know who it had been, whether she might have even spoken to them during the festival, but she cut those questions off.

Survive until dawn.

That was the only thing that mattered.

The footsteps passed beneath their shelter again. They were accompanied by a slow, scraping noise. A body. Being dragged along the worn paths. Back to the beach, to be added to the cleansing.

And then they were alone again, kept company only by their shallow breaths.

Ruth focused on the rain, letting the rhythm consume her. Trying to ignore the pain, the thirst, the tiredness. Trying, as hard as she could, to not visualize what was happening to the rest of the guests.

She wasn't sure she could hear Hayleigh's breathing any longer. Sounds were magnified inside their shelter, but the space beside her seemed too quiet, and that terrified her.

"Zach?" Her voice was so light she could barely hear it herself.

She felt him tilt his head a fraction.

With everything that had happened, the question shouldn't matter any longer. It felt inconsequential, even ridiculous. But...

"I got one of the red-circle rocks for the first game. You said the staff wouldn't let us swap them." She hesitated, wet her lips. "Did you really ask?"

She'd watched Zach approach a staff member, hands gesturing as he asked a question. The staff member had smiled as she shook her head. But she'd been too far away to hear.

"No," Zach admitted.

Ruth nodded, her chest aching.

It had never been a coincidence that she was picked for that first game. She was the reason they'd gotten their tickets, after all. Zach had needed her to participate. To perform.

He'd done it so smoothly too. Instead of trying to force the game, he'd made her feel like she had choice. He'd encouraged her to drop out. Only then had she felt safe enough to agree to play.

She'd thought Petition had taught her how to identify manipulation. It hurt to realize how badly she'd failed.

Something moved outside. Ruth stopped breathing.

More footsteps.

They came from her right and passed beneath their shelter.

This set was different, though.

Faster. Lighter. Hesitant.

A guest. Someone gambling on finding a better hiding place.

Ruth waited, her heart aching, hoping she wouldn't have to listen to another stranger die. They circled beneath the medical clinic. Then a sudden sound cut through the rain. Ruth pressed her eyes closed, bracing for the screams.

The sound repeated.

Metal on metal.

Picking, scraping. The heavy clunk of tension failing. Like a crowbar, straining against a lock.

The stranger was at the medical unit's doors, and they were trying to break in.

She could feel Zach tense beside her. She could follow his thoughts. It was a bad choice of hiding place; the staff had placed the locks. If they saw they'd been disturbed, the unit would be scoured.

And that was if the sound didn't draw them in like wolves to a wounded deer.

There was a heavy clunk as the crowbar slipped. Again and again. Metal on metal, scraping, growing louder with each attempt.

They were compromising not only themselves, but also Ruth, Zach, and Hayleigh.

Ruth squeezed her eyes closed, her heart thundering. Braced for the rush of footsteps, the *whick* of a knife through air.

Instead, she heard panting. A woman swore under her breath.

Ruth's eyes snapped open. She recognized the voice.

"Makayla."

46.

Heather twisted. Her fingernails scraped at her shoulders, leaving long red lines.

She was gasping. Her body convulsed. And as she turned, Logan saw it.

Her back. A gash cut from her shoulder blades down to her hip, two inches wide. It oozed with every flinching movement.

It was why she was in the tower. Why she hadn't taken part in the hunt.

She'd already been involved in a struggle. Possibly with Lisa. Possibly with Trigger. And they hadn't gone down easily.

Sounds burst out of Heather's lungs. Like a bellowing animal, heavy and reverberating in the small space.

She swiped at them with an arm. Petra stepped out of reach. Bumped into two of the hanging bodies. The ropes creaked as they swung like pendulums.

"What's happening to her?" Eton asked. He raked his fingers through his hair. "Pet? What do we do?"

"Run," Logan hissed.

He had not gone far down the Petition research hole. But he had been far enough to learn exactly what the nerve toxins had done to the cult.

An aching howl ricocheted through the space. Heather staggered. She was between them and the doors. Her fingers clawed at her flesh: her shoulders, her abdomen, her breasts. Her feet slammed into the floor as she staggered.

And Heather's short, tidy nails dug deeper. Through the soft outer layer of her skin. Blood oozed. Pockets of tissue and white fat gleamed.

Her eyes rocked in their sockets, the pupils blowing out, and then fixed on the group.

Logan grabbed his companions and pulled. "Run!"

"It's Makayla," Ruth hissed.

"Shh." She could feel how rigid, how petrified Zach was.

He was making the correct choice. Stay quiet, stay hidden, no matter the cost. It had been their unspoken pact when they entered the roof. They couldn't save the people outside, no matter how loudly they screamed.

But it was Makayla.

Ruth had watched her being dragged across the rocks.

And she'd watched her survive.

Were they really going to let her die that night?

"Makayla," Ruth hissed, louder, loud enough to be heard outside, and the scrape of metal fell silent.

Zach clutched at her hand, squeezing, furious, desperate.

"Makayla," Ruth repeated, and she ignored him when he pressed harder. "Up here. I think we have room for one more."

"I don't want to hide with you." Makayla's voice was a raspy whisper, filled with anger. "I'm trying to get us help."

Metal clanged. Ruth could picture a crowbar jamming against a lock.

Zach's grip on her hand eased off a fraction.

"How?" he asked.

"I spent a full day in there," Makayla spat back. "And Dr. Coleman? He was pretty excited to have a chance to show off his satellite phone."

Ruth felt Zach's breath catch.

A satellite phone meant contact with the outside world.

Rescue.

She couldn't see Zach's face. But she could feel the energy, the indecision. He was running through the options, trying to gauge whether the risk was worth it.

He'd found a good hiding place. He thought it would keep them safe until dawn, and Ruth believed him. The safest bet, at least for their group, was to stay hidden.

And listen to a massacre that was planned to last for hours.

She'd done that once before.

And this time, she was being offered a way out.

"Stay here." Ruth shoved on the metal sheet before Zach could stop her.

"Wait," he hissed.

She shimmied out of the gap and onto the roof.

Rain hit her, unexpectedly cold and hard. She slid to the roof's edge and looked over.

Makayla stood below. Her clothes were torn. Her hair was in her face. Horribly, a clump had been pulled out, leaving a fist-sized patch of raw, red skin on the side of her skull.

Her body still bore the patchwork bruises. They were deepening and darkening as they settled. A row of new scrape marks ran across her arm, inflamed and clearly painful. The bandages around her hand were peeling off.

Ruth had pictured her with a crowbar. Instead, she carried a narrow metal pipe, torn from one of the buildings. She'd jammed it into the chains lashed through the double doors' handles and was trying to apply enough pressure to break them. The pipe had already started to bend.

"Be careful," Ruth whispered. "The staff keeps sweeping through here."

"It's you. I didn't realize." Makayla's bruised lip twitched as she lifted her head, squinting into the rain. "I have a minute, at least. Friends are keeping watch."

She leaned against the pipe. Shoulder muscles strained and shoes dug into the slick ground. The chains pulled, quivering. But they were thick. Fresh. And Makayla grunted as the pipe slipped from its notch.

Ruth bit her lip. Around her, she could see the other buildings, glossy with rain. No sign of the friends who were supposed to be keeping watch.

At her back, Zach had the metal peeled up, braced on one hand, his eyes glinting in the shadows as he watched. And behind him...

Skylights. About two foot by three foot each.

Glass was less sturdy than metal.

"Throw me your pipe," Ruth whispered, arm reached out.

A hint of hesitation passed over Makayla's face, then she tossed the bar to Ruth.

She slipped across the roof to the nearest skylight. It was set into the metal, held in place with a frame, and Ruth jammed her knee against its edge to hold herself steady as she raised the pipe and slammed it down.

The corner of the skylight chipped.

Ruth, breathing hard, aware of just how visible she'd be on the roof, raised the pipe again.

The sound was painfully loud. Louder even than Makayla's. A hazy white scuff appeared where the pipe cut through decades of patina, but the chip didn't widen.

She raised the pipe again, then flinched as she sensed movement. A figure slipped across the roof, reaching toward her.

"Here," Zach said, putting his arms around her, his hands joining hers on the pipe.

They lifted it between them, then slammed it down.

The crack splintered across the glass.

Up again. Down, as hard as they could. The skylight shattered inward.

Ruth threw the pipe aside, then slipped both legs through the hole. "Makayla? Tell me where to find the phone."

"Go," Logan hissed. "Go!"

Heather's body convulsed as she clawed at herself. Holes appeared in her stomach, across her hips, over her throat. Glass crackled under her staggering feet.

She stood between them and the door. But it was only going to get worse if they hesitated.

Logan shoved his hands into Eton and Petra, physically cramming them forward.

Heather sucked in a wailing, gasping shriek, then came at them.

They peeled aside. Heather's damp fingertips grazed Logan's arm. She hit the hanging bodies, sending them spiraling, trails of liquid dripping from their shoes. Shadows careened across the walls as the three struggled to hold their lights.

Eton hit the door first. He scrambled, shoving it, trying to get it wider, but it was jammed. He turned his body sideways to get through.

Heather swung. Blood trailed over her jaw, and Logan saw, with sinking horror, that she was chewing her own lips off. Her hands rose to her face. Fingers pressed in on either side of her eye. Pushed through, stretching the lids, squeezing the eyeball. Spittle and blood flew from between her teeth with every rushing, haggard breath.

Petra was through the door. She grabbed Logan's arm, dragging him with her, and he had just enough time to see Heather pop her eye out before he made it through.

The gasping, moaning sounds were growing louder. No longer frightened but filling with outrage.

"The door," Logan whispered, snapping through the shock. "Help me!"

He knew the stories about Petition. About how the cult members had turned, not just on themselves, but on one another as well.

He shoved his shoulder into the metal. Eton pressed in beside him. The old, aching door ground closed, crunching into place.

A body slammed into its other side. The reverberations rushed through

Logan's arms and into his shoulders. He reached for the latch, pulling it down, sealing the tower. The lock had been broken, but Heather didn't seem to have the presence of mind to turn the handle.

Another slamming shock wave passed through the door as they reeled back from it.

And then another, and Logan swore he could hear skin splitting.

Another.

And another.

And again.

They stood back, shivering and voiceless, as they listened to Heather beat herself to death against the door.

"Ruth," Zach hissed. "Once you're in, there might not be an easy way out."

"It's about as safe as any other hiding place, then," she said.

Her legs were through the skylight. She couldn't see the floor. Her feet kicked for purchase as she lowered herself. They bumped into something small, knocking it over. A lamp? She took a breath, then let go of the roof.

Her hip grazed something solid—a desk, she thought—then her feet hit solid floor. She took a second, trying to find her balance in the near perfect darkness.

A horrible smell infused the room. She'd caught some of it while hiding beneath the metal, and she'd assumed it was just rot and mildew. Inside, it was a hundred times stronger. She swallowed and switched to breathing through her mouth.

"I need a light," she whisper-called to the hole in the ceiling.

Her own phone had been dead when she crawled out of the ocean.

Light appeared above her, then Zach reached his phone through the hole. Ruth caught it as he let go, then felt her heart skip beats.

The doctors were still inside the medical unit.

They occupied the beds. Six of them, one for each bay.

She only knew they were doctors because of the scraps of uniform that had been left trailing off the bodies.

Beside each bed was a small tray on wheels, the kind that might be used for surgeries. A large metal bowl had been placed on each of them, next to an array of tools. The trays and scalpels were drenched in red.

The doctors had been skinned. The flesh had been peeled back, like a layer of clothes being discarded. Sinew and muscle and fat exposed.

Their rib cages had been carved open. The sharp edges of bone shone in Ruth's light.

She didn't need to approach the bowls to know what they held.

The heart.

In Petition, the human's essence lived in their blood. The brain was a corruption, a rot. It longed for temptation, for evil, for sloth and self-service. A dangerous but unavoidable link to the corrupted world. You were expected to master it, to control it, or it would control you.

The blood, by contrast, was the purest part of a human. It infused every millimeter of the flesh, cleansing it, healing it with every pulse.

The removal of the heart symbolized the corruption of its owner. An insult, almost: it implied that a person had so little humanity left in them that they did not deserve their most valued organ.

Petition had viewed doctors as the antithesis of purity. They'd saved their worst punishment for the island's medical team.

And then Petition had left them, laid out on the beds, arms hanging limp and skin shed, as a message for whoever searched the island once their business there was done.

"You all right in there?" Makayla whispered.

The sound seemed to come from behind Ruth's shoulder. She shivered, drawing in on herself, as she turned the light away from the corpses. Metal walls and plastic storage compartments lit up under its glow. Streaks of red coated the surfaces. Fingerprints. Reaching hands. The storage boxes were scattered, plastic-coated tools and swabs spread across the floor. Rain came through the newly broken skylight, creating a patch of dampness that was beginning to spread.

Ruth backed toward the double doors. She stopped short of touching their blood-streaked surface. "Where's the phone?"

"Dr. Coleman kept it in a leather satchel." Makayla's voice floated through the metal, magnified and echoing. "Brown, a bit smaller than a pillow. It's old and worn; he said he's been bringing it to remote jobs for years."

Ruth raised her light as she scanned the room. Seconds were precious. Her eyes jumped from scattered cotton swabs to a lost shoe to an overturned chair.

Did Petition take the bag? Did they know there was a phone inside?

She moved, skirting around the debris, shoving desks away from the wall to check beneath them.

Was it even here to begin with? Or did Dr. Coleman return it to his room or put it in one of the lockers or…?

Panic rose. They were taking a serious risk by making themselves so visible. If she couldn't find the sat phone after all that…

Desk legs shuddered as Ruth pushed furniture aside. Beneath were the shattered remains of a laptop. A coffee mug, broken.

And a brown leather satchel.

Joel's breathing was thin. Painful in his throat. He chewed on the corner of his thumb, wearing the skin down to bloody scraps.

His laptop was open on the floor ahead of him. A cable ran from it, looping through the rain and half hidden by the mud.

Camping Quest's gear. Frustrating to pack, heavy to carry. But designed to cope with any obstacle the wilderness environments created.

The cable was plugged into the back of the festival's surveillance system nearly two hundred feet away.

The surveillance room had been too risky, too close to the jungle's edge. Joel had watched a group try to set up base inside that room, believing they'd found the advantage they needed, only to be ambushed and killed within ten minutes.

The two hundred feet of space their cable bought them amounted to about twenty seconds of warning if they needed to run.

Barely anything.

But better than nothing.

Mirror images of the security feeds played over the screen. He and Mitchell hunched shoulder to shoulder, watching them.

Watching Makayla. And watching the woman from the roof. The one who had vanished into the medical clinic.

Most importantly, watching the pathways that led to the staff area.

Joel's chest squeezed.

He slapped Mitchell's shoulder, getting his attention.

Three bodies moved through the rain, their bare skin gray and shiny under the pixelation.

They were coming toward the staff area.

Mitchell waved a hand at Brent.

He was crouched by the window, in the most exposed location, his pupils reflecting beads of light in the dim room. He rose just high enough to see through the glass. Aimed a laser pointer. Snapped it on and then off again.

On the screen, a dot of light appeared on the medical unit's door, next to Makayla. Her head jerked toward it, then she swiveled to stare up at the camera, her eyes wild.

47.

Ruth wrenched the satchel open.

Inside were notebooks, spare batteries, a flashlight. What looked like an emergency water filter. Space for the laptop. And a pocket with a thick, blocky phone in it.

Makayla's fist slapped against the door. It was probably only a light tap, but inside, it seemed shockingly loud.

"They're coming," she hissed.

Ruth dashed to the space beneath the skylight. "Here!"

She tossed the phone upward, through the curtain of rain.

Zach's silhouette moved. He snatched it out of the air as lightning shot the sky into sharp relief. Thunder rattled the walls, and Ruth backed away from the cascading rain as Zach vanished.

"Go. *Go.*"

Each word came out with a puff of breath as Joel shoved the laptop underneath a bed.

His last glimpse of the screens showed a swarm. At least twenty of them, slinking through the jungle, following the paths, cinching in from every direction. Metal and wood swinging in their hands, blood painting their flesh.

How are there so many? Why all at once?

He and Mitchell were at the door. Out into the rain. Racing for cover, for the jungle.

Because we're not the only ones plugged in to the surveillance system.

The realization felt like a kick to his chest. He was fighting to breathe. They were between the trees, racing, and he didn't see the figure until it was on top of them.

A man. Skin slick. An enormous hook balanced in his palms.

Lightning reflected off his eyes as they fixed on Joel.

And then they were past one another.

The man didn't even try to raise the weapon. He kept moving forward, face toward the staff clearing, leaving Joel to vanish into the jungle.

He was only interested in one specific prey.

<hr>

Petra could barely hear anything over her pounding heart.

Eton's breathing was shallow, frantic. She held on to his slick wrist, afraid she would lose him in the darkness otherwise.

"The tower's dead." Logan swiped a hand over his face, clearing rain. He led them through the forest, but Petra wasn't certain he knew where they were going. "What else? What are our alternatives?"

A scream sliced through the trees. They pulled up short, pressing so close together that Petra could feel their body heat radiating through wet clothes.

"We're too exposed out here," Eton whispered. "We need to find shelter."

Rain trailed off Logan's hair as he shook his head. "Any hiding place will be turned over a dozen times over before dawn. Right now, the staff is still hunting down the easy targets. There's enough chaos and enough noise to buy us some cover. It's a brief window and we can't waste it. Now, *think*. There has to be some other solution."

Eton turned on Petra, his expression tight, wanting her to side with him.

And she did. Mostly. Until they took cover, their small group counted as part of the *easy targets*.

But she also knew what Logan meant.

Out of everyone on the island, she and Eton had the best knowledge of the layout and logistics. Which meant they had the best shot of anyone to stop the slaughter.

"We find someone with IT knowledge to get the staff network back online," she said. Her tongue was dry. Hurt flashed over Eton's face, and she willed herself not to look at it. She was gambling not just her own life, but his as well. "I don't know enough to troubleshoot it myself. But maybe a guest will."

"Okay." Logan swallowed and began leading them forward again, angled away from where they'd heard the scream. "That's something."

"You saw what they did to the storm warning tower," Eton hissed. "I don't think we'll have much chance of salvaging the actual official network."

He was right. Heather had made it clear that none of them planned to survive the weekend. They wouldn't show any restraint in what they did to the systems.

"What about satellite phones?" Logan's voice was low and quick, his head moving in response to any sound, benign or otherwise, that came from the jungle.

"We had two. The staff took them." *But what if we could find them? There are eight employee bunks. Maybe the phones are hidden under a mattress or inside a suitcase—no. Of course not. They'd have been destroyed as well. No loose ends.*

"What about the guests?" Logan shot her a meaningful glance. "Some of the VIP invites do remote travel. What about that travel vlogger, Melody? Or Camping Quest? What's the chance they'd have some kind of satellite system?"

She felt Eton twitch. A small spark of hope, mirroring her own.

"Maybe." Petra yanked her satchel around and tugged the tablet out. "We'd need to find them."

"The communications room video feeds," Eton said. "They were still working when we were last there."

Even with that advantage, everything was pinned on hope. Hope that they could find the right guest. Hope that the guest actually had a sat phone. Hope the guest was still *alive*.

The tablet screen was blindingly harsh. Eton threw up his hands, trying to screen the light from outside eyes, as Petra switched the brightness settings to their minimum. She tabbed to the database of VIP guests.

"Think if there are any other VIPs who produce travel content," Logan said. "We'll go to the communications room first. It might be necessary to make a desperate play."

"How desperate?" Eton asked.

"I'm thinking we try the PA system, in case it still works, and put out an announcement."

Eton shook his head, his jaw rigid. "You'd be calling them straight to us."

"Like I said. It's a desperate play."

Petra shot her arm out, halting them. Drops of water filtered through the heavy canopy to trail around them in thin rivers. They were submerged in a muted cacophony: the storm, the insects, the jungle itself. They'd been relying on it to mask their voices and their movements.

But it had been masking more than just their group.

"Ah-ah. Ah-ah. Ah-ah!"

Not quite words. Not quite a laugh.

Petra turned. Through the trees, she saw a shimmer of something pallid. Flesh, shiny in the rain. Eyes, pupils blown out.

"Ah-ah! Ah-ah!"

The glint of a cleaver from the kitchens.

Every muscle in Petra's body stiffened.

She still had her post, with its blunt metal tip, hooked into the back of her pants.

Three of us against one. Do we fight? Or do we run?

The choice was made for her.

Eton bolted.

"Ah-ah!" The gaunt figure threw itself toward her, and Petra felt a miserable stab of recognition. His name was Declan. He'd stayed late to help her process invoices right before they traveled to the island. Over a coffee break, he'd quietly told her that his mother had been diagnosed with early-onset Alzheimer's, and had thanked her for the job opportunity.

And now he raised a meat cleaver as he ran at her. Mud and blood streaked over his legs and torso. He'd been hurt already; a flap of skin hung loose on his stomach, a small river of blood trailing from the gash.

His face showed no recognition. No softness or grief. Only hunger.

Petra couldn't turn off her emotions in the same way. She couldn't wipe the gentle, quiet coworker from her mind.

She clutched the tablet to her chest as she threw herself away from Declan and raced for the trees.

"Ah-ah! Ah-ah!"

Logan sprinted a half step behind her. She could hear Eton crashing through the plants ahead. A stitch burned in her side and wet hair clung to her face as she flew after him.

Then Petra sucked in a sharp breath as the smothering jungle broke apart, and they plunged into a clearing.

The staff area. Logan had said he was aiming for the communications room; Petra hadn't believed his sense of direction was strong enough to get them there.

Declan's pace was chaotic. He ricocheted between trees, bare feet slipping in the mud. They'd gained ground. But not much. Not enough.

Eton balked. His legs kicked at the mud, sliding out as he fought to stop his momentum. He landed on his side, hands slamming into the wet earth.

Ahead, a cult member stood in the center of the clearing.

Lightning seared the scene. The figure's eyes shone white as she reached an arm upward, as though to snatch the lightning out of the sky.

Not a staff member. A guest. Her clothes were drenched, her face and arms spackled with blood.

And she was reaching toward a second figure. One poised on the medical clinic's roof, silhouetted against the canopy. He held a small blocky object. No…not just held; he grasped it like a lifeline.

"Pet." Eton grasped her sleeve, mud streaking over the fabric. "Pet!"

Declan was almost on them. They needed to move. But Petra couldn't tear her focus from the two figures as thunder built into a shuddering, rolling crescendo.

The man on the roof threw his treasure. It arced overhead: small and rectangular, its metal surface catching the light.

They'd been trying to guess whether any VIP guests could have brought long-range communication devices. But didn't their lead doctor regularly work as a field surgeon in remote areas?

"Pet!" Eton shouted.

She spun. Declan was right there. Close enough for her to see his dilated pupils and the string of frothy saliva connecting his lips.

And then Logan shoved in. She heard the rush of his post cutting through air, then a soft thud as it hit flesh. Declan's hatchet swung down, but the momentum was cut short as Logan forced him back.

"Hold him back," Petra yelled. "As long as you can!"

Then she threw herself forward, tearing free from Eton's grip, as she ran toward the guest in the clearing.

She already held the tablet. Her pen flew over the surface as she exited the list of guests and opened the core files.

Logan grunted as he wrestled with Declan. Ragged laughter burst from the man. It wasn't the only sound. Voices rose from the jungle. No words: just syllables. Barking shouts of anger and glee and wildness, coming from ahead, behind...everywhere. So many of them.

Petra didn't tear her eyes away from her goal. Makayla, she realized. Holding a sat phone. Her jaw twitched as she powered it on and pulled out the antenna.

911 wouldn't work; they weren't in the U.S. And Makayla wouldn't know the local emergency numbers.

But Petra did.

They'd taken out the internet, but Petra's pad stored its notes offline. Every safety document, every memo, every completed task was at her fingertips.

Her emergency protocol, carefully built over months in the lead-up to the festival, splashed over the screen as Petra tapped it open. The emergency contact details were bolded at the top.

A fresh wash of lightning cascaded over the clearing as bodies emerged from between the trees. Cruel metal tools reflected the light as the shouting, chanting voices rose into a cacophony.

"Here!" Petra shouted, hand outstretched as she neared Makayla.

"Now run," Petra snapped as she snatched the phone from Makayla. Her fingers shook as she punched in the numbers with a series of sharp stabs. There was no room for mistakes. The cultists were closing in, pouring around the buildings, all running toward her. She had only seconds left.

As the phone began to ring, Petra searched for her allies.

Makayla darted away, pressing close to the buildings. The cultists ignored her. They seemed prepared to let her escape, as long as they didn't lose Petra.

Declan had joined the throng. Logan must have given up on holding him back; there wasn't anything he could do to help Petra now.

She couldn't see Eton. She hoped he'd gotten away.

The staff she'd so carefully trained were just feet from her.

The computer-generated ringing cut out. A voice answered the phone.

Petra began speaking, not even allowing the other party the chance to greet her.

A meat hook stabbed into her upper arm. Pulled.

Unimaginable pain lanced through Petra. She closed her eyes, icy sweat blooming over her. But she kept speaking, spitting out her script. Staying focused, the way only she could.

Something sharp pierced into her back.

A blade stabbed into her thigh, toppling her to the ground. She clutched the sat phone in both hands, refusing to let it drop.

And she kept speaking, spitting out the words as clearly as she could manage while the hook pulled, and the knives moved in around her. She had to make sure she got her message out, no matter how badly it hurt.

Her job involved overseeing the island's activities to the best of her abilities.

And she never did anything by half measures.

Ruth froze as voices rose outside the medical clinic.

Chanting, growing louder, growing closer.

She pressed Zach's phone to her chest, smothering its bulb as she fumbled to switch it off.

His silhouette appeared in the skylight, his arms braced on the metal frame. "Ruth."

She couldn't see his expression, but his voice was eerily shaken. "I'm here. I can't stay any longer. Good luck."

He hesitated, and she could hear a thin, unsteady smile in his voice. "Let's find out if your sighting comes true."

He vanished. She heard him sliding over the roof. Heard the moment his feet left its surface. The impact as he landed behind the clinic and began to run.

The voices outside were growing in pitch, fervor.

Loud. Angry.

Ruth reached for one of the desks. If she got it under the skylight, she might be able to boost herself out.

She stopped, hands on the wood.

Climbing out would only make her more visible.

Worse, it would draw focus to the roof. To the sheet of metal where Hayleigh was still hidden.

Ruth ground her jaw. She couldn't see anything. She could only hear.

A voice, shouting.

The slap of footsteps. The ring of metal.

The shouting grew louder, more frantic.

Then there were hands on the clinic's doors, tugging, rattling the chains.

Breaking them open.

Ruth backed away. There was no time to hide. No *space* to hide, not even underneath the beds and their flayed corpses.

The doors rocked open, shuddering as the hinges maxed out.

A crowd stood in the opening. Their faces were vacant, wild. Staring eyes. Limp hair. Flesh stained pink from the massacre they'd wrought.

At least, Ruth thought, her mind ringing with dull terror, *at least we tried.*

They flooded through the doors. Wet hands were on her. Grabbing her clothes, grabbing her skin. Pulling her, bruising her.

Dragging her back through the open doors.

Through the haze of rain, Ruth saw a figure in the mud.

Makayla, she thought, but that wasn't right. Makayla had been wearing a singlet, not a jacket.

The figure seemed strange. Stretched, somehow. A hand was too far away. A leg was a meter past where it should have been.

She lay prostrate. Spears, so much like the ones Gilly had taken, extended from her back.

As the family dragged Ruth past, she saw the face, open mouth seeping blood, eyes vacantly filling with rain.

Petra.

The sat phone rested next to her severed hand.

One of the family stepped up to it. Inhaled. Raised their weapon.

Their implement—a ragged flat of metal, sharpened on both sides—smashed down into the phone, shattering it.

48.

Ruth licked rainwater that trailed over her lips.

Her shoulders ached from the angle they'd been pinned at. Ropes rubbed skin raw around her wrists.

She couldn't tell how long she'd been there. The storm had spent itself. Spits of water still hit her face, gathered on her chin, but the brunt of its force was gone. The beach's floodlights burned through her closed eyes.

The family had knelt her in the sand, her hands tied to a stake behind her back. They'd faced her toward the crossbar and the tub.

She refused to watch. But she could still hear everything. The shudder of bodies being dragged through the sand. The creak as they were pulled up by ropes around their legs. The slice of a knife through skin.

The steady drip, drip, drip of their blood into the tub.

It had been nearly half full when they'd brought her there. She wondered how much closer to the rim it would be by now.

She'd taken part in two cleansings in her lifetime.

One, she'd been too young to remember. Just vague images, a sense of unease, of being scolded by one of the mothers when she squirmed.

The second had been just two days before Petition's end. She'd been seven. She could recall it vividly.

A middle-aged couple had come to their commune.

Visitors weren't prohibited. Barom talked often about how they needed to welcome the lost ones who came to them.

But he also talked often about persecution, about how the world

loathed them for what they believed, about how they had enemies everywhere who longed to corrupt them and tear them apart.

About how the followers had to be careful not to let those forces into
their lives.

Ruth had felt both fascination and fear when she saw the couple step
out of a shiny black car. Neither of them wore head coverings. The wife's
curly hair was cut short, and her skirt stopped at her knees, unthinkable
in their commune.

Ruth had been especially fascinated by her heels. Less than two inches
tall, kitten heels, she later learned. In Petition, heels were a shorthand for
vanity, for hedonism, for earthly corruption.

And as those heels clicked against the path, Ruth had felt a twinge of
curiosity, of longing, and she'd hated herself for it.

The couple was there about their son. Barom had warned the commune
about it over the previous weeks. They were jealous and shamed that their
son had escaped the world's rot. They were trying to drag him back into
the mire, back down to their level.

They would be cunning, Barom had warned. They might fake tears.
They might promise any number of impossible things. They might say
they were there for love, but they did not know what love was; they could
only pretend.

Ruth stared, in silent fascination, at their wrinkles and their gray hair
and the wife's gold jewelry, as they entered the building.

They stayed inside for hours. When they left, they were both crying
and angry.

But they didn't stay away. They returned the following afternoon.
Ruth, gutting rabbits with the other girls her age, heard shouting through
the walls.

That night, the commune had a cleansing in the barn.

They entered in single file, silent as the ceremony demanded, and
gazed up at the sacrifices hung from the ceiling.

The last of the couple's blood dripped into the basin. Their faces were slack and gray. The wife's jewelry was gone; so were the envy-inducing heels. Her skirt had been tied to her legs so it could not fall down and shame her.

Ruth hadn't known it at the time, but that moment solidified Petition's end.

The couple refused the leave the compound without speaking to their son. During the inquest, it was revealed that he had perished the previous winter. His family had never been told.

Barom had enacted his own laws.

People inside his family could die and be buried with very little attention from the outside world.

But an outside couple? A wealthy couple?

A couple who had told friends and family their plan?

Barom's warnings of persecution were about to rear up, suddenly all too real and utterly inescapable.

Two days later, they had a feast.

All the food they loved. As much of it as they wanted.

And afterward, honey.

"Hey, dearest one."

Ruth cracked her eyes open.

A man crouched before her. His skin seemed as pallid and gray as a corpse's under the harsh floodlights. He smiled, and his wide mouth was filled with irregular teeth.

"How are you feeling?" he asked. "Are the ropes too tight?"

Ruth kept silent.

He tilted his head, concern creeping into his expression. "You must be thirsty. Here."

He held out cupped hands. One of the others unscrewed the cap on a bottle of water and poured it into his palms, and he held them up to Ruth's mouth.

She hesitated, but her thirst was immense, and she was so close to the end that not much seemed to matter any longer. She dipped her head and drank from his hands.

"There, that will help." He waited until she was done, then flicked his hands to dry them. "There's a while to go until dawn, dearest one. Let us tend to you until then."

Ruth wished she'd been given more water. She would have spat it into his face.

"You might notice something familiar about me." His smile was very wide, and it showed too much of his gums. "I asked my beloved family to refer to me as Barry this weekend, but you can call me Barom."

Quiet shudders passed through Ruth. They felt like cold, squirming worms, corrupting her limbs and turning them heavy.

"I've sought justice for Petition since the day of its sacrifice. Barom saw my devotion. He chose me as a worthy vessel. He allowed me his name and assigned me the greatest honor and hardest task: that of finishing his work."

He looked so young. He would have been a child when Petition collapsed. Ruth's mind raced. Could he have been there? Was he one of Barom's many children? She didn't recognize him, but a lot could change about a person in twenty years.

They'd told Ruth she was the only survivor. But were they *sure*?

"We couldn't speak before now. It wasn't safe. But, you know, we've been taking care of you, even if you didn't know it." The creases around his eyes deepened as he smiled. "When Gillian Davies caused you distress, we had her removed. When the man who called himself Trigger hurt you, we kept score."

Trigger's limbs were silhouettes against the dark ocean. Ruth had forgotten that he'd bumped her while playing games at lunch.

"We're so glad you came back to the family." The man reached out, running a hand across her hair, down onto her cheek. "Finally, all can be

made right. We will lie down alongside you, and together, our sacrifice—
our gift—will be enough to shake the foundations of evil. To save the
others, the corrupted ones, the rotted ones. A great cost for us—and
received without gratitude—but more valuable than any gift this world
can give."

The words took a moment to register. When they did, they came with
faint confusion, then low, burning, blooming shock.

"Can you tell me something?" she asked.

"Of course." He beamed, his canines like fangs. "Anything for you,
precious child."

She used her chin to gesture toward the basin. "Why are you performing a cleansing?"

There was a hint of hesitation, gone so fast she nearly missed it. "To
make ourselves clean and forgiven. To ensure our sacrifice is pure."

"And why today? Why this weekend?"

"It is twenty years exactly since the first sacrifice." His smile widened.
"We're closing the loop, at last, on its anniversary."

Thin spits of rain grazed her face. She stared into the night, barely
feeling them.

The man's words sank in slowly. Dripping into her mind, seeping down
her spine and into her heart.

They moved through her as slowly as a scalpel carving out a tumor.
Agony, but also relief. Each cut unbearable, but signaling the end of a
nightmare.

Her mouth felt strange as she let a smile grow. Then she said, quiet and
calm, "You're a joke."

The man tilted toward her. His brows rose a fraction.

Shocked laughter escaped Ruth. She felt lighter. As though the tumor
had been lifted out.

"You're a joke," she repeated, almost intoxicated by how true the words
were. "You're not Petition."

Gentle concern had settled over the man's face. "Dearest one—"

"I'm not your dearest one. Barom didn't like me. Did you know that? When our paths crossed, I was supposed to get out of his way."

The man started to lift a hand but then left it hanging, as though unsure what to do with it.

"Cleansings aren't to purge your sins," Ruth said, relief running through her nerve endings, making her giddy. "You perform a cleansing to renew your knowledge of the evils of the world, to remember what corruption tastes like."

A faint sound caught in his throat. He wanted to tell her she was wrong.

But she wasn't. She'd been there. She knew Petition's rules better than anyone.

"Did the twenty-year anniversary feel significant? The important number was *seven*. We only acknowledged milestones that were based around seven."

A figure had approached, hands clasped at her naked waist. "Barom?"

"One moment." His smile was cracking around the edges.

"I should have realized sooner." Ruth wasn't really speaking to Barry any longer. "Barom never talked about *saving the world*. Barom thought the world deserved everything coming to it." She breathed, flooding cold, salty air into her lungs. "Did you cobble together your knowledge of Petition from what the media released? From the scraps of paper in Barom's rooms? I hope not, because those were mostly fiction."

His silence was damning.

"I'm so glad." She laughed, breathless. The ache of relief was overwhelming. "I thought that Petition had survived."

Frustration bled into his voice. "It did. We are. We follow Barom's teachings. Petition was rebirthed through us."

"No," she said, and met his bitter, panicked eyes. "You're not Petition. You're just a fan club."

He raised his hand to slap her.

There were so many of the others around them. Staring, silent but fixated. No longer smiling.

He carefully lowered his hand.

"You're testing us," he said, loud enough for everyone to hear. "You're seeing how we respond when you sow doubt. Don't fear; we're strong enough not to waver."

"Oh, look at that, you're trying to spin a narrative. Barom was better at it." She didn't care if he hurt her. She was dead either way. At least she didn't have to die afraid of Petition, afraid of the past. It was over. The best Barry and his followers had managed was a shambling imitation. "Barom would have loathed you."

Barry stared at her, his expression ice.

The woman behind him shifted. "Barom?"

"Not now."

"It's important." She fidgeted, heel dragging into the sand. "Ships are coming."

"What?"

Ruth shuffled, pulling strained muscles a fraction tighter, to see the ocean.

Through the fading rain, through the gloom and the clouds and the sea spray…there were lights.

Petra had died. But not before making her call.

Barry stood. He stared from Ruth to his followers to the horizon. Then his face hardened.

"Call the others. Dawn happens *now*."

49.

An alarm played from every speaker. Ruth could hear echoes of it coming from all across the island.

The final body was discarded from the cleansing rig. The tub was two-thirds full. Staff crowded around it, drawing the bound lamb in the sand, trying to set a stage. They had probably planned to dedicate hours to the ritual, to making it feel symbolic, special.

Under a time crunch, they looked stressed and frightened.

She was glad. They wouldn't get to have the indulgent ceremony they'd wanted.

The sirens cut out. The last of the staff jogged out of the jungle, answering its summons, but Ruth was sure they were missing numbers.

Some of the guests had fought back.

They shuffled around the basin of mingled blood and rainwater. Ruth didn't want to watch, but she couldn't bring herself to look away either.

Under the harsh, artificial lights, they dipped their fingers into the slurry. Stirred. Raised their cupped hands and drank.

She still remembered the taste from that last cleansing. She'd thought of the kitten-heel shoes while the blood slid down her throat.

The staff each brought up a second cupful of liquid, then poured it over their heads, letting it drip through their hair and down their backs.

"Sacrificial blood will wash you clean."

The mantra. They'd repeated it so often, been *reminded* of it so often. Every time they walked beneath the image of the bound lamb above the doors.

She could see how they'd conflated it with the cleansing. But they'd gotten it wrong, yet again.

The sacrificial blood referred to their *own* blood.

The people in Petition sacrificed themselves to Barom, to serve him unquestioningly.

And their blood, purified, washed the corruption out of their cells with every lap through their veins.

"Sacrificial blood will wash you clean," the followers murmured, stepping back to make room for more at the basin, and Ruth was filled with misery at how many lives had been culled for their ignorance.

Someone brought out a wooden tray. On it were rows of small glass bottles. The first batch of staff, the ones dripping blood, each took one and uncapped it.

Ruth closed her eyes.

Of course, no reenactment of Petition's darkest moments could be complete without the honey.

The inquest had never released the chemical makeup of the neurotoxins used to kill the commune. But she knew there had been whisperings online, scientists and armchair chemists theorizing on how the effect was achieved.

She felt pretty certain this new Petition could create a recipe that was at least similar.

They drank, each of them closing their eyes and clasping the vials tightly as they swallowed.

They believed they were making a sacrifice. To offer themselves up to save the rest of humanity.

If they'd wanted a more accurate reenactment, they would have no idea what was actually in the honey.

The original family had been promised a quiet death, a gentle death. Barom had said they would lie down together like lambs. And then, once they had joined in death, they would rise, their bodies purified and immune to the world's rot.

The fake followers had gotten one thing right, at least. The deaths had been a sacrifice. But not a selfless one. Not for good.

They'd been a sacrifice to a man's ego. And to his refusal to let any of them outlive him.

"Your turn, precious child."

She'd known this was coming. She still wouldn't go down softly.

Ruth kicked. Writhed. Clamped her mouth closed.

Fingers pried at her lips. Knuckles pushed into her jawbone, applying pressure until her teeth were forced apart. Two of them held her legs and another two fixed her head as their leader uncorked a bottle and raised it over her mouth.

"You were the only one missing last time," he whispered, taking delight in the retribution as he tipped the fluid into her mouth. "With this, the sacrifice is complete."

Sweet, bitter. Flowing over her tongue. Ruth jerked her head, trying to spit, but hands forced her mouth closed again and tilted her head back, giving her no choice. The liquid began to trickle past her tongue and down her throat.

"There, it is done," the man said, cleansing blood trailing over his face, dripping from the tip of his nose. He uncorked his own vial and swallowed its contents before stepping back.

They let her head go. Ruth spat, and spat again, but there was very little of it left in her mouth.

The ropes pulled tighter around her wrists, then released. Her fingers tingled as blood flowed back into them.

They'd let her go.

She wasn't sure if that was a mercy or a final punishment. Bound, she would be forced to writhe in agony until her nerve endings died and her heart split. Free, she would claw at herself and those around her until they were all dead.

Ruth turned away and retched. Bile came up. A little of the water they'd given her. Not enough.

The honey was quickly absorbed.

The pretend family had finished their cleansing. The tray of bottles was set aside.

They stood in loose lines and held hands as they faced the ocean and hummed. They had probably planned to do this as the rising sun bathed them in warm colors. They would need to sing to the blinking ship lights instead.

They didn't even know any of Petition's songs.

That was a comfort. For all the world's obsession with the cult, for all its speculation, almost nothing of Petition had survived. Ruth was the last holdout, the only person who could remember those events. And she could ensure those secrets would be buried with her.

She pulled her legs up, arms wrapping around them, chin on top of her knees.

Some of the figures began to twitch. The blood dripped from their hair and trailed down their backs as their breathing became labored.

Ruth closed her eyes, feeling anger, grief, and emotions she couldn't even name.

Despite everything that had happened.

She still wanted to live.

50.

One of the cultists jolted.

His head snapped to the side, left shoulder rising high, as his grip on his neighbors tightened.

Twenty years before, Ruth had watched from beneath a table as her family, one by one, began to convulse like that.

The new version of Petition continued to sing, swaying lightly. Their arrangement, informal rows with hands held, made them look like paper chain dolls. Another one spasmed, and Ruth pictured an invisible hand reaching out and crumpling them.

Her heart galloped. She flexed her fingers and realized they were numb. Other parts of her seemed to be growing more alive. Tingles spread through her cheeks, her jaw, and into the tip of her nose. She shuffled her knees up closer to her chest, fighting to stay calm. Panic would make the poison spread faster.

Her last few moments on earth were going to be hell, but she still wanted to hold on to them as long as she could.

A woman buckled to her knees. Her neighbors kept their grip on her hands, raising their heads and their voices to drown out her groans.

Someone closer to the beach screamed, but the shout was cut off before it could finish.

The group's tranquility was collapsing. Nearly all the bodies were beginning to shudder. They doggedly held their rows, but feet scuffed through the sand and heads flicked erratically.

The original Petition had tried to hold its composure too. Sat at tables with the remains of the feast, their outfits clean and freshly pressed, their heads bowed in reverence, and pretended not to care as their bodies twitched and their breath hitched. The women had hummed one of the commune's songs. Two decades later, that melody still had the power to rear out of Ruth's subconscious. Both the words and the tune were simple to the point of being childish, and yet impossible to forget.

"We sing…we sing…we sing to you…"

On the beach, the new cult's song was already petering out into labored breathing and groans. More bodies collapsed to their knees.

"Today…" Barry's voice was loud but ragged at the edges. "We close the loop. Today we fulfill—"

A scream cut over him. The first of the informal rows broke. A woman wrenched her hands free from her neighbors and staggered toward the water, fingers digging into her scalp, clawing, clumps of hair drifting down her back as she fought to get relief.

"We…we fulfill…"

Barry was trying to finish his parting words, but his own body was jerking, one leg rising up repeatedly as muscles cramped.

It was just one more way he'd fallen short of the original Petition. One more way he'd failed to live up to his idol, Barom.

He'd taken the poison.

Ruth remembered being hidden under her table, frozen by terror as her family lost control of themselves. One of the mothers slammed her head into her metal plate, again and again, as the women around her fought to hold up the song.

"You hear, you hear, when we call to you…"

A man had begun clawing at his arm. Spots of blood appeared on his freshly ironed white uniform.

Voices shouted, chairs scraped, hands beat against wood tables and stone floors and fleshy limbs. On the Petition dais, where he presided, stood Barom.

Calm. Watchful.

As the room's atmosphere grew frantic, he turned, unnoticed by everyone except Ruth, and quietly vanished through the side door.

It took hours for everyone to die.

They spread through the commune like a virus. Blood spilled across every hallway, every wall. Everything became a weapon, including fingernails and teeth. Some sought to destroy themselves; others sought to destroy those around them.

As the honey's agony deepened, many ran, searching for a way out of the compound, trying to escape the hell they found themselves in. The elders had already sealed the exits, and piles of bodies built up against the locked doors.

Not a single one of them died quietly or easily.

Except Barom.

He sealed himself away in his private bedroom, surrounded by his comforts, as the commune collapsed on the other side of the door. Even Mother Aama, the favorite wife, had taken the honey. But Barom, the man who demanded his lambs lay down their lives for him, had saved a painless exit for himself.

"Ha." The sound slipped out of her now, full of bitterness. Barry wanted so much to be like Barom, without ever truly understanding the man.

Barom would never have subjected himself to his own ceremony.

"We ful...*fill*..." Barry's final attempt at his speech petered out. His neighbor twisted away, breaking their line, as gurgling moans rose into shouts and then into screams.

Barry's upper body jerked, convulsing backward at a ninety-degree angle and pointing his face to the sky, and the moonlight flooded over his bulging eyes and the froth about his lips.

There was no more singing. Only shouting, only howling.

They were turning on one another.

The woman who had broken away first had pulled out the last of her hair. Blood-matted strands hung from her arms as she turned back on her community, twitching fingers aiming for the nearest body.

A man shoved his fingers into his mouth, pulling his jaw wider and wider, exerting more strength than any human should have, until the bones snapped.

Two followers wrestled in the sand, gnawing at one another's face. Lips and cheeks and eyelids tore away between their teeth.

The honey consumed them so wholly that no other pain seemed to register.

Just like twenty years ago, some of them were reaching for weapons.

This time, the weapons were not just whatever object lay closest at hand. The followers had designed their own weapons to hunt the island's guests and had laid them down in neat rows in the sand. Blood-streaked fists closed around them.

Ruth looked down at her own hands.

She shook. Her fingers were numb. The pins-and-needles sensation that had started in her face now spread to the rest of her body, like ants filling every vein. They burrowed into her lungs, her stomach, her feet, her heart.

Ruth drew a slow, deep breath into her lungs. It tasted of blood and brine and smoke.

She shifted onto her knees. Got one foot under herself. Then the other.

Then she stood and began to shuffle forward, following the beach's slope toward the shore.

She remembered these sensations from way back then. The numbness, the pins and needles. She'd felt them while she crawled through the darkened halls, over her family's bloodstained bodies, searching for a way out.

The toxins would absorb through the mucous membranes within a matter of seconds. Even a small amount would be fatal.

That was what the scientists at the inquest had said.

Ruth had believed they'd gotten it wrong. She'd held the honey in her mouth until she could scurry into a corner and spit it out. And she'd survived.

My sacred child carries my gifts. Their sightings light the darkness ahead of us. No animal and no poison are capable of harming them.

Those were Barom's words.

"No." She spoke out loud, even though she didn't know who she was speaking to.

Sightings aren't real. The sacred child was a lie.

And yet.

She continued to walk. Shaky, her heart heavy and aching, her body both numb and electric. But still alive. Still in control of herself.

And she entered the fray.

Blood gushed into wet sand as the new family tore themselves apart.

They were past speech, but they vocalized. Screams. Howls. Grunts. Thick, fleshy moans. So loud, from every direction.

Limbs swiped and clawed and contorted. Digging into the sand, gouging it into an alien landscape.

A flash of dull light caught her focus. Glass. The empty honey vials: they'd found them, and they'd used their jaws to break them.

Ruth didn't flinch as she walked over the shards.

Ahead, three women crouched over a man. The skin over his stomach had been torn open and pulled back, revealing a maw of red and white.

The women dragged his organs out, biting into them and then throwing them aside, as though hunting for some cure to the poison's pain.

As Ruth stepped closer, she saw the man's face.

Barry.

His eyes were open. Dilated pupils flicked from side to side as his blood-filled mouth quivered.

His gaze latched onto Ruth for a heartbeat, then shifted away.

She didn't know if he recognized her. Or if he even knew what was happening to his body.

She stepped past the feasting women. They ignored her, fighting over Barry's intestines.

Ahead, a man staggered. He held one of the group's handmade weapons. A blade, carved into ridges like a saw. It was slick with blood. He stabbed wildly, slashing at the air, fighting monsters she couldn't see.

Flecks of hot blood landed on Ruth's throat. A woman lurched past her shoulder. She'd chewed her fingers off. Her palms were held up, showing the stumps to anyone who would look, as she wailed.

Then she burst into a run. Straight into the man's saw-carved blade.

Ruth moved around the pair as they drove themselves into the sand, the man hacking, the woman's wails turning thick.

A man staggered toward Ruth. He held a shard of glass in his mouth. One of the broken vials. Blood poured from his lips and over his fingers as he sawed his tongue out.

Ruth waited as he stumbled past her. His eyes were already missing. Red streams trailed down his cheeks like tears.

They fought one another. They fought themselves. But not even one of them seemed to see Ruth.

Men and women stumbled within inches of her. Flecks of blood, hot, sprayed across her arms and face. She didn't react. Her focus turned toward the moonlight rippling across the water—and on the distant flashing lights.

The beach was a cacophony: a screaming, shuddering hell. But she felt none of it.

She stepped across bodies. Across limbs and clumps of hair and organs that had churned into bloodred sand until it was impossible to tell what was beach and what was human.

She passed through the carnage.

Just as it began to feel as though it would never end, she emerged from the other side.

Right there was the ocean's edge.

Cool water swept up the sand and flooded across her bare feet. It was as soft as a caress, and Ruth let her body soften as the wave drained away.

The family continued to destroy themselves, but it seemed easy to let the sounds fade into the background until all she could hear was the whispers of each frothing wave and the thump of her own aching heart.

Ruth stepped forward again, into the shallows.

While preparing for the ritual, the followers had discarded the drained corpses into the ocean.

The water was thick with bodies.

Floating hair, limp limbs. Clothes rippling beneath the surface.

Ruth waded through them, letting the water rise over her knees and then to her waist.

She knew what she was going to find. It still hurt, more than she'd imagined it ever could.

Zach floated in the water. Body broken. Face bloodless. His open eyes stared sightlessly as salt water lapped over them.

Ruth pushed bodies aside to create a space for herself, then knelt. Her arms went around Zach, holding him in place. Her cheek rested on his chest, just below his chin, half submerged.

"I'm sorry," she whispered. "I really didn't want the sightings to come true."

Water lapped at her. A distant horn sounded, an early warning from the approaching ships.

She closed her eyes. Zach was cold, but his shape was still so familiar.

"I wasn't even the prophetic child," she said.

He'd so desperately wanted to know about her past. Now that it was all over, all gone, she would give him a piece. Something she hadn't told anyone. Not the caseworkers, not the people at the inquest, not the psychiatrists.

"They believed a child had prophetic powers. But it wasn't me. It was a boy, a year older than I was. Barom's son."

She smiled through the grief, and salt water washed over her lips.

Barom had many children, but parentage was never discussed at Petition. Ruth had sometimes wondered if she herself was a descendant of the cult leader.

"I had sightings too. I tried to whisper them to people sometimes, but the mothers always told me to be quiet, to mind my place. Barom wouldn't let a girl hold any power in the commune. Never. Only a boy, only his son. So I learned to keep them to myself. Until those last days, after the final cleansing, after the visiting couple was killed. And the sightings were so bad I couldn't lie about them anymore."

Ruth had approached one of the kindest mothers while they were in the kitchen. She hadn't realized Mother Aama was in the shadows, listening.

Mother Aama, who had always been so watchful and cold.

Mother Aama, mother of the commune's true prophetic child. A child who was supposed to be immune to poison. A child who eventually succumbed, twitching and howling, to the honey.

"When they searched the compound, they read Barom's writings. I talked about my sightings, and they made the connection that I had to be the special child. The one who gave the prophecies. They thought I'd been spared on purpose. I never told them the truth. I don't know why. Maybe…I wanted to feel like my family had loved me. Even if it was just pretend."

Ruth closed her eyes.

The salt water seeped into every cut on her body, stinging, but she felt it less than she should have. Bodies shifted around her, limbs bumping against her back and sides as they moved in the currents. Some of their faces would have been familiar, if she'd let herself look at them. She might have played against them on the raised maze, or passed them in the shipwreck house, or sat next to them in the audience that first night.

Sightings began to nudge at the edge of her consciousness. Ruth pressed her face against Zach's cold body and let them flood over her.

Black plastic against sand. Body bags lined up on the beach. So many of them. Even more are being brought out from the forest.

Searchlights, passing over empty rooms. Shelves, desks. Scattered papers. The lights turn toward the room's corner. There's a figure there, wedged into the gap between a shelf and the wall. Eton. His eyes round with fear. He reaches toward the light.

Sheets of metal. They're pried up, shuddering. Being moved off the roof of the medical unit, exposing the cavity underneath. A woman lies there, her face half missing, her limbs slack. Her blue eyes shimmer as they turn toward her rescuers.

Men and women are brought onto the ships. Thermal blankets hang from their shoulders. Glimpses of familiar faces: Makayla. The ghostlike man. One of the three friends from Gilly's group. Logan.

Some are covered in blood. Some stare into nothing, their faces empty. And some take out their phones. Calls to loved ones. Messages sent and received. A symphony of mechanical chimes ring through the space as photos and videos from that night flood into the outside world.

And they keep flooding. Like ripples, growing larger and larger, not losing power but becoming stronger as they bounce off one another. Three hours after the ships arrived at the island, those ripples have reached every corner of the online world.

Ruth let her eyes open.

It was all about to start again. The public fixation, borne half from trauma, half from morbid curiosity. The inquests, the trials. A deluge of news headlines following every fresh revelation. Statements from politicians, statements from celebrities, opinions flooding social media. Outrage and grief and blame and fear.

She was no longer a child. There would be no sealed records this time. No hiding.

"Okay," Ruth whispered.

She'd begged for another chance at life. She'd been given her wish. And if this was going to be the cost, so be it.

The sounds from the beach had faded out. If any of the staff was still alive, the toxins would finish them before morning.

The second version of Petition had destroyed itself as thoroughly as the first.

And just as with the first, Ruth had survived.

The ship's horn sounded again, deep and long and mournful. They were closer, no longer distant lights but growing silhouettes, blocking out the stars. Figures crowded at the railing, straining to see the island.

Everything was about to change.

But not yet. Not for another few minutes.

She tightened her hold on Zach.

She'd stay until they pulled her away.

• • •

Hi Logan,

I've given a lot of thought to what you said.

For most of my adult life, I've had filters on my computers and phones to screen out any mention of Petition. A week ago, I took those filters off.

It's about as bad as I expected. Half-truths and mistruths are spreading like fire—and the more they're repeated, the more people believe them. My counselor suggested limiting my intake, but it's so hard to step away.

Some of the lies are familiar—the ones that sprang up around the original Petition—but now there are new ones, as well. Videos from people claiming they were on the island but describing events that never happened. Theories about Petition being some global community that secretly runs governments. One video claimed I spent my life in a maximum-security psychiatric hospital. That one hurt. It had nearly eighty thousand views before I stopped looking.

Most of my life was spent hiding from the lies. Now, I'm trying to focus more on the truths. And the more I look for, the more I find.

Did you see the interview with a court security guard who was at the original Petition inquest? His account of what happened mirrors my own memories almost exactly.

And there have been videos and posts from people who really were on the island. I remember a lot of their faces. Some of them didn't understand what was happening or didn't see much. But others have explained the events more calmly and clearly than I could ever hope to. They're doing a good job of pushing back against the fakes.

Now that my identity is no longer secret, the media's trying to reach me. They were calling my phone until I turned it off. My inbox is a flood of all-caps interview invitations. I've never had social media accounts, but apparently there are some other Ruth Phillipses out there who are getting a lot of eager messages.

The voicemails and emails keep repeating the same phrase. A chance to tell your story.

But it's not, not really.

Those mistruths and half-truths? The videos of people pretending to be on the island, or coming up with new theories? They spread because they're exciting.

The news outlets want that too. They want to hear about a tyrannical leader and the bodies piled in the hallways. They'd slice up my interview to take the most shocking parts—the really disturbing, taboo, tantalizing bits—and lean on them so heavily that everything else would be forgotten.

Petition has been mythicized for my whole life. It doesn't deserve it.

I want to share what it was really like living in the commune. The whole story. How boring it was, and how ridiculous, and how monotonous and mindless.

I want to talk about the times Barom took to the pulpit while he was drunk, and we could barely understand him. Or how often he contradicted his own teachings, likes telling us butter was sinful and then ordering cartons of it the next month.

He sent us to dig the foundations for a new building, forgot about it for weeks, and then had to come up with an excuse for why the project was canceled. He kept rewriting one of the songs because he wanted to be a musician but wasn't good at lyrics. Two of the elders hid behind the grain shed to smoke forbidden cigarettes and thought no one could tell.

My life was spent pulling weeds, skinning rabbits, pumping water, hanging laundry. That was true for all of us. The ending was horrendous, but the daily living was menial and unrewarding.

I want people to know about that. Not just the exciting parts, but everything.

You're one of the few people I think I can trust right now. I want to do an interview, and I want the entire conversation to be shared. Even if it takes hours. No cuts or edits, not even for pacing, without my consultation.

Would you agree to that?

I think, from our conversation last week, that you would.

Let me know.

I'm ready to talk.

–Ruth

●●●

Eton's island festival was "a disaster waiting to happen" claims employee

How lax safety standards and inadequate security contributed to the unprecedented tragedy…

Cupcakes and Murders podcast interviews festival survivor

In a shocking two-and-a-half-hour episode of the smash-hit podcast, hosts Alyssa and Maggie interview festival guest Blake Fischer…

Sophia Holmsten signs six-figure deal for biography

The controversial model's new unfiltered account of her harrowing ordeal surviving the festival massacre is set to hit shelves this fall…

"Diabolical": Eton slammed with shocking new grooming accusations

Police are now investigating claims that internet celebrity Eton also sent inappropriate messages to a minor in 2019…

Did she do it? The Petition Child's secret role in the festival

Questions continue to swirl about Ruth Phillips's potential involvement in the festival massacre with internet sleuths uncovering further clues that link her to the cult…

The festival massacre's complete timeline

Chronological infographic detailing all major events from the festival's announcement to present day…

HOW BAD THINGS CAN GET

Petition Child: everything we know so far

Where she lived, where she worked, and her secret double life. "I had no idea," says shocked former coworker…

"He fought like a champion"

Lisl Pollock reveals the heart-wrenching final moments of fellow festival guest Mark Charmers as he used a plank to defend his friends from the cult…

Viral meltdowns, drug possession charges, and rehab: the fall of an internet queen

Travel and lifestyle influencer Kia Rayleigh has voluntarily entered rehab just a week after her unhinged video about the festival massacre went viral for all the wrong reasons…

Further arrests in festival massacre case

Charges have been laid against two brothers who allegedly had links to the infamous Petition cult, bringing the number of arrests to twenty-nine…

SummitRide apologizes: "We made a mistake"

Indie game development company SummitRide has released an official apology after backlash to their announced VR adventure that let players experience the festival massacre…

"I just want to bury my baby"

DNA testing is still underway for many unidentified partial remains from the festival massacre. Mother Leslie Farrow speaks of the heart-break of not having a body to bury…

Why internet celebrities deserve our scrutiny

As allegations of grooming, employee mistreatment, and dangerous negligence mount against internet superstar Eton, critics are waiting to see how he plans to pivot his career…

ABOUT THE AUTHOR

Darcy Coates is a *USA Today* bestselling author of *Hunted*, *The Haunting of Ashburn House*, *Craven Manor*, and more than a dozen horror and suspense titles. She lives on the Central Coast of Australia with her family, cats, and a garden full of herbs and vegetables. Darcy loves forests, especially old-growth forests where the trees dwarf anyone who steps between them. Wherever she lives, she tries to have a mountain range close by.